Agog! Terrific Tales

This book is dedicated to the memory of Elsie Mullineaux
1904–2004

Other Titles by Agog! Press:

Agog! Fantastic Fiction: 29 New Tales of Fantasy, Imagination and Wonder, Edited by Cat Sparks, 2002/2006

AustrAlien Absurdities, Edited by Chuck McKenzie and Tansy Rayner Roberts, 2002/2006

Agog! Smashing Stories: New Australian Speculative Fiction, Edited by Cat Sparks, 2004/2006

Daikaiju! Giant Monster Tales, Edited by Robert Hood and Robin Pen, 2005

AGOG! TERRIFIC TALES

NEW AUSTRALIAN SPECULATIVE FICTION

EDITED BY CAT SPARKS

Agog! Terrific Tales © Cat Sparks 2003
Design, layout and cover art by Cat Sparks
Typeset in Bookman Old and Century Gothic

Second Edition © Cat Sparks 2006

All stories © 2003 by their respective authors, printed with permission of the authors.
All stories are first printing, original to this anthology, except for:
Lacey's Fingerprints © Chris Lawson
First published *Borderlands: The World Within* [Borderlands convention program book], ed. Hepworth, Oxwell & Watson, November, 2001
In translation as 'Les Empreintes de Lacey' in *Galaxies* [French]ed. Stéphane Nicot, vol 26, 2002,
and
The Butterfly Merchant © Sean Williams
First published in *The Stone Mage and The Sea*, HarperCollins Publishers, 2001.

Published by Agog! Press
PO Box U302
University of Wollongong
NSW 2522
Australia

in partnership with
Prime Books
www.prime-books.com

ISBN:
0-8095-5631-6 (hc)
0-8095-5632-4 (pbk)

CONTENTS

FOREWORD

PEOPLE OFTEN SAY they no longer have time for reading. Today's world is a frantic place—everything's always go go go, shops bursting with curious and exotic distractions competing against traditional books for our precious recreation dollars. With this in mind, it's a wonder that the short story format is not more popular. You can read a short story while waiting for the bus, standing in line at the delicatessen, or microwaving your dinner.

But alas, people don't tend to do so, and the short story is going the way of the dinosaur. Few of the major publishers are willing to gamble on anthologies because they don't sell as well as books by single authors.

The short story has always been an important element in the literature of speculative fiction. Indeed, many ideas are best expressed in three pages rather than three volumes. Short stories allow an author to experiment, be rebellious, dangerous, naughty or just plain weird. Short stories don't have to seek the approval of marketing departments, or earn back their advances by appealing to the lowest common denominator. For these reasons and more, short stories have fallen into the domain of the independent presses (some may argue that they were never really comfortable anywhere else).

Agog! Press is proudly dedicated to keeping the tradition of short speculative fiction alive and kicking. I hope you enjoy these twenty one new tales of Australian speculative fiction at its best.

Cat Sparks,

Wollongong, 2003/2006

KIJIN TEA

KYLA WARD

THE WESTERN DRESS RUBBED ABOMINABLY, but her husband had made it clear she must abandon the kimono. Utako shifted as she looked out across the garden in the evening brightness of Small Heat.

'Sute,' she called, 'It's time to watch television.'

Her daughter was barely visible amongst the hollyhocks at the far end of the garden. Above the brazen flowers the hills rose in soft, mottled waves, like a forest pattern on a kimono's train. She walked forward, feeling the light breeze in her hair.

'You must come in. Your father will be disappointed if you do not watch television.'

'I can't come Mama. Lord and Lady Tooth are here for tea.'

And who, she thought, would want to watch grey pictures flickering in a box when the garden was here? Lord and Lady Tooth were frequent guests when Sute was alone, which as the daughter of a Company Director she often was. There were no other children of her status in Port Kujira. Both of them, these days, were so often alone.

'What are you having, Sute?'

'Sweet dumplings. Lord Tooth says I perform tea ceremony very well now.'

Utako smiled as she thought of the curled leaf bowls and flower heads set out for dumplings. 'He is kind to say so. What is Lady Tooth wearing?'

'Three layers; white, red and hollyhock pattern. Her hair is dressed with flowers. Lord Tooth is in white with a golden cloak and his forehead is like the rising moon.'

Sute remembered everything, even descriptions from a story she might have heard months past, she noticed everything and used it in surprising ways. She was so quick, so clever; if Yorimasa would only stop and see. There were good girl's schools in Tokyo and if he moved them there, Sute might have real friends.

Again the breeze set the trees to rustling and Utako turned her face to catch it. She caught a glint amongst the distant pines and realised it was a building, yet more new houses or, by the position, it could even be preparations for the dam that was to go across Raimei gorge. She could remember when the upper reaches of the gorge had been a sacred place.

She did not want to go to Tokyo, with its grey buildings and maze of streets. But it would all be the same here soon enough. The only difference was whether she would still be the wife of a Company Director, or a cast-off living in her brother's house—if he would take her.

'Lord Tooth is very handsome,' she said. 'And now Sute, make your goodbyes and come in. It is your father's wish that we watch television.'

Japan had lost the war, Yorimasa said when he still deigned to discuss such things with her, not because it was Japan but because it was not modern Japan. Against an old America they would have won. Japan must become not another America, but modern Japan with its own companies, its own democracy and its own programs on the television. And so he worked, first on the reconstruction at Kujira harbour and then, with his promotion, in Tokyo itself. He took the new train line and stayed there for weeks at a time. Tonight he came home, driven from the station in the company car, to see his wife and daughter seated on the matting watching a broadcast play, a lavish supper awaiting his presence. He spoke barely a word, but ate and then went to the Wysteria Room to see his mother.

Utako put on the red nylon slip he had bought her for New Year, and waited for him in his chamber.

Afterwards, she returned to the room she shared with Sute. Not for the first time she thought of him eating at restaurants, sleeping in hotels, and about the women he might meet there.

Utako woke knowing something was wrong. As she lay on her futon, the darkness around her seemed threatening. Then she heard the choking sound, perhaps it had awoken her. She was already up and pushing through the mosquito nets, her body feeling heavy.

Sute was by the chamber pot, vomiting. Utako put an arm around her, soothing and feeling her skin. She was clammy in the warm night. Utako went to get the water she kept on her desk and she also lit the lantern. To use the electrics would waken the whole house.

She set the lantern down carefully, pink light bathing her daughter's face. 'Oh dear one, did you feel ill after dinner?'

Sute coughed. There was something black on her tongue.

'Come now Sute, drink and spit.' Sute spat it out and Utako looked in the pot.

The rice and fish had come up almost undigested. But there, slick and sticky with bile were black feathers and bones and the whole, eyeless head of a bird. Crusted with rice.

Sute rubbed her mouth weakly. 'They said it would taste however I liked. And it did Mama, it tasted good.'

The first thing Utako did was upturn the washing basket on the veranda outside the sliding door. The precaution was worthwhile, although the One-Eyed Boy usually took the form of a Buddhist novice. It seemed more likely that Lord and Lady Tooth were fox kijin or snake kijin. All took children.

The second thing was to go to the kitchen and take pickled plums, rice cakes and some of the cold adzuki soup that had been made for breakfast. She made Sute promise not to leave her futon—she was weak and sleepy now—and took the bowls out into the garden. All around, the darkness was heavy with scent and alive with the sound of crickets. She placed the food at the edge of the hollyhocks and hurried back inside.

'Where were you Mama?' said Sute.

'I took a gift to Lord and Lady Tooth,' she answered. 'To make sure they are not offended.'

Sute began to cry. 'I didn't meant to be sick, Mama!'

'Shush, it's alright, it's alright.' She held her daughter through the netting, rocking her, feeling her breathing calm slowly into sleep.

When Utako was not much older than Sute was now, the ten-year- old son of her family's neighbours disappeared one evening from the back of their farmhouse. His friends confessed they had trespassed on the sacred reaches of the gorge that afternoon, so as Headman, her father decided he had been taken. That night and the next day, the hills echoed to the sound of beaten drums and shouts as the people searched for him. That they found nothing made it only more certain. If he had fallen to his death or drowned there would have been a body; he had been taken, or eaten for his offence. That was why she had to return a gift for the gift the kijin had given, in their foul way. Without that, they could claim her daughter with the justification of being shown no respect.

But the kijin were wild things. Despite the heat, which the lantern increased, and the child in her arms, Utako shivered. If they wanted something, they would find a way to come at it. And her parents were dead now—years since the bombs had fallen.

She let the lantern burn.

The best precaution was to have Sute exorcised at the Buddhist temple on the headland. But this presented problems which, in the light of morning, seemed all but insurmountable.

Madame Tohoi, her honourable mother-in-law, found fault with the adzuki soup; it was tainted, she said, the lid must have been left off. She called upon Yorimasa to admonish his stupid wife. Utako could hear Madame Tohoi shouting from her room as she brought Yorimasa breakfast in his, but he sat silently, eating as though he neither heard nor tasted. He was already dressed. In answer to her inquiry, he said he must go early to view the works in Raimei Gorge. Timidly, she asked if the company driver was taking him. Yes, he would here soon. Did he desire his wife and daughter to accompany him? They were already dressed. They could pass by Kujira temple and leaving offerings for the soul of his father.

'What, is it the Bon festival already? I've no time.'

'May we expect you for lunch?' she asked, gazing at the matting.

'I'll be home this evening,' he said.

Sute sat on the veranda outside their room to watch the car. Utako watched and tried to steel herself. To walk to the temple would take hours, and to be absent so long she would have to obtain permission. Madame Tohoi's complaints had subsided and the house was quiet. Perhaps she should wait until after lunch, although it would be hotter then.

'Utako!' The sharp voice cut through the screens. 'Utako! Come and help me find my pins!'

'Stay on the veranda, dear one,' she said to Sute. 'Don't go into the garden.' She went to the Wysteria room.

Madame Tohoi was 60 years old and she sat fanning herself as Utako searched the room for the enamelled hair pins. Madame Tohoi dyed her hair and the jet black looked curious, falling in strands across her wrinkled face.

'Why are you looking in my jewel boxes? Don't go anywhere near them! I still have eyes, you know, I can see!' Utako switched to the futon, rolling it up as she searched, to put it away in the cupboard. 'And that should be aired! Every day when it's humid they should be laid on the veranda and turned, and you can do that. One thing you aren't is weak Utako, you've got arms like a rice miller. Oh sweet Buddha it's hot, and so early in the season!'

'Would you like a drink from the refrigerator?' Utako offered, bundling the futon into her arms.

'Find those pins, that's what I want. Ah, this house is a shambles, and my son no sooner home than he's off again. Why is that, now? Why is that?'

The pins were in the clothes chest, jabbed carelessly into the tortoiseshell kimono she had worn three days ago. Utako combed and pinned the old woman's hair, and held the mirror for her to see it this way and that. She seemed pleased.

'Honourable mother-in-law, I have a favour to ask.'

'What is it?'

She hesitated. She couldn't say what really happened, reveal her daughter's shame. 'Your grand-daughter was ill last night in her belly.'

'Probably snuck out and drank from the soup.'

'She had ill-omened dreams, of kijin. I ask, may I take her to Kujira temple?'

'You want to go to the temple in this weather?' For a moment Madame Tohoi looked genuinely astonished. Then a more familiar expression settled across her face. 'The child is ill, you say?'

'She was.'

'And well enough now to walk to the headland and back?'

'She is scared, scared of the kijin—'

'For a child's dreams. You're too fond of going out to this place and that,' said Madam Tohoi, 'You'd think a peasant's daughter would understand about work.'

'My father was Headman,' Utako couldn't stop herself, 'We were not samurai but we have a long lineage—'

'What's that to me? Our family were samurai and you had the honour to join us! And what gratitude have you shown? A miserable daughter, and sickly too.' Madame Tohoi reached for her cane. Automatically, Utako bent to help her rise. 'Leave me alone!' She banged the cane against Utako's legs. 'My son stays away because he can't abide to look on the dull creature he married, who can't even give him a son! Where's your lineage, girl? Water in your blood.'

Utako bowed, feeling the heat burning across her cheeks, feeling it burning in her eyes. She bowed respectfully, a daughter to her mother-in-law, and made to leave.

'You should know I've told him to divorce you. He can do better, my son. Ah, he is doing very much better, in Tokyo!'

Utako returned to the veranda and stood there, blinking ridiculous wetness from her eyes.

Was that really what it came down to? In spite of all his talk of modern Japan and shaking off the past, she was beneath his rank and had not given him a son. It had been a formal marriage with introductions and gifts between the families, but she and Yorimasa had known each other for years. It had been at the end of the war when there was so much destroyed and so many dead, especially the young. Her lineage had been good enough then! People had cheered at their wedding and said they were the future of Port Kujira and its good luck. But nine years on and no son. Did those people, her neighbours who sold her fish and rice, think of her that way as well? And what by all the gods was she supposed to do about it?

She straightened up and rubbed her eyes, for she would not let Sute see her crying.

Where was Sute?

Her stomach suddenly chilling, she scanned the garden—
the azaleas, the arrowroot bushes, for a scrap of pink, a little
girl's dress—.

'Mama, look at this.' Sute's voice came from the half-open
screen into the main chamber. 'It's the book for the television.'
She stepped out from the dimness studying the printed
broadsheet. 'The lady in the play was a man dressed as a lady.'
She giggled.

'Sute, where have you been?' she said sharply, though she
knew it was foolish.

'I went inside.' Sute looked up at her wonderingly, 'You said
not to go into the garden.'

'Yes. Yes, good girl. I just—didn't know if you had been good.'
Sute dropped her eyes back to the television guide.

'Grandma was shouting,' she said, 'I don't like her.'

'You must never say that Sute! Never!'

'Lady Tooth said she didn't like her.'

'Sute,' she said slowly, 'I don't think you should listen to
Lady Tooth. That was a bad thing to say.'

'Why?'

'Because it is! Sute, have Lord and Lady Tooth ever asked
you to do anything? To come visit them?'

'They live in a palace,' said Sute, 'Of cedar wood and cypress
thatch, and inside the walls are golden. Servants wait on them,
bringing them tea and delicious cakes. The rarest flowers bloom
in their garden.'

'You mustn't believe what they say. It isn't real, and they
may want you to do bad things. Now Sute, I want you to go into
our room and stay there. I have work to do in the garden.'

'I'll help!'

'No, you will stay in our room. Read your number book.'

'But Mama, I don't—'

'You'll stay there and keep quiet so Grandma won't shout
again!' She regretted the words as Sute's face fell. But still
holding the television guide, Sute passed down the veranda, slid
open the door and went inside.

Utako set her face firmly. If she couldn't have the help of the
priests she would have to help herself. There were things anyone
could do when bad spirits came too close. A little hard work with
her peasant arms. But she would have to find an excuse . . .

Shortly after lunch, Madam Tohoi went into the bathing
chamber to sit with her feet in water, and called her daughter-
in-law to bring her iced persimmon juice. She was drinking it in
a big, western glass when the first explosion came.

'Bombs!' she squawked and the sticky red juice spilled
down the front of her open yukata. Another muffled bang, then
another. 'Utako! What's that noise? Stop that noise!'

Swiftly Utako appeared at the door. 'Honourable Mother-in—oh dear. Let me bring you a cloth.'

'What's that noise? I can't stand it!'

'Oh yes, isn't it dreadful! I think it's coming from Raimei Gorge—they must be blasting. That must be what Yorimasa went to see.' She smiled and held out a damp cloth. The old woman took it and made no further complaint.

She had taken the New Year's fireworks and bound them into balls, so each would be a single, large bang instead of the usual many small ones. She set them off in the bushes at the edge of the trees, under the veranda steps and by the lavatory, keeping a careful eye out for sparks.

She had already cut away the long grass and pretty much every plant next to the house. Fox kijin or snake kijin; as fox or snake they would be uncomfortable with the lack of cover, as spirits the noise and smoke would scare them away. As a final touch, she took her mirror and the shiny lids from tins in the pantry and nailed them at every corner of the foundations. No shape-shifter could bear to see its true reflection.

She had knocked on the door after setting off the first bomb and told Sute not to be scared, there was nothing see. Sute had stayed inside the entire time, without a sound. Utako was sweating and wondered longingly whether the bathing chamber was free yet. But first she had to let Sute know she was no longer in disgrace.

After the brilliance of the afternoon outside, everything was floating dimness and she could scarcely make out Sute on the floor, playing with something. White dots. Black dots. Oh, she had the go stones out, which she shouldn't do but under the circumstances, Utako didn't care. Sute didn't play go as such; she played child's go, moving the stones into pretty patterns. But as her vision cleared, it seemed to Utako that what was on the floor before her was a real go pattern, a game considerably advanced.

Sute moved a white stone. 'Hello Mama.'

'Is this what you've been doing all this while?' A real game, with black in the lead.

'Only after lunch, once the bangs started.'

Utako knelt down. Her wondrous, clever child. She looked at the black pieces, thinking that she might make the next move.

'Don't Mama.' And her hand touched—it was wet. Covered in slime.

Each a globular, black egg in a slimy packet. Spread over the chamber floor, using the lines in the matting as a game board. A small piece of blackness, not a globe, was inching its way along the inner wall, a wide, gleaming leech.

Her shoe was badly aimed, it bounced off the wall and the leech humped on. There on the floor, where they laid their futons—

'They didn't like the noise in the garden, so they asked if they could come inside. They had to come along the roof because there were mirrors. I said I couldn't do anything bad and they said we could play go. And you play go Mama, and Grandma and Papa do. I can play now too.' She smiled. 'Only not the black pieces, 'cause they might hatch.'

When Yorimasa came back in the company car, the sky was indigo and the crickets had begun their nightly chorus.

'Tell the driver to wait.' Utako ran across the lawn. 'Please Yorimasa, we need the car.' As she reached him, she became flustered and bowed.

'What's wrong?' he asked, 'Is Mama ill?'

'It's Sute, she's—' Utako forced herself to look up at him. His brow was furrowed. 'She must see a priest, now. Tomorrow may be too late.'

'Sute's ill? Then you should have called a doctor—'

'She's been with the kijin, Yorimasa. She's eaten with them. At first I thought it was just a child playing, but today there were things in our room, see?' She thrust forward the bucket containing the black eggs, now shrunken and dried and looking more like mushrooms in the twilight.

'What are you saying? You think the kijin are going to take the child?' Yorimasa glanced sideways at the driver, and she realised she had embarrassed him and that he was angry. Very angry.

'Yes,' she barely whispered.

'You think shape-shifting animals are going to come out of the woods and make a seven-year-old vanish in front of you?'

She nodded.

'You're as bad as the workmen! Kijin take their tools, kijin cause the rockslides, and now that man has drowned—go inside Utako, now!' She bowed and walked slowly towards the house. Behind her, she heard him tell the driver to wait.

She heard him catching her up. Then he seized her arm.

'People have been saying the work on the gorge is cursed. Are you one of them? Have you said anything?'

'No, nothing. Yorimasa, I would have gone to the temple today only your mother refused me—'

'Good! Good to keep you home when you're talking like an idiot, an ignorant peasant!'

'I would have said nothing! She needs to be exorcised!'

'You need to be exorcised! Or I do! Maybe I'm cursed; I marry, I work hard, and what do I get? A house full of nothing but women. I'm ashamed to bring my superiors here! You and my mother are good company for each other, you know; both always on at me—I'm not sleeping here, not one more night,' and he strode back towards the car, sitting there with its engine running.

'Yorimasa, please stay with me!'

He turned his head, smiling nastily. 'Why? Are you pregnant? Because you're no good for anything else!'

He slammed the car door behind him and the car began to move. She couldn't move, couldn't speak until the headlights had passed over her and it was gone. Then she put the bucket down and walked down the veranda, and opened their chamber door.

The lantern was burning and Sute was sitting there, wearing one of her father's jackets. Thank the Buddhas he hadn't seen that.

'I'm dressing as a man,' she said, 'Then I can learn to drive. I'll drive to the city.' She turned an imaginary wheel and made puttering noises. 'Mama, why are you crying?'

Feeling as though her stomach was filled with lead, she sat down on the matting—the fresh piece she had put in to replace the one that was soiled. The tears wouldn't stop. 'Oh Sute,' she said, 'I love you so much!'

'I love you too Mama. Stop crying.'

'Promise,' she choked on the words, 'Promise you won't go with Lord and Lady Tooth, even if they say it's just for a little while. You have to tell them that you're sorry for what your father is doing, but you are your mother's child and she will miss you very, very much!'

'Mama—'

'Say we will give them offerings, that we will set them in our family shrine if they don't take you.'

'They don't want to take me, Mama.'

Outside, the crickets were singing. Sute stretched her arms inside the jacket sleeves and the shadows writhed across the wall like huge serpents. She looked at her mother. 'They want to come with me. To Tokyo, to the girls school.'

Even now part of Utako was marvelling; see? She remembers everything—'What do you mean?'

'They don't like what's happening at the gorge but they can't stop it. Things have changed. So they want to come with me and learn as I do. They'll learn how to live in the streets and buildings, and television. They like television.'

Utako was sweating in the stiff, stupid western dress. But she could feel a cold spot at the back of her neck, like a pinprick or a tiny, tiny eye. 'That's why they talk to you. Teach you.'

'Yes.'

'Then—I have been very rude.'

'They don't mind.'

'Sute, are they here now?'

'They're close,' said the little girl. 'They're watching us.'

'Then I say I am sorry. And that I am afraid we will not be able to help them, though I gladly would. We may not—Sute, your father doesn't like me now. I think he will not take us to Tokyo.'

'He would if I had a little brother,' said Sute. Heat in her face, cold on her neck, Utako dropped her eyes.

'They can fix that,' Sute added, turning the steering wheel once more.

Behind Utako, in the garden, the blanket noise of crickets stopped.

'Of course, it wouldn't really be my little brother, but it would look like him and act like him as he grew up. Papa would never know. And I'd help. It would be really good.' She paused a moment, as if listening. A floorboard's crack? A hiss from the lantern? 'They say it wouldn't hurt you. Like I hurt you. Did I hurt you?'

'Not much,' she whispered, 'And you were just a baby.'

There was no sound from the rest of the house. Madam Tohoi should have been calling down the wrath of the Hell-Gods by now, but she was silent. Utako had the feeling that if she were to go to the veranda and look for the lights in the hills and on the headland there would be none, just the vast, dark stillness of the forest and sea.

'How would they do it?'

'Lord Tooth would come to you. And they'd make it sweet, Mama, however you want.'

She reached out and snuffed the lantern wick. Darkness flooded the room, darkness that felt charged, alive. She could smell the heavy scents of the flowers at night and she thought she could hear something now, a faint sliding on the veranda.

'However I want.'

Something large.

'Sute. Go watch television.'

'Yes Mama.'

'But first—tell them. Tell them I want to see a handsome prince in white with a golden cloak, and a forehead like the rising moon.'

Kyla Ward's short fiction and poetry has appeared in gothic.net and shadowedrealms.com.au, *Borderlands*, *Aurealis* and *Abbadon* magazines, and the anthologies *Passing Strange* and *Agog! Terrific Tales*. She has written articles for *Dragon* and *Viewpoint* magazines, and far, far too much roleplaying material for the likes of White Wolf. Her first (co-written) novel, *Prismatic*, is appearing in the Dark Suspense series from Lothian Books in 2006. She shares a website with her partner, writer David Carroll, which may be found at www.tabula-rasa.info

Waiting at Golgotha

SIMON BROWN

THE TOURIST BOAT FROM DAVAO arrived at Tongay Island two days before Good Friday and the annual Celebration of the Crucifixions. It carried pilgrims mainly, and three television crews from Japan. They were taken out of Puerto Santa Cruz and up into the hills by jalopy, away from the mosquitos and the worst of the humidity, and distributed among the various lodges and hotels scattered throughout the island. Santa Anna, a small guest house resting on stilts almost at the top of Tongay, took the last of the passengers, an English woman called Sydney.

She was greeted by Maria, short and round and happy, and showed to her room on the second floor.

'It is a long trip on the boat from Davao and you are very tired,' Maria explained in English. She said this as she pulled down the bed cover for Sydney, giving her instructions the weight of maternal authority. 'Come down at seven—that is when we eat, and afterwards we'll say prayers. Remember, seven.'

'Seven,' Sydney echoed after the retreating woman, setting her bags down. It took a conscious act of will to ignore the bed and make her way to the French windows opening out to a narrow balcony. Stepping onto the balcony, she was greeted with a view of Tongay's steep slopes descending to Moro Gulf. In the far distance she could make out the green fringe of Mindanao, a vague promise of firmer land. She stared at the sea. She'd never before in her life seen anything so intensely blue. In Liverpool the sea was a cold, threatening grey that promised violent winter storms and death by drowning. But here the waters held out a promise of new life, rejuvenation. *Resurrection.*

'My God, halfway round the world,' she said, startled by the thought. *Halfway round life itself,* she added silently. She still didn't really believe her eyes. *How could anything be so open? The sea is as deep as deep can be, and the sky has no end. We are just ants here.* She closed her eyes and saw how Tongay was linked with all the other islands, large and small, that floated in the amniotic waters of the world. *We are pilgrims blown to this place by the breath of God.* But a part of her mind made her remember Klong Toey and the reason for her pilgrimage, and it occurred to her that they were not seeds but survivors who'd been washed up on this shore by fortune alone, yet to be proven good or ill.

Shortly after seven, Sydney went down to the dining room, a small area with half-a-dozen tables. They were all being used and she turned to leave when Maria ambushed her.

'You look much better after your rest,' Maria told Sydney, taking her by the arm and leading her across the room to a small, square table with two chairs, one of them occupied by a man. 'You will sit,' Maria instructed, and Sydney obediently sat. 'Don't be embarrassed. Nobody knows anybody else here; isn't that right, Father Saavedra?' The man looked up, his gaze catching Sydney on its way to Maria.

'Yes,' he answered in a soft voice, his wide face unsmiling but open.

'Father Saavedra, this is Miss Sydney.'

'Ms,' Sydney said quickly and extended a hand.

'*Ms* Sydney,' Maria corrected herself, her tone faintly disapproving.

'She is English.'

'I am Spanish,' the priest said, saying the first thing that came into his head, and gently shook Sydney's hand.

Maria beamed. 'That should give you two plenty to talk about. I will get you some food.'

Father Saavedra watched Maria's back as she left for the kitchen. His plain blue shirt was open at the throat, revealing a long thin neck that appeared too frail for his large head. His eyes were round and dark, his nose long and narrow, suggestively aristocratic. Black glossy hair was cut short for the tropics.

'I'm sorry about the intrusion,' Sydney said.

'Oh, it is no intrusion, Ms Sydney,' he assured her.

'I wonder why she thinks we'll have plenty to talk about?'

'The Filipinos think political union has turned Europe into one nation like their own, with Spain and England reduced to provinces. Maria probably thinks we have friends in common.' Sydney laughed, and Saavedra smiled in return. 'Which part of England do you come from? Maybe we do have friends in common.'

'Liverpool.'

'Then it is unlikely.'

'Anyway, I haven't been in England for several years.'

'So where have you come from?'

'Thailand,' she replied quickly. 'Are you here for the Celebration?'

Saavedra stiffened slightly. 'Yes, like almost everyone else, I suppose.'

She recognised the cue. 'And me,' she added.

'What do you do in Thailand?'

'I'm a stringer for two British newsnets. I cover the Far East for them from Bangkok.'

'A journalist?' Again his body tensed. 'So you are here to cover the Celebration?'

Sydney quickly shook her head. 'My interest is personal, not professional.'

'Ah,' he said, relaxing.

She worked hard to suppress her journalist's curiosity. That was what had gotten her into this fix in the first place.

'And why are you here?'

Saavedra shrugged, appeared to be searching for the right words. 'I have come to see if I have a cross to bear.'

'That's an intriguing answer,' she said.

'Like the Church itself, we men and women of the cloth strive to project an aura of mystery.' He offered the slightest of smiles. 'It's a convenient cloak to hide us from the real world—and the real world from us.'

She looked at him blankly.

'I have confounded you, Ms Sydney,' he continued, his tone mildly apologetic, 'when I only intended to deflect your reporter's instincts.'

'I left those behind in Bangkok.'

Saavedra nodded, seeing the truth of it in her eyes. 'I am here to test my love for God.'

The priest's sudden frankness made her feel awkward, and they waited in silence for their meal.

Knowing sleep would be difficult to find, as it had been now for a year, Sydney busied herself by unpacking suitcases and carefully arranging her clothes in the room's closet. She had a cold shower to wash away the day's sweat, and spent ten minutes studying herself in a long dress mirror. She saw a short, thin woman approaching middle age with little grace but great speed. Her sandy hair had been infiltrated by grey wisps, her skin was beginning to sag seriously under her eyes and her arms, and her small breasts seemed less a part of her body than a pair of sad, white alien growths.

I don't like myself, she realised, and at the same time understood it wasn't so much the effects of aging that repulsed her, but the need for her mind to belong to something so utterly physical and corruptible. She finally went to bed, crawling under the mosquito net and tucking down between two crisp, white sheets. A cool breeze wafted in from the open French windows, bringing with it the sound of insects and fruit bats, the smells of the rainforest. She struggled to find sleep, but her mind dwelt instead on the coming Celebration and its attendant crucifixions. She'd always assumed they were something the locals did to enable them to wear the scars of martyrdom without first having to make the ultimate sacrifice of dying. She vaguely remembered reading stories about some crucifixions going horribly wrong, stories of shock and sudden and bloody death, but every year the three century old Celebration seemed to get bigger and bigger, and to garner for itself more attention and notoriety.

All the world's major newsnets sent crews to cover the occasion. It was the planet's most popular event shown live on television. More than 2,000 years after his death, the crucifixion of Jesus still fascinated humanity, and an audience that numbered in the billions now watched its re-enactment every year from their electronic ring seats.

And why am I really here? she asked herself. *Am I spectator or suppliant? Heretic or true believer?* She realised glumly that the questions had no proper answer.

Sydney woke just after dawn. She dressed quickly in light cotton pants and a t-shirt and went downstairs. There was no one in the dining room except a maid preparing the tables for breakfast. The thought of food made her hungry but she decided she needed a walk first. She stopped on the front veranda, suddenly confronted by a forest filled with the sounds of birds and insects. *It's a lure. The sounds draw people into the jungle and they're never seen again.*

'You are up early,' said a voice to her right. Sydney turned and saw Maria and a man sitting on cane chairs. Thin morning shadows criss-crossed them like the threads of a spider's web.

'Did you sleep well?'

'Yes, thank you,' Sydney lied.

Maria waved at the man sitting next to her. 'This is my husband, Miguel. He helps me run Santa Anna, but he is not well and cannot do as much as he would like.' Miguel smiled vacantly at Sydney. He was a short man, as thin as Sydney, who looked as though he'd been mummified in the recent past and was having trouble coming to terms with the fact that he was still alive.

Sydney smiled back. 'I thought I'd go for a walk ...'

Maria pointed to her right. 'Follow the veranda to the south side of the house. From there you will see a trail that will take you to a lookout. The view is very pretty, and you will be back in time for breakfast.'

Sydney found the trail easily. It was narrow but well worn, winding south for five minutes before bending to the east.

Another ten minutes and Sydney found herself in a clearing at the top of a cliff offering spectacular views of the lowlands and Moro Gulf. From here she could see Puerto Santa Cruz, Tongay's only town, its single jetty protruding into the sea like the finger of a skeleton.

Several people were already in the clearing, their heads bowed in prayer. She felt uncomfortably out of place. *Why? I have as much right to be here as they do.* But she couldn't throw off her sense of being present under false pretences. One of the worshippers stood up, brushed down his knees and made to leave. It was Father Saavedra. He saw Sydney and walked over to her.

'It is a beautiful morning,' he said pleasantly. 'From here you can see the Butig Mountains quite clearly.'

'What are they?'

The priest pointed east towards Mindanao. 'The chain of mountains just inland from the coast. That is what we see of the island.'

Sydney's mouth formed a silent 'oh.'

Saavedra laughed. 'I can tell the information interested you a great deal. Forgive me, but a memory for trivia is my one great weakness.'

'Only one, Father? Most of us crawl through life with a truckfull.'

Saavedra stared at his feet, suddenly unsure of himself. 'I have lots of minor faults to make up for it,' he told her, and then paused uncertainly. 'Most people assume priests are halfway to saints.'

'That must be a burden,' she said sincerely. 'Some people think that journalists are halfway to demons. It's harder to disappoint someone when their expectations of you are so low.'

'You don't like living up to people's expectations?'

'Especially my own.' She cursed herself for being so honest. *I don't know this man ...* The confession seemed to embarrass Saavedra. He turned away. 'I'll let you get on with your prayers.'

'I came up for the exercise,' she said, following him down the trail. After a while Saavedra said over his shoulder: 'You do not seem to me to be much like the other pilgrims.'

'Did I say I was a pilgrim?'

'No, but last night you did say you were here for personal reasons, and not professional. I merely assumed you were a pilgrim.'

'It's the word I don't like,' she said after a moment.

'The word?'

'Pilgrim. It sounds medieval. *Canterbury Tales.* Not of this world. Not any more, anyway. There should be another description, something more modern. "Religious tourist".'

'Is that what I should call you?'

'You should call me Sydney,' she said firmly, and then, from curiosity: 'Would you describe yourself as a pilgrim?'

'Oh, yes. We Spaniards have no objection to the term. We are Catholics living in a Catholic country, brought up in a Catholic tradition. You are English, and England is very different, very C-of-E.'

'Liverpool's more Catholic than Rome,' she told him, 'but you're right about the tradition. The first person I heard use the word 'pilgrim' was John Wayne. For years I thought pilgrims were cowboys.'

'Very well, you are just Sydney and you are here for personal reasons. We'll leave it at that.' A minute later he cleared his throat. 'What are you doing today? It is only that I thought I would see some of the island, and I was wondering if you'd like to accompany me.'

Sydney smiled. 'Are you asking me for a date?'

Saavedra returned the smile. 'If you like.'

'I don't even know your first name.'

'Ariel.'

'Alright, Ariel, I'd like that.'

A jalopy arrived soon after breakfast, and several of Santa Anna's guests clambered aboard for the trip down to Puerto Santa Cruz. It delivered them in the town's main square, a paved area dominated by a church which had been built by Spanish monks four centuries before, using local stone and timber and the bones of their dead brethren. Virtually everyone in the world had seen the Chapel of Bones on television, but the pilgrims were still keen to see it for themselves and as a body they marched towards it. They were intercepted by a dozen local guides, each trying to corral his own herd of visitors. Saavedra grasped Sydney's hand and forced a way through the crowd and up the stairs into the dark church.

Sydney looked around, expecting to see skulls in the roof staring down at her, but instead was surprised to see smoothly whitewashed walls, a high curved ceiling with exposed beams of a dark brown timber—the rib cage of a whale, she told herself— and frescos that shimmered with bright colours despite the gloom. The altar was made from a simple stone bench covered with a cotton cloth. Gold candelabra and a golden pyx rested on the cloth, and to Sydney they suddenly seemed to be strange symbols of an alien and exotic faith. Again, she felt like an intruder.

Saavedra tugged on her hand. 'Hurry, before all the others come.' He took her through a side door and into a passage that led to a narrow flight of descending stone steps. At the bottom they were met by an old man sitting on a stool and carefully nursing an offering box on his knees. He glanced at his visitors, meekly responding to Saavedra's greeting, and shook the offering box. Saavedra made a donation and the guard reached behind his head to flick a switch, bringing light to the Chapel of Bones.

Sydney gasped in surprise.

Columns were made from long femurs, cornices from a collection of scapulas and pelvic iliums, the walls from smaller, more fragile bones, while phalanges made brackets for verdigrised cups of holy water. When Sydney looked up she saw a ceiling of dry, grinning skulls with most of their teeth missing.

'This is ...' but she couldn't find the words.

'Incredible,' Saavedra finished for her, his voice filled with wonder.

'No,' she said.

Saavedra looked at her, his expression puzzled. 'No?'

'*No*. This is ...'

Just then the other pilgrims and their guides arrived, excited, babbling, overwhelming the old man and his offering box.

'... horrible ...' The word was smothered under the noise of the crowd.

Sydney turned and fled back up the stairs. She burst into the church, startling an old woman dressed all in black. She drew in large gulps of air. Sweat prickled her face like the bites of tiny insects. When her heartbeat slowed she sat down at the end of a pew. She noticed the old woman staring at her with a mixture of concern and disapproval.

Sydney laughed nervously, feeling foolish. 'I'm alright,' she said. The old woman turned her attention to a string of rosary beads which she passed through her fingers like small coins. *She must think I'm an idiot. God, maybe I am.* The thought made her want to giggle. She stood up and left the church as quietly as possible.

There was no one in the square. She walked along a road that passed a series of shop fronts until she came to a line of trees. There were sounds coming from up ahead. She walked on past the trees and found herself on the edge of a soccer field, a level stretch of dirt with nets at either end.

The field was full of people, most of them locals, but many were foreigners single-mindedly erecting gantries for television cameras, satellite dishes and broadcasting posts. The locals watched the foreigners with intense interest. Sydney joined a group of them, mainly women and children.

'What's going on?' She asked them.

'It is for the Celebration of the Crucifixion,' one woman explained. The children looked curiously at Sydney, as if she should have known better than to ask. 'Everyone in the world wants to see it.'

Sydney counted at least six television and newsnet crews setting up their gear. As she watched, one of the technicians shouted she had established a satellite link to a broadcasting station in Tokyo. The crowd cheered. 'That is the first,' a second woman told Sydney, her eyes shining with excitement. 'Soon they will all be working and the whole world will be watching us.'

The children escaped from their mothers and began jumping and shouting in front of the camera, now online. The crew smiled, waving encouragement.

'Golgotha,' said a voice behind Sydney. She turned to see Saavedra. 'This is the place of skulls,' the priest continued, staring over her head. 'Jesus was crucified on Golgotha.'

'I thought it was Calvary.'

'Golgotha is the Aramaic word, and Jesus spoke Aramaic.'

Sydney sighed. 'I've had enough of skulls for one day.'

'I missed you in the Chapel of Bones. I did not know you had gone.'

'I was feeling claustrophobic.'

'I understand,' he sympathised, still not looking directly at her.

'I'm going back to the square. When does the jalopy return?'

'Not until midday.'

'I'll go back to the square anyway.'

'I know a cafe where we can get coffee.'

Sydney wanted to be by herself, but didn't know how to say so without offending the priest.

'Something is wrong, isn't it?' he asked as they started back.

Sydney didn't answer. She was watching locals pass as they drifted back from the soccer field. *Golgotha*, she reminded herself.

'I do not mean to sound melodramatic,' Saavedra persisted, 'but I get the impression that you are in trouble. You are running away from something.'

'Are you looking for a confession?' she asked sharply.

Saavedra raised his hands. 'No no! I was not implying you had done anything wrong. Just that *something* is wrong, and it is affecting you.'

'No one can help me,' she said simply.

Saavedra changed the subject. 'Did you know there are chapels in Portugal and Spain also made from the bones of monks?' Sydney shook her head, but wasn't surprised. The last year had been full of unpleasant revelations of one kind or another. 'They are strange testaments to faith, don't you think? I sometimes wonder what it is that makes us express our faith in such extreme ways.'

'It was horrible,' Sydney said emphatically.

Saavedra looked sadly at her. 'Ah,' he said softly. 'That is why you left the Chapel of Bones so quickly. It appalled you.'

'Yes.'

'And yet you have come all the way from Bangkok as a pilgrim—sorry, I know you do not like the word, but I can think of no other—to watch the crucifixions? Surely this is a most extreme expression of faith? Perhaps even more extreme than our habit of using the remains of our dead to build temples to God.'

'I came to Tongay because I thought I'd find something I need, but I was wrong.'

'What is it you are looking for?'

'Salvation,' she replied evenly. 'I have lost my soul, and I want it back again.' *God, why am I telling him all this?*

Saavedra's eyes widened. 'That is some admission. How did you lose your soul?'

'It was taken from me,' she replied grimly.

'Can you tell me about it?' Sydney shook her head. Her whole body was tense. Saavedra changed tack. 'Do you doubt God's love for you?'

'No. But I don't know if I can love him.'

'I, too, suffer from doubt. I often call into question my own capacity for love and compassion.' He sighed deeply. 'In a strange way, Ms Sydney, our missions are similar. Like you, I seek salvation. Salvation from doubt, which I believe is the greatest sin of all.'

'Why are you telling me this?'

'I want you to know you are not alone.'

'You're one of those to be crucified,' she said, suddenly realising the truth.

'Yes. We clerics have as much to prove as the laity—maybe even more.'

'But crucifixion ... ?'

'Nothing more than a few hours physical suffering, which I willingly accept to find answers to my questions.' He looked at her with calm certainty. 'We should expect nothing without sacrifice.'

'I wonder if you're not really looking for absolution,' she said sharply, and almost immediately regretted it. He had given her no cause to question his faith. She realised too late the question was better asked of her own motives. She placed a hand on Saavedra's arm and apologised.

'Whatever for?' he asked.

'I've been a failure as a date.'

Saavedra stopped, blocking her way. He studied her carefully. He raised one hand and gently stroked the line of her jaw. The contact was brief, but Sydney felt blood rush to her cheeks.

'You have nothing to apologise for, Ms Sydney. Today has been filled with small miracles.'

She dreamed of Bangkok nights. The river called Chao Phraya gurgled somewhere in the darkness. The slum of Klong Toey slept around her. It was a rude irony that the only signs of life were here in the abattoir, a place where Thai Catholics performed the work Thai Buddhists were forbidden to do.

Her feet splashed in water. She looked down and saw the water roiling with blood and oil. The pens around her stank of pigs and refuse. A terrified squeal vibrated in the air as a blade sliced through flesh and windpipe. The squeal turned into an obscene whistle. Unclean endings for unclean animals.

She forced herself to watch. The butcher was quick and agile; head thrown into one sack, guts into another, the body sent down a chute. Blood slopped into a trough. Sydney looked down again, but gagged at the mess on the floor—a hairy ear, a trotter blackened with stale gore.

This is pig's hell, she told herself. *They must fear this place from birth.* The animals were not large and round and pink like the overbred Western pig, but hairy, compact creatures. *This is the source of all pain for pigs.*

And it was hell for humans, too. *My brown-skinned Catholic, Thai brothers in God.* She imagined them, night after night, wielding long knives like flyswats, cutting, slicing into warm panting animals. *The world is full of carcasses.*

Some of the Thais became aware of her and stopped to stare. She realised they were seeing her simply as a white woman and not as a fellow Christian. *What does God matter in an abattoir?* But she too found it difficult to see them as anything more than Thais. *Why should I expect Catholics to be white? It's my Irish avatar, centuries stained with Celtic prejudice. It's supposed to be the universal church.* Still, she was surprised, even jealous. They wore their small gold crosses with flair and pride, like German air aces must have worn their iron ones. *What shame a Catholic in Bangkok?*

Did Jesus die for them? That's as absurd as Jesus dying for me. But yes, if he died he must have died for something. In the end we all die for something: a cause, a failure, an ulcer . . . a question.

She walked on until she was surrounded by larger pens filled with waiting cattle. They rumbled and stamped impatiently. Small insects hovered around their heads like particles of smoke.

She tried to keep her mind on the job by conjuring up a

suitable hook and header for her story on the Klong Toey slums for the newsnets, but the presence of so much animal carnage made it impossible for her to think clearly.

There were shouts behind her. She turned and saw him. He looked fourteen, maybe older. To Sydney the Thais all appeared young until they hit forty when they all turned into Methuselahs. There were no shades in Bangkok.

At first she thought it was a game. Two youths were dragging him along, and he seemed to be laughing. But there was a tension in his stare, and his laugh turned into a scream. He sounded like a frightened pig.

It was over so quickly she had no time to react, and afterwards realised there was nothing she could have done anyway. The captive was put on the block. He twisted his head around to plead, but before he could say anything the blade sank deep into his neck. The butcher had to swing a second time to finish the job. The body jerked, fell to the floor, and was lifted onto the block again. Blood blossomed out from the jagged neck in a bright hissing spray, drenching the abattoir workers. Then more cuts with the long knife. Head in one sack, guts in another, the carcass sent down the chute, disappearing behind a leather curtain.

Before she could stop herself she was doubled over and retching. She emptied her stomach in a few seconds, and it was the stink of her own vomit that gave her the strength and will to stand up and step away. A heavy hand fell on her shoulder and she froze, now afraid. The hand turned her around. Its owner was not much taller than she, but almost twice as wide, and he was white.

'You didn't see anything,' he said, and then, absurdly: 'Will you be alright?'

'What do you mean 'I didn't see anything'?' she demanded, her voice rising with anger and fear.

The man appeared vaguely disappointed. He grabbed her arm almost casually and pulled her away from the pens and out onto the street. She tried to resist, but he was too strong for her. He twisted her around until she was facing him again. The open, bright moonlight revealed details she hadn't noticed before, and she saw the dog collar for the first time. She gasped in surprise. 'Who are you?'

'My name is unimportant.' Sydney automatically tried to place the accent; it was French. 'As you can see, I'm a priest, and this,' he continued, sweeping one arm around him, 'is my parish.'

'They murdered a boy . . . !'

'Shut up,' he ordered.

Sydney swallowed, made an effort to lower her voice. 'They *murdered* a boy ...'

'It wasn't murder,' he told her, his voice insistent. 'It was self defence.'

Sydney stared at him. His face was partly covered by a tough, black beard. His eyes were dark and without expression.

'He was a pusher,' the priest continued. 'He was selling heroin to the kids in this neighbourhood. Whenever a pusher is caught in Klong Toey he's brought to the slaughterhouse for execution.'

'They have no right ... !'

'Listen to me! Peddling drugs is a capital offence in Thailand. The authorities execute a dozen pushers every month, and no one lifts a finger to stop them. But they don't care about the pushers in Klong Toey. The people that live here are untouchables. They take care of themselves. There's nothing else they can do.'

'But the body ...'

'Is treated the same as every other carcass.'

'Oh, God.'

The priest pushed her away. 'Leave Klong Toey. You don't belong here. You're not *wanted* here.'

'I don't understand,' she said wearily. 'You're a priest, for Christ's sake.'

'Yes, for Christ's sake,' he sighed, his blank eyes staring right through her. 'This is God's work we do.'

He spun around and headed back to the abattoir.

She woke with a start, her sheets moist with sweat, the smell filling her nostrils. She sobbed. The memory was as sharp as ever. She felt no pain or sickness, but every night she died in Bangkok.

There was a knock on the door. 'Yes?'

The door opened slightly, and Saavedra's head appeared. 'I was coming to see you, but when I knocked no one answered and I thought you must be asleep. And then I heard you cry out. I was worried for you.'

'It's alright. I'm fine.'

'Are you sure?'

'Yes. It was a dream. I'm fine now, really. Why did you want to see me?'

More of Saavedra appeared. 'I thought you might want someone to talk to.'

'For God's sake, Ariel, come in. You look like a trapped rat, half-in, half-out like that.'

'But are you decent?'

'I have a sheet over me, if that's what you mean.'

Saavedra entered the room and quietly closed the door behind him. He stood there like a timid servant, eyes cast down, hands clasped behind his back. 'I do not want you to think I'm being presumptuous ...'

Sydney turned on the bedside lamp. Saavedra glanced up, blushed and quickly threw his gaze down again. 'It is just that when you talked about salvation earlier today ... well, I am a priest. If you think it would help ...'

'You *do* want a confession,' she accused, her tone defensive.

'No. But perhaps you are worrying needlessly. Perhaps your soul is in no danger at all.'

Sydney laughed without humour. 'My soul is gone entirely, Ariel. I am only body.'

Ariel came forward until he was standing next to the bed. 'I cannot believe that. I cannot believe that of any person.'

'Your faith is too strong,' she said.

'Because I believe in my God, and in his eternal love. He would not desert anyone.'

'You misunderstand. It is I who deserted God. I have no stomach for the sacrifices he demands in exchange for his love. I have seen too much.'

'You can change.'

'Undoubtedly, but I don't want to change. That's what I've learned on Tongay. The Chapel of Bones, Golgotha ... the cost is too high. I must live my life, for whatever it's worth, without faith.'

'And without hope?'

'Without compromise, at least.'

Saavedra shook his head in disbelief. 'You have been wounded very deeply. I thought I might help, but I cannot see how to reach you.'

Sydney's face softened, and she brought her knees up to make room on the bed. 'Sit down,' she commanded. Saavedra sat. 'You have helped me, and reached me, simply by caring. I'm grateful, but just don't expect me to be grateful to your God.'

'I must be honest. I think you are wrong.'

'Of course you think I'm wrong. Your faith leaves you no choice.' She reached up and touched him gently on the cheek. He looked at her, his expression confused. She laid back then, letting the sheet slip down. At first he glanced away, but his head slowly turned back until he was looking at her once more. He timorously extended one hand, palm downward, and placed it in the middle of her chest. She lifted the hand and placed it over her left breast. 'For me,' she said.

He smiled sadly and returned his hand to where it had been. 'For your heart,' he said, and leaned over to kiss her.

In the morning he was gone. For the first time in over a year Sydney didn't want to leave bed the moment she was awake. She shut her eyes and tried to find sleep again, but the sunlight streaming through the French windows was too strong, and with a sigh of regret she slowly eased herself into a sitting position. She smiled as she remembered the night. *Perhaps this is how I find God*, she thought, but immediately shook her head. *No, that's ludicrous.*

Maria's voice called from outside the door. 'Ms Sydney, do not take too long. The jalopy will be here soon to take us to the Celebration. We must all go down to Puerto Santa Cruz together.'

Sydney was startled fully awake. *Oh God. It's Good Friday, the day of the Crucifixions. That means Ariel ...*

You can't Ariel. Not now.

She got out of bed and dressed quickly. By the time she got downstairs the jalopy had arrived and people were boarding. Saavedra was waiting for her.

'I didn't want to wake you,' he said into her ear.

'You don't have to go through with this,' she told him fiercely.

He shook his head. 'That is *why* I must go through with it.'

Maria and her husband, dressed in their best clothes, came up behind them. 'We must not be late,' Maria told them, sounding slightly flustered, and ushered them both aboard.

Puerto Santa Cruz was awash with people. Two large ferries were docked at the jetty, and several commercial VSTOLs had set down in the town square. The pilgrims from Santa Anna kept together, and within fifteen minutes of leaving the jalopy were at the soccer field, eagerly awaiting the start of the Celebration. Sydney found herself toward the front of the group, Saavedra on one side and Maria and her husband on the other. In the crush no one noticed that she was holding Saavedra's hand.

She tiptoed and whispered: 'You've proven you can love. It's not too late to go back.'

'I have proven I can love you,' he corrected her. 'Now I must prove I can love God, as well.'

Her mind was almost overwhelmed with a bitter sadness, and an aching chill filled her bones despite the day's heat.

The first sign that anything was about to happen was given by the television and newsnet crews, suddenly alert, their equipment flickering with red and green LEDs. Batteries of cameras, like heavy machine guns, turned on mounts and pointed toward the centre of the soccer field.

'It has begun!' Maria whispered urgently to her husband. He looked vacantly at her. 'Pray, Miguel, pray!' She clasped his hands together for him. 'Pray to God.' Miguel nodded, began mouthing some words. Sydney turned away. She of all people had no right to question their faith. She squeezed Saavedra's hand a little harder; he squeezed gently in return.

Ten crucifixes the colour of old bones were laid out on the ground. Locals milled about the field, mallets and sacks of nails in their hands, ropes tied around their waists.

From Sydney's left, immediately beneath one of the television stands, a Filipino wearing nothing but a loincloth strode across the field. He raised his arms in salute as the crowd cheered. He was taken to a cross. He laid down on it, shut his eyes and muttered prayers as his wrists and ankles were tied securely to the beam. The crowd fell silent. One of the helpers placed a nail over an open palm, raised a mallet, paused dramatically, and brought it down with great accuracy. The nail was driven through flesh and wood with a dull thunk. A cry of pain escaped from the suppliant's lips, but he cut it off by biting down on his tongue. His other hand and both feet were quickly pinned to the beams, and others gathered around the completed crucifix to help raise it. It fell into its hole in the ground with a gentle shudder. Blood streamed down the arms of the new Jesus.

Sydney swallowed a mouthful of bile, gripped Saavedra's hand even harder, but he was so busy shouting his approval with the others he didn't notice. Maria was alternatively cheering and weeping, and her husband looked on, mystified, muttering repeatedly '... gloria ... gloria ...   gloria ...'

A second man walked onto the field. The cameras panned to show him to the world.

But Sydney could watch no longer. She squeezed her eyes shut, forcing sudden tears of grief down her cheeks. *Will I ever know God again?* she wondered, and then with something of a shock realised it no longer mattered to her.

Sydney lost track of time, but when she opened her eyes nine crucifixes stood in the field like barren, bloody trees. The cameras, the people, seemed to be looking at her now. The world waited. 'No,' she whispered hoarsely. Saavedra tugged his hand free. 'No,' Sydney repeated more urgently, but someone was holding her by the shoulders. She reached out for the priest's hand. 'Ariel, you have nothing to prove. Please don't leave me ...'

It was too late. He was already on the field. They removed his sandals, his pants and his shirt, his watch. Stripped, they laid him down on the last cross and tied his limbs to the beams. As one of the workmen raised his mallet Sydney caught her breath, and when it came down hard and straight, plunging the nail through the flesh of the man she had shared, her scream of anger and defiance was swallowed by the ecstatic wailing of the people around her.

Sydney reeled back. The iron that pierced Saavedra's palm had impaled her heart. Once again she was nothing but body. Her gaze wandered over the crowd. She saw Maria jumping and clapping, saw Maria's husband staring vaguely into space still mouthing: '... gloria ...   gloria ... gloria ... ', and finally she saw Ariel raised high on his wooden chariot for all the world and its God to cheer.

She didn't wait for the end. She found a jalopy driver who took her up to Santa Anna. She packed and took the jalopy back down to the port where she boarded one of the waiting ferries, finding refuge of a kind at the stern of the boat. An hour later the ferry, loaded with day pilgrims, left the island to return to Mindanao.

Sydney kept to herself. She stood alone, staring back at Tongay, a small dark pyramid rising from the sea. Toward evening she glanced up at the island's summit, and for a brief moment she saw hundreds and hundreds of crosses silhouetted against the setting sun, stretching from one end of the island to the other, but the offerings were too late—the last of her faith had spilled from her soul like the blood from Ariel's hands.

And she knew, too, that she would never again dream of Klong Toey. Now she would dream of dark wooden crosses, crosses waiting for her at Golgotha.

Simon Brown's latest novel is *Empire's Daughter* (DAW), the first book in the Chronicles of Kydan. The second volume, *Rival's Son*, will be published in 2006. He lives on the NSW south coast with his wife and two children

RUNAWAY

LUCY SUSSEX

'TEN, NINE, EIGHT ...'

Counting down the New Year is always something special for us Runaways. We have a big BBQ, the whole of the family staying up till midnight, even the babies. However, we don't hold our New Year's parties at anybody's house, but out in the open, in the hill country, because that's our home, every stone of it. And we don't recognise new-fangled calendars like the Julian, or the Chinese, because we have our own New Year's day.

'seven, six ...'

Great-Gran Mowra stood on a big stump, leading the countdown. We had the lookout and its picnic ground to ourselves, just like we wanted it. The sheer volume of music coming from the boom boxes, the sight of the beat-up utes and the milling crowd of Runaways, in plaid shirts, jeans, barefoot, or in moccs, showing their (missing a few) teeth and tatts, with dogs and kids running riot, the general message being don't-you-mess-with-us ... well that scares others away. Nobody wants to picnic with trailer trash, nobody looks too closely at trailer trash. It's useful camouflage.

'five, four, three ...'

To one side the kids were ready with the home-made firecrackers. Just in case, I took a firm hold of the rope that held the Handies, though they should be used to fireworks by now, with all the training I'd given them.

'two, one!'

The night exploded with light, dogs barking and Runaways from all generations yelling at the top of their voices. The rope jerked a couple of times—Dimmey, of course—and then was still. We kept up the pandemonium as long as we felt like it, and then Great-Gran Mowra waved for silence.

'Ahem,' she said. 'Now for the Runaway family's New Year's resolution.'

She paused, as if listening, although the only sound was the crackling of the flames, the wind in the trees, a soft Handie snort.

'Well!' she said. 'Tough times, indeed, at the mo'. From the news you'd believe the end of the world was coming, or maybe just the end of *their* blessed economy. We've got trouble to either side of us, just like the days of the river family and the plains family all over again. Under the circumstances, the resolution has to be ... the same as ever. Lie low, prosper discreetly and above all, SURVIVE!'

The family cheered, every one of us. We weren't expecting anything different, just the Runaway family 40,000-year-old plan, but it was always nice to hear it again.

And with that, the celebration was over. We Runaways had work to do, some of us, and the rest needed our sleep. The boom boxes were switched off, the fire doused, dogs, kids, oldies packed into utes and vans, and we gradually and quietly disappeared into the night. We Runaways are good at disappearing, running away, that's how we got the name.

I sat, holding onto the rope and saying goodbyes. When I was the last Runaway at the picnic ground, I stood up, and whistled: work time!

Six large pairs of eyes reflected the moon's full light back at me, six pairs of ears pricked. I had prepared earlier, for the night's run, and each Handie carried a pack. I fixed the rope to my harness and said:

'Hey ho, let's go!'

There was silence all around, apart from the sound of Uncle Tich's muffler, a receding roar. The nearest non-Runaways were ks away and there was nobody to witness a slightly rough looking citizen leading—how cute!—six shetland ponies into the bush.

And immediately down a steep incline, enough to make any watcher think their eyes had been playing tricks, and that they'd mistaken the ponies for shaggy and agile mountain goats.

The bush is full of tracks, if you've got the right knowledge. Go off the dirt or macadam and you'll find the roads for the creatures of the bush—wombat, wallaby and the Runaway family. Some, like the wombats, are well-marked, like the tracks of a mini-tank, if a tank left square turds behind. Others, well, they're invisible unless you're a Runaway. We can follow them with our eyes closed. It's like an old and much loved tatt—you can follow the curves of it around in your mind without looking at or touching it. Don't ask me how. If I live long enough to be an Elder, then one day Mowra'll tell me.

Some of the Runaway tracks lead to secret places, plantations and workshops for small illegal things. Couple of the

Great-Uncles dig for gold somewhere down that left fork and over the hill; I've seen another uncle, who's got a sideline in seasonal produce, wild magic mushrooms, on that track sometimes. But if you take the right fork for five k or so, and climb over the fence to the water catchment area, that's where the younger cousins grow their ganja crop. But if anyone's snooping, it's for private use only, Mr Officer sir! Mr Mafia sir! We Runaways always stay on the good side of the powers that be, official or not.

'Lie low, prosper discreetly and above all, SURVIVE!' It was a good motto, dreamed up who-knows-when, when the Runaway family first found themselves in the hills, squeezed between larger, fiercer families—what the anthropology types would call tribes—on richer, more attractive chunks of land. So we made do, adapting anything that came along to our use. If that meant trade goods, fine, if that meant the occasional couple from another family, eloping in a wrongheaded marriage, fine—we don't mind new blood! If that meant runaways pale like blossom and wearing bracelets hard as meteor stone, walking to some place they called 'China' ... well, they too joined the family, and shared what they knew with us.

Course, things got tough when the rest of the Blossom family arrived with their suitcases, chattels and guns. However, we were on land nobody saw much value in but us (unlike the land of the poor old plain and river families). So we learned a lot of new skills in a hurry, lied a lot (specially to the missionaries), and stayed around the hill country. When it became a problem that we weren't pale in colour, we found Blossom family members who had the Runaway sort of attitude, and *intermingled* with them. Now, couple of centuries and a lot of sex later, we were olive-coloured, with skinnier legs and darker eyes than the norm. But nothing anyone could get personal about.

Next fork in the path I went left, following a thread of track along the side of a hill, the Handies padding behind me. This was an old, old route, where Runaways went carrying goods to trade with the other families. Some things don't change—it's just the goods and the value put on them that does. Once a shell from the distant seashore was worth its weight in ... something or other. Now a shell was worth nothing much; I carried gold dust, mushrooms, ganja, and other stuff, valuable to various people. Call me a courier, call me a black marketeer, call me a smuggler, if you must. Just don't call me girlie ...

In a gum tree just above, a possum let out a territorial roar. Hi, fellow Survivor! I thought, then, Oh shit! From behind me came a fearful whinny, then a frantic scrabbling. I turned to see the line of Handies kinked: the second last Handie was half on, half off the path, and teetering.

Dimmey! Might have known it. When Aunt Gidj had passed

on the Handies to me, I'd assumed the naming, which tended to simple descriptors: Sturdy, Shagpile, et cetera. Most folk couldn't tell the Handies apart, but I could see the subtle differences, in looks and personality. All of them had sound horsesense or better, except for one. Dimmey was trouble, which nearly became his name with a capital T, until I decided he was just dim. Anything that could go wrong, would, if he was involved. Now the Handie on either side was supporting his weight, stopping him from sliding any further down the hillside.

The rope was Smart, being liberated from a bungy-jumping business in one of the gorges. It had all sorts of interesting properties, but hadn't been made with sheer brute dimness in mind. Worse, there was no room for me to edge back along the track, unless I climbed over the intervening hairy backs. I called to the hindmost Handie: 'BigGrrl! Stay put!' Then I patted the muzzle of the leading Handie, Trusty (because unlike Dimmey, he was reliable) and took a couple of paces forward, leading the line of Handies with me, except for BigGrrl. The Handies pulled, BigGrrl stood fast, and we dragged Dimmey safely onto the track again.

When we got to the nearest open space, on a small hilltop, I paused, thinking what to do. If Dimmey was going to be a scaredy-shier all the trip, then I might as well leave him behind hobbled, to be retrieved later. On the other hand I had a full load of packs, and an eager client. I sighed, and went on into the night.

Coming down the hill, I saw moonlight in front of me, reflected off the window of a small mudbrick house. I knew the people living there were squatting illegally; and if they knew I sometimes went walking by their parsnip patch at night, they didn't show it. Them that asks no questions isn't told a lie, I thought, and then came the rest of the words, long forgotten, read aloud from a picture book by some teacher:

> Watch the wall, my darling, while the Gentlemen go
> by!
> Four and twenty ponies
> Trotting through the dark—
> Brandy for the Parson,
> 'Baccy for the Clerk;
> Laces for a lady, letters for a spy,
> Watch the wall, my darling, while the Gentlemen go
> by!

Well, I wasn't carrying grog, smokes or spy info—not this night. And if there was any lace around then it certainly wasn't on *my* knickers. Nor were there any gents involved, nor 24-pack carriers, only six. Maybe, if the business expanded, one day. If wishes were Handies …

Shooting star overhead, something else to wish on, if I'd wanted to. I followed the speck of light with my gaze, until it dropped behind the steep rockface, just ahead. The little valley with the squatters was some distance back now, yet I waited for a minute, listening to the night sounds around me. It never pays to be too careful; but all seemed clear. 'Hup!' I said to the Handies, and we started the short climb up the rockface.

The steep slopes on this track were the reason for the rope; that and Dimmey's fondness for wandering off. Mostly the Handies would follow you like dogs, though no dog could climb like this. The old rhyme was running through my head again, I just couldn't seem to get rid of it. Not four and twenty, nor pony either, not entirely ...

The Handies didn't look unusual, just short, shaggy little horses, though a bit out of proportion, with a bigger head, ears and eyes than the pony-norm. But it was the feet that were the giveaway. If you bothered to look under the long footsocks of fetlocks, there was no hoof, just a bunch of toes, with little stubby claws. We Runaways hadn't bred them, we'd *acquired* them, or rather their mamas, two pony mares in foal. Acquiring, Runaway style, usually meant outside the official economy— from trade, fencing, favours owed and done. It wasn't that the mares had fallen off the back of a horsefloat and Aunt Gidj just happened to be passing by, but ...

After the foaling was over, at Gidj's little farm, she needed a lie-down. Six live young and mutants to boot ... I mean, to foot. Then she summoned the Runaway's animal experts for a conference. There were four of us, Great-Gran Mowra, Gidj, me and Uncle Tich, who'd once been a jockey.

'And just where did you get those mares?' he'd asked Gidj.

'I guess ... it was middlemen I dealt with.'

'Middlemen?'

'The body language said the goods'd been liberated from somewhere. I smelt a bit of fear, too. But not enough for me to look some cheap horseflesh in the mouth, well, no closer than usual.'

The heap of blanket on Gidj's lap had stirred then, and she'd stuck a feeding bottle into the little mouth that appeared between two folds. The runt of the litters, had to be revived, needed special care. Dimmey, of course ...

Uncle Tich thought a bit. 'I heard some talk about the Ag College over the hills. They got all sorts of money from the racing industry, to *experiment*, I heard.'

'On ponies?' I'd asked.

'Starting small ... Just like horses did, with Eohippy.'

Gidj looked at me. 'Movies, you ever seen anything like the foals before.'

'No, not even in Hollywood.'

Runways are good with animals, that's how I'd blagged myself into a job with a film crew doing a wildlife documentary. At first it was opening cages and picking up poo, then serious animal training for commercials and features. Film work had taken me around the world; until I got homesick for the hills, and fellow Runaways, even if they'd taken to calling me Movies. But better that than Girlie.

'Sorrow,' Tich'd said. 'That's the word—sorrowgacy. The foals aren't with their mamas, not that these mamas know.'

'Blossoms is just too clever for their own good,' Gidj had muttered, rocking her bundle gently.

I'd gotten up at that and walked over to the stalls, looking at the mares and the foals, teetering on their long legs, just like any other equine baby. They didn't look like children of sorrow.

Tich had rubbed two fingers together. 'Sorrowgacy means money, maybe big money. Someone might pay to get their property back.'

'I'm not sure I'd want to deal with the folk who did this,' Gidj had said, pulling out a small foot from the blanket, and displaying it in her palm.

Tich had rocked in his seat like it was a saddle. 'It'd have to be racing folk did this. What's stopping horses from going any faster? Mostly foot design. So maybe they spliced in some greyhound genes, or a monkey's ...'

We had talked and talked about it for hours, until Mowra, who hadn't said a word all night, settled the issue.

'Family rule: big money usually means big trouble. Don't let's go looking for it.'

Gidj had added fiercely: 'Nobody's taking these babies away for experiments.'

Tich had sighed. 'Well, in that case looks like we're keeping 'em. But I only work with horses I can ride. So I guess that leaves Movies.'

There was a long silence.

'OK, Movies?' said Mowra.

'Er ...' I said.

'OK, Movies.' It wasn't a question now, more an order.

OK. I lifted up my hand and made the sign, forefinger and thumb meeting for the 'o', the rest of the fingers splayed like the top of a 'k'. It was the way I'd learnt on the film sets, when what with all the bells and whistles going off, the signals for the trained animals, you could hardly hear yourself think, let alone speak.

'Guess they'll come in handy somehow,' I said.

Gidj had stroked the little foot in her palm. 'Hand-ies.' And the name had stuck ...

It wasn't long before I found out just how handy the mutant foals could be. A pack of feral dogs had gone on a rampage through my farmlet one night, and in the general mayhem I didn't notice at first that the Handie paddock was empty. Gate was shut, the fence was too high, surely, for them to leap: so where were they? I walked around the paddock in the dawnlight, clutching my shotgun, now and then coming across the results of my sharpshooting—a dog-corpse in the grass. Then I noticed the windbreak trees looked cankered and craned my neck upwards to see, in the branches, seven dark lumps, the foals and one really pissed-off cat, hair on end.

Hmn, good night vision for a horse, hmn, good climbers. At that time I was going up this cliff regularly, though not with Handies, but tourists. Adventure Bushwalks, my business was called, and I led parties along tracks that weren't special, or secret to the Runaways. For a while it was a nice little earner, nothing like the film industry, but OK. Shame the world economy had to go pear-shaped, for suddenly people didn't have the yen, or dollars, for holidays anymore.

We were nearly at the top of the rockface now, a line of climbers and ropes. Another metre, and I clambered onto the hill saddle, followed by Trusty & Co. At this point in the tour I'd have been handing out water bottles but Handies were a tougher breed. I began to jog, and they trotted behind. The ridge was flat and wide enough for an ATV (as the tourists never failed to remark) ... except that jeeps and the like weren't leaving the city much, what with the fuel supplies alternately dribbling or droughting.

The first big fuel drought saw the Ganja cousins on my doorstep. Could I help them out? They needed to get supplies to market, and they'd lucked onto someone who could help, who lived on a tributory to the city-bound river, and had a boat. Trouble was, he was leaving tomorrow and he lived on the other side of the hills.

'C'mon Movies, you climb, and you know all the routes ...'

'Yeah, but carrying that load?' Then my gaze fell on BigGrrl, a yearling now, like the rest of the foals, and a hefty filly indeed. I did some weightlifting experiments. It nearly killed the cousins laughing, the sight of walking haybales with a Handie underneath. Hmn, strong little beggars. First trip I took BigGrrl and Trusty, for obvious reasons. They did just fine, which set me thinking, and then training my charges hard as I could. They responded well to commands, good as a dog, they were brighter than the average equine (Dimmey excepted) but still I had the feeling I'd only scratched their hairy little surface.

Next drought, I was ready, and started tendering for business, as you might say. Of course, this meant dealing with folk outside the Runaways, from all the Blossom families that had come and settled among us. We had Survivalists in one valley, busy hoarding everything they could lay their hands on and guarding it. Next valley along were ferals, and a little further down the tax lurk winery mob, alias *The Mob*. Someone had burnt down a bridge? Fine, I'd circumnavigate it. Somebody had some hot property they wanted moved to a safe place without anyone knowing? No worries. Some consenting married adults were having a long-distance affair? Fine, I'd play post-box Cupid.

Of course, this meant people outside the family would see the Handies and might start noticing they left some odd tracks. The best Runaway minds brainstormed, then made, galoshes, as we called them, to fit over the little feet and make them look like hooves. It was a devil of a job getting the Handies used to them, but by sugar bribes, bullying and cajoling, we managed it. Even though Dimmey still kept losing his ...

I called Gidj round for tea, and to show off the troupe in their nice new galoshes.

'They might look like ponies now,' she said. 'But don't you forget they're something more.'

'Yeah, but what?'

She shook her dreadlocked head. 'I don't know yet. We can't tell what they can do, because they're still babies. You take a baby, a helpless whinging lump, give it a few years, and you'll find it teasing the hogs or going out rabbiting. Runaway babes, that is.'

'Handies ain't interested in hogs or rabbits.'

'They will be.'

OK, I signed at her. Have it your own way ...

We were over the ridge now, heading down again into land that I'd have preferred to avoid, as the family here wasn't you-mind-your-own-business-I'll-mind-mine. But that was where the handover point was, agreed in advance, so I had to stick to it. I was just the messenger, no need to shoot me, no need to think about what was a pretty lucrative load. Even if I didn't know what the recipients were going to do with it. 'Them that asks no questions ...'

I took a wombat's track down to the road, which was silent and empty—it had been blocked and guarded, some ks ahead. No chance the Handies and I'd run into Old Man wombat, for he strolled this section of his track at sundown, keeping to his own regular body clock. My rendezvous point was the old graveyard on the other side of the road, something that unnerved me a little. Trust the Blossoms to be blind to the bad vibes.

Down to the macadam now, on which a horse's hooves would have clip-clopped, but a Handie just pad-padded. And there, in the graveyard, shone a torch, the signal, the beam shaking slightly as it turned on and off. Nervous of Blossom ghosts, I decided—but then the nearest Handie gave a sudden soft snort and stopped still in its tracks. Each one of them halted with their ears up and their nostrils dilated, as if they didn't like what they smelt or heard. I got a whiff of it too ... there was a whole group of folk waiting for us, when the understanding was that this was a small, private deal, between me and my client only. If he wanted a load of guns ferried over the hills to deal with his uproad neighbors, then that was my business only until the goods were delivered and I got paid.

'Movies?' That was my client, all right, but with a strangled sound to his voice, as if he had a knife at his throat. The smart rope was still attached to my harness, with its control pod: I tapped the code that broke it into sections, and felt it part and retract, each Handie stepping free. Then I whistled at the top of my lungs, the command that meant: Scatter! And go home fast!

One Handie charged up the road, another down—a third and fourth went crashing into the undergrowth, and what the other two did I don't know, because I bolted for the wombat track. Yells came from behind me, a shot cracked in the darkness, but I was moving at speed on the smooth-trodden earth of the track. I didn't stop until I was over the hill, and then only momentarily, because feet were pounding up the slope after me. I glanced at the starry sky, checking my bearings, as a volley of shots spat into the night. There was another path leading off the wombat track, special to us Runaways, invisible to anyone else. If you weren't an elder like Mowra, it was for emergencies only, like *now*! I hightailed down it, moving as quietly and quickly as I could.

The interference being run by the Handies was spot-on. I guessed the ambush had been for the load of guns in the packs ... and the Handies had all gone in different directions, divvying up the pursuit. Smart work that, smart as their troublespotting; without the early warning we'd have been surrounded as soon as we entered the graveyard. 'Teasing the hogs or going rabbiting,' was what Gidj had said. Well, they weren't doing *that* yet, but they were certainly going up the learning curve like it was a rockface.

I could hear the crashing and swearing behind me reach the hill-top, see torches sweeping through the bush. Moving as silently as I could, I looked for cover, and found it: a feral blackberry bush. I crawled under it, biting my lip at the thorns. Then I just laid low and watched the pursuit head off in another direction. When their racket had passed, I extricated myself slowly and painfully from the spiky embrace.

Once out, I moved on down the track, ears and eyes at

the alert. A leaf cracked behind me, and I froze, listening, my heart pounding and adrenalin surging up and down my body. Inwardly I counted to 50, then again, but nothing stirred. I went on, after ten paces pausing again, then after another ten, stopped for longer, listening or sniffing as hard as I could. Hell, I was being so careful it was almost paranoia, though after this night, paranoia might just seem sound good sense.

Who had gazumped my client? The bunch blocking the road, I guessed, his Survivalist enemies. I stopped again, holding my breath, but all that happened was that a frogmouth swooped overhead, chasing a large moth. Teach me to traffic in guns; but I'd carried all sorts of illegals before and nothing had happened. Ten paces on and I froze once more. Was that a faint vibration on the track behind me? Again a long wait, for nothing, not even wildlife. Hell, I was getting worse than Dimmey for scaredy-shies—at this rate I'd take years to get home across the hills. Better to ignore the paranoia and just keep walking on.

I was following a curve now, the corner of the hill, a rock outcrop jutting out. I stopped, realising why this route was elder-only. There was old, old story stuff here, the rock being something else, once. If I lived long enough, if I lived past this night, Mowra might tell me all about it. I touched the outcrop, paying my respects. Though it was still and cold under my hands, from somewhere within it I had the sense of something like a beat, maybe the artery thump of Runaway country lifeblood, what had kept us here all these eons. I connected to it ...

When I lifted my hand my inner duststorm of fear and stress had settled; and I also had the distinct sense that I'd been read a lecture, as elders do to the silly young. Now I could think of something else besides the big Me, Movies. Like what it might be like to be a little horse, running through the night, guns on my back, guns behind me. Were the Handies scared, wounded, even dead, because of the error of judgement I'd made, in carrying a dangerous cargo? I'd tried the scatter command a few times in the bush; the Handies had responded well, but never with real danger after them.

Just because my family are runaways, doesn't mean we're cowards. We help each other, in a fix. I hoped the Handies would have had had the wit (just how much wit, was something I'd probably have to revise upwards) not to get themselves in a fix. But at least I should try and find out whether they'd all gotten away or not.

From the outcrop I could sense the path ahead. A little way on it met another, quite well-travelled, an everyday Runaway route. If I kept to this track I'd have a long walk home, curving around what the Survivalist family thought was their land, but was really Runaway country, as it had been long before and would be long after them. The other way curved back through old growth forest, towards the folk who'd tried to kill me and my horses. I took it.

In the forest was a super-gloom, the only light from snatches of starry sky seen through the leaf canopy overhead. And that was how I got myself in a right mess. My boot met something which gave, flesh over bone, and living flesh at that. Next moment I grappled in the dark with something, no someone, waking from sleep with grog on his breath, but nonetheless wiry and strong. We rolled over and over, bumping into tree roots and what felt like the metal and wheels of an all-terrain motorbike. I did what I could, wrestled and bucked, but still ended on the ground, him sitting astride me, as if we were doing a spot of *intermingling*. A torch shone in my face.

'Girlie Runaway!'

First girl born for several generations in my branch of the family, and what did my parents call me? Yep, you guessed it.

The voice sounded familiar, vaguely.

'And who are you?'

In answer he shone the torch up at his chin: a local.

'Well, Girlie, after all these years.'

I knew the face, but not the name. 'What are you doing here?' I said.

'Well, I'm with the Survivalists now.' As if that explained everything. 'And you're with the Runaways, as always. I usta be friends with a coupla them, we dealt in ganja. They'd take me walking through the hills on the Runaway tracks—until we had a little argument about the proceeds. Your cousins owe me.'

'I'm not my cousins' keeper.'

He ignored that. 'Fact, when I heard about this little op, I figured they were doing the gun-running, right down their alley, it would be. So I started wondering how I might get my dues. Survivalists are new around here, they don't know that it's hard to catch a Runaway. They didn't ask me and I wasn't going to tell them that the graveyard ambush was daft. I've seen your cousins do the scatter and scarper trick.'

I was going to have words with them, if I ever got out of this mess, for being indiscreet ...

'Now, your cousin Wombat, know how he got the name?'

I knew, but wasn't going to tell him. It was for Runaways only, even if he trotted out that tired joke about eats, roots, shoots ...

'Sticks to certain paths, he does. And he's fond of this stretch. So, I thought, lemme volunteer for outer sentry duty, then get lost ... on Wombat's fave trail, so I could get my dues either coming or going.'

He belched, the smell of a home-distillery thick as a fog.

'While I was waiting I passed the time with a little tipple. Musta overdone it, because next thing you fall over me. Nothing coming, but something going?'

'I'm not Wombat.'

Long pause. 'Runaways stick together, everyone knows that.'

Yes, drat it.

He sighed. 'It's not much I'm owed, not really. But is it worth your value to the family?'

'I won't be worth much if you keep crushing me.'

He hiccuped. 'Point took. But Girlie, you aren't gunna do a bolt on me, areya?'

I could feel something in his pocket, digging into me, and no, it wasn't because he was pleased to see me, either. If this was what I thought it was ...

'No tricks,' he said, rising slightly. Immediately I twisted beneath him. The torch went flying and I aimed a distracting blow with one fist, with the other hand trying a spot of pick-pocketing. Damn, not a gun, but still better with me than with him ...

It was safely underneath me when he plumped down on me hard, knocking the breath quite out of my lungs. For a little while we just sat there, me panting, he sitting there on my back like he was Uncle Tich, out training his hopeless racehorses.

'I said, Girlie: no tricks.'

One of his hands reached down, fiddling in his pants. Oh gawd, he wasn't getting randy, was he?

'Where's me bike key?' he said.

Underneath me, buster. He felt in all his pockets, reached over and retrieved the torch, using the beam to rake the surroundings. I saw, close by, a disused wombat hole, almost overgrown ... but also a faint movement, something ducking out of sight.

'Musta dropped it.' He thought some more. 'Oh well. Changa plan. I'm not carrying you Girlie, you ain't skinny no more. And I gotta make sure you stay put. Since I can't ride me bike, I gotta walk. I need something like yer little ponies, to carry you back to this hidey hole I've got. And there you'll stay until your cousins pay up.'

His fingers gripped the harness on my back and all in one movement he got up, pulling me with him. The torchlight skidded wildly, my feet ruffled up the leafmould ... and with that noise as cover, I threw his precious key down the burrow. You'd need an earthmover to get it out now, or a tame wombat.

'Rope attached, hey. That's useful.' The torchbeam shot all over the place again, then he focussed it. 'Oh, one of them clever ropes. Know how to deal with those.' He held the torch in his teeth, grabbed the rope's control, and squeezed it flat as a roadside tinnie. 'There. Now it's just ordinary rope.'

He wound the rope around me and also the nearest treetrunk, not a forest giant, but still thick and strong. My hands were trussed in front, the remaining rope then tied at the back like an apron. I tensed, testing the knots—they felt sloppy. When he'd finished he frisked me, and I blessed the instinct that had me dispose of his key. But he took everything useful to me right now: knife, torch, matches. The rest, like the sugar cubes for the Handies, he strewed at my feet.

'Never was a boy scout,' he said. 'And I know how you Runaways get outa things. I also know how they can't hold their liquor either—'specially you, Girlie. Sorry about this, but business is business.'

He held a bottle in his hand; now he took hold of nape-hair, and pulled my head back hard. I gasped, and the lip of the bottle slid between my teeth. Foul-tasting pot liquor cascaded into my mouth—it was swallow or choke. It burned a trail down my throat and into my belly. When the bottle was empty, he released me. Ever feel the bite of the snake, and know that you have only a few minutes to save yourself, before the poison takes effect? That was how I felt, and there was nothing I could do.

I watched as the beam of his torch receded, growing fainter, then finally disappearing around a turn of the track. Cursing was something only Mowra did, and then reluctantly, but nonetheless I sent a nasty wish after him. Break a leg, or better still, your neck.

I tried to think, before the grog fuddled me, what the hell to do. How to get out of here ... *with or without help.* I had seen movement in the torchlight: there was something out there. Now I could hear, very faintly, sounds approaching me. No wild animal would do that, and a human, unless they were a Runaway, would make too much noise. I didn't know what was coming, but I'd chance that it was friendly. I stood and waited, all I could do, while the liquor burnt its way through the walls of my belly.

A dim shape neared. I held my breath, listening hard to: a scrape against tree trunk, a long exhaled breath, then, when it was less than a metre away, a snort. A moment later rough horsehair, covering iron-hard muscles and flesh, rubbed against me. A Handie! but in the dark I couldn't see which one. Its head lowered as it scoffed the spilt sugar at my feet. I reached out a hand as far as the rope would let me, felt the leather of the pack saddle, but no load. Well, after tonight I wasn't trafficking in guns again, but they could have been useful now, assuming I could have got one out, loaded it, and shot my bonds off before the grog hit.

'Do you a deal,' I murmured, when the crunching of sugar had stopped. Shit, I was slurring my words already. 'Get me out of this tangle and it's double sugar ration. *Zhu-ga*, *Zhu-ga*, you know what that is.'

It was whistling in the dark ... but the Handies responded to whistles. I felt it sniffling upwards, following the sugar trail back to my empty pocket. It brushed past me, following the line of the rope around the tree. Silence. Then the rope jerked, even the tree shuddered, as the Handie began a determined onslaught on the knot.

Smart rope wasn't just hemp, but all sorts of other things, mostly not the stuff you'd chew on or even sever easily. But I couldn't blame the Handie for trying; they had a vicious bite on them, as Cousin Wombat had found out when he teased them. Serve him right. I'd have the Handies more than bite him when I got out of here ... if, that is. Yeah, when the Handies took up rabbiting, maybe.

Or maybe they would, real soon now! The rope pulled, cutting into me, then started to give. I flexed my arm muscles, then next moment the ropes dropped loose from the trunk, and I stepped away, and free. First thing I did crouch over and stick my fingers down my throat. I vomited hot bile, but not much of it. And now my head was spinning, my wits dulling with nausea. I worried the loops of rope around my hands, but they wouldn't give and I couldn't see to work out the knots. Nevermind, I still had my feet free. I stood, took a step—and fell over.

Beside me the Handie snorted again. I grabbed at its tail, pulling myself up, then collapsed half across the small wiry body before I could—sort of—stand again. I had just enough sense left to loop my bound hands over the pommel of the pack saddle. The shaggy head turned and I felt hot horse breath on my face: it was smelling me.

'Yeah I'm sick', I muttered, 'real sick. Which means that for once, you're the boss. Get me out of here, any way you want.' Then, very softly, I gave the whistle for home.

We started off, me half-crouched over, half-supported by the Handie, concentrating on keeping on my feet, keeping my feet moving. All I could hear was the sound of leaves crushed under our footsteps, the faint creak of leather and rope. All I could smell was dried horse sweat, all I could see was the dark mass beside me, ears pricked, as if pleased with itself. The horse boss took us off the Runaway trail, going cross-country, following a maze of different animal tracks, wallaby, wombat, and smaller. I barely comprehended them, so grimly determined was I on keeping my body under control. The night had contracted around us, just me and the Handie, all alone in the universe.

I know I passed out at least once. The consciousness flicked off, and next moment I was kneeling on some hard and nubbly tree roots, dangling off the Handie by my bound hands. One hurt like buggery, and I felt blood drip down my wrist. The Handie nudged me with its muzzle, hard: on your bike, mate! I knew then it had bitten me awake, but better that than drag me like a stunt man in some western. I pulled my feet under me, forced myself to stand, and on we went again, the constant ache from my hand like a strong and horrid coffee, keeping me walking wounded.

It was a hell of a journey, measured only by the different terrain under my feet: leaf mould, dry earth, tussocks, and rock. The only way I knew that hours had passed was that very slowly the nausea, the discombobulation turned into the mother of all hangovers. But I was getting my brain back, even if it hurt. I started to see shapes more clearly, although they were all a shade of dusky grey. Now, in the pre-dawn light, the first dawn of the new Runaway year, I could get the sense of the land around me. We were moving out of the old forest, and into the beginnings of the serious hills. Soon, we'd be out from the canopy, soon it would be light enough for me to see and sort out the knots.

The trees thinned, became scattered, and finally fell behind us. We were climbing now, on exposed pastureland littered with rocks. Ahead I could see an outcrop, one I knew. From it my house was visible, but better still was that part of the outcrop formed a bowl, where rainwater collected. Beneath my feet all sorts of tracks converged, for the rock pool was dry only in the worst droughts. When we reached it, I unlooped my hands from the pommel and knelt. The Handie lowered its long head to drink. The water might be brackish, and with little wiggling things in it, but it was the best thing I had ever tasted.

When I had drunk my fill, I hunkered back, wiping my mouth. I tasted blood again, and inspected the wound. Vicious but fair, under the circumstances. Then I stared at the ends of the ropes. They were not chewed, like I was, but neat. Somebody had gone and *untied* the knots. I stared at the Handie again, seeing now that it wasn't big, not like Sturdy or BigGrrl, nor hairy like Shagpile, nor ...

'Dimmey!'

He looked at me from under his straggly forelock, ears still pricked. Then he lifted one foreleg almost to my eye level and lowered it. It was naked, the hand plain to see—he'd lost his galoshes again. The toes on it flexed, then touched. Well, I'll be, opposable digits. No wonder he could get his galoshes off so easily, or get rid of his pack, which had been securely fastened. Or untied the rope. The runt of the litter, who'd always got special attention, always played up, played stupid, as when he got lost (exploring?), or fell off the track (a pretence to test the smart rope?).

The outermost toe of the Handie touched the next one in. 'Yes,' I said. 'I know you're clever, I know you untied me.'

Then my hair stood on end as the three remaining toes straightened, splaying like the arms of a K. OK, my OK. For all I knew the Handies had not only picked up the sign from me, but were also aware of its meaning.

It repeated the gesture. OK—and there was only one answer. With my good hand I made the O and the K, showing I understood ... that you're more than I thought you were, that I was in a fix and you got me out, that I owe you. OK? OK.

Wait until Gidj heard about this, I thought, or Mowra. We'd got used to the other families, and their little ways, even the Blossoms. Now here came along another family, not even human, but with funny agile feet and even more agile brains. Well, it'd be a learning curve for us, but I figured the Handies already had some of the Runaway attitude, which was what was most important. Give it time, and we'd all go rabbiting together, just like Gidj said. Even though I wondered if the boot, I mean, the galosh, was on the other foot, er, hand now.

But in the end, we'd probably lie low, prosper discreetly and survive together quite well.

Then I held out my hands in supplication to Dimmey-no-more, waiting to be untied.

Lucy Sussex was born in New Zealand, and is a Senior Research Fellow at Melbourne University. She has published editions of crime writers Mary Fortune and Ellen Davitt; and four anthologies, including *She's Fantastical* (1995), shortlisted for the World Fantasy Award. Her award-winning fiction includes five books for younger readers and one adult novel, *The Scarlet Rider* (1996). She has written two short story collections, *My Lady Tongue* and *A Tour Guide in Utopia* (Mirrordanse, 2005), with another forthcoming. Currently she reviews weekly for *The Age* and *West Australian* newspapers. She is also completing a book on early women and crime fiction. http://lsussex.customer.net space.net.au

MOONFLOWERS AT THE RITZ

MARIANNE DE PIERRES

O NLY THE INDOLENT, YOUNG RICH stay at the *Carmine Island Ritz*. With its wide verandahs, white linen and staggering views of the rainbow-coral reefs, it's the perfect place for afternoon daiquiris. Or, on the back of a generous tip, thimbles of pink and white amphetamines, served on a silver platter with martini chasers and slivers of lime melon.

On my infrequent visits to the lobby bar with the *Carmine Island Tourism Auxiliary,* I watch them at their entertainments.

The meetings themselves represented a great farce—encouraging tourism on an Island transformed by an air-born canopy of dangerous spores. Had the wider world understood the true nature of the threat, *Carmine* would have suffered an imposed quarantine, followed by an infestation of recognition-hungry scientists.

Like all the other residents, my almost pathetic need for separateness, and the desire to preserve *Carmine's* seductive quality, ensured my collusion in its secret.

Meanwhile, the wealthy, youthful faces of the Ritz blended into a morass of prematurely softening features and casual sneers peculiar to those who never need concern themselves with money.

Mid mornings the young surfed the break past the rocks at *Mestiqua Beach,* under the watchful eye of Island lifesavers on twin-motored *Harbinger's.* Late afternoons they took chairlifts to the top of the dunes and careened wildly back down on sleek broad-backed sandboards. Or, on an ethnic whim, toured the protected sacred sites at *Black Swamp* and *Ningil.*

The rest of their time was spent in a pleasure-seeking haze in the Lobby Bar of the *Ritz.* That was where one evening, Lauren Carson and I met Blade Reeves.

Fellow *Auxiliary* members had drifted off early to other appointments, leaving us to our pink champagne. I sat admiring Lauren's sophistication. With her sleek blonde hair and Dolce Gabbor sunglasses, she seemed perfectly at home in the *Ritz*

Lobby Bar—despite her concealed sightlessness.

Unlike me!

'Katrin won't come here anymore. She says the odour of wasted money sickens her,' Lauren commented, idly, with a hint of gentle humour.

Katrin. Untamed. Spore-immune.

'Another glass?' I leaned forward to pour, curious to hear more about Lauren's lover but a figure brushed my arm. The bottle tipped, its contents staining my Sari.

'Please, you must help me ...' A young man stood there, shirtless, ghost-faced and distressed, hands out flung. His face seemed familiar.

'I've heard the Curlews.'

Behind him a solicitous servant hovered with a white shirt and sports jacket, as if hoping to ensnare him with the clothes. 'Master Blade, please calm yourself—'

Lauren turned her attention to him, her lovely voice soothing. 'The Curlews are a feature of *Carmine Island*. They are steeped in myth. But truthfully, they cannot harm you.'

'They fly with death. I know—she told me.'

'She?' Lauren voiced my thought.

'Shaka, the *Voyant*.'

Voyant. Kino-psychics. According to Katrin the latest, most fashionable leech on society circles, usurping the domain of therapists. Even the *Carmine Ritz* had engaged one, Shaka, a bitter-lipped woman, with skin discoloured the unnatural orange of pigment enhancement —an affectation to render her more authentic.

Katrin disdained her.

The mere mention of Shaka's name chased coherency from the young man's tongue. He reached for his pockets and shakily retrieved some capsules, jamming them into his mouth. Then he snatched the remnants of our champagne bottle and swallowed convulsively.

After moment of uncertainty, he took a shaky breath.

'Forgive my rudeness. Blade Reeves.' He held out a hand, grasping Lauren's as if a lifeline.

Blade Reeves, son of Interstellar Communications magnate, Gertha Reeves? Wealth even I was aware of—despite my disinterest in the larger world.

I noticed Lauren tremble—whether at the young man's touch or in recognition of his pedigree, I didn't know. The legacy of Lauren's encroaching blindness—a consequence of her contact with the spores—was an extraordinary intuition about people. It mired her in the tedium of their habits, something for which I had no patience. It also blessed her with an empathy that made rest of the world seemed pitiless.

'Lauren Carson.' She replied. 'And my friend, Tinashi.'

Friend. Her claim left me sweating slightly. I had no wish for intimacy or its pains.

'We live at *Glimmer-by-Dark.* A most marvelous, secluded beach. You must come and visit us.'

My mouth opened, astonished at her impulsive invitation. A disturbed billionaire's son! What would Katrin say to that?

'You are most generous. But please, do me the honour first of attending a room party tomorrow evening. It's my birthday.' He uttered the last with an endearing bashfulness.

Lauren clapped her hands. 'How wonderful, Tinashi. A birthday party at the Ritz.'

But Blade was already distracted, eyes drawn toward the heavy, pirouetting doors of the lobby and outside toward the hammering surf. 'Tomorrow, Lauren Carson,' he whispered. 'Please don't forget.'

Katrin was furious. Her rage soared.

They sat on my patio oblivious to the scarlet sunset and the playful, warm fingers of *The Bara.*

'What would you have me do at such a party?'

'But he is lost, Katrin. Hallucinating, poor boy,' beseeched Lauren. 'He needs help. Someone to dispel his fears.'

'Tinashi?' Katrin turned to me.

They'd done this before. Tried to draw me into their disagreements. Katrin with her demanding anger, Lauren with her pleading.

I resisted—as I always did, shrugging.

'I'm going for a walk. There's a *glitter rose dusk,*' I said.

I left them there, and wandered over the dunes to the beach, feeling the thrill as a rose colouration tinged the sand and the mysterious spores began to reproduce beneath my feet.

Visitors to Carmine Island were warned off the beach at *glitter rose* with stories of possible contagion and mutation. But I knew *Carmine's* secret—knew that indeed I had been infected from having first set foot on the pontoon under the hazy canopy—that *glitter rose dusk* could harm me no more than simply breathing the air.

Now I waited for the spores to change me.

Would it be my eyes? My facial contours? My senses? Would I become blind like Lauren Carson? Or would it be something deep within? Something to renew my soul? I hoped for the latter. Anything to alter my barren gloom. Anything that would stand between me and my past.

In the distance I heard their voices, gentle insistence and uncompromising passion. To and fro, like the tide. Lauren would go to her party at the Ritz, and Katrin ... who ever knew what Katrin would do?

Katrin found me much later, as the last pink streaks faded to dark in the sky and *glitter rose* muted.

She slumped alongside, digging furrows of sand with her feet, tensely knotting the long wings of her dark hair with an agitated hand.

'Go with her, Tinashi. The spores have made her vulnerable.' Her voice was hoarse from arguing.

'What do you fear?'

'Her empathy. It will trap her when the Curlews carry him over.'

I stared at her. The madness was never far away, in her voice and the wild inner landscape she inhabited. It frightened and fascinated me. I couldn't help myself, provoking this strange woman. 'Why don't you come then?'

But she stood in one restless movement and was gone into the darkness.

Lauren chose antique silk and ribbon lace to wear to the party. Delicate, old-fashioned and utterly feminine.

Alongside her I looked gauche in a dated tunic dress— remnants of my wished-to-be-forgotten life. While I absorbed the light, Lauren shone with gaiety and warmth.

Katrin's smoldering anger followed us down the tourist path to Mariners Drive and The Ritz. I didn't understand it, but in some way I respected it. She was the most extraordinary of all the *Carmine* residents, and yet the only one untouched by the spores, immune to them by some quirk of biology. While her beloved ...

Even now Lauren leant lightly on my arm, to avoid stumbling. Her sight worsened daily, yet she bore it with grace and serenity. While the spores diminished her sight, they had also offered her life, providing a mysterious antidote to the terminal illness she had brought with her to *Carmine*.

Blade Reeve's manservant greeted us at the door of his suite with a single, elegant bow that drew us into extravagant opulence. Soft Persian carpets, glowing wood and vase upon vase of jasmine, bouganvillea and bauhinia flowers.

Framed by the French doors of the balcony, egg-yellow wattle and burnt orange bottlebrush spilled from brass urns. Butterflies jinked about them like tiny kites.

Lauren stopped and breathed with delight.

'The moonflowers will bloom out on the balustrade later this evening. Perhaps you would care to see them with me.' Blade Reeves was behind us, his hungry gaze fixed on Lauren, devouring her rapture.

'Oh, Blade,' she sounded breathless, 'I'd be charmed.'

For a second I felt a sliver of Katrin's unease. Something in this young man ensnared her.

'But first you must meet my friends,' he said.

As we followed him into the heart of the *grand suite* I could not help but acknowledge the exquisite cut of his silk-slubbed dinner jacket and the virile, ebony curls nestled above his cravat line. An aura of boy-ish allure eddied around him.

'Comtesse Yvonne Plessis-Belliere—Vonny—may I present ... Madame Lauren Carson and Demoiselle Tinashi.'

Then, 'Freddie the Frog, Earl of Cornwall and the Territories, esteemed holder of three Quoffer titles ...'

I suffered tedious introductions to a flotilla of gaily decorative young who chivvied around each like challengers at the onset of a yacht race. They talked in brazen, gadabout tones without listening to each other, and swallowed, sniffed and swabbed substances I had never seen.

By mid-evening the noise crescendoed into a drumming tattoo of conceit and self-delusion. I searched for Lauren in the smoky haze having lost track of her while engaged in a one sided conversation of clicks and rapidly sequenced grunts by the MalconFunk music sensation, *Aloys Along*.

> *'Be<click>me. Want<click>me. <Click/Grunt>make me your*
> *night.'*

Unsure of his intent, I staggered from the cloyed atmosphere out onto the balcony. Pausing by a pillar clad with climbing moonflowers, I drank their scent.

Outside, by the glow of a distended moon, Lauren swayed in the arms of young Reeves. His head cradled into her shoulder.

Oily waves lapped *Mestiqua* beach below. An amber light—so unlike *Carmine's* usual glitter-rose incandescence—drowned the night.

He cocked his head. 'Save me, Lauren Carson,' he pleaded. 'The Curlew comes for me tonight. I feel it.'

'Hush,' she placed a calming hand to his lips. 'Your imaginings frighten you, poor boy.'

He kissed her fingers fervently. 'I love you, my Lady. Do not let them send me over, and I swear before this moon, that forever I am yours.'

'Why should you think this?' Lauren whispered, clearly disturbed by his declarations. 'What could be so dire?'

Madness, Lauren. Can't you see? I thought, but never uttered the words, guilty of wanting to see what transpired.

He fell to one knee and whispered. 'I have rifled a *Midden*.'

With that declaration the air rushed from the night.

Becalmed by the awful nature of his crime, I stood, witnessing the next.

'A sacred *Midden*?'

'Aren't they all?' His bitterness stripped him of his glamour, like a movie star barefaced in harsh sunlight.

'But why?'

'The *Voyant* instructed that in the native refuse piles on *Carmine Island*, I should begin to seek my salvation—my life's purpose. And that, you see, is what I must find. I *must.*'

His confession continued. 'I took my shovel, a small collapsible type, to the *Midden* at *Black Swamp*. When the guide readied to leave, I slipped him money to count me as returned with the rest. My valet covered my absence among my friends. Not that they would concern themselves.'

With taut bitterness he plunged on.

'When the tour left me, I dug from the base of the far side, my feet sinking among the reeds of the swamp. At first the digging was easy. But soon small cave-in's occurred.' He shrugged, showing her white, fresh calluses on his hands. 'Being not familiar with such work, I made a poor job of it.'

'What did you find?'

'I dug long into the night. Swamp noises did not dissuade me. I became single-minded, obsessed with finding my way. But in the end there was nothing. Only shells and bones.'

'Bones.' Lauren's voice was the faintest of all whispers, barely carrying to me.

'By dawn I was spent, unable to even attempt to hide my desecration. So now you see, why you must intervene.'

'Me,' even fainter now, her voice.

His expression became sly. 'There is one part, still, to my story. The *Voyant* foretold that only blind compassion would save me from damnation. Only then would I find my purpose.'

His confession spent, Blade Reeves lost semblance of sanity. He clutched Lauren violently, shaking her.

'You will help me, lady. It *shall* be.'

Abruptly a hot wind blew in, raking us, slamming doors, snuffing candles. It carried with it the mournful cry of the Curlew.

The sound paralysed me when I should have run to Lauren's aid—as did the deepening amber light and the sudden fierce crashing of the waves.

As sea spray flung up at us from the cliff and beach below, the Curlew cry whipped away like a ghost lost in a storm. From somewhere that I could not fathom, came an amber-clad figure, a man-creature made entirely of light, spear raised.

With words as unfamiliar to my ears as those of the performer *Aloys Along*, he incanted in tuneless song. Testing the spear's weight, he drew back to throw.

Reeves clung to Lauren, screaming, thrusting her smaller body before him as a screen. She spread her arms to the creature in a sacrificial gesture.

His show of cowardice uncoiled me from my role as bystander and I lunged.

Too late!

Katrin was there, climbing the balustrade like a wild thing. Wrenching Lauren away from Reeves perfidy, she barked incoherent words of fury.

A second later the spear stabbed through him—a clean, sharp display of penetrating light.

And then the moment passed.

The figure dissolved into the night, the wind dropped to a breath and the waves stilled.

Guests poured onto the balcony, a cacophony of curiosity. Without explanation Katrin steered Lauren through them and away. Reeves lay bathed in a pool of moonlight and bruised moonflowers. Still, but alive.

Aloys Along helped the young man to his feet, coaxing him inside, thrusting a brandy tumbler into his hand. Nobody had quite seen, nobody quite knew what had happened, and Blade sobbed inconsolably.

Suddenly the party was over and I slipped away.

Katrin came to my patio later, as dawn reckoned.

'Lauren?' I asked.

'Sleeping.' A shudder passed through her. 'I should have stopped her.'

'From what?' I couldn't help myself. 'What happened tonight, Katrin?'

She paced a little. 'There are two ways to tell it,' she reflected. 'One is that young Reeves disturbed an ancient *Midden* on the bidding of a malicious *Voyant*. There is a legend that says that if you dig to the bottom of a native collection site, you will gain much personal power. But to survive it you must be wrapped in the arms of blind compassion when the Curlew heralds and the *feather feet* come for you.'

'Reeves thought Lauren was his blind compassion?' I said.

She nodded. 'Perhaps Shaka twisted the words to cause mischief. Perhaps Reeves misunderstood.'

'But Reeves lives. The *feather feet* spared him.'

Katrin shrugged and loosened the cork on a bottle of pink champagne. It popped quietly, without celebration, and she trickled the fizz into two glasses.

We toasted the dawn in silence. Then we walked. Down past the breakwater and the majestic, spore built sandcastles of *Bara Beach*, seemingly drawn back to *Mestiqua* and the fading lights of the Ritz.

Along the rockwall, underneath a familiar balcony, a small crowd had gathered. The Island doctor, the police, and the tuxedoed, distressed Ritz night manager. They hunched over a lifeless form, fallen from above, tangled in seaweed, and the refuse of the sea.

A chill of perspiration broke across my body.

In mutual unspoken agreement we stopped and returned the way we had come.

We reached the breakwater without comment.

'There is the other way to tell it, Tinashi,' Katrin said suddenly. 'A dissolute, wealthy young whelp attempted to seduce an older woman on his birthday night, away from the watchful eyes of his overbearing mother. For in truth he was still a virgin and feared the mirth of the women of his own crowd.'

While she spoke she flicked the heavy wings of her hair as if she might use them to fly away.

'As he executed his deed he was caught on a low balcony of the *Carmine Island Ritz* by a freak of nature—the sudden onset of a mild tsunami—that played havoc with the water and the ambient light.'

'But what of you and me?' I said.

'A friend witnessed the ordeal but had unwittingly imbibed spiked champagne which rendered her powerless to help. Fortunately the woman's *aficionado* intervened in time to prevent harm to her loved one. The young man, however, suffering unbearable sickness of spirit took his own life ...'

I digested her logic, remembering the liquor I had consumed at the party, and my conscience eased.

Until she turned her eloquent, questing gaze on me.

'Was that it, Tinashi?'

Marianne de Pierres is the author of the Parrish Plessis series: *Nylon Angel, Code Noir* and *Crash Deluxe. Nylon Angel* was shortlisted for best SF novel in the 2004 Aurealis Awards, and *Crash Deluxe* was shortlisted in 2005.

Her short fiction has appeared in various book anthologies and magazines. She has been an active supporter of Australian genre writing and was the co-founder of the VISION writers group, and ROR—wRiters On the Rise—a critiquing workshop for Australian professional genre writers. She is currently working on the first book in The Sentient's of Orion series, *Dark Space*, which will be released by Orbit Books in 2007. In her spare time she is writing a film treatment for Sydney-based production company, Enchanter, called *Stalking Daylight*.

LOUDER ECHO

BRENDAN DUFFY

*'The intelligence which can reproduce the lost claw of
a crayfish can reproduce the entire animal.'*
Nicolaas Hartsoeker, 1722

M Y ENRAPTURED THRONG OF LESSER ANIMALIA had finally formed
their sections and were warming up under the chair.
Crickets and beetles, moths and frogs, all rehearsing scales,
practising squawks and squeals, creaks and croaks; a brilliant
pre-operatic cacophony abuzz with acoustic anticipation. I
tapped the baton to the lectern, and the hubbub gradually
quietened as compound and complex eyes turned to focus on
me. Finally there was silence. I threw to the string section and
opened my favourite Opera, *Il Barbiere La Seviglia*.

I commanded the chirping woodwind with decisive fervour,
lifted the percussive beating of wings to punctuate the tempo,
and introduced the toad's croaking baritone. Through my baton
the cicadas and crickets of the string section hinted at more
complex motifs to come.

I conducted this magnificent orchestra with a poignant
aplomb, and built the piece to its aria, 'Largo al Factotum',
where Figaro sings his famous solo. Of course, I was Figaro.
It was ecstatic and I found myself singing the aria, modified to
accommodate my ultra falsetto, with a passionate gusto. I had
just thrown across to the big bugs of the brass when I was prised
from my reverie.

Something new: a smell. A new smell. My Master had
just bought some strange kind of food. It was fresh and richly
aromatic, hypnotic, reaching even this deep into the cellars to
find me. Wrenched from my solo I ditched the philharmonic and
scampered across cold flagstones in dark workshops. I rushed
upstairs, crept past the kitchen and larders, ran through empty
halls with closed doors, then stole into the parlour.

There was no one to be seen, but the room was warm: a

welcoming fire crackled in the hearth. My Master had left this wondrous thing up on the table, so I climbed arm over arm up the table leg, then hauled myself over onto the table top. Before me was a sight I had never before beheld, but I had my suspicions. I guessed it was a gigantic cob of bread, because I'd heard tell of such things. The giant loaf, still steaming from the baker's oven, rested on a wooden cutting board.

My mouth watered. I looked about; shadows danced across the walls, urging me to eat. Little grains embedded in the crust stared seductively; they winked at me in the flickering light. Mesmerised, I couldn't break their gaze. I staggered toward the awesome boulder of bread and embraced it, hugged a warm wall of food!

I was so hungry and it begged me to eat it, so I quietly chewed a window through the crust, then burrowed into the fluffy interior. By the time I was sated I had eaten my way to the centre of the loaf and lay in a cosy hollowed den. It was soft, warm, and dreamy. Feeling tired from my repast I belched, rubbed my swollen purple tummy, then curled up with a soft lump of fluffy and slept.

I awoke to the sound of My Master's voice and another more authoritative tone—a resonant voice used to unquestioning respect. It spoke thus:

'Lazzaro, the Church's views on generation are founded on the teachings of Aristotle and the Ancients. All this talk of Preformation is dangerous! I don't like the unrest and division it's causing. Tell me of your investigations. Do you think it's true, or is it just some new Protestant blasphemy?'

'I have long suspected the truth in Preformation,' spoke My Careful Master. 'The works of all of the Church's great scientists actually imply this axiom, if you look carefully.'

' Continue.'

'All animals of all species that would ever walk God's earth were formed *ab origine mundi* by the Almighty Creator's loving hand during the six days of Creation, and tenderly placed inside each other, within the first of each respective kind, preordained to unfold down the generations to come. The Preformation was a work done at a single stroke by His Adorable Will.'

'Ah, a beautiful theory.'

'It's more than a theory. I have made some interesting observations using careful modifications to Leeuwenhoek's microscope and method-ologies.'

'The Protestants are saying that semen contains little animals. Tell me, have you seen these Eels of Man?'

'I have seen them. But they are not eels; they're animalcules, spermatick vermiculi. Worms.'

This subject was My Master's passion, but his enthusiasm

was dampened by an impatient, patronising tone. It meant he was speaking to someone who didn't agree with him. Sometimes he called them 'People Who Don't Use Proper Scientific Methodology'. Other times he called them 'Priests'.

He despised the clergy for their blind heavy handedness: proposing interpretations of the Bible and calling all else heresy. My Master had rigorously taught me Proper Scientific Methodology, and I wondered if I should likewise educate this Priest. 'Make exhaustive observations of different sides of the argument, then interpret them by the shining light of the Bible so you aren't executed by ignorant zealots.'

My Master and I had spent many an evening in the laboratory, examining diagrams drawn by Europe's finest scientists and worst blasphemers, poring over secret texts by alchemists and investigators. My Master had performed experiments on generation many times, and had documented what he called 'The Empirical Proof'. Together we'd repeated the experiments of Buffon and Needham, My Master precisely determining where they went wrong, and carefully demonstrating it to me, he often cursing and swearing, me often joining in, once I learned how.

My Master told me that I was his Magnum Opus.

I practised my sourest condescending expression while this obviously foolish Priest continued to dispute with My Master:

'It's just as Aristotle says! And Buffon!' exclaimed the Priest. 'When higher animals die they decompose and spontaneously revert back into the lesser animals from which they arose: worms and flies! Vermiparous generation, all life springs forth from worms!'

'No, not like Aristotle. Well, a little,' spoke My Master. 'But there is no spontaneous generation. Meat left protected in a mesh enclosure does not spontaneously sprout worms and flies upon decomposing, and infusions of broth enclosed in glass bulbs do not spontaneously ferment. Aristotle is wrong! Something cannot spring from nothing, thus the theory of Preformation must be correct. Just as the caterpillar contains the chrysalis, which contains the butterfly, and the tadpole unfolds to become the frog, these spermatick worms are human worms that generate humans—the head of each spermatick worm contains a little Preformed manikin waiting to be born. In woman they find nurture to become Man. I have seen it.'

'You have seen the Little Man!'

'Yes! As have others. Dalenpatius documents that he has even seen spermatick vermiculi throw off their skins to reveal complete miniature men dancing! In fact, I have examined the testes of many animals and have seen smaller animals of their type within their spermatick worms. But I have also examined the ovaries of many animals. They also appear to contain small animals. I need a better lens. Preformation is true. The only question remaining is whom God chose to bear this burden. Man or woman? Animalcule or ovary? Adam was the first man, but we are all born of woman, like a great unfolding.'

'Bah! It's obvious! The race of Man is not called Woman. A woman's role is to bear a man's children. If Preformation is true it must be through the male.'

'But to provide conclusive proof of Animalculist Preformation I must also disprove Ovist Preformation. Ovism must be fully investigated to be refuted, just to be sure.'

'That is not necessary. Ovism cannot be true. You've seen the Little Man! You said so yourself! Why would God choose sinful woman to be the bearer of body and soul? Six thousand years ago God created Adam in Eden. Adam was the first man, Eve was made from him, as are all God's children. Preformed in Adam's testes was the body and soul of every person that would ever walk God's world, down through the male lineage, through all of God's children until judgement day.'

He coughed wetly before continuing. 'Lazzaro, I don't much care for science, but those cursed Protestants are investigating Preformation. Garden has made progress documenting the Eels of Man! He's a Bishop in the Church of England! We cannot let the Protestants feather their caps with scientific innovation. Catholic superiority must be vigorously maintained and demonstrated. What notes have you made?'

'These are diagrams of my observations.'

I peered through my crusty window at the decrepit Priest as he flipped through one of My Wonderful Master's notebooks: secret drawings of dissected animals, ovaries and testes, the microscopic secrets of semen.

'Lazzaro, isn't the collection of semen a sin against God?'

'Normally yes, but when it's for science God doesn't mind.'

The old Priest frowned and turned to the well-thumbed *Essai de Dioptrique* by Nicolaas Hartsoeker, an early Animalculist, with the renowned drawing of the Little Man curled up in the head of a spermatick worm. The first picture of me! He fixed My Master a worried stare, and then saw the forbidden recipe by Paracelsus the alchemist.

'The Generation of Homunculi,' he gasped. 'This recipe is from a banned book!'

'Yes. But I have proof of Animalculist Preformation. I have made an homunculus!'

'What! Is it dangerous? Is it an abomination in the name of Our Lord?'

'No, but I made it from spermatick worms that have never touched a woman.'

'Then this is all we need!' hissed the Priest. 'We've beaten the

Protestants at their own game: the ultimate proof of Animalculist Preformation. The body and soul carried within man alone!'

'I'm not so sure. I don't think it has a soul.'

My ears pricked up. What was My Master saying?

'But it must have a soul,' said the Priest, 'if Animalculist Preformation is true.'

'It failed the Turin Test,' answered My Master.

'Ahh, those questions they found imprinted on the Holy Shroud, with the image of Jesus of Nazareth!' said the Priest.

So that was what all those questions were—a test to see if I had a soul! The Priest looked at the notes.

'Some of this writing is Arabic! Imagine if the Moors could do this! Or worse, the Protestants! Are we likely to face an army of homunculi marching in the name of the heathen? I want to see the homunculus!'

I crawled out of the loaf and picked up the breadknife. I marched across the table toward the Priest, singing a reveille and spinning the knife in my hands like a halberdier on parade. He stared in astonishment.

'Shalom Allah!' I said, and stood to attention before the Priest, saluting.

'Oh the Lord and Holy Land, it marches for Islam!' He crossed himself and staggered backwards. I dropped the knife and poked out my tongue, making faces and waving my hands at my ears.

'By God, it has no genitalia! Why all the purple birthmarks? It looks like a tiny adult baby—one that should have been knocked on the head!'

He was very rude so I did a little dance, turned around and poked my bottom out at him, wagging it about, pointing at it.

'Wicked little monkey!' The Priest whipped out a wooden staff and smashed it down on the table exactly where I was, but I had dashed back into the loaf. I hid deep inside and buried my head in the warm fluffy, shaking from this violent outburst. That bad Priest had tried to get me!

'Ecce! Behave yourself. Come out and apologise,' said My Master.

I slowly peeked out, then rushed to My Benevolent Master, quaking with fear, hiding from the bad Priest behind My Master's huge fleshy hand. My Master patted my head until I was smiling. The Priest stared.

'Can the homunculus see the future?' he asked. 'Does it summon demons!'

'No, no. It has knowledge of math and speaks many languages. It has much innate knowledge.'

'It could scour the earth with pestilence and hellfire! It's happened before!'

'Signore,' I said with a bow to My Master, then addressed the Priest. 'The homunculus apologises, Your Grace, and wishes to report that it cannot see the future, and nor does it summon demons.' I held my hand out to the Priest. 'Je m'appelle Ecce Homo.' We shook, and he snatched his hand back.

'I'm feeling sick! It must be working its magicks on me!' He searched his hand for magick marks. 'It's an abomination with no parents.'

'And how many parents do you have, Your Grace?' I asked from the security of My Master's loving hand.

'Two, of course!' he spat, insulted and uncomfortable.

'And how many grandparents?'

'Four.'

'How many ancestors from ten generations ago?'

'Umm,' he paused, looked at the ceiling and counted fingers off.

'One thousand and twenty four,' I answered for him. Shortly he nodded, quiet now. 'And how many ancestors did you have at the time of Adam and Eve?'

He looked at me blankly.

'According to the Archbishop James Ussher of Armargh the world was created at noon on the 23rd of October, 4004 BC.' The Priest looked nonplussed. 'Say, 230 generations ago,' I reminded. He flashed me an annoyed glance then resumed staring at the ceiling, petitioning Our Lord for mathematical assistance in His loyal servant's moment of need.

While the Priest was searching the ceiling My Bemused Master looked at me, smiled, and quietly shook his head; the Priest, My Master's Patrone, was a fool. I could tell My Master appreciated me. He loved me. I did this for him.

I gazed back at My Beautiful Master and he scratched behind my ear, then down my neck. It was really good, so good I stretched my head up into the air. My Master obliged, scratching under my chin. My foot started tapping up and down, in time with the scratching, then he hit the sweet spot and I suddenly snapped and bit his forefinger, not hard though. I just softly brushed my teeth on the giant finger. Just enough to let him know without breaking the skin. He laughed and patted my head.

'That's enough,' he whispered, indicating the still counting Priest.

I approached the Priest.

'How big was Eden? Bigger than Zanzibar?' I laughed. 'Standing room only! No room to move! But where did all those people go?'

The Priest looked at me with scorn, then turned back to his fingers, determined. I did a little dance behind his back. I'd put him out of his misery soon. I readied the sword for the mercy blow.

'At some stage the number of ancestors you have is larger than the number of people alive on God's earth.'

'True!' He turned and looked from me to My Master. 'But how could that be so?'

'Ancestors traced down one line are also ancestors traced down others, so they're multiply represented.'

'Oh, I see,' he nodded, then looked confused again. 'But how can that be?'

I held him there for a moment, then brought the blade down.

'They were all having sexual congress with each other!'

The Priest's mouth fell open.

'Holy Lord, it is a Protestant!' He crossed himself again. 'Oh my, this is complicated! Tomorrow I'll give it a Catholic baptism. Him, him, give him. And get it into a confessional! He talks like The Devil himself!' The Priest stood and hurried to the door, shaking his head. 'We must beat Garden! Animalculist Preformation is true, so it must have a soul. Make it sit the Turin Test again.' He looked back. 'And Lazzaro, my son, if it fails the test, it is not one of God's Preformed, therefore it is an abomination and you are a blaspheming alchemist, and I am an alchemist's exchequer, and we're all in trouble. I will have a new Venetian lens ground to your specifications. Use it to further science wisely.

'As for you, little Ecce, it was very crowded in Eden. Every one of God's children was there. Even you!'

With a toothy smile I scampered across the cold flagstones to where My Glorious Master worked. The workshop floor was strewn with straw and sawdust, offcuts from his contraption. I crept up behind My Master's towering form. He was hunched over some blueprints at his bench, cursing Leeuwenhoek for a buffoon. He sat amongst a confusing system of callipers and vices, wires and cord, all strung about a wooden framework of dials and pulleys. A great many lenses of specially ground Venetian glass hung in the web, sparkling like morning dew. The largest, the new Great Lens, was like a smooth aquamarine from a king's crown, as large as an eyeball.

This would be funny, and My Master would think me very smart. It should help him see the ridiculous nature of Ovism. I could barely contain my mirth as I carried the huge doll in my purple arms. The anticipation was too much; a snigger escaped my thick red lips and I froze, hand on mouth, almost dropping the wooden doll. Fortunately, My Master didn't hear because just at that moment he fussed with the microscope settings. The sound of my glee was covered by the clatter and creak of cords and pulleys as My Clever Master lowered one of his new lenses into the microscope.

I almost burst out laughing from my joke. My Master would love it! All would be forgiven and he would pronounce me of soul. He turned away from his workbench to face whence I had come. I crept behind his towering form, snuck under the workbench and saw a weird knot of wood protruding from the chair leg. It smelt like some strange animal: exotic and hairy. Distracted, I put the doll down and rubbed my head back and forth against the knot. I closed my eyes and got stuck into an itchy bit behind my ear. It was so exhilarating I found myself singing Figaro's aria from where I'd previously left off with the philharmonic. Somehow my *sotto voce* must have become *grosso*, and My Master looked about.

'Ecce! Ecce!' My Master called, deep and rumbling. I grabbed the doll and climbed up the bookcase, shelf by shelf, finally lugging the heavy doll out onto the bench top. Exhausted, I leaned on the doll while catching my breath. My Master had his back to me, facing the door.

'Ecce!' he called, 'Ecce. Come help align the lenses!'

Oh, My Master was a genius! The greatest thinker in Europe, patronised by royalty and the Church. Beneath the microscope a doe lay on blocks of packed snow, limbs bound. Her sleek fur was brown with small white spots. Etherised to insensibility, she lay with her side flayed open, layers of skin and muscle pinned back to reveal her internal workings, God's secrets. And an ovary, the subject of My Master's study.

'Master, what have you found?' I called, trying to obscure the doll with my body.

'Eh?' He spun about to face me. 'Oh, there you are. I think it is as I suspected, Ecce. Something is carried by the female line in the ovary.' He noticed I was hiding something. 'What have you got there?'

I was biting my lips, trying not to laugh. 'Oh, Master, I have a present for you!' I hoisted the Russian matryoshka doll in my arms and carried it across the workbench to him. He took it in a great fleshy hand and examined it while I burst out laughing and danced with glee.

'Did you make this doll, Ecce?'

'Si. Si, Maestro! Per voi!'

My Master wore his full winter costume, and puffed little white clouds into the air. He turned the doll over in his great hands, admiring the craftsmanship. I had painted it to resemble an English maid. I sang a crazy song, hopping from one foot to the other, waving my gangly arms in the air. Soon he'd get the joke. But I had to try to control myself; this was serious. I tried to concentrate. The doll should keep him occupied for a while.

While My Master examined the doll I slunk across the workbench to the semiconscious deer. It was twitching and would shortly awaken. I tipped some surgeon's ether onto a rag and held it to the deer's nose. It relaxed and I examined My Master's apparatus. The fog of My Master's breath usually condensed on the lenses as he worked, and he needed me to polish them clean. The cold didn't bother me, and my breath didn't fog, so I often worked with him and was familiar with the operation of his tools and subject. Indeed, I was a product of them.

I looked down the microscope eyepiece and fiddled with the fine focus dials as I had seen My Master do. Set on medium magnification I saw the doe's ovary in amazing detail: great swirling images of a hidden world. I swung another lens into place and focussed. Inside the doe's ovary were little animals, like in My Master's drawings of spermatick vermiculi. They were pretty little deer, exact and precise, though not yet fully unfolded: not yet born. About the size of rice grains, they appeared as though formed of a translucent primordium. I could see their gelid insides as though each had been laid open to cross section by My Master. Eight miniature deer stood in two rows on the ovarian scaffold, presenting their innards for inspection.

So it was true, something of God's Preformed was carried down the female lineage, too. Behind me My Master opened the doll to reveal another inside, exactly the same but smaller. He laughed, but I ignored him. I had to know more.

I looked at these miniature deer, little does and bucks. I focussed onto the ovary of a miniature doe. I grimaced and increased the magnification, engaging the Great Lens. Within the gelid ovary of the miniature doe was another ovarian scaffold, and seven more deer stood upon that scaffold, tiny, awaiting their eventual birth. Deer within deer within deer, all Preformed, through the female lineage. I stared down through three generations, as far as I could see into the future.

But what of Animalculist Preformation? I swapped back to the lenses of lesser magnification and scanned across the ovarian scaffold to a miniature buck. I saw the confusing vesicles in its testes, just like the drawings from My Master's vivisection notebooks. I swung the Great Lens into place and saw turmoil. The spermatick worms were moving too fast, but I found some sleeping ones and focussed on their heads. It was hard to be sure, but inside one I glimpsed odd swirling shapes: legs kicking, a tail twitching. Was that a deer's head? I saw antlers!

I played the fine focus and there it was, a perfect little buck, hale and robust. Eager to be off, it stamped its foot and brandished its antlers, then leapt away. It vanished! There was nothing discernible left inside: no little buck staring back at me, nothing. I gave chase, hunting the deer in other spermatick worm heads, but it was gone, like a ghost, an echo. I kept searching but found nothing. Just mushy lumps at a dead end in the chain of life. It seemed that Ovism was correct, Animalculism was not.

I beheld God's great plan with my own eyes. It didn't include me.

My vision swam, I pulled the focus back; pretty little deer danced on their scaffolds, so miniature and perfect. I looked up at the ceiling timbers until my vision cleared. My Master laughed with delight as he opened more dolls to reveal yet more dolls.

'Ecce. You've even painted them to look like English maids!'

'Yes, Master. It's an English Russian doll!' I walked across the bench top to My Master. 'You could have it delivered to Garden in England! As a present to his pregnant wife, Master. From you! From Lazzaro Spallanzani. The Ovist.'

My Master bellowed, but I wasn't laughing. I rubbed my head in my leathery hands. The Animalculist investigators were wrong. Garden the Protestant Bishop was wrong. Males were dead ends. Dear God, the Ovists were correct. My Master would soon prove his new theory true and demonstrate it to everyone.

'Yes! It could be Garden's wife! And a daughter. Bravo, Ecce!' He held my gaze with a quizzical expression. 'You're a clever one!'

'Yes, Master, yes! Very clever! Let me sit the Turin Test again!'

'Ecce.' My Master chided. 'We've been through this before. You failed.'

'But Master, remember what the Priest said! Give me a second chance!' I fell to my knees before My Master, hands clasped together in supplication.

'Ecce. Second chances don't come into it. You're either conscious or you aren't. I administered the Turin Test and caught you cheating. You had answers written all over your arms!'

'But Master, I'm conscious! And I'm smart and can make you laugh.'

'Ecce, you're not conscious. The natural beauty of flowers can inspire rapture in a man, but it doesn't mean they're conscious and have a soul. Ecce, you are as wood, live, but with no soul.' My Master placed the Russian doll before me. It leered at me with its garish, painted face.

'No, Master! I want to sit the test again!'

'No, Ecce. It doesn't matter now. I'm currently proving that the body and soul are in the ovaries, not the spermatick worms. So you can't possibly be conscious!'

'But Master, maybe the body is in the ovary and the soul is

with the spermatick worm!'

'Ecce, you have no soul. I'm sorry.' My Master meant that I wasn't human. I was a monster, an abomination. 'I called you Ecce Homo because I was sure that Animalculist Preformation was correct. I thought you would grow to be a man, and that your innate knowledge heralded the person God had ordained you to become. I thought you were the future, but I was wrong. I'm renaming you Echo Homo, for your knowledge is merely a reiteration of the past; you are simply a lesser version of your template, the man whence the seed was collected and you were made. A travelling musician, a vagabond, now dead.'

My Master walked to the door. He called back over his shoulder.

'I'm going to make a new homunculus, this time from ova. I want you to mix the reagents.'

I scowled and spun away from him, to look straight into the eyes of the garish Russian doll, still leering at me, mocking my hopes. This joke wasn't funny any more. I slapped it off the table and simmered.

Not the future, just a reflection of the past. My Master would replace me with something better.

And he wanted me to help.

The Priest administered my Catholic Baptism in a private vestibule, but it didn't make me feel any more human or closer to God's Glory. I just felt like an awkward initiate to some esoteric venerable fraternity—a soulless impostor.

Afterwards I sang Handel's baroque oratorios in my perfect ultra falsetto, higher than any castrato. Notes hung in the chamber like pure crystal spheres, and the Priest closed his eyes and wept passionately. Later he was quite jovial and we made jokes in Latin; then I prompted the discussion toward the intrigue of Church politics. He told me that he didn't really care about scientific theory, just the advantages that could be secured through it. Everything has its uses, he'd said. Except Ovists and Protestants.

My Manic Master wouldn't let me repeat the Turin Test. He rushed about, ignoring my petitions. He was too busy now and had driven me out of his life so that he could concentrate on The Important Things. I read through his old notebooks and followed after him, clutching his early drawings of me: the Little Man in the head of the spermatick worm. He wasn't interested any more.

I kept out of his way, quietly trailing behind, collecting his flotsam. I occasionally observed him from my lurk in the rafters or espied him through some ratty hole. Late one night whilst skulking in the corridor I heard a curious noise behind the oaken door to My Master's chambers. I lifted back the escutcheon and peered into the keyhole-shaped light.

I gazed upon My Master entertaining a lady friend in his boudoir. They were talking and laughing. Deep into the wee hours I spied them through that tarnished, brassy hole, and the things I saw: hurried whalebone fumbling, riotous shrieking, the slap of quivering, pink flesh. Oh, My Lascivious Master! He beguiled her into quaffing copious amounts of absinth, then sniffing from his bottle of surgeon's ether. She fainted and he quickly had her up on the table where he had his way with her.

Now I watched My Wicked Master do unspeakable things! I guess the collection of ova isn't a sin against God, either, when it's for science. There would be trouble with the Church if My Suicidal Master continued these dangerous investigations into Ovist Preformation. When I could watch no more I closed my eyes and saw bundles of kindling being bound with twine by cackling, toothless hags.

The next morning My Master hurried about the hallways with notes and a quill. He found me moping about near the larders. He wanted me to mix a new range of liquors, some of which I'd never heard of. He'd even made a list. I knew he wanted me to mix these reagents to generate a new homunculus. What would it be like playing second fiddle to some Ovist homunculus? My Mistaken Master already had a perfectly good homunculus and didn't need another. He sensed my reluctance.

'Ecce, if you make these reagents, we'll repeat the Turin Test!'

'Really! And then will I have a soul?'

'We'll see.'

'But what of this new homunculus you wish to make?'

'No, I've changed my mind. I'm not making another. It's too dangerous in the current political climate,' said My Surprising Master. 'I've given up on Ovist Preformation and stopped all my mistaken investigations. I was wrong.'

'Really? N'est pas? Pourquoi?' I followed after him.

The workroom seemed different. I climbed up onto the workbench. He had packed most of his equipment away! Only his precious microscope remained. Maybe it was true! A sheaf of papers lay neatly on his workbench, designs for a large glass bottle, some kind of complex fermentation tank for brewing.

'We're going to continue our early investigations cataloguing microscopic life,' he said.

'Oh, Master, it will be just like old times!'

'Yes, Ecce, yes,' he gathered up his diagrams and left.

I explored his bookshelves with renewed vigour, scanning through standard church issue—safe, recommended reading—but also scientific texts. Among the recipe books were some interesting works: seminal texts by the Ancients on spontaneous and vermiparous generation, experimental investigations by fringe alchemists, how to generate different dog breeds, how to spawn monsters, create golems, summon demons! I saw some works on Animalculist Preformation, and Paracelsus' recipe: The Generation of Homunculi.

I found recipes for vital fluids and prolific liquors and collected the things I'd need from the materials cabinets: solids, powders and liquids, mixtures and compounds, although I'd also need some more arcane ingredients. My Master kept human specimens and essences in a special cabinet. I took the key from his desk drawer and unlocked the cabinet to reveal a glass jar atop a notebook and a formidable old leather-bound tome with brass fittings.

I picked up the jar and a chill passed through me. I was looking at three gelid babies, the size of rice grains. Preformed foetuses extracted from the ovarian scaffold of that shrieking harlot.

I opened My Master's notebook and surveyed the evidence of his recent investigations: detailed drawings of rabbit and mouse vivisection, exposed ovaries. My Master had drawn the fully laden ovarian scaffold of a doe—three generations deep, just as I had seen.

I examined the old tome. The gilt title read *De Generatione*. The solid cover was engraved with a picture: Jove holding an open egg, from which sprang forth many different types of animals. Underneath was written the Latin inscription, *Ex Ova Omnia*, 'from the egg, everything'. The incriminating book was penned by William Harvey, a blasphemous Protestant Englander. It was the legendary first work on Ovist Preformation and was banned by the church soon after its release. I leafed through the pages; it discussed oviparous and viviparous generation and set the theoretical foundation that led to Ovism. My Meticulous Master's dirty bookmarks were all through the section detailing the manner in which an Ovist homunculus might be made.

In a glass fermentation tank.

I couldn't believe my eyes. My Deceitful Master had lied to me. He hadn't stopped his investigations into Ovism, he'd finished them and was now moving on to their more practical application—not brewing ferment for microscopy but brewing my replacement. My Lying Bastard Master was an Ovist scoundrel. He'd never give me the Turin Test and I'd never be pronounced of soul. He didn't care, he just wanted me slaving away on his potions so he could generate his Ovist Homunculus.

The Priest would be interested to know of this! There would be trouble. I'd see to it.

☆

I wandered about the deeper sections of the cellars, feeling betrayed and desperately alone, while My Master busied himself upstairs with his new glass fermentation tank. I crept between stacks of discarded notebooks and explored the piles of abandoned glassware that lay strewn about. I recognised equipment from My Master's now forgotten past—experiments I had helped with.

It was damp and cold, and I was hungry. I chewed at the bottom of my candle as it burned, but it provided grim succour. The prey I stalked was behind a heap of old microscope pieces. I heard the tinkle of glassware and doubled back, then saw it: a hideous monster twice my size! No, just an ordinary bug magnified behind a glass bulb: a tasty meal.

My prey scuttled from the glassware. I froze: a statue, David—the perfect man. Two fingers on my right hand twitched, testing the air like antennae. The bug halted, then carefully responded, and an antenna dance ensued. I played it with my lure, enticing it closer with all the right promises. Mesmerised by my lying semaphore my prey courted its treacherous mate, and slowly climbed up onto my outstretched statue arm. I sprang, ripped its head off and scoffed it down, holding its body like a tankard of juice with six twitching legs.

Sated, I leisurely sipped at the tangy juices while searching among the piles of junk. I heard a desperate tapping and found a pile of sealed jars, each containing a prisoner—victims of My Cruel Master's experimentation in regeneration. I couldn't prise the lids off so I smashed each jar in turn and liberated the hungry, motley crew, naming each after one of My Master's rivals. I freed a tailless skink, a one-clawed crab, a three-legged salamander, a one-eared rat, a one-eyed mole, a snail missing its entire head, and a mouse with a human ear on its back.

They were happy to be freed and vowed to help me. We danced in circles around smoky chemical fires, cheering and making merry. Feeling heady from the bug juice I summoned my throng of Lesser Animalia and assembled the philharmonic orchestra. My New Chums gladly joined its ranks. We spent the evening discussing generation and feasting to song, the philharmonic supplying all our needs, although the arias were getting pretty thin with the decimation of the string section.

Amidst the revelry I fixed a candle onto one of My Master's notebooks and lit it. My shadow, big and impressive, almost a man's, fell onto the wall before me. Laughing, I danced to the music and watched my shadow dance. I scattered handfuls of sulphur and saltpetre across My Master's open notebooks and waved my arms over intricate diagrams of animalcules and ovaries, dissected beasts, ink pentagrams, sigils and magick numbers, singing my favourite operatic excerpts.

I danced before a mirrored glass, making faces. I turned around and wagged my arse in the mirror. Looking back, I saw it wasn't my arse but an ugly arseface. I spun around to check my arse but I couldn't see it properly; I had to run in circles to catch up. When I caught it I saw that it was just my arse, and the mirror was just the mirror. With a shrug I eased my way back into the dancing—and saw arseface in the mirror again.

'Ciao! Ciao!' it said. I spun about but it was gone. I poked my arse in the mirror again. 'Ciao amico! Si parle Italiano?'

'Si, si,' I said.

'Echo Homo, reflection of man!' It laughfarted in an old Calabrese dialect.

'No, no. Ecce Homo! Behold the man!'

'Echo, you don't have a soul! Do you want one?' asked my arsehole.

'No, I already have one! A Priest said I do!'

'A Priest said! Ha! He's playing you like a pawn! You don't have a soul and you know it! Now pick up that chalk and draw! Left, left, now straight ahead ...'

Under its rude direction I chalked a pentagram onto the flagstones and arranged five candles. Upon lighting the last there was a great sulphurous explosion. A slopping wet pile of offal fell out of the air and filled the pentagram. Atop the pile of putrefying entrails and scabrous bat wing was a stinking-furred goat head. My eyes watered from the stench. Its flesh pulsed, glistening with heat sheen, and motion stirred its evil eye. The philharmonic dashed for cover. It appeared that Those Stupid Priests were correct about some things.

'Ciao, bello!' I said in my oldest Italian.

Laughing, it metamorphosed into an extremely handsome youth wearing the gilt and bejewelled dress of an impeccable Calabrese noble, exquisite and ostentatious.

'Hail Caesar! Cicco Ghibbeline,' he said in Italian older still. He held his immaculately manicured hand forward and we shook. 'Your Master, Lazzaro Spallanzani, is doing interesting work.'

'He's a great Catholic scientist, a devout and learned man, once a Jesuit Priest! I'm going to get him in trouble with the Church. Maybe banished or burned at the stake!'

'Get him excommunicated and you will be in my favour.' Cicco examined his fingernails and smiled with indulgent pearly-white beattitude. His halo brightened—a band of bright antiworlds orbited his head: coloured souls slowly tumbling through the air like tiny glowing babies, each softly screaming distant, high pitched Latin woes.

I stared at them. 'Oh, I want a soul!'

'Hmm ... No.' Cicco shook his head and the little souls

jangled in my face. 'That won't be possible.'

'What would it take?' I begged.

'What have you got to offer? Nothing. Forget it. You would have to summon hellfire for me to pronounce you of soul.' He was a seasoned horse trader—diabolically cocksure. My arsehole was right—as far as pronouncing me of soul, My Master didn't, the Priest couldn't, and Cicco wouldn't.

'Then I want a microscope to see further into the ovaries than My Master can.'

Cicco made a play of patting down his pockets. 'Unfortunately, I didn't bring a microscope with me …'

'A Great Lens, then. Better than My Master's!'

Cicco waved his hand. 'Only what I have on me. Anyway, why a lens? Do you think that will make him like you again?'

'No. I already know how to make him like me,' I laughed. 'Give me a Great Lens, and I will get him excommunicated.'

'Hmm,' Cicco raised an eyebrow, then nodded. 'So be it!' He surrep-titiously looked about then opened his pantaloons. He held his perfect penis in his immaculately manicured hands and winced in red-faced pain as he strained and pushed. A huge lump slowly, agonisingly, moved down the length of his distended member. He grimaced and gasped as blood dripped from his urethral opening. With a final demonic bellow Cicco peeled back his foreskin and passed the gigantic kidney stone into his hand, buffed and polished from its tight journey. He wiped the blood away.

'Whew!' Cicco dabbed the sweat from his brow with a gilt embroidered pocket kerchief. 'To excommunication!'

He vanished, leaving me holding the shiny, clear lens.

I was the apprentice, but it was time for me to become the Master. I knew how to make My Fickle Master like me—I'd continue his work and generate my own homunculus in my new laboratory underground. I'd show him how clever I was! I explored every corner of the dark catacombs, collecting bits and pieces, the legions of my philharmonic dragging them back to the new lab we created at the bottom of the staircase. I located much of My Master's original equipment and recreated his early workplace, the beakers, bulbs, and burners, all arranged according to his diagrams— candles and condensers, burettes and pipettes, droppers and stoppers. We reconstructed a microscope and fitted the Great Demonic Lens.

The philharmonic played my favourite pieces while we worked. We ground solids to Albinoni's harpsichord concertos and mixed liquids to Mozart. I made My Master's potions, his prolific liquors and vital fluids, and when the passion seized me I conducted the philharmonic with one hand, while directing manufacture with the other, as my industrious insects carried weighed portions of powders to mortar and pestles, measured ounces and drams, and stirred and simmered, while vapours flowed through the condenser to form precious essences.

The vapours cascaded through my head as I commanded the philharmonic to perform *Don Giovanni*, a disturbing piece about a lusty, deceitful scoundrel blinded by pride. With a stroke of my baton a bevy of bugs placed the crystal birthing dish before me. I brandished the baton as though smiting foes as the Lascivious Don slew and seduced his way through the men and women of Seville, and was finally confronted by the statue of a man he murdered. I laughed hysterically as he fearlessly invited it to dinner!

With each ominous parry and riposte the orchestra conjured minor chords of sinister portent. I conducted with oblivious fury as bottles oozed oily fluids into a swirling puddle in the dish. With the baton in one hand and a dropper of human essence in the other I built to the moment when the colossal statue arrived for dinner. As it dragged the Unrepentant Don down to the fiery pits of Hell I let the drop of human essence fall into the pearly puddle.

It splashed into the greasy swirling rainbow and the liquids changed and congealed. By flickering candlelight I glimpsed anatomy, a gathering nativity. Form condensed in scintillating colours: hands, a face, then were gone. I sprang back and resumed conducting the piece with added fervour, pouring my energy into it, barking commands at the philharmonic.

Something took shape in the liquid! A head. Eyes staring straight at me, lips smiling savagely. He slowly rose from the rainbow liquor as new anatomy congealed: shoulders, chest, hands already on hips—a little man, just like me! I laughed. He laughed, too, as his legs formed and he rose further from the liquid in the dish. He looked like me, but smaller. His skin was pinkish-grey with purple birthmarks, just like mine. He stood before me, whole, glistening, dripping from his spawning. He looked at his body, flexed his arms, and stepped from the birthing dish.

'Grazie, Maestro, grazie,' he said. I administered the Turin Test.

'Are you Homo sapiens?'

He flexed his little muscles, 'I am an echo of Man, an echo of the man I am!'

'God made Man in His image, but you're an echo of Man made more in mine.'

'Then I am an echo of an image of God, made more in the image of an echo of Man!

'I name you Piccolo Eco, the Little Echo of the man you are.'

'Grazie, Mio Buono Maestro.' Piccolo bowed to me. We held hands and danced in a circle, singing while the philharmonic played faster.

'I'm an echo of the man I was!'

'And I'm an echo of the man I am!'

'Quiet everyone,' I yelled. 'Quiet!' The hoards of chattering homunculi quietened, and I looked upon Friedrich, the little man who had just arisen from the birthing dish. At two centimetres tall he was the smallest yet, a tiny echo of a man not yet born. The deeper we delved into the scaffold for our samples the smaller were the homunculi we made, and the quieter they spoke—but the more bizarre their stories became. Generation seven spoke of the strangest wonders. We hushed as he told of the entire world at war. Again.

'Oppenheimer, Julius Robert, born in 1904.'

'And what did he invent?' I asked.

'The first atomic bomb.'

'And what is that?'

'A piece of the sun.'

'Hmm,' I'd heard this chilling story a few times now. 'And your brother?'

'He designed the fuel injection for the Messerschmitt 262 jet engine.'

'So this was your youngest brother, Hans, born in 1909?'

'Yes.'

The gelid foetus I had stolen from My Absent Master's locked cabinet now lay beneath my microscope, submerged in a preserving buffer. My microscope, equipped with the Great Demonic Lens, was trained onto its ovarian scaffold, focussed seven generations deep into the future: the Guenther family scaffold.

I looked down the eyepiece.

'A gauche, a gauche, a gauche ...' A hoard of our smallest homunculi carefully adjusted the fine scrolling of the stage, scanning across from Friedrich, past siblings, to his youngest brother, the last male on the Guenther scaffold.

'Halt!' I was looking at Hans Guenther. I gave the command. My Miniature Technicians began the process of delicately extracting spermatick worms from this foetus. We'd find a manikin in his spermatick worms and in a few hours his echo would be arguing with the others about future history. Together they may remember enough to draw up plans for a flying machine.

I joined Piccolo and examined our map of the ovarian scaffold. We'd made homunculi from each generation and asked them about their family, the world, and anything they could remember. Piccolo was a meticulous bookkeeper, penning in names and professions as we explored this expanding family tree, cataloguing them for later reference. He also recorded a detailed history of the future they described.

We never made Ovist homunculi because My Master might be right. If Ovist Preformation was true, they would be real people born too early. It would alter the timing of God's divine plan, and He may send an avenging angel to correct things. We would have to replace this foetus soon, so it could bear its fruit.

We only made Animalculist homunculi, soulless echoes of the future, copies, using spermatick vermiculi samples taken from the testes of the male foetuses on the scaffold. We were always careful not to injure or harm the foetuses, as they were yet to fulfil their destiny. One day Hans Guenther would be born, ignorant of the echoes made from him 130 years prior.

We heard noises. People were descending the stairs. Pandemonium erupted as everyone ran and hid. I stood there, dumbfounded, looking at books, recipes, chemicals, scales, measuring cylinders, pipettes, bubbling vials—every stage of the process accounted for. I'd even automated the process by rigging pipes and taps straight to the birthing dish. It was an homunculus manufactory, and looked like one.

The squeaking and tittering died down and all was quiet. A small pool of ink spread across the table. Tiny ink footprints across an open page recorded the first homunculus stampede. I turned the page.

The Priest stepped forward into the light. 'Ahh! Here he is!'

'Your Grace.' I bowed deeply.

'Dear Ecce! The proof of Animalculist Preformation!' The Priest patted my head. 'How wise I was to fund this research. The Papacy shows me favour. Although, imagine what would have happened if I'd been caught funding research into Ovist Preformation!'

We both laughed. My Shadowy Master huffed and stepped into the flickering light, shaking his head.

'You shouldn't discount Ovism too soon!' he said. I heard that impatient, patronising tone taint his voice; he would unthinkingly reiterate the tired empirical rhetoric. He waved his forefinger. 'Other options should be investigated before being discounted. Rigorously apply proper scientific methodologies: make exhaustive observations of all aspects of the argument, then interpret the results making the least assumptions.'

'You proved Animalculist Preformation,' said the Priest.

'You proved Animalculist Preformation,' I echoed. 'So say I have a soul!'

My Master scowled at me so I backed behind the Priest's hand.

'But what of truth?' My Master asked the Priest.

'Animalculist Preformation makes the most sense,' said the Priest. 'It combines the beauty of Preformation with a theory already endorsed by the Church: Aristotle's vermiparous generation.'

'Ha! Worms! Ridiculous! There is only oviparous and viviparous generation,' My Master scoffed, 'and I think that even viviparous animals actually use a form of oviparity. Ex Ova Omnia!'

'That is a dangerous catch-cry, Lazzaro.'

'But what about maternal inheritance of traits like polydactyly? It is well documented and supports the theory of Ovist Preformation! Also, there is parthenogenesis in many aphid and skink species! No male is needed for generation!'

'So now you're comparing us to insects and lizards, Lazzaro?'

'But I have seen the ovarian scaffold!'

'You've seen an optical illusion caused by refraction! Lazzaro, I paid you to revive Animalculism and refute this growing Ovism! God would not have chosen woman. It's against the Church! We are the moral guardians of the flock. They are incapable of making correct choices without our guidance. A place for everything, and everything in its place, Lazzaro, or we'll have women as priests and scientists! And where would that get us?'

'Your Grace,' I said, 'he possesses many arcane tomes! The intricately described works of schismatic dissidents and deluded alchemists! Blasphemers! I've seen *The Second Book of Natural Magick* by Giambattista della Porta. It contains the recipes, 'How to generate preti little dogs to plae withe', and 'How living creatures of divers kinds may be mingled and coupled together'. It's a treatise on how to warp God's creatures. He wants to create life himself! Abominations! Monsters, golems, and demons!'

The Priest looked to My Wayward Master.

'It's nothing,' said My Master. 'I never made any of them.'

'But you do not deny this?' said the Priest, more an accusation.

'No. It was an early work that contributed to the formulation of Animalculist Preformation theory. I had to read it to do the study you asked for! It has the original recipe for vital fluid.'

'He has a book,' I said, 'called *De Generatione*, it is an Ovist tome dedicated to making Ovist homunculi!'

'It's just another old book.' My Master shrugged.

'It's a dangerous work of blasphemy by an enemy of the church,' I said.

'So was *The Generation of Homunculi*, but you don't seem to care about that!'

'*De Generatione* was banned by the church,' I said. 'Penned by an Englishman! A Protestant!'

'What!' said the Priest.

'It's in a locked cabinet in his workroom, along with samples of ova he removed from a harlot he drugged one night and operated on! Here is the key.'

'Lies!' My Master made to grab it, but the old Priest held him back with a wave of his hand.

The Priest took the key. 'Continue, Ecce.'

'He is growing an Ovist homunculus in a glass tank in his workroom!'

'Lazzaro! After all the help I've given you, this is how you repay me?'

'He means to use it to prove Ovist Preformation theory and bring you down!'

'This is outrageous!' said the Priest.

'No, no, it's not true!' said My Lying Master. 'Ecce! Why are you doing this?'

It was time to play for checkmate. My Foolish Master's Ovist days were over.

'Your Grace,' I said. 'The Ovist homunculus—My Master is trying to generate a pure person, untainted by desire and sin, the physical act.'

'Yes,' the Priest was fuming. 'What of it?'

'Derived from woman only.'

'Yes ...'

'With no father. When else has this happened? Immaculate conception!'

The Priests mouth fell. 'The Messiah! He's trying to resurrect Jesus Christ!'

'It's a Protestant conspiracy!' I said. The Priest staggered and leant on his staff, wide eyed. I played him with my lure. 'A soulless Antichrist summoning demons, hellfire, and pestilence!'

He choked and spluttered, clutched at his chest, then crossed himself with the cabinet key. 'This has gone too far! I will not protect you now, Lazzaro! I'm calling for an inquisition! You will be investigated!' He hurried up the stairs, calling for his escort. 'Excommunicated!' He bellowed. I smiled.

The look of death simmered in My Murderous Master's eyes. I ran for cover. I saw an old box and crawled inside. Piccolo and the others were cowering in the corner. I cowered, too.

'Ecce! What is the meaning of this? Come out! I'll get you!'

My Master's great arm reached into the hole and patted about inside, feeling its way around the rubbish. A team of us slid a large nail from the wood as the hand approached. I charged the hand and stabbed it in the forefinger, yielding a resounding yelp. The hand ducked around wildly and grabbed Piccolo. He screamed and flailed about helplessly as it dragged him from the box. I rushed to his aid too late, and was left peeking from the hole.

My Evil Master clutched Piccolo tightly around the torso. Piccolo struggled but couldn't escape; his arms and legs were trapped. Only his head and shoulders protruded from the top of My Seething Master's fleshy hand, and his little purple feet kicked back and forth underneath. He held Piccolo at eye level and stared, more furious than I had ever seen.

'After all I've done for you! Why are you doing this? You've wrecked everything!'

'Let me go! Let me go!' Piccolo screamed and struggled in his grip.

'Ecce! How could you do this! I made you!'

I walked from the box, across the bench top to confront My Ignorant Master. 'No, I made him.'

My Confused Master looked from Piccolo to me and back again, stunned, then surveyed the lab, noting the equipment.

'You've made another!' He suddenly snatched me up, too, clutching me in his other fleshy fist. I screamed and pummelled his hand with all my might but to no avail.

'Which one of you is Ecce?' He scowled at us in turn as we both struggled in his clenched fists. I conjured my throng of Lesser Animalia. They swarmed around us like a plague, and My Rationalist Master saw spontaneous generation occur before his astounded eyes.

'Attack!' I screamed. Wasps stung his head as he ducked about, spitting them from his mouth. Bugs and ants crawled among his clothes and over his skin. Then I summoned my Greater Animalia, 'Malphigi, Maupertuis! Allez! Allez! Attendez-moi!'

All My New Chums ran to the rescue. Malphigi Mouse snuck into his sleeve while Maupertuis Mole disappeared up his cavernous pants leg. My Ex Master jumped from foot to foot, then Cruikshank Crab scuttled up his collar and pinched him on the earlobe while Reamur Rat sunk incisors into his big toe. Leeuwenhoek Lizard and Swammerdam Salamander rushed into his robes.

Lazzaro hopped about, swearing and bumping into chairs, crab swinging from his ear, rat hanging from his toe, snarling homunculus in each hand. Swarming with insects, he wailed:

'Ecce! How could you? I treated you like a son!'

'The son you didn't want!'

'But I gave you life! I made you!'

'And then I made you!' I said. 'In my image!'

Lazzaro followed my gaze to the homunculus in his other hand.

'Don't you recognise me?' Piccolo laughed. ' ... Papa!'

Lazzaro's eyes widened. His blotchy, insect bitten face paled as he stared into Piccolo's blotchy homunculus face and saw an echo of his own. We tittered.

'I know what you're thinking!' said Piccolo, then bit him on the thumb, hard. Lazzaro yelped and dropped us.

We ran.

'And how many brothers and sisters did Olge have?'

'There were three older sisters, then Olge, then a younger brother and sister.'

He gave us their names. Piccolo looked up and nodded. It was the right family.

'What region of Wurttemberg was this?'

'Neustadt.'

'And what was her mother's name? Think, think!'

'I can't remember, I was too young when she died! Umm ... Helscha? Helschen?'

We were making a generation map that led to the man called Robert Oppenheimer. We had traced his family tree from the future back to the current generation, the one alive now. Somewhere in Europe his great-great-great-great-grandmother was living her life with him packed seven generations deep inside her ovaries. Helscha of Neustadt? We would find her.

Piccolo penciled in the last step of the generation map.

'I wonder what it's like in the Alps this time of year?' I said.

Piccolo looked up thoughtfully, 'He feels cold and unhappy. You know, we should mail him that English Russian doll as a memento.'

It sat on the desk, leering at the both of us with its wooden glare.

We tittered.

I closed my eyes and beheld the future: cinders—cities scoured with searing atomic hellfire, and Cicco with my bright and shining soul.

Brendan Duffy has worked as an optometrist's assistant, printer, packaging maker, furniture finisher, chromeplater, waiter, kitchen-hand, storeman, forklift driver, brickie's labourer, photographic sales assistant, escort driver, market stall holder, telephonist, orchard hand, fruiterer, science practical demonstrator, personal tutor, scientist, public servant and writer. Brendan has a doctorate in the molecular evolution of mammalian sex chromosomes. He is a member of SuperNOVA writers' group, and lives in Melbourne with his partner and two cats. http://mc2.vicnet.net.au/home/bduff/web/index.html

LACEY'S FINGERPRINTS

CHRIS LAWSON

'G̲O AWAY,' I SAID INTO THE PHONE. '*But I'm from the Press Office!*' She was a young woman with a Bachelor of Journalism and she could not understand why we had done everything in our power to avoid an interview. She was still young enough to think that everyone wanted to tell a story.

'*Please don't bother us.*'

She said, '*The Commissioner himself told me I should talk to you. Do you want me to call him and say you wouldn't talk to me?*' She wasn't so young after all.

I told her to meet us for lunch and that she was paying. Logan and I got there ten minutes early. As soon as she walked in the door, I knew it was her. Young, tall, pretty, wearing a short skirt and tailored jacket, she clutched a clipboard and a tape recorder. She looked around the diner for us. It took her a while. I've changed a lot since my personnel file photo was taken and Logan was wearing his stupid cowboy hat. Finally she recognised us and clattered over on her pinpoint heels.

'*It's so nice to meet you. Real heroes,*' she said.

'*I'm no hero,*' said Logan. '*And I don't want it said in print. Neither would the Commissioner if he knew the whole story.*'

'*Well, he thinks it's a great story,*' said the girl from the Press Office. '*Real PR material. The Detectives Who Solved The Kilsyth Mystery! It's a precooked headline.*'

I said, '*We didn't solve it. The Corpsegrinder did. And if you think he'd be good for PR, just think for a while how he got that nickname.*'

She smiled as she opened her clipboard and set the recorder on the bench. '*We can spin it.*'

Logan said, '*No you can't. You couldn't spin it with a corkscrew.*'

She had large pleading eyes, just like my cocker spaniel, so I said, '*We'll tell you what happened. But it goes no further. Understand?*'

Logan took the batteries from her recorder and flipped her clipboard face down.

The house was larger than our precinct station, and the master bedroom was the size of my apartment. There were separate servants' quarters and tennis courts and a pool with a mosaic dolphin and a five-car garage, all set in an award-winning 'landscape', which was a fancy way of saying the garden cost a fortune. It would have been cheaper, I imagine, to use a row of Mercedes convertibles as planter boxes.

Amanda Kilsyth-Besselt's body had already been taken away, but the impression her body left in the bed was still plain to see. The forensics team was at work dusting the walls, collecting hair and skin samples from the bed, and sealing in plastic the tumbler she had used to wash down her last drug cocktail.

'Face down in the bed like that, we're not sure if she OD'ed or suffocated while intoxicated. The Corpsegrinder will sort it out,' said Harvey from Crime Scene. 'There's no sign of a struggle or forced entry and only a few sets of fingerprints. Everything is consistent with suicide.'

'Thanks, Harvey,' I said. 'How's the family?'

We exchanged the usual pleasantries and gossip until Logan broke up the conversation.

'Hey, Sis!' he called to me, knowing it would irritate me. 'Check this out.'

He placed a leather notebook in my hands. I opened the book at random. The page was filled with neat handwriting. At the top was written FAVORITE FOODS, followed by a list in five columns. *Pumpkin. String beans. Apple pie. Chicken soup. Pear stew. Peanut butter and jelly sandwiches (white hi-fibre bread). Banana.* And so on.

'Weird, huh?' said Logan.

I flipped the page. FAVORITE TOYS, it said. *Barbie. Snooks. Action Horse Figures.*

'Looks kind of obsessive,' I said. 'Like she was documenting everything about her daughter.'

'Spooky,' said Logan. 'Probably flipped out because some drug was slipped in her drink, just like Frances Farmer.'

'Enough of the conspiracy theories,' I said. 'Let's just register it and move on.'

Logan registered the leather notebook in the evidence log. By now the house was swarming with uniforms. Somehow they had all found time to tear themselves away from other work. It wasn't often they had an excuse to ransack the home of a mysterious and reclusive celebrity, even in the Hills precinct.

'This place is covered,' he said. 'Let's go talk to the ex.'

☆

On the way to the ex-husband's place, a call came through to Logan. He picked up his cellphone and talked while I drove.

'Yeah. Logan here. What? Tell him she's at the house.'

Logan folded the phone closed and said it looked like we were in charge of the case.

'How did that happen?' I asked.

Logan shrugged. He unfolded his phone and dialled.

'Hey there, Stu. Is the girl still there? Gone already? OK. Thanks.'

He hung up. He looked pensive.

'What was that all about?' I asked.

Logan looked out the window, watching the city go by and thinking to himself. He didn't seem to hear me.

Damon Besselt's house was a mansion, but smaller than his ex-wife's. He was only middling wealthy by local standards. His last good box-office was nearly a decade ago. Just as he was about to break into the thirty-million-per-film club, he divorced. His embittered ex-father-in-law was Fletcher Kilsyth — not a good choice for an ex-father-in-law. Kilsyth was one of the most powerful media moguls on the planet. Besselt's career sank along with the marriage. I might have felt sorry for Besselt, except that he had a butler answer the door.

The rich are different. Besselt lived in greater luxury than any of the ancient Roman emperors, but by the Kilsyth standard he was poor. Besselt had a mansion, but Kilsyth owned half of Vermont. Besselt had a collection of vintage cars. Kilsyth had an assortment of multinational media companies. Besselt liked skiing in the Italian Alps every winter. Kilsyth's hobby was horses, but not just any horses. Kilsyth's taste ran to multi-million dollar thoroughbreds; his preferred arena was the international circuit; his rivals included Saudi princes.

We showed our badges.

'I'm sorry, but Mr Besselt can't speak right now,' said the butler.

It must have been hell wearing a suit at ten on a Sunday morning, I thought. Then I realised Logan and I were wearing the same.

'Well that's too bad,' said Logan.

The butler considered for a moment then allowed us into the foyer. He asked us to wait, then slipped into the house, pausing only to bark an order for coffee as he passed the kitchen.

The coffee was brought in by a maid just as Besselt himself appeared, looking like he could do with a maid to carry him in, too. He stepped gingerly down the stairs into the foyer, wearing a bright silk dressing gown of Japanese design over bike shorts and tennis socks. His face had last seen a razor three days earlier, which was probably the same day he had last dressed in presentable clothes. The bags under his eyes would put a bloodhound to shame. This was not the matinee idol I remembered from the movies. To think I once had a crush on him.

'Jesus, is that coffee?' Besselt asked. He reached for a cup with trembling hands. The maid passed him a steaming cup, laid the tray on a side table, and slipped away into the house, discharging her duty in ghostly silence.

Besselt took two deep mouthfuls from the cup and, oblivious to the heat, swallowed. 'I don't know why you're here, officers, but I'm happy to co-operate provided you keep your voices down. At the first loud noise, I'm claiming cruel and unusual punishment.'

I said, 'I'm Detective Lindamuller and this is Detective Logan. I'm afraid we have some bad news. Please take a seat.'

'Damn,' he said, 'I knew that was a speed camera on Sunset.'

'No, Mr Besselt, this is not a traffic offence. I'm sorry to tell you your ex-wife died this morning.'

He looked shocked. 'Are you sure?' he asked, then shook his head. 'Sorry. You probably get the same stupid question all the time.'

'Her face is well known,' said Logan. 'Still, we'd like you to come down and formally identify her for us. There are rules, you see, even with well-known folks. When you're ready, of course.'

Besselt nodded. 'I'll get dressed if you can just...' He stopped and put his head between his knees. I thought he was going to throw up, but then I saw that his heaving was actually a chain of deep sobs. He sat up straight again and his face was smeared with tears and mucus.

Logan said, 'Don't worry. We can get her father to identify her if you'd like. We won't need to ask your daughter.'

'What do you mean? I don't have a daughter.'

'Madison is at the station right now. She was the one who called 911.'

Besselt sat bolt upright. 'There must be some mistake,' he said. 'My daughter died eight years ago. It must be someone else's little girl.'

'She says she's Madison Lacey Kilsyth-Besselt.'

Besselt's mood shifted swiftly. 'Madison died of leukemia. She died in my arms, for God's sake. That cannot be my daughter.'

'But...' said Logan.

'Don't you get it?' Besselt was shouting now, his earlier warning about noise levels completely forgotten. He jumped to his feet. 'That's what all this is about. This house, the divorce,

Amanda's freaking out, the end of my career. It all started with one damn cancer cell. You think I could be mistaken about that?'

A pulse beat a rhythm on his temple. He stopped, rubbed the side of his head and leaned against a slender Greco-Roman column. 'I'm sorry for shouting,' he said. 'My analyst says...' He took a deep breath and steeled himself. 'Madison got leukemia and died despite the efforts of the best physicians in the world. She's buried on the Kilsyth Ranch overlooking a beach she loved playing on.'

He drew another breath. 'Amanda and I got counselling, but the one useful thing we learned was that more than half of all marriages break up when a child dies, and Hollywood marriages are hardly known for their stability in the first place. Although I think we would have made it if Madison had lived, you know, with the whole grandchildren and diamond anniversary schtick.'

'I'm sorry,' said Logan.

'You know Kilsyth doesn't let me visit her grave? It's his property, the Kilsyth Ranch, and he won't let me set foot on it. And it's weird. He buried her in the family plot. On the left of Madison's grave there's room for Amanda, which is where I guess her body will end up. But there's no room on the other side of Madison's grave for me. I'm not part of the picture.'

Logan asked, 'So who's buried on the other side of Madison's grave?'

Besselt laughed. 'It's not who. It's what. The other grave holds the remains of Don't Knock.'

'What?'

'Don't Knock. It's a horse. It won Papa Kilsyth his first Kentucky Derby.'

'We'll sort it out back at the station,' I said. 'Sorry for intruding. I think it would be best if Mr Kilsyth makes the identification. Come on, Logan.'

Before we were off the lounge, Besselt's butler returned. 'I'm sorry to disturb you, sir, but Mr Kilsyth is waiting at the front door.'

'Damn it, no I'm not,' came a bellow from the foyer. 'I'm coming straight in. There's a damn cop car in the drive.'

Papa Kilsyth burst into the room. His silver hair and weathered face did not suggest mellow old age and quiet wisdom so much as battle-hardened remorselessness. Over navy trousers, he wore an angora sweater that would have blown my MasterCard limit yet had the audacity to be called casual. He went straight for Besselt and grabbed him by the lapels of his dressing gown.

'What have I told you about talking to police without a lawyer?'

'Mr Kilsyth,' said Logan. 'Please take your hands off your son-in-law before I arrest you for assault.'

Kilsyth laughed. 'Right. Like he'd press charges. Now, Damon, tell these nice officers you won't consult with them anymore without legal representation.'

'I'm sorry, detectives,' said Besselt.

'Good boy,' said Kilsyth, releasing his grip on Besselt's gown.

'I'm sorry to interrupt,' I said, 'but Mr Besselt is not a suspect for any crime we are investigating. Why does he need a lawyer?'

Kilsyth snarled. 'You want to talk to him, you arrest him. And then you can wait for his attorney.'

I picked up my bag and tucked away my notes. Clearly we were not going to get anywhere with Kilsyth around. He ushered us out the front door like we were Hare Krishnas doorknocking in Utah.

As we came out onto the veranda, we heard a helicopter *whoop-whoop-whooping* in the distance. Kilsyth ran out onto the lawn shouting, 'Anyone see that chopper?' The butler pointed to the northern sky, where a blue-and-gold helicopter circled.

Kilsyth flipped open a mobile phone. 'Lachlan, it's Fletcher here. Get your goddamn people away from Besselt's house. I don't want to see any of this on the news tonight. Yeah, yeah. Journalistic independence, my ass. I'll give you journalistic independence. I'll get on the phone to my EP from LA and you can guess the pictures you'll be discussing with your family over dinner. Thank you, Lachlan. That's very understanding. Give my regards to the wife.'

He snapped the phone shut. Pointing to us, he said, 'Now get off this property and take your damn cop car with you.'

'It's an unmarked vehicle!' Logan protested.

'Listen, boy,' said Besselt, 'I've run a TV news corporation for nearly forty years, and believe me, when a helicopter sees a clean white middle-class sedan parked across the driveway of a celebrity mansion, you <u>know</u> it's a police car. Get it the hell out of here.'

As we drove out, Logan said, 'Well Kilsyth's a major league arsehole, eh?'

'Yeah. What can you do about it?'

Logan laughed. 'Plenty.'

He had a look on his face that I had seen before.

'Don't do anything stupid, partner.'

He just grinned.

Quick coffee stop. Logan needed nicotine and I needed caffeine.

'Did you notice how young the girl looked?' said Logan.

'What I noticed was that Kilsyth's daughter has just topped herself and all he seems to care about is keeping a tight leash on the media.'

'She's supposed to be ten years old,' said Logan, who had a habit of not listening to me when he was thinking up a theory. 'But she looks like she's only six or seven.'

'Maybe she's just a small girl,' I said. 'You know, short for her age.'

'You really don't know anything about kids, do you?' asked Logan, who had four micro-terrorists of his own.

'No, but I know a lot about contraceptives.'

On the road back to the station I tried to keep talking, knowing full well that Logan was cooking up one of his grand conspiracies. Lieutenant Ziegler had paired us up not to play good cop/bad cop but girl cop/weird cop. He must have got the idea from *The X-Files*. I hoped that I could distract Logan, but it was no use. After ten minutes of me prattling on about the weather, the traffic, and Lieutenant Ziegler's bald spot, Logan whistled and said, 'I've got it!'

I groaned. There was no stopping him now.

'Cryonics.'

'What?'

'Cryonics. Freezing people until a cure comes along. You know, Walt Disney's head.'

'That's a myth.'

'Yeah, so says Disney Corp. Like they want little kiddies thinking about ol' Uncle Walt's head sitting in the freezer like a popsicle. They covered it up.'

'Oh come on. Can you come up with a single shred of evidence that Disney Corp covered up the decapitation and freezing of their beloved founder?'

'Lack of evidence is the mark of a really efficient conspiracy.'

Rationality was no barrier to Logan's conspiracy theories. In his mind, lack of evidence only confirmed the theory, and the less evidence to be found, the greater the confirmation.

I surrendered to the moment. 'So what's cryonics got to do with Kilsyth-Besselt?'

'The girl was cryonically frozen.'

'What?' I nearly hit the side of the road.

'Think about it,' said Logan. 'The girl was born ten years ago, but is physically only six or seven. That's three or four years missing. The father says she had leukemia. So she was frozen until a new treatment for leukemia came along. Wasn't there that new treatment for kids with cancer a few years ago? Maybe she was thawed and cured.'

As a theory, it was more coherent than his usual efforts, but it still had a gaping hole in the logic. 'So how come the father says she died in his arms?'

Logan answered straight away. 'All sorts of drugs can fake death. Notice how Besselt didn't know about the girl? I bet the Kilsyths concocted this scheme as a way of saving the girl's life and dumping Besselt at the same time.'

'Why would they want to dump him?'

'Just look at him. He's hitting the bottle pretty hard. Judging by his appearance this morning, he's drinking in an afternoon what I do on New Year's Eve. They couldn't rely on him.'

'He says all that came after the girl's death.'

'Yeah, yeah. Alkies have a million excuses.'

I was about to raise the improbability of keeping something like that quiet, until I remembered Kilsyth scaring off the news helicopter like he was swatting a dragonfly. It was still ridiculously implausible, but for once Logan's theory was self-consistent, and that scared the living daylights out of me.

As we pulled into the station, Logan took another phone call.

'We're nearly inside,' he said as we walked. 'OK. I know she's not at the house. Yeah. I know I told him she was there. She was there when I told him. Yeah, yeah. Tell him she's being looked after in the interview rooms.'

He hung up then opened his phone again.

'Hey there, Cliff. Logan here. The girl still there? Great. Can you take her upstairs to the overflow rooms? Yeah, I know it's a hassle, but it's important. She needs to move now. Like the next two minutes.'

Logan had accrued a tangle of favours owed and nod-and-wink friendships. It was an education seeing him go to work on his network.

'So what's going on?' I asked.

'Just shuffling the deck,' he said.

As the only woman in the squad, I always got the interviews Lieutenant Ziegler considered 'emotional', and as expected, he gave me the Kilsyth-Besselt girl to interview. Ziegler dragged the girl's nanny in to the station to be the responsible adult. Logan and I knocked and went into the interview room. The nanny looked up from the task of brushing the girl's hair. She was tying braids for the distraction.

'Is this really necessary?' she asked. 'I've signed a non-disclosure agreement.'

Logan said, 'I'm sorry, but I think you'll find a police investigation trumps a non-disclosure agreement. And we have to talk to Madison.'

'Lacey,' said the girl. 'My name is Lacey.'

Logan looked down at the file and frowned. Her name was marked as *Madison Lacey Kilsyth-Besselt.*

Without looking up from the braiding, the nanny said, 'She has insisted on being called Lacey for the last few weeks.'

'Madison's a stupid name,' said the girl. 'I don't want to be named after an avenue. Should be the other way round.'

She was such a beautiful girl modelling agencies would kill to put her on their books. Blonde hair fell down to her shoulders. A porcelain face drew the gaze to her enormous jet-black eyes. She was dressed in a button-up blouse and an ankle-length linen skirt. She bit her lip in a manner that was just a bit too deliberate—she had learned how to look adorable in the way that other kids learn how to play piano or throw a curveball.

'Lacey,' I said. 'My name is Detective Lindamuller, and this is Detective Logan. We need to know what happened.'

'Sure,' she said, and then went through the events of the day before, all in a quiet monotone. She had a fight with her mother. It was over something trivial, as usual. This time it had been the way she wore her hair to go horse riding. The nanny confirmed that the mother and Lacey had been at each other constantly for the last few months. They could both be mule-stubborn, and the fights kept escalating.

'It was getting unbearable,' said the nanny. 'I was ready to resign except I knew Mrs Kilsyth would never give me a good reference if I left her. She could be a manipulative cow sometimes—sorry, Lacey.'

The girl just shrugged.

For the last few months, Amanda had become increasingly obsessive. She would insist on certain activities, such as horse riding, even when Lacey said she hated horses. Amanda had bought her a blue swimsuit, and insisted that blue was Lacey's favorite color, even though Lacey insisted she preferred yellow.

The night Amanda died, the nanny had been on her Saturday night off, which meant Amanda was with the girl all by herself. The conflict had gone nova.

'It was Snooks,' said the little girl.

'Snooks?'

'My purple elephant doll. I burnt it.'

'You burnt it?'

'Yep. I was bored with it.'

It didn't occur to me at the time that this was anything more than a little emotional drama that the girl had played out for the benefit of needling her mother.

Not much else came out of the interview other than a few details of Amanda's steady descent into oblivion. Because of her money and power, none of her staff was brave enough to approach her. I suspected that Kilsyth was going to sack them *en masse* once he learned about his daughter's last four weeks. If Amanda had not been surrounded by 'supportive' staff, then she would have been forced to seek the psychiatric help she needed. If Howard Hughes had not been insanely wealth he might not have gone insanely phobic.

The Corpsegrinder was sitting at his desk, hunched over a magnifying lamp and a chunk of someone's tooth. He was a tall, bony man with a gleaming billiard-ball skull. There was scarcely any more flesh on his frame than on the skeletons he examined.

He heard the elevator doors open and turned to inspect the visitors.

'Logan. Lindamuller. You seem to have become the chief investigators by default,' he said. 'I thought you hated celebrity cases.'

'Too damn messy,' I said.

'Too many lawyers,' said Logan.

The Corpsegrinder put down his *objet d'art* and wiped his bald and sweat-glistened scalp with one hand. His sweat smelled of formalin. Squad members used to joke about him reeking when he left the mortuary, until Logan pointed out that he had never been seen outside the place. The story doing the rounds was that the Corpsegrinder slept in the stainless steel drawers overnight.

'Come over here,' he said. He opened Amanda Kilsyth-Besselt's drawer and drew back the sheet. Her skin was tight. Under the mortuary lights and without her makeup, old cosmetic surgery scars inched like pale worms along her chin, behind her ears, and under her eyes. She was a beautiful woman. Yet here she was, disfigured and self-mutilated by her fortieth birthday. How could someone so exquisite have such poor self-esteem? Now she bore scars from more recent work. Black stitching ran up her sternum.

'Nice needlework,' said Logan. 'Looks like the seam on a football.'

The Corpsegrinder smiled. 'Thank you, Detective Logan. Always a pleasure to sample your humor. Anything else I can sample while you're here? Your frontal cortex, perhaps? If you have one?'

'So what's the story?' I asked, breaking up the bull elephants' territorial display.

'Definitely overdosed,' said the Corpsegrinder. 'All the pills came from her own prescriptions. Toxicology matches the bottles found by the bedside. Benzos and stimulants. Terrible mix. Users get on a rollercoaster ride where they swallow an upper to get stimulated and overshoot, so then they take a downer and overshoot again. Up and down they go until the oscillations get out of control.'

'So she might have accidentally OD'ed?'

'Not a chance. She took every pill she had, both uppers and benzos, and a half-bottle of gin, and a few random tablets in the medicine cabinet. Given her state of mind, I couldn't say she was in control of herself, but the OD was no mistake.'

The Corpsegrinder flicked the sheet back to cover Amanda's face.

'You called us down here to tell us that?' asked Logan.

'Oh no,' said the Corpsegrinder. 'Any idiot could have figured that out just by checking out the scene.'

Logan bridled. I put a steadying hand on his arm.

'What's so interesting then?' I asked.

'The girl. You said she looks six or seven but was born ten years ago.'

'That's right. She must have been cryonically frozen,' said Logan.

The Corpsegrinder looked at him for a full five seconds, then said, 'You know, that's absurd. But better than your usual efforts. She had some disease when she was younger, didn't she?'

'Leukemia,' said Logan, chuffed at drawing ahead of the Corpsegrinder in their game of Look Who's Smarter.

'Well,' said the Corpsegrinder. 'We'll see who's right, then. All you need to do is check a few pieces of evidence for me. Consider it a challenge.'

'Right about what?' asked Logan. 'What are you suggesting?'

The Corpsegrinder just smiled. 'You ought to check for any photo albums. If the girl was cryonically frozen, there will be a gap in the photo sequence of three or four years and then she'll reappear again.'

Logan nodded and wrote down PHOTO ALBUM.

'And check the hospital where she was treated for leukemia. They won't give you her records without a warrant or a waiver, but if you hustle, you ought to be able to confirm her date of 'death.' Check the family's travel records about that time. And one other thing: check the Kilsyths' security system for new users in the last seven years.'

Logan added HOSPITAL RECORD, TRAVEL, and SECURITY SYSTEM to his list. 'What is all that supposed to prove?' he asked.

The Corpsegrinder didn't answer. He went back to the magnifying lamp and the tooth. 'Let me know what you find.'

I had to drag Logan out of the room before he imbedded the cadaver's tooth in the Corpsegrinder's smile.

Logan was on the phone again.

'Yeah. I know. She is in the interview rooms. We just interviewed her. Yeah I moved her to the overflow room. I know we weren't that busy. She's a little girl and I thought it would be nicer for her if she was well away from the hustlers and the junkies. Yeah. So it's not *the* interview room. It's *an* interview room. That's what I told him.

'Well that's hardly my fault. No, she's not there anymore. We moved her to the medical suite for the doc to check her over. Yeah, sure.'

He closed his phone and grinned.

'Seems Kilsyth is getting antsy,' Logan said.

He made another call. 'Hey there, Stu. Logan here. Yeah. Time to leave the medical suite. Like now. She's been looked over? Good. Get out of there now. Call me when you're in the car. Thanks, Stu. No, you won't regret it.'

Despite having strict regulations about confidentiality, the hospital was the easiest to tap for information. All we had to do was to demand to know why Madison Lacey Kilsyth-Besselt's death had not been reported to the coroner. The administrator refused to hand over the records, but he was more than relieved to tell us that she had not died in the hospital. She had been discharged against medical advice. They had nothing to do with the poor girl's death, and would vigorously defend any malpractice suit or coronial investigation. Logan made a song and dance about needing to see the records just to make the administrator sweat, and then we left on a promise to return with a warrant. It was pure theater from Logan—the hospital had given us what we needed.

The travel records were harder to track down, not because the airlines were uncooperative, but because the Kilsyths had covered their tracks well. The day they pulled Madison from hospital, they had travelled under assumed names to New Mexico, where Kilsyth held a large property.

Tougher still was the security log. We had to lean on Kilsyth's chief of security, who was an ex-cop. We reached out to his old squad, where it turned out he had resigned hours before he was sacked. Some dubious friendships with some dubious colleagues allowed him to break into the security industry at the high end of town rather than at the door of a nightclub. The lieutenant at his old squad was happy to give the circumstances of his resignation, off the record. We then approached the security chief with our information, off the record. He had a couple of kids in expensive schools and a wife in an expensive car and Kilsyth was not going to keep him if the whole truth came out. He gave us the information we wanted, off the record of course.

The Corpsegrinder was onto something, because a new user file had been opened for Madison a few years earlier.

The photo album was impossible. Kilsyth had already sealed off the house and filled the moat with lawyers. We couldn't have got through them with an armoured truck and a rocket launcher, although the thought did cross our minds.

Stu was on the phone.

'You're driving? Yeah. Good stuff. Just keep driving. Don't go back to the station. Take her to the park. Enjoy yourself. Just make sure you don't answer any calls unless it's me.'

Logan grinned. He hummed one of his favourite Waylon Jennings songs. He was happy. Logan was almost never happy.

As soon as we came into the squad room, Lieutenant Ziegler pounced. 'What have you got?' he asked as he ushered us into his office. Logan rattled off the evidence we had accumulated.

'So it's a suicide. What's taking your time?'

'There's still the kid to sort out.'

'Surely it's just a clerical error,' said Ziegler. 'Some idiot got the birthday wrong.'

'No chance,' I said. 'We've seen the original birth certificate. There's also the fact that she had terminal leukemia when she was three, was discharged from hospital against medical advice, flown to the Kilsyth's ranch in New Mexico—under an assumed name—and now there's a three-year gap between her reported age and her physical age. This is no clerical error.'

'Could you close the case now?'

'Sure, it's a clear suicide, sir, but I think we ought to pursue this.'

'Do you have a theory?'

Logan started to speak, but I stepped on his foot before he could mention the magic word *cryonics*. 'Nothing confirmed yet, sir.'

Ziegler smiled at Logan. 'You were about to fly me one of your pet conspiracies, eh, Logan? Probably say she was frozen or something.'

'Hey! The Corpsegrinder thinks it's a possibility!' Logan protested.

'So you've spoken to the Corpsegrinder about it. I don't want to sound like I doubt you, but I'd like to know what *he* thinks is going on. Logan? Lindamuller?'

Logan coughed. 'He won't say, sir. Not until we report back to him.'

'And why haven't you?'

Now Logan was looking down at the floor, scuffing his shoes. 'We thought we'd check with you first, sir.'

'You mean you were stalling for time until you figured it out for yourself. I have no time for games, especially considering the chances of you matching wits with the Corpsegrinder. There are another five cases on the board with your names next to them. Get this one off your plate and move on.'

'Yes, sir.'

As we were leaving, Ziegler said, 'By the way, I haven't heard from Stu. You don't know where he is?'

Logan shook his head and I shrugged. It was no lie. We didn't know where he was. Well, not *precisely*.

The Corpsegrinder was looking mighty pleased with himself. Every line of investigation he had suggested came up trumps—except the irretrievable photo album, and he insisted it was unnecessary with the rest of the information at hand.

'Look,' said Logan, 'I don't have time to muck around. Just tell us what you're so self-satisfied about. I'll be sure to put in a commendation.'

The Corpsegrinder said, 'So you have a sick little girl who isn't responding to treatment. Rather than let her die in hospital, the family pulls her out and flies her to a secluded property. She dies thereabouts, as the father attests, and is buried somewhere near the Gulf of Mexico overlooking the ocean. Then, she reappears looking three years too young.'

'She didn't die. She was frozen.'

'Forget that, Logan. She was not frozen. She died.'

'So what the hell is going on?'

'A little story that might help you,' said the Corpsegrinder. 'Have you ever heard of Chang and Eng, the first Siamese Twins? They were identical twins joined at the chest and abdomen, which means they had shared a single placenta. Since they were conjoined their entire lives, they shared almost the same experiences. They had exactly the same genes, exactly the same intra-uterine conditions, and as close to the same environment as is humanly possible. Despite this they had distinct personalities and tastes. Chang was a heavy drinker while Eng was a teetotaller, although it's arguable how much difference this made since they shared a blood pool. They once came to blows over a piece of music.'

The image of Siamese twins in a fistfight with each other flicked across my mind. 'What's your point?' I asked.

The Corpsegrinder gave his death's-head smile and said, 'Even when you control for genes, intra-uterine conditions, and environment, you still can't direct the development of an individual person with precision. Identical twins don't have the same fingerprints.'

'Fingerprints?' said Logan. 'Fingerprints! They had to add a new user to the security system because the girl had different fingerprints.'

I was confused. 'You mean she was an identical twin? But...'

The Corpsegrinder and Logan turned to me.

'You tell her,' said the Corpsegrinder.

'You figured it out,' said Logan. 'You tell her.'

'All right. Kilsyth Ranch is stocked with some of the best racehorses in the world. A straw of semen can be worth a fortune, but insemination is still unreliable. Even with the best semen and the best mare, you can still end up with a dud foal. The Kilsyth Ranch has pioneered a way of guaranteeing a first-class racehorse. They sell embryos.'

I shook my head. 'I don't follow you.'

Logan sighed. 'Embryos. Fully-fledged embryos. Kilsyth Ranch leads the world in *animal cloning technology*, for chrissakes!'

'Cloning,' I echoed.

The Corpsegrinder and Logan slapped a high-five. It was the first time I'd seen them exchange a friendly gesture. They were laughing together, delighted at their cleverness. The Corpsegrinder was a frustrated Sherlock who had just cracked a case, and Logan had stumbled across a genuine *News of the World* vindication of every paranoid thought he held dear. They were beside themselves with joy.

All I could think of was the little girl upstairs.

'We've got to make a decision,' I said.

'About what?'

'The girl. It's time we brought her in. We can't play hide and seek with Kilsyth forever.'

'I guess so. Plus Stu will be going crazy.'

'And we have to make a decision.'

Logan got my meaning at last. 'No way. I'm not going to take that responsibility,' said Logan.

'Not making a decision means Kilsyth gets the girl. Pretending there's nothing to be done is just the same as taking a position, only without the guts.'

Logan unfolded his phone and handed it to me. 'OK, but you make the call.'

Damon Besselt knocked on the PA's desk. I saw him first and went over.

'Thanks for coming in, Mr Besselt.'

He had brushed himself up for the visit to the station. Showered and shaved and wearing a crisp Armani suit and a polo neck, I could see the looks that had once made him hot property in Hollywood. But the bags under the eyes and the look of pain when he took off his sunglasses reminded me of the human wreck we had met that morning.

'I wish you had explained over the phone,' he said.

'We honestly didn't know how.' I waved to Logan, who stood up from his desk and joined us. 'Please follow me,' I told Besselt.

We went into the observation room.

'There's something I have to ask,' said Logan. 'Just to clear my mind on an issue.'

Besselt shrugged. 'Ask away.'

'Why did you travel to New Mexico on fake IDs?'

'It was Kilsyth's idea,' said Besselt. 'He said it would help throw the press off our tails. And it worked. Hardly a soul knew about Madison's death. We chartered a private jet. It's not illegal is it?'

Logan and I looked at each other. He seemed genuine, and gut feeling was all the corroboration we were going to get.

Logan drew up the blind that covered the one-way window. Through it we could see Lacey in the interview room with a uniformed policewoman. Lacey was playing with a doll from the box of toys we kept in a storage cupboard.

Besselt rubbed his eyes.

'You don't recognise her?' asked Logan.

Besselt shook his head.

'She doesn't remind you of your daughter?'

Besselt tilted his head. 'Sure. Madison might have grown up looking like that, but she was only three when she died. It's hard to know.'

'Sit down please, Mr Besselt. I have something to tell you.'

Logan and I went through the whole story from when Madison died. Amanda hadn't trusted Besselt to go along with her, and it was easier to break off the marriage than risk him sabotaging the plan. Her father, Fletcher Kilsyth, probably knew nothing of the plan until it was too late, either. In all likelihood, Amanda was already heavily pregnant when she told him. She knew how to play him. Once he was committed to her protection, he would fight like a bulldog. The shutters had <u>really</u> come down on the media. They travelled rarely, and always with some cover for young Madison. Security was anaconda tight. Nobody was to find out the truth. For seven years, the Kilsyths had managed the impossible.

Besselt was staring at the ceiling and taking deep breaths. Abruptly he stood up to leave, but Logan blocked his way.

'Listen, Besselt. We didn't call you here for a social. The girl in there is your daughter.'

'Madison is dead.'

'*This* girl is alive. If it makes you feel any better, think of her as a child from by a long-forgotten lover who has just turned up on your doorstep. But she has half your genes, so she *is* your daughter.'

'And you want me to take her? I can't do that!'

'It's you or Fletcher Kilsyth. Do you really want her to grow up as screwed up as Amanda?'

'You think I'm going to do any better?'

I said, 'I don't know, Mr Besselt. Pardon my honesty, but you're a bit of a loser and a lot of an alcoholic. But I guess you weren't always that way. And you couldn't do worse than Kilsyth.'

'Jesus! You can't dump this on me and expect me to decide in the next five minutes!'

'Kilsyth knows his daughter is here, and any moment now he is going to walk through that door with a phalanx of attorneys,' said Logan.

Besselt sat down and covered his eyes to think. After a few seconds I saw him lift his gaze to watch Lacey playing dolls.

'I don't get it,' said Besselt.

'Amanda wanted her little girl back,' I said.

'No, I mean why did Amanda kill herself? She had everything the way she wanted it.'

Logan shrugged. 'She was using uppers and downers. Maybe she was just depressed. People don't always have a reason.'

'That's not true,' I said. 'She had a reason.'

I remembered what the Corpsegrinder had said about Chang and Eng, the Siamese twins with the same genes, the same womb, and the same environment, and how they had vastly different personalities. And then I saw the scene clearly, as if I had been right there in the Kilsyth mansion when Amanda crawled off to bed with her pills and a glass of water.

Months of fighting over Madison's likes and dislikes had reached a crisis point. Madison would say she wanted to go skating, and Amanda would look it up in her book and say: 'You hate skating. Why don't we go riding? You can wear your blue suit.' And the girl would scream back about how she *hated* riding. How horses were *disgusting* and *smelly* and *stupid*. And how blue was a colour for *boys* and she wanted to wear *yellow*. And they would scream at each other until Amanda broke down crying for the girl she had failed to resurrect. She had been delivered an impostor despite giving her the same genes, the same womb, and as close to the same environment as possible. But this was not Madison. She didn't even have the same fingerprints.

The girl had started to call herself Lacey. She wasn't going to be Madison, a stupid name for a stupid street in New York. She had never been Madison, so she wouldn't answer to Madison. And her mother had got on the rollercoaster about then. Up and down and up and down and out of control.

Finally that night, the substitute daughter had torn Amanda's world beyond repair. High or low, it didn't matter; Amanda was in no shape to cope with the girl's emotional assaults. Amanda had staggered in from the lounge, soaked in gin to numb the pain. There in the lounge was Madison, waiting for the perfect moment when her mother was close enough to see exactly what she was going to do, but not close enough to do anything to stop her. Madison picked up her 'favorite' toy of all time, the purple elephant called Snooks, and tossed it into the fireplace.

Amanda would have kept the toy vacuum-sealed until her new daughter was two years old, which was the age the first Madison had received it. To Amanda, the toy was the most precious thing in the world, the thing her daughter had loved, the thing she had held to her in her grief, and now it was bathed in flame. The nylon caught fire in an instant. Before Amanda could even cry out, the toy was a puddle of black plastic and blue flame.

In my head, I could hear Amanda screaming, half in fury, half in despair. And Madison, I could see her turning to her mother and presenting a face as blank as marble—the face of a stone cold angel of destruction.

The clarity of the vision was overpowering. Maybe the fight had been over hairstyles or movie preferences rather than horses and colours. But I knew I had the principle.

That night, Amanda gulped her life away. And in revenge for her daughter's increasingly surgical acts of emotional violence, Amanda made sure the girl found her in the morning. *See how much I can hurt you?* she was saying. *You cuckoo!*

I controlled my voice. 'Amanda finally realised she could never have Madison back. Not for all the money in the world.'

Besselt looked again at the child in the other room. 'You told me your pathologist figured it out.'

Logan nodded.

'I want to speak to him.'

'We don't have time.'

'I need to ask him a few things.'

Logan pursed his lips. We were running out of time, but Besselt couldn't be expected to make his choices completely blind. Logan took out his phone and pressed autodial.

As he handed the phone to Besselt, he said, 'Make it snappy.'

'Now do you understand?' Logan said.

'I still don't see why you can't tell the story.'

The Press Officer still wasn't getting it.

'Look,' I said. 'If Kilsyth ever hears the details, he'll pour a ton of lawyers on us. He knows well enough what happened, but if we confirm anything in an interview he'll have us. I don't know what you need to tell the Commissioner, but say it, whatever it is.'

The Press Officer still looked confused. 'I don't see what Kilsyth could do.'

Logan sighed. 'We'll have to spell it out for her.'

'We stonewalled Kilsyth,' I said.

'You what?'

'We delayed him. Deliberately.'

'Oh,' said the Press Officer. 'I see.'

'Tell her the rest, Logan.'

Besselt spent half an hour with the Corpsegrinder, and then headed back to the interview room. He sat, staring at the girl for what seemed like an eternity.

Lieutenant Ziegler knocked and came in.

'The PA just called to say Kilsyth's limo has pulled up outside. I've just had Kilsyth on the phone and he's in a very bad mood. Besselt will have to leave through the compound.'

'Last chance,' said Logan.

Besselt breathed deeply. 'Bring her in.'

Logan tapped on the one-way window. The uniform brought the girl round to the observation room.

'This is your father,' I said to her. 'Damon Besselt.'

'My father? But he's...' She never finished the sentence, so I never learned what lie Amanda had told her.

Besselt crouched down and held his arms open. The girl took a cautious step into his embrace. She was going to take a long time to trust anyone. I wasn't sure Besselt would manage but at least the girl had a chance with him, and if he screwed up, Kilsyth's lawyers would take the girl out of his hands soon enough.

Besselt held her tight. 'It's nice to meet you, Madison,' he said.

'My name is Lacey.'

'Lacey,' he said, straightening up. 'I think I can handle that.'

'Come on!' said Logan. 'They've stalled Kilsyth as long as they can.'

The girl's ears pricked up at her grandfather's name. She looked at Logan, then back at Besselt, the father who was a stranger to her. Goodness knows what her mother had said about him, but it was unlikely to be flattering. I could see her working out the options. It was a big decision for a seven-year-old.

'It's up to you,' Damon Besselt said to Lacey. 'But you have to choose now.'

A worried frown darkened her face.

Besselt extended his arm, and Lacey, after a moment's hesitation, reached up and took his hand.

'You're right. I can't use the story. Pity.' The Press Officer finished her coffee and waved for the bill. 'But I still think you're heroes for standing up to Kilsyth.'

Logan smiled. 'We're not heroic—just sentimental and impulsive.'

The Press Officer packed up her things and left.

It can't have been more than a minute between Lacey taking her father's hand and Kilsyth bursting into the interview with two lawyers, a court order, and a cold look in his eyes.

'Where's the girl?' he demanded.

Logan shrugged. 'She's been signed out already,' he said.

The old saying about possession being nine-tenths of the law is as true of family law as property law. The moment Besselt walked out of the station house with Lacey, he staked a claim for custody. And Kilsyth had his problems — namely that he was an accessory after the fact to an illegal cloning of a human being. There are some legal principles that money just can't cut through.

Besselt turned out to be a pretty decent father, as far as anyone could tell, despite having a daughter with some of the Devil in her. Lacey settled down surprisingly well, even after the world's editors decided the CLONE GIRL! headline was worth braving the wrath of Papa Kilsyth, and a stolen photo of her face echoed around the planet.

We had given the Press Officer the happy ending, but in our line of work it's never that simple. There's always a downside. Or two ...

The Corpsegrinder told me about it. His reading on identical twins revealed an interesting study. It turns out that identical twins raised together are less similar, psychologically speaking, than identical twins raised apart. Humans, it appears, have a deep need for personal identity. If Lacey's mother hadn't tried so hard, she might have raised the Madison she wanted.

The Corpsegrinder had an even more disturbing revelation. There are genes that predispose to leukaemia. He said the real tragedy was that Lacey's mother had recreated a child who could die of leukaemia all over again. In fact, he said, it's remotely possible that the gap between Madison the First and Lacey was not due to the difficulty of adapting equine technology to humans. Maybe, just maybe, there was another short life in the interim, a Madison the Second. Maybe a Third. Maybe more. Nobody knows and nobody wants to find out. Not even the Corpsegrinder and his morbid curiosity wanted to dig there.

Lacey is now ten, and the older she gets the less likely it is that she will get sick, I guess. Not that there's anything anyone can do about it. I just hope Lacey's name doesn't turn up in the news again.

And Besselt? He talked to the Corpsegrinder. He knew these things. He knew the girl was more than a little broken. A girl who could grind you down like steel wool. A girl who could drive her mother to suicide. A girl who could fall prey to leukemia all over again. A girl who would bring Papa Kilsyth's fury down upon him—and Besselt knew Kilsyth's resourceful ferocity better than anyone.

Logan was right. We weren't the heroes of the story. We were just sentimental and impulsive. If anyone could be said to be the hero, it was Besselt.

Chris Lawson is a doctor with an interest in genetics, paediatric medicine and epidemiology. His stories have appeared in *Eidolon*, *Asimov's*, *Event Horizon*, *Spectrum SF*, *Dreaming Down Under*, *Under Centaurus*, *Gathering the Bones*, *Realms of Fantasy*, and several times in various Year's Best Science Fiction anthologies. He has won the Ditmar and Aurealis Awards, and his story 'Unborn Again' has been optioned for feature film development.

http://members.ozemail.com.au/~claw/frankenblogger.htm

In the Days of the Red Animals

KATE ORMAN

Europe: 30,000 years ago

GRANNY SCRATCH WAS PERCHED atop the tilted rock, looking for the lights in the sky. Sister Two Scratch clambered up behind her, cupping a lamp in her hands, her stomach growling loud enough to hear. Up here it was crisp and clear, wind sharp as a spear through cloth and fur alike, but it never seemed to bother Granny. Hunger didn't seem to bother her much, either.

The old woman glanced over her shoulder. There were lines around her eyes, and her hair was just starting to gray. 'Anything?' asked Sister Two, settling in a hollow on the rock.

'Nothing,' sighed Granny. 'Plenty of shooting stars. But none of the low, fast green lights.' She fished in her pocket for the bone calendar, and ran a chipped thumbnail along the pattern of grooves. It was smaller than her hand, intricately patterned. 'Three moons, less four days,' she announced.

Sister Two shivered, wishing the lamp was a real fire. 'And it's never happened before.'

'My grandmother told me they stopped coming for almost a whole moon, once. But never for this long.' Granny gave her a sharp glance. 'You think it's to do with the red animals.'

'They come from the east,' said Sister Two. 'Same as the lights. And they started coming when the lights stopped.' Sister Two tilted her head back, scanning the sky. 'Do you think they're ever coming back?'

Granny shrugged. 'Come on, girl, let's get you back by the fire.'

The red animals had begun as a trickle. One came from the east, then two, then more than you could count on your fingers and toes. They blundered. They trumpeted. They knocked over trees and fell in creeks.

They were tall, twice as tall as a man. They had three legs as thick as tree-trunks, and round, flabby feet. Their bodies were covered with spiky scarlet fur, visible for miles across the cold plains or through the spare forest.

Their crashing and hooting frightened animals all around. Rabbits and foxes bolted randomly through the forest, missing their usual runs and the snares set there. Nests fell from trees, becoming twiggy messes of crushed eggs. Elk and sheep stampeded out of the red animals' path and away from the women's nets.

Dawn had arrived when Sister Two and Granny Scratch joined Sisters Three and Six by the fire near the cave entrance. They were working on a net that needed repairs. Most of the women and kids were already out gathering nuts and roots, and the men had gone off to see if they couldn't spear a reindeer to make up the food shortage. The quartet of women were surrounded by babies wrapped in cloth and laid out on furs.

'Maybe we could use the red animals to flush out game for us,' piped Six, picking at a knot. She was still too young for babies, too young even to braid her hair. 'Grab anything they send bolting.'

'Hurh,' said Three. 'Tried something like that when they first showed up—followed 'em around with the bunny nets. Problem was, the rabbits ran in all directions, 'cos the red animals run in all directions too. You dunno where to wait.'

'Something's happened in the east,' said Sister Two. Granny gave her another piercing glance. 'Something's driving the red animals into our range.'

'What do they eat?' asked Six. 'Maybe they've run out of it.'

'I've only seen them eat trees, or bushes,' said Two, frowning as she unhooked a tangle in the coarse fibers of the net. 'Maybe the trees have stopped growing over there? Whatever it is, we're in trouble.'

One of the infants started mewling. 'That's for sure,' said Three, picking it up and tucking it into her beaded shirt. 'We're not gonna be able to feed this lot without them bunnies and sheep.' She poked Sister Two gently in her stomach. 'Starting to show.'

'Do you think we could make a net big enough for one of those things?' said Six.

'You know,' said Granny Scratch, 'one of them's dying down by the stagnant waterhole. Why don't you three go and take a look at it?'

The red animal looked like an unlikely fallen tree. It lay on its side, its three legs sticking out ridiculously, its head in the half-frozen mud at the edge of the waterhole. Its long red ears trailed pathetically into the water. Its flanks rose and fell sharply.

'It's starving,' said Sister Two quietly.

The three sisters and their Granny stood at the top of a rise, looking down at the wreck by the waterhole. 'It can't be starving,' said Six. 'They eat more than a flock of sheep! I watched one chewing up a whole tree—leaves, branches, bark and all!'

The red animal raised its egg-shaped head as they edged closer, then let it fall back into the mud with an uncaring squelch.

Three said, 'Bones stickin' out all over.'

Sister Two hefted her club, but Granny Scratch said, 'Can't you smell it? That thing's not fit for eating.'

'We've got to eat something,' said Two. 'Why waste it?'

Granny tweaked her ear. 'Does it smell like anything you've ever eaten? You wouldn't eat a funny plant just like that, would you?'

'Give it to Mammoth Killer,' giggled Six. 'He'll eat anything.'

'How can they be starving when they eat so much?' said Two.

'Could you live on leaves and bark?' said Granny.

Three laughed. 'Hurh. Hurh. Things are so dumb they dunno what they're supposed to eat.' She poked Two in the arm.

Sister Two let her club fall by her side. 'I'm going east,' she said.

'You're what?' said Six.

'I'm going to head east. See what's over the mountains.'

There was a long silence. Finally, little Six said, 'But nobody goes there except the Bluefaces.'

Mammoth Killer wasn't the biggest of the men, or the strongest. But he was the fastest runner, and by far the best with a spear. He wasn't a greyhair yet, but only because his hair was thinning like a worn cloth.

The community sat around the fire—27 of them now, plus babies. Mammoth Killer sawed off juicy, charred chunks of mutton and passed them around, deciding who got what piece. Eight years ago, in a desperate winter, he had been the one to launch the spear that finished off a mammoth, and he had never let anyone forget it. He still had the spear.

Sister Two Scratch waited until everyone had eaten enough to get their minds off their hunger. Then she stood up and explained her plan.

'I'm going to head east,' she said. 'Half a moon's walk should take me as far as the mountains. I'll see if I can find out where the red animals are coming from, and why. Maybe I can even find out what happened to the lights in the sky.'

There was a companionable silence for several minutes while the community digested that. Scouting missions were far from unusual, but these were strange circumstances.

'You'll pass through the Bluefaces' range for sure,' said one of the men. 'We found one of their campsites only the other day.'

'You can't go alone,' said a woman, around a mouthful of meat. 'Take someone with you. Take one of the men.'

'Take a group,' pleaded Sister Six.

Sister Two said, 'The more people that go, the harder it'll be to keep us fed as we move, and the more attention we'll attract. A lone woman would have a much better chance of making her way through Blueface territory without getting spotted.'

Mammoth Killer cleared his throat, and everyone fell silent. 'If they get hold of you, girl, no one's coming to rescue you. No one wants to get close to those cannibals.'

There was a murmur of agreement. The Bluefaces were scavengers, living in small and hungry groups around the edge of the other tribes' territory. Prey was scarce in their margin of land in the shadow of the mountains. It was well known that the Bluefaces would eat anything they could catch.

'Just let them try and catch me!' said Sister Two.

But Mammoth Killer shook his head, and now the other men shook their heads too. 'We need everyone we can right here, out looking for food.'

Sister Three said, 'We're 'bout as far east as we go each year. Those red animals'll starve before they get west of us.'

'We'll move west a little,' Mammoth Killer said. 'And wait for them to die off.'

'But what about the lights?' said Sister Two. She found herself sitting down again, her voice becoming a murmur. 'Things like this just don't happen. What's going to come next? What's happening to the world?'

Mammoth Killer was watching her, sucking the marrow out of a bone. I mean what I say, his glance told her. If she tried to disobey him, walk out, he'd be right behind her with his famous spear.

So she didn't walk. She ran.

She let it go for a week. There was plenty of work to do; the red animals kept coming, more and more of them, scaring off the herds, filling the forest with noise and panic when they needed quiet and calm. The catch stayed low. There were enough nuts and berries and mushrooms and roots to keep them alive, but everyone's stomach was grumbling, everyone's mood was bad.

So it wasn't hard to pick a fight with Sister Three when their best net tore. They held the net taut and ready, waiting for Six to flush out whatever she could from the undergrowth. 'Oh, look what you've done!' exploded Sister Two.

'Just caught on a thorn,' grunted Three.

Sister Two snatched mesh from her hands. 'Look at this! We can't afford to wreck our nets now!'

Three sat down on a stump and folded her arms. 'Not my fault,' she said. 'Rant and rave all you want.'

'Look at you, just sitting there! Oh, we're never going to fill our bellies this way!' Three was unmoved, picking at her teeth with one of the thorns. Sister Two gave an angry grunt and threw the net on the ground. She stomped off into the trees.

And then she ran. The moment she was sure Sister Three wouldn't hear her bolting through the undergrowth, she was gone.

She headed for the river that ran down a steep hillside on the other side of the forest. Get over that, get over the ridge beyond it, and she could disappear into the warren of caves on the other side. It would take days for the community to search them. Time they wouldn't waste when food was so short.

Shouts! Somewhere behind her—and there, the sound of feet crashing through the undergrowth. They were onto her already. Sister Three must have realised what was going on right away.

Sister Two Scratch knew how she looked—a silhouette flashing through the trees, like any reindeer in its panicky flight from the spears. She could hear Mammoth Killer roaring her name. The baby was a small weight low in her belly, no more hindrance than carrying a basket of food. But if she couldn't outrun the others, her only chance was that he wouldn't bring down a pregnant woman.

Somewhere close ahead, she heard trumpeting. She changed directions in an instant, bounding over a fallen log, heading for the echoing hooting sound.

She exploded through branches into a clearing that hadn't been there the day before, and almost ran straight into the red animal.

She was barely more than an arm's reach from the thing. She backed up, fast, getting out of range of its heavy legs and its gaping mouth.

It looked down at her with its flat black eyes, its head drooping. Skin hung from its legs as though it was melting. She could see it had been stumbling about, trampling the small trees, chewing up branches and bushes. There was a great mass of chewed-up leaves and wood at its feet—Sister Two realised it was vomit.

Sister Two stepped in a wide circle around the creature, faster than it could turn to follow her, took out her butchering blade, and jammed the sharp stone into the flesh of the monster's hindleg. The red animal trumpeted and staggered sideways. Its thin bulk crashed against a tree, the roots groaning as they tore loose from the earth. Sister Two poked it again with her knife, and the red animal started to run, back in the direction she had come, awkward legs smashing the trees and the undergrowth.

Sister Two turned back towards the river and kept running, her trail covered by the blundering beast. It had no chance of killing any of the others, not with its weak body, its burning color so obvious through the trees. But it would slow them, confuse them, give them something else to worry about.

She burst from the forest and half-stumbled, half-slid down to the cold river. Her grin at her own cleverness faded. Her babies would be fine, but she wished she could have said goodbye. She had escaped her own people. If she came home with the answers, would they ever take her back?

She could draw a map of any of the community's hunting grounds in the dirt, from memory. But not here. The landmarks were new, she didn't know by heart where to find water or food. She moved slowly, sniffing the air, combing the frozen landscape with her eyes.

The corpses of the red animals were scattered across the ground, their hot color burning like campfires against the grays and greens of the empty plain.

Twice she saw the spoor of the Bluefaces. A patch of charred earth, a chunk of cloth torn loose on a thorny bush. But that was all. She never saw the blue-painted cannibals themselves. It was easy to slip between them, even on the wide open plain.

The land began to rise, a little at a time. After just a week Sister Two could look back out over the entire valley, see the rim of mountains on every side. It was like looking at the whole world. Somewhere in there, her sisters and her babies were tiny dots. One day she would find them again, she and her new child. She sang to her growing baby about the community as she strode across the plains. She sang about the red animals and the green lights. She promised her baby she would find the answers. She'd be like a granny, full of knowledge to keep the community fed and safe. She knew their grounds, where they hunted and camped, and when. She would find them.

At least here the red animals weren't frightening away her prey. Once she bagged a fox while it sniffed round a scarlet carcass. It was the same with each of the red animal corpses she found: they were little more than skin draped over bones.

Except for one. Its body was slumped across a rock, one of the worn and naked chunks of gray that thrust out of the rising ground. There were two spears in its hide.

She spent long minutes crouched behind a rock on the rise, peering down at it. There were no people down there, not even bodies of hunters killed by the red animal. It couldn't have been much of a fight. Probably they'd left it because its flesh was inedible. But why leave the spears?

She couldn't resist slipping down the hillside to take a closer look. Her boots crunched across frosty grass as she drew nearer to the pitiful carcass.

The Bluefaces came from nowhere. There was no hiding place—they seemed to rise up out of the earth, all around her. She spun on the spot, darting back and forth, but two of the men had spears and two of the women had clubs. If she ran, she'd wear one of those spears in her back.

She realised what she was seeing—they had hidden under blankets, covered with grass and twigs. If she had been looking properly she might have seen the suspicious lumps in the landscape. The Bluefaces must have watched her, followed her, and gone ahead to set up this trap.

Sister Two sank down in a crouch, next to the body of the red animal, showing her submission. There was no help for it now. She was bones and flesh now, and her baby too, both of them a rich meal.

A month went by and they still hadn't eaten her. Twelve of them lived in the shadow of the mountains. They had no nets. Every day Sister Two Scratch spent hours showing them how to catch rabbits and foxes with hers. She wanted to keep their bellies full.

They were skinny and bad-tempered, scowling at everything from behind their masks of blue paint. None of the women were pregnant. No one spoke to her, except the one-armed brute who bullied around the rest of the group, and his painfully thin grandmother. The granny followed Sister Two like a shadow, always close behind. Even they wouldn't answer her questions. They didn't care about what was happening to the world. All they cared about was getting enough to eat to stay alive.

One morning Sister Two sat down to do some much-needed repairs on her net. There were only two children in the group; they were left with her and the granny while the others went out to scrape the rocks for moss. And granny stayed behind too. Even her bony face was smeared with the blue paint. Tiny bird skulls hung from her clothes instead of beads.

How could these primitives survive? Sister Two didn't look at the infants while her fingers worked over the net. Such a small group, so few kids, such poor hunting grounds. She had never been so hungry in her life. If she couldn't get loose, she'd probably die with them when a bad winter came.

At least they hadn't made her eat anybody yet.

Granny Blueface curled a spidery hand on Sister Two's stomach. 'Long time since we snatched a mamma,' she said. 'Good, good.'

Sister Two pushed the old woman's fingers away, cupping her own hands over her belly. It wasn't strange for the different communities to steal one another's people, especially pregnant women. But surely the hungry Bluefaces wanted flesh to feed mouths, not more mouths to feed?

Sister Two stood up to stretch, gazing up towards the mountains. They loomed so close here, like the walls of an immense tent. She had been making a map of them in her memory.

She put her hand on Granny Blueface's shoulder and pointed up to the pass she'd marked out in her mind. 'That's where they came from, isn't it?' she said. Granny squinted up at the gap in the mountains. 'Through there. The red animals came through there.'

Granny Blueface slapped Sister Two's face. It was like being hit with a handful of twigs. Sister Two blinked at her. 'That's tabu for you!' snapped the old woman.

'You do know!' said Sister Two. She grabbed the granny's hand before she could land another blow. 'You have to tell me!'

'No more questions, cannibal girl!'

Sister Two grabbed the granny by the shoulders. 'I don't eat people! You do! You bluefaced baby-eater!'

Granny shrugged herself loose. 'We know. Know what happens when Bluefaces get too close to your people. So we tell you nothing. Nothing.'

'Right,' said another voice. It was One-arm, back from the hunt, looking grumpy as ever. His bald scalp was marked with a single handprint in thick blue paint. He gave Sister Two a casual shove, sending her sprawling tail-first onto the rocky ground. 'Only Bluefaces know. Only. Right?'

Sister Two nodded at him, rubbing her bruised behind. The bully was just like Mammoth Killer at his worst; he wouldn't hesitate to deliver a beating, or even to crack her skull if she made him too angry. It was too dangerous to talk back.

But she knew she had guessed right.

At night they all crammed into a single tent, literally sleeping on top of one another. Sister Two didn't mind the extra warmth after cold days spent trailing around with the women, chucking her net at bunnies or hacking roots out of the frigid soil.

She spent the whole night working her way to the edge of the tent. It meant a roll this way, a turn that way, nudging someone until they moved their arm, moving her leg when someone else grunted at her in annoyance. Little by little she shifted through the pile until she was by the edge of the tent.

Close to dawn she slid a hand under the skin wall of the tent and started, carefully to lift it up.

'Don't!' said granny, at the edge of the human heap. 'You're letting the cold air in.'

'Sorry,' said Sister Two. 'I've got to pee.'

Granny Blueface waved at the entrance. 'Go out,' she muttered.

Sister Two went out.

The sun was halfway up the sky before she saw them coming after her. She was clambering up towards the mountain pass. They must have known a shortcut, because even with her long head start, they were bounding over rocks to the side of her, spears out, shouting curses.

She kept heading upwards. The child in her womb was weighty enough that it slowed her, but she was used to running and climbing with a swollen belly. There was a ridge above; if she could reach it, she might be able to get a glimpse into the next valley.

She made it to the ridge. The shouts were close behind her, now, women's voices as well as men. She wasn't just escaping, she was breaking their tabu. They might well kill her for it. It was too late to worry about that now.

She ran along the ridge, crouching so she wouldn't make an inviting silhouette against the sky. There was nowhere to go—wait, there was a thicket ahead, narrow trees huddled close together. She dove into them, ducking and weaving. She would be safer from spears in here, but she must still be visible through the skinny trunks.

Someone hurled themself on top of her, slamming her into the ground with the full force of her run. She yelped as the breath was driven out of her body.

She tried to wriggle and wrestle her way out from under her assailant. It was one-arm, holding her down easily with his brute weight.

She got hold of a good round stone and held it until he started to get up. He yelped as she slammed the weapon into his arm, his ribs, his shoulder. 'Flesheater!' she shouted, as he fell on his knees. She scrambled away from his searching hand and bolted, half-panicked, through the trees.

Moments later, she ran straight into a net.

Sister Two Scratch screamed and rolled, feeling the rough fibers of her own net closing around her. She snatched for her knife, grabbing at the net and trying to saw at it, but a woman smacked her hands away with a club. She yowled and sucked her bruised fingers. They had her.

The women spent several minutes disentangling their captive, looking obscenely pleased with themselves. When she was finally loose, One-arm hauled her up by the waist of her dress, and slung her over his shoulder, easily, as if she'd been the carcass of a young doe. The other Bluefaces hovered nearby, waiting to see what he was going to do.

He headed up, up, towards a rock shelf that jutted out into the gap between the mountains. Sister Two started to struggle again. Was he going to hurl her from it?

One-arm dropped her onto the ground and nudged her with his foot. A moment later, he kicked her, and again. 'You want to see. See.'

Sister Two got up and started walking, up towards the rocky shelf.

The next valley began to come into view. From the first she could see that the light was all wrong. It looked hot over there, not the cool grays and greens of the plains, but hot like the sunset, the gold and pink clouds.

At first she thought she was seeing a forest. Then she thought she was seeing tents . . . big tents, orange-red tents, square tents. More of them than she could count. More tents than she had ever seen. They started somewhere close to the mountains, and filled the plain, filled it completely. The glare of orange and red hurt her eyes.

She squinted, taking in more details. Tall tents, round tents, all manner of shapes and sizes. There were no forests there, there could be no herd animals—except the red animals.

'No one lives there,' she breathed.

'Nobody,' agreed One-arm. 'Five, six moons.'

'Why didn't they come over the mountain?' gasped Sister Two. 'They could have driven us off our ranges. So easily. So many of them.'

The Blueface grunted. 'We leave land for you people to hunt,' he boasted, waving his remaining hand magnanimously. 'They leave room for us all to hunt. He pointed across the valley. 'Bluefaces hunt all round the rim, near the mountains. Yes?' She nodded numbly. It was the longest speech she'd heard him make. 'Red tents like these are over that mountain, and that mountain.' He pointed north, then south. 'And over the west mountain, we think. Everywhere but here.' He flattened his hand to indicate the valley the Bluefaces shared with Sister Two's community. 'Our place.'

Sister Two's head flooded with the image of a whole world filled with the red tents, every patch of soil covered except their valley. Their tiny world. Left for them by the kindly strangers who didn't want to see them vanish.

Her skull felt too heavy. She let it drop down to the earth. One-arm delivered another bruising kick to her leg, but she barely felt it. 'Now you see.'

After a while she realised they were carrying her away, down the mountain, but she didn't care.

When Sister Two came back to herself, it was night, and she

was curled up beside a low fire with five of the Bluefaces. Her hands and face were too hot. She mumbled and shifted, sitting up, hunched over.

The Blueface granny sat down with her, next to the fire. 'You've seen. You're one of us.' She thumped the soil with a wizened hand. 'Home,' she said firmly.

Sister Two just nodded. It didn't seem to matter any more.

'My granny told me,' said the old Blueface woman. 'She saw them come. She said, we follow the reindeer, those people follow the red animals.' Generations ago, thought Sister Two. They've been here all that time, and my people never even knew.

'Gone now,' the old one was saying. 'No more sky lights. Nobody there.' She gestured at the mountains. 'Just red animals looking for something to eat. They got left behind.' The granny reached into the pocket of her skirt, pulled something out, and put it in Sister Two's hand.

Sister Two held it up in the firelight. It was a piece of carving, a good one made of serpentine, the yellow-green stone polished smooth. 'You did this?' The granny nodded.

There were two figures, back to back, joined at the head, shoulders, and feet—Sister Two had seen this kind of design before. One of the figures was a woman, maybe the granny herself. The other . . . Sister Two held up it close to her face. The second figure had a head like a snake, a striped body like a wasp, small, misshapen arms. Were those horns on its head? Or feelers, maybe?

'That's what they looked like?' she breathed.

Granny nodded. She let Sister Two hold the carving until her hands dropped down, then took it from her palms and tucked it back in her pocket.

'Why did they go?' murmured Sister Two, staring into the flames. 'Where have they gone?'

Granny Blueface grunted. 'Home.' Her hand patted the earth again. 'Our home.'

Sister Two huddled closer to the fire. 'But what if they come back?' she said, and the old Blueface didn't have an answer.

Kate Orman lives in Sydney, Australia, with her husband and collaborator Jonathan Blum. Best known for her numerous 'Doctor Who' novels, Kate has also written a number of fantasy and SF short stories, and is currently working on a pair of original SF novels. Kate has a degree in biology, a graduate certificate in English literature, and recently completed a summer school course in the Akkadian language of ancient Babylon.

JAM JARS

ROBERT HOOD

WHAT THE HELL'S IN *THEM*?' Jordy Firth was pointing at the ornate jars lining the back shelf of Emmanuel's Street Emporium. He was of average height, podgy and, even from a distance, a bit too smelly for everyone's liking. Dressed in stained trackies, a frayed Megadeth t-shirt and sandals so soggy with sweat they'd gone fuzzy and made a squishing sound as he walked, he was no one's idea of an attractive human being.

'JAMs,' said scrawny old Emmanuel without moving his attention from the book he was reading.

'Jam?' Jordy frowned. 'Why the hell are you selling jam? Deal in electronics, don't ya?' As always, the stall was crowded with strange gadgets and cheap electronic gizmos that had been made some place OS by cheap labour and would break down as soon as Jordy got them home—assuming he'd condescend to buy one of them. He intended to, all right. Every weekend he window-shopped, flirting with the possibility that he just might buy something ... one day. But you couldn't be too careful, he reckoned. Had to study the market.

Emmanuel looked up. Even his eyes seemed wrinkled. 'Not jam,' he said. 'JAMs. New from ...' He waved vaguely. '... long way off. Very rare.'

'What sort of jam?'

'Not jam ... JAMs.'

Jordy couldn't fathom the difference, though he tried for a moment. Patience finally exhausted, he huffed derisively. 'Whatever,' he muttered. 'What's so special about this jam then?'

Emmanuel raised his eyebrows thoughtfully. 'Oh, the manufacturers reckon their JAMs'll change the way you look at things. Hell, they reckon their JAMs'll change the world.'

'Change the world?'

'They're *that* good.'

'Yeah, right.' Jordy squinted toward the closest of the

jam jars. If the knobbly glass contained jam, it was the most unappetising-looking jam he'd ever seen. Too dark and lumpy. Jam normally had fruit bits in it, but this looked like it had wires, nuts 'n' bolts, and rocks as well. 'Strawberry?' he suggested.

'Na.'

'Plum?'

'Na.'

'Some sorta marmalade?'

Emmanuel shook his head. 'Not fruit. You're not listening. Each one is an individual JAM. What its particular configuration is you'll have to find out by opening it.'

'You reckon?'

'Yep.'

Annoyingly intrigued despite himself, Jordy growled, 'What's one of 'em cost then?'

'Nothin'.'

'What?'

'JAMs don't cost nothin',' said Emmanuel, slumping back in his chair.

'You mean they're free?' Jordy was suddenly looking at the jars with a spark in his eye. 'That's stupid. I don't believe it. Can't be worth shit if they're givin' 'em away free.'

'Ten cents then! It's a promotional deal.'

'Ten cents? That's just as stupid.'

'You drive a hard bargain, mate. How about a dollar?'

'Done!' Jordy slammed a dollar coin onto the counter and held out his hand. 'I'll regret this, I reckon, but I wanna see what's so wonderful about this jam. Come on. Gimme!'

Emmanuel smiled secretively, as though everything had gone the way he'd expected. 'Which one?' he said, indicating the row of jars. 'Which one d'ya fancy, eh?'

Jordy studied them. They were all opaque, thick with a suggestion of hard lumpiness. One looked a little less inedible than the others. 'That one!' he said, pointing. Emmanuel drew a thick gardening glove over his skinny fingers and reached for the jar.

'What's with the glove?' said Jordy. 'The jar hot or somethin'?'

'Just delicate.' Emmanuel held it out. 'For maximum quality, only you should touch it.'

Jordy eyed it suspiciously. 'Is it dangerous? You settin' me up?'

'Settin' you up? Me?' Emmanuel's face crumpled in mock disappoint-ment. 'Hey, how long've you known me, eh?'

Jordy frowned. 'I dunno. Not long.'

'Yeah. Well, I've been here in these markets for the past three weeks. And have I ever ripped you off?'

Jordy shrugged. 'I haven't bought nothin' before.'

'See? Now you have. You're a customer. I value customers. Want 'em to come back. You've chewed my ear every weekend since I been here. Hour after flamin' hour. I call that commitment. I'm not gonna rip you, am I?' He manipulated the jar with his gloved hand, placing it in a clear plastic bag and then taping it up. He handed the package to Jordy. 'Take it. If you ain't satisfied, you can bring it back, even if it's opened. I'll give you twice what you paid for it.'

'Really?'

'Guaranteed.'

Jordy grabbed the bundle. It felt heavy and cold. He held it close up and peered through the translucent plastic. His hand pulled at the tape. 'Not here!' yelled Emmanuel. Jordy frowned, pausing mid-rip.

'What?'

'Don't unwrap it here!'

'Why?'

'Open it at home.' Emmanuel glanced up and down the street as though checking for spies. He tapped the side of his nose. 'For god's sake. Secret stuff, mate. Top secret.'

Jordy nodded. 'Oh, right.' He thought about it. 'I'll need bread anyway, won't I? Or a muffin maybe. To put it on.'

Emmanuel smiled grimly and went back to his book.

Jordy headed for home. Halfway there, dodging market-day crowds through the Mall, he got the feeling someone was following him—a shadow spied out of the corner of his eye. But, no, that was just dumb paranoia, he reckoned. He scanned the crowd for suspicious behaviour. Nothin'. With sudden cunning he ducked into a nearby comic kingdom and then peered out to see if anyone reacted. When no one did, he bought the latest issue of *Space Police* and read it as he shambled back onto the street. Who'd want to follow him anyway?

JAM Surveillance Report 45-8C: Agent Catre Dee in field. '10.49, local time. Contact made. Typical SAGO perp. Will follow. Risk that device will be activated pre neutralisation is estimated as 10.6% only. Worth the possibility of finding local nest? [PAUSE] Approval acknowledged. Out. Say hi to the kids, Gajspir.'

A message was waiting for Jordy on his answering machine. It was his friend Warren. <*A flamin' idiot, Jordy, that's what you are. 'Struth. Do you know how hard it was for me to get you that job?*> Damn, the boss had changed Jordy's shift at the local bookshop and Jordy had forgotten about it. Warren hadn't, of course. He was the size of a refrigerator but he fussed like a nervy chook whenever he did you any sort of favour. Yet he meant well and Jordy hated disappointing him. <*I covered up for ya—just get down to the store by 11. Okay?*>

Eleven? The Book Dump was half an hour away at least. Jordy glanced at his watch. 11.16. Shit! But his Darth Vader wall clock indicated it was 9.57. Jordy liked that better. Still early. Plenty of time. He unfastened his wristwatch and tossed it behind the sofa.

Now he had time to try out the jam. Not that he expected much. A dollar? Still, how bad could it be?

He found two slices of bread on the bench—mouldy, but he cut off the worst bits and stuck what was left in the toaster. Heat'd kill any germs, he figured. While he waited, he tore off the plastic Emmanuel had wrapped around the jam jar. The glass it was made of was covered in some sort of writing, though Jordy couldn't recognise the language. The writing was engraved all over the glass surface and looked a bit like mathematical formulae. There was no label. The jam itself appeared dull and unappetising. Funny business, Jordy thought. Revolutionary jam they couldn't even bother to make look appealing. Well, he'd soon find out how special it was. He reached to twist off the lid then stopped, puzzled.

There was no lid. The jar appeared to be solid.

'What the hell!' he muttered.

He grabbed one end and twisted, just in case it was simply a tight fit. Nothing moved.

The toast popped up with a CLUNK.

'Put down the JAM!' yelled someone behind him.

Jordy staggered around with a grunt of surprise, his heart thudding. His fingers clung onto the jam jar, holding it to his chest.

'I said, put down the JAM!'

It was a woman. She was wearing a dark knee-length coat. Black hair foamed around her oval face. She was holding what looked like one of those toy space guns you could buy in any el cheapo import store.

'Who are you?' Jordy said. 'What're you doin' in my flat?'

She snarled. 'Put down the JAM, SAGO boy! Now!'

Jordy could barely see her face under the mass of her hair, but what he could see was pretty cute. He lowered his eyes, checking out the rest of her. Hard to tell, but the coat had fallen open slightly and the shadows through the gap suggested a halfway decent bod. Her legs were covered by baggy trousers and she wore army boots.

'Um ... ummm ...' Jordy mumbled, distracted and unnerved.

'Put the JAM down!'

Jordy looked at the object in his hands. Why was she so spooked by it?

'It's just—' he began.

'I know what it is, freako.' She stood in combat stance, her toy ray-gun covering him. 'Put it down or I'll blow your ugly head way back to Mordalcor.'

'Look, I dunno what you think—'

At that moment, the jam jar heaved. Its surface pushed outwards. Jordy shrieked and opened his hands to let it fall.

'No!' the woman cried. Her voice—in tone and volume—was suddenly urgent, even scared. Chill shot through Jordy's nerves.

He spread his hands.

The jam jar was attached to them. It hadn't fallen. Long fibres had squirmed out of it, burying themselves in his flesh. The strands were so fine he could barely feel any pain. It was as though he'd been touched by a spray of ice water, that's all.

The woman fired her gun. Jordy glanced up as some sort of beam shot toward him, like a wrinkle in the air. He could feel its heat as it approached. But before it hit him, a metallic armature erupted from the jam jar, straight into the path of the beam. Deflected, the line of disturbance ploughed into the ceiling, scorching it, ripping the plaster apart.

With a curse, the woman leapt aside.

Something barely tangible crushed outward in a line from the jam jar, tearing up the carpet so that dust flew high. The edge of the line struck her a glancing blow. She groaned and crashed out of sight into the corridor.

By this time Jordy had had a chance to decide he wanted nothing, absolutely nothing, to do with this jam jar any more. Hell, he doubted very much the object contained jam at all—and as far as he was concerned that was a violation of his rights as a consumer. He'd been conned. Wait till he saw Emmanuel again! He tried to toss the thing away. But by now the threads coming from it had thickened, eating their way right into him, and it had no intention of letting itself be tossed anywhere. Jordy whimpered, tripping backwards as though trying to jump away from it. The surface of the glass oozed, bulged, shooting out articulated arms and pincers that grabbed Jordy's tumbling body and dragged it upright again. Some of them—like long, jointed needles—burrowed themselves into his arms, legs, belly. Jordy still couldn't feel any pain though, despite appearances. What he could feel was the movement of the metallic appendages as they wrapped themselves around his bones, joined with his muscles, filled him with their cold growth ...

He screamed, trying to thrash his way out of its grip.

His feet weren't even grounded now. The jar had produced metres of chaotic mechanical tangle that was growing as he squirmed—a greater mass than could ever have existed in the small jar it had emerged from. It lifted him into the air as it surged around and into him. Soon it would consume him completely. What would happen to him then?

Just when he thought he would inevitably find out, he saw something hopeful out of the corner of his eye. The woman—the one that had barged in on him—had bought it, or so Jordy'd believed, but there she was, sticking her head around the corner, checking out the state of play. Jordy groaned, his lips refusing to produce the words his mind had sent their way. He couldn't get them to work. But she knew he needed help, surely. She stepped into full view, raised her ray-gun ... and then paused. Jordy saw her frown, as though considering. After a second, she reached to a panel on the side of the weapon and tapped at the buttons there.

She took aim again.

Jordy felt the cables that were woven through him become aware of the imminent attack. How they could possibly do that he had no idea. Were they alive? His body twisted, painfully, forced to follow the motion of the metallic framework. The woman fired and he yelped.

The world flared into white-out. Heat shot through the strands and filaments and cables, burning his flesh, searing his innards.

He blanked out.

Yet nothing is blank, not even a mind flash-burned into obscurity. Jordy's contained images of a childhood spent mainly indoors, in front of the telly or hiding in the cupboard when his drunken father came home. Images of school, too. Jordy had done badly there—he hadn't been able to work up any sort of interest in his classes, finding his attention veering off to outside interests, especially the Roleplayers Club, where at least his imagination had a chance of overcoming the limitations of his podgy flesh. Images of days and nights spent eating chips and stale pizza. Hanging with the guy he'd for years considered his best friend—Jack Agar. High laugh and dark, sardonic eyes. Jack always became a Thief, and in most campaigns they played together, betrayed Jordy to the Dark Lords or the Satanic Sorcerers with aggravating consistency. Later Jack talked Jordy into helping him rob a store for real. Naturally it was Jordy who got caught, thanks to Jack's subtle deflection of responsibility at a crucial moment. Jordy was convicted and, though he got off with a warning and a fine, the record stood. How often had that record cruelled his chances of getting a decent job? Jack's last words to him were 'You're a loser, Jordy. I got more important things to do than to hang with losers.'

Jordy woke up.

'Ah, you made it back.' The voice was female, but hard. Was it coming from the telly?

Jordy lay on his sofa, feeling like a beached whale. Must have dozed off and had a nightmare. But if that were the case, who was this woman towering over him, peering down with a sneer?

'Who are you?' he asked.

'My name's Catre Dee. I'm a Federal agent,' she replied.

Jordy tried to sit up, but his body didn't want to bend yet. He felt prickly all over, as though some sort of anaesthetic was only now starting to wear off.

'Federal agent?'

'Anti-JAM squad.'

It all came rushing back. The jam jar! 'What's with that friggin' jam?' Jordy managed. 'It went berserk.'

'It was unzipping itself. Seeking a bio-host.'

'Wasn't really jam, was it?'

She shrugged. 'It was a JAM, yes. But I think you have no idea what that means. At first I considered you to be part of a centralised nest of symbios. But I quickly realised something was wrong. You didn't seem to know what you had.' She manipulated her shoulder, making the bones crack. Then she stretched. Jordy realised that she'd removed her coat, but the loose shirt she wore didn't offer any extra insight into the nature of the underlying landscape. 'That's what saved you,' she continued. 'Otherwise I would have fried you both.'

'But what's a jam,' Jordy asked, 'if it's not jam?'

She scowled. 'Jettisoned Amorphic Mechanism. Very nasty.'

Jordy scowled back at her. 'Jettisoned ... what?'

'Amorphic Mechanism.' She sighed. 'A semi-sentient programmable metal alloy created as a by-product of certain quantum drive functions. Not all drives, of course. But recalcitrant planetary blocs have repeatedly refused to upgrade their technologies because, they say, the costs involved are prohibitive. Anyway, their ships tend to jettison JAM waste when it becomes too difficult to control, and pirates trail them to collect it. Sometimes the governments involved sell the junk themselves. There's an extensive blackmarket network of Ferro Sculptors that deal in JAM programming and one of their arms has recently reached into your System. I'm here to track them down before the contagion spreads.'

Jordy screwed up his face in disbelief.

'Yes,' the woman said, 'I'm an extraterrestial.'

He rolled his eyes. 'Look human enough to me.'

'Our species are genetically related through subspace osmosis.' She paused. 'Have you heard of Particular Cross-Spatial Twining?'

'No.'

'Well, that's what does it. It's not common, but makes the genetic coincidence more plausible than it seems.'

Jordy decided to let that one go. He could dredge up other objections. 'You speak English, too. What's the chance of the same language developing both here and ... wherever you come from, even if we have similar genes?'

'Infinitesimal,' she admitted. 'But I've been on your planet for ten years. I can speak 31 native languages.'

'You said the JAM-smugglin' dudes only came here recently.'

'They did. About ten years ago. That's pretty recent. After all, I'm over 300 Earth years old. What's ten years?'

Yeah, thought Jordy, right. 'Really? Ya look pretty good for an old lady.'

'Thanks. It's the nano-bacteria.'

By this time, Jordy was pretty sure he'd undergone a fugue blackout of some kind. He'd wandered around and had ended up being sucked into playing a Space Adventure game with friends of his Book Dump buddies. This Catre Dee chick—whoever the hell she was—was pretty good at it, too. She'd responded to his questions in character and had managed to construct some reasonably believable technobabble in the process. Very cool.

'So what d'ya reckon this JAM crap was tryin' to do to me?' he asked.

'JAMs can be programmed to achieve certain configurations— exploration, combat, decoration—when they meld with a body donor, usually what we call a SAGO—Symbiotic Alienated Gangelionic Organism—'

'What's with all the acronyms, eh?' Jordy scoffed. 'Same everywhere, you public servant-types!'

She ignored his comment. 'The JAM wants to become a coherent entity through joining. SAGOs have more complex motives, in case that was your next question.'

Jordy scratched at something prickly on his forehead. 'Such as?'

'Self-extension, virtual suicide, an inability to resist the JAM's psychic seduction—'

'What?'

'Never mind. Look, time's short in regards to the local supplier. I need to know how you came by the JAM ... now!'

Jordy tried to sit up. Took a bit of effort, but he made it this time, and only then noticed the tangle of fused metal in the middle of the lounge-room floor. Supposed to be what was left of his JAM, no doubt. Cute.

As though reading his mind, Catre Dee said, 'Some of it's still viable, but its programming was aborted in time and now it's dormant and more-or-less under control—'

Jordy glanced at his arms, belly and legs—flesh visible through tears in his clothes. Jagged metallic ends stuck out here and there among the sores and scratches and bruised lumps.

'Most of the JAM came out of you when I scorched it. You're stuck with the rest. You'll heal up soon enough, though, even your eye.' Jordy blinked his left eye. It felt gritty. Vision through it was blurred and distorted. 'I injected you with a slew of bio-repair nano-bacteria.'

Jordy poked at a lump of JAM half-buried in his belly. 'I don't believe this!' Panic quivered in his voice.

'Don't you?' Catre Dee stepped closer. 'What do you think all those bits and pieces sticking out of you are? Once the JAM bonds with you, which it partially had, total separation would've meant death.' She glanced at a device strapped to her arm. A monitor or timekeeper, maybe. The urgency in her voice increased. 'It'll retreat from your epidermal regions eventually. The internal constructs are fused to your muscles and organs. You'll be able to control it, with practice—maybe even modify it.' She'd moved still closer during this harangue. 'So where'd you get the JAM?' she snarled suddenly, irresistibly impatient, as she grabbed his shoulder.

Jordy's body reacted a fraction of a second before his brain could consciously issue instructions. His hand—his ordinary flesh-and-bone one—shot out to knock her arm away. At the same time something hard, grey and finely articulated sprouted from the base of his neck, slashing up at her as its tip area bunched and flattened to form a blade. Catre Dee's trained reflexes gave her barely a millimetre's grace. At least it saved her. The JAM-blade sliced through her cheek, out and into her hair. Black tufts and blood splatters danced around her.

'Watch out!' Catre Dee cursed, wiping at her cheek. 'You could kill someone with that! Control it, for shit's sake.'

'Sorry.' Jordy stared aghast at the whipping metal tentacle. His haunted eyes turned to the woman. 'Am I on drugs?'

'Naturally.' Catre Dee kept her distance now, back to the wall. 'The JAM injects an anaesthetic. Otherwise the pain of fusion would cripple you. Should last long enough for the nano-units to build up some bio-interfaces and form clean-exit channels for—'

'That's not what I mean!' Jordy yelled. The JAM-blade quivered with attack eagerness and other bits of the JAM within him pushed toward his skin surface. He felt as though the insides of his body were squirming. 'Am I tripping? LSD or some shit? How are ya doin' this to me?'

'I'm not *doing* anything.' Catre Dee's tone was so contemptuous it cut right through the last threads of Jordy's fantasy. Any hope of relative normalcy he'd had fell away.

'This is real, ain't it?' he whimpered. 'You're not a gamer at all. You're a friggin' alien!'

'As I said. So? You catch on slowly.'

Jordy sank onto the sofa, burrowing into its spongy cushions. The extended armature disappeared into him and he frowned and prodded at the spot. The skin there was already healing. 'Impossible,' he muttered. 'Friggin' impossible.'

Catre Dee sat on the arm of a tattered one-seater across from him. 'I don't want to rush your pathet—' She reined herself in, groping about for some long-disused diplomacy. '—Perfectly understandable attempts to adjust to all this. But I really need to know where you got the JAM. It's vital I—'

'Street huckster!' Jordy snapped. 'Emmanuel's Emporium or somethin', it's called. Down the city markets. Had lots of the things. I wasted a whole dollar on it.'

'What are you saying?' Catre Dee nearly leapt for his throat, but pulled herself back when his flesh twitched. 'He *gave* it to you?'

'Sold it! For a dollar.'

She snorted. Simultaneously her scorn mutated into anxiety. 'Programmed JAMs sell for thousands of dollars in your local currency. Tens of thousands, depending on the complexity of the embedded configurations. A dollar's nothing!' She began pacing. 'What are they up to? I don't like this at all.'

'Don't like what?'

'Don't you see? This isn't just a random market-supply phenomenon. This could be a planned infiltration.' She clenched her fists. 'An invasion. Various sociological commentators have warned of this possibility. Planetary conversion, they call it. If I hadn't interrupted your JAM, you might've become a soldier of whatever cadre's behind this.' She came at him. He pulled back, but held his suddenly activated JAM appendages steady. 'The vendor had lots of them, you say? How many?'

'Dunno. Maybe a dozen.'

'Good. That's good. Maybe they're just performing a trial. Thank God we found out about it in time.'

'Makin' some big assumptions, aren't ya?'

'Come on!' Forgetting the danger of it, she grabbed his arm and jerked him toward the door. 'Take me to this Emporium. We'll do some nipping in the bud.'

Jordy let himself be dragged. Frankly, he was too numb to fight back. He rose to his feet, JAM implants grinding and stretching.

And the doorbell rang.

Catre Dee dived for her coat, fumbling through its folds to extract her ray-gun.

'Jeez. Calm down!' Jordy growled. He staggered toward the door. 'Who is it? What d'ya want?' he shouted.

'It's me ... Warren!' came a deep, slightly indignant voice. 'What the hell are you still here for, Jordy? You're s'posed to be at the damn shop. You know what time it is?'

Jordy swore under his breath. 'Friend of mine,' he whispered back at Catre Dee. 'What'll I do?'

She ground her teeth. 'Talk to him. Get rid of him.'

'But I look like shit! He'll be suspicious.'

'Tell him you're sick. Contagious. Say you can't open up.'

Not a bad idea. 'Hey, man,' he shouted through the door.

'Jordy? You got someone in there with ya?'

'No! I'm real sick. Came down with somethin' bad. Doc reckons it's catchin'. So I can't let you in.'

'Sick? What sorta sick?'

'Plague or somethin'. I dunno. I'll give you a call, okay?'

In the silence that followed, Jordy leaned toward the door, listening for his friend's departure. Or maybe for a verbal response. But there was nothing. He frowned. 'Warren?' he shouted. Still no reply. Then the wood ruptured around him, flinging him back. Catre Dee yelled as the door disintegrated. Jordy tried to get his balance, to see what had happened.

'Your friend's been JAMmed!' Catre Dee cried.

If the thing smashing its way into his flat had anything to do with Warren, it was only as a distant relation. True, there were signs of Warren among the tangle. Bits of recognisable flesh, bulging eyes embedded at the end of telescopic tubes, certain contours that were familiar. The rest of it was no friend of Jordy's. Metallic planes and angles, jagged protuberances, blocks of material fitted into each other with precision: this was no failed hodge-podge the way Jordy's JAM had been. This one was neat and functional. It seemed to make sense in a military sort of fashion, though the exact nature of that sense was beyond Jordy's ability to decipher.

'Out of the way!' shrieked Catre Dee from behind him.

Jordy stumbled sideways as she fired. Heat from the blast scalded his arm. But her aim was off. The Warren-JAM lunged through the peripheral haze emanating from the heat-ray, extending a long spear of JAM matter. The spear thudded into Catre Dee's abdomen, pinning her to the wall. She screamed and fell silent. When it withdrew, her body collapsed in an insensible heap.

Jordy lashed out at the Warren-JAM with a metallic bludgeon he grew from his side. The monstrosity grabbed it easily and pulled. Jordy felt his whole skeleton wrenched forward. He could sense the pain of it despite the anaesthetic numbness that still infused his body. The Warren-JAM slammed him to the floor and loomed over him.

'Don't fight me, sibling,' the Warren-JAM spoke through what was left of Warren's lips. 'Your growth has been stunted by this agent of the tyrannic Galactic Governors—' A tentacle gestured at the motionless Catre Dee. 'But she can't hurt you any more. The amorphic-matter inside you can still be released. At the moment it's been blocked, frozen in sub-molecular coding, but it'll come out if you let it. Why be a pathetic freak when you can join me against the pitiful uni-flesh creatures of this planet, and make their world your own?'

A good question, and a fair one.

'Who are you?' Jordy asked. 'Not Warren. Warren didn't talk like this.'

'He didn't speak truth?'

'He spoke crap, often and a lot. Just like you. But harmless crap. Not fascist bullshit.'

As he spoke that final word, Jordy let the JAM matter inside him thrash outward. Articulated limbs unfolded from every side, tearing through his flesh and skin. Some of them were clawed and spiked like weapons. He struck at the Warren-JAM with a war-cry that caused the ceiling to flake.

The Warren-JAM was knocked backwards. But it didn't stagger far. It re-established its centre of gravity a metre or two further away—whereupon it hit out at him with an arm so fast-moving it was barely visible. The force of the blow crushed several of Jordy's JAM-limbs, sprayed past and ripped a huge hole in the outer wall, exposing the room to a few startled people in the residents' car park. Jordy crashed to the floor again, a tangle of uncoordinated appendages. He tried to straighten up, but tripped over himself. This was harder than he'd thought.

'Loser!' the Warren-JAM called. The sound echoed, split apart, turned to a low, bone-grinding rumble.

It was, perhaps, too much. Everything had always been too much for Jordy. He began to withdraw. His dangling JAM limbs pulled back, grinding into his body, reconstituting themselves as out-of-phase sub-molecular potentialities. It didn't matter to them. Unlike the JAM in Warren, and unlike Jordy himself, the JAM in Jordy had been aborted in the moments before true sentience, so now it was content to simply wait, painlessly, for the order to re-emerge. Jordy, on the other hand, would agonise and fret and rationalise as he waited for a potential he knew would never come.

As Jordy curled into himself, the Warren-JAM lashed out again, gouging a hole in Jordy's shoulder. Another limb struck him a powerful blow so that he crashed against the wall. The Warren-JAM reared back, then leapt at him. Jordy held up one pathetic limb in defence—something he grew from his chest but suspected would be ineffectual—and to his surprise caught the

Warren-JAM off-guard. Jordy's limb stabbed into the Warren-JAM's gut, crunching through a network of artificial arteries. The Warren-JAM howled, stumbled from its intended trajectory and crashed away to the side. Jordy felt a crack. The tip of the limb he'd used to defend himself had broken off. It remained in the Warren-JAM's gut. The Warren-JAM rose again, sounding more annoyed than ever. Now it had a shrapnel wound that would plague it in its old age as JAM arthritis set in ...

'I will absorb your JAM-fragment,' it hissed, 'have no fear of that. And then I'll consume you as well. You may not join the struggle of your free will, but join it you must, one way or the other.'

Calmly, Jordy waited for the final attack.

No, not calmly. That was illusion. Inside, he was seething with emotion: fear, anger, sorrow among the foremost. This alien thing had killed his friend Warren. And Catre Dee, who wasn't his friend, but might've been. It was part of an invasion force. JAM had turned him into an even bigger freak than he had been before. He hated it for that, just as, somewhere deep down inside his human guts, he hated the world for making him the freak he'd been all his life. All that burning emotion, nurtured over many years, gave him the careless exuberance he needed to ... to ... to what?

Fight back?

No, he thought, I've given up.

But beneath his fear and resignation he felt something, something distant yet familiar. It spread, moving like a eager cancer. As it did so, it sent out tiny telepathic waves that resonated inside Jordy. He recognised it. His JAM matter, separated from him but still his. It was inside the Warren-JAM. Spreading through his enemy's veins.

And Jordy could speak to it. Control it. Make it grow. He could tell it to reach out, to dominate and exploit the quantum ocean in which it swam. To defile the Warren-JAM with its own Jordyesque structures. To take it apart from the inside.

'Do it!' he snarled.

And it did.

The Warren-JAM ran. Leaving a trail of disintegrating molecules, it crashed through the door, stumbled downstairs, wove across the car park screeching, staggered down street after street. In its death-throes it was heading for the markets. Seeking help from its Supplier.

Emmanuel.

Jordy grabbed up Catre-Dee's discarded ray-gun and followed eagerly. Though still under his conscious control, the JAM in him was raging with barely restrained glee, sniffing out the game. Wanting action.

Pedestrians reared back in terror at the sight of him. They ran. They hid. Jordy wasn't worried. He didn't have time for concerns over secrecy. Cars honked, swerved, lost control. A green sedan mounted the pavement near him and ploughed into a glass shopfront.

As he entered Market Square, the bustling crowds were already retreating. Through the parting wake of the Warren-JAM's flight, Jordy caught a glimpse of the Warren-JAM itself, now more like a torn, bloody corpse than a fighting mechanism. The destruction of Warren's JAM hadn't saved him. Warren was long dead. Only a few ragged networks of JAM matter in his body's muscles and bones kept the pathetic remnant on its feet.

But not for long.

Jordy had caught up enough to see Emmanuel's face as the Supplier noticed first Warren's tattered corpse and then JAM-enhanced Jordy, both bearing down on him.

Shock. Fear. Panic crashed over him.

He pushed himself up from his chair, letting the book he was reading fall to the ground. He stumbled against the crowded table. Tripped on scattered packaging. Recovered. Made to retreat into the curtained-off rear of his stall.

Jordy fired.

His first shot shattered the skeletal remains of Warren, exploding them into powder.

His second shot scorched the flesh off Emmanuel's metal framework, from the waist up.

Emmanuel had been JAMmed, too.

Now he was fucked.

The market crowds kept well away as Jordy, torn and bleeding, knocked aside the piles of electronic crap cluttering the display front of Emmanuel's Emporium and pushed through to check on Emmanuel himself.

The Supplier was still burning, his JAM endoskeleton sizzling with absorbed energy. Jordy aimed point-blank at the remains and fired until they turned to ash.

He checked the shelf above. Only a couple of JAM jars were gone from the row—his own and, presumably, Warren's. Thank god. He'd caught the invasion in time. Catre Dee might have died, but at least Jordy had been able to complete her mission. He felt justified, perhaps for the first time in his life.

Police sirens blared in the distance, approaching fast.

Hurriedly, Jordy scorched the remaining JAM jars into molten blobs. That should end the threat forever.

A murmuring rose from behind him. Jordy glanced back. The crowds, no longer intimidated by the sight of monstrous rampaging bio-mechanisms, had edged forward. The path through had closed up.

Jordy didn't want to be identified. He was full of JAM and had a duty now. How long would it be before Catre Dee's superiors realised that she'd been iced and sent a replacement? Maybe they'd *never* send a replacement. Who knew what politics played into the organisation she'd worked for? She'd called herself a Federal agent, but Jordy was pretty sure she'd been talking about some intergalactic agency, not the local-space national one. So their workings would remain a mystery and Earth might be left to suffer under some future JAM infestation.

It was up to Jordy now. He'd been given a purpose. This was no game but he knew he could be a player. After all, how hard would it be? The likelihood of combat might be minimal. No more JAM jars had been sold or given away. Maybe the pirates would consider the trial a failure and head off somewhere else.

'Hey, you!' someone called. 'What's goin' on?'

Jordy didn't answer. Wanting to disappear, he ducked through the curtain at the rear of Emmanuel's Emporium. The stall had been constructed on a footpath, pushed up against concrete barriers. There couldn't be much space there, but there might be a gap, a hidden way out.

In the sudden gloom Jordy stopped, disoriented.

The space was huge, more like a warehouse than a gap. How could such an expanse exist in the small area available? The whole impossible space was packed with row upon row of crates—dozens of them, most with their lids ripped off. On the side of each, in rough stencilled lettering, were the words: JAM UNITS, 24 PER BOX.

Aghast, Jordy rushed over and looked into one. Then another. Then another. His JAM trembled, deep inside his flesh. He felt sick.

Every single crate was empty.

Robert Hood has been writing stories within the SF/horror genres for several decades. Among his books are the short-story collections *Day-dreaming on Company Time* (FIP, 1988) and *Immaterial: Ghost Stories* (MirrorDanse Books, 2002), as well as novels such as *Backstreets* (Hodder Headline, 2000) and the *Shades* series (Hodder Headline, 2001). In 2005, he co-edited *Daikaiju! Giant Monster Tales* with Robin Pen (Agog! Press), which is a unique collection of stories from around the world inspired by the Japanese tradition of giant monster films. His website can be found at www.roberthood.net.

BONE DOG

KAARON WARREN

IN THE PORN INDUSTRY, models don't usually get to choose the venue for photo shoots. I guess 'Fat Slits' has to be a bit more flexible than other magazines; some of us just can't get too far from home. They agreed to send the photographer to me, agreed to my price; their attention brought tears to my eyes.

When I heard the photographer's van at the end of my long driveway, I walked slowly to the vast tree stump where I sometimes display the gifts Bone-Dog brings me. I had the tree cut down and turned into doors—very solid doors that will never slam shut and lock me inside the house.

I like my doors open.

I could see the photographer's lips twitching as he walked towards me. Controlling his laughter. Bone-Dog growled deep in her throat. I motioned her away.

'I'm Melody,' I said as I gave him a beer and he drank it in one. He was not a talker. He wiped his mouth with his shirt; I could see silvery snail trails on the sleeve. This was a man who did not bother with handkerchiefs. He was bony, too. I hate bony, skeleton showing through.

'Where do you want me?' I said, winking. He squinted, as if he wasn't sure what he'd seen. I couldn't be flirting with him. Not possible.

'Just there'll be fine,' he said.

I waited until he was set up, then let my robe fall.

He didn't actually shiver; he was protected by the camera lens.

He lifted his head, though, as I began to arrange my bones. I know so much about bones I can hear my own glide and click as I move. Naming them is easy. All you need is a good memory. My memory is very good.

He lifted his head and stared.

'Oh, yeah,' he said. It's nice when their voices sound like that. I leaned against the stump. It creaked a little.

His breathing reached me. He wasn't looking in the lens, but he was clicking, shooting me.

I arranged my bones this way and that for him. My fans would love these ones.

I like to get fan letters. It keeps the postie coming, every day, and if I don't collect my mail from the box he'll tell someone. That keeps me safe from being locked inside the house with my Bone-Dog. Even though I've taken precautions, I don't want to be locked in.

'Your film's run out,' I said. He stepped from behind the camera and towards me. He reached for me. Touched me, stroked my forearm, the childhood scar there shiny and puckered. Blood and fat and bone and I screamed when it happened.

'Ha ha, scared of blood,' kids said.

I had to tell them the truth. I said, 'No, I'm scared of bone.'

I wanted more photos afterwards, but he was ashamed and out of film. He stumbled about packing up; he almost stepped on Bone-Dog.

'Sorry little fella,' he said, glad of the distraction.

'She. Baby.'

'Baby the dog?' he said. I shrugged. I liked him for seeing her. He couldn't have known how kind that was. Not many people admitted to seeing her. Hearing her rattling. It's not in my head. That little dog found me, sniffed at my ankles and followed me home. At my feet, snap snap, bones jumping like a little dog.

It would be a good set of photos. He had seen Bone-Dog; he understood me.

He bent to pat her but she trotted over and squatted at my heels.

'Pretty, isn't she?' I said. 'Prettier than me?'

He nodded. Shook his head.

'Another beer?' I said. I wanted him to stay. I wanted to suck his fingers, lick his ribs.

He shook his head. 'Gotta develop these.' He lifted the camera. I saw his elbow flinch. He wanted to snap Bone-Dog.

'You're out of film,' I said.

Bone-Dog was on her haunches, ready to bite. Snap snap go her teeth. I can hear it even if she's not with me. Snap snap of a little sister wanting her bones back.

He leaned down to pat her.

'I wouldn't. She doesn't like strangers.'

He ignored me. Leaned closer. Stepped back when he saw, it became clear, that she was a Bone-Dog.

He sucked breath. She leapt at him, bit his little pointing finger off and spat it out, sucked clean of flesh.

The wound didn't bleed. I could smell burnt flesh. He stared at his cauterised hand. He walked backwards to his truck, 'You should control that thing,' his jaw snapping. Then he left me with her.

There was plenty of food but I didn't feel like eating. Sometimes, after I have my photo taken, I don't feel like eating. I want to stop being a fat woman. Bone-Dog lay at my feet, all bone, skeleton, and I went to the kitchen and made an eight-egg omelette and ate it standing there.

We've lived here many years, the perfect place for us. Paid for with porn. Bone-Dog doesn't approve of my work, but she is happy to sleep in the house I paid for, sleep in my bed, refuse my shameful food. She found the place herself, bringing me the paper and staying so quiet as the real estate man showed us around I almost forgot she was there. It was a quick, eager sale; most people were put off by the old graveyard, partly uncovered, so close by. Not Bone-Dog; she loved the sense of all those bones, so close. I allowed myself the fantasy that our mother was buried there, and in the early days would visit with offerings of food, laying it at the graveyard's collapsed brick entrance. I haven't been back for a long time, but I remember the mess of it, the jumbled, forgotten nature of it.

I slept until the moon and Bone-Dog woke me. Looking out my bedroom window I could see the bones in the yard, how well I've lined them up. They shone silver in the moonlight. If I stared long enough my eyeballs quivered and the bones jerked and danced.

Those bones, so carefully laid out. 'Thank you, Melody, for being so careful with our bones,' their thin voices said. Whistling like the wind so Bone-Dog howled at the noise. 'Melody, Melody,' their voices tuneless. Melody and Baby. My little sister was Baby because Mum hadn't thought of a proper name yet.

I called her all the names I could think of but she didn't blink. Dolores. Jemima. Janina. Godliness.

Bone-Dog leapt at my feet. I reached down to pet her and she snapped her jaw together. She hadn't forgiven me for letting her die. She thought I let her starve to death. She thought I let her bones be jumbled up, and that I should have escaped earlier.

Bone-Dog thought I liked being locked in that childhood house, but the smell of it has never left me.

I have a very sensitive sense of smell. A hint of rot and I have to leave the room, waste the food. Mould on bread, rotten meat and vegetables, sourness of milk. Fresh food is all I can abide. The smell of rot is a warning. Do not eat this. Do not be near this.

Bones left in the sun for long enough will lose their smell of rot.

My mother left when I was five. Went out for a run to get back in shape. Gotta get back in shape. I was old enough to stay by myself. She deadlocked the door so we would be safe and she ran away, her smooth long legs tan against her shorts, her shoulders muscular but slim, the keys hooked to her waistband.

'Back soon. Gotta get back in shape,' she said. I'm still not sure it was an accident. Perhaps she left us there because she wanted me to be thin when she got back. She ran away, a long run, because she had not been running since Baby was born

It was a hit and run driver. I hit and ran at school, once I got my weight back. I could hit hard and run fast for my size. I still can. I can run and surprise people so their jaws drop.

It's not good for my ankles, though. The driver hit and ran and moved her body to a river or a lake.

They didn't know who she was and no one claimed her. I knew who she was; I saw her once on television and told my little sister. She stared at me. She didn't blink. She didn't move after the first three days, just lay there. She was one month old.

There was food in the fridge. I liked to eat. There was some cake and chicken and cheese. There was beetroot, pickles, potatoes and one carrot. There was plenty of food. There was chips and chocolate and lemonade.

I gave the carrot to my sister but she wouldn't eat it. I didn't want to eat, either, once the things started to rot. I put off opening the fridge because of the terrible smell, but the house smelled bad, too.

I didn't eat very much. I chose from the fridge the least rotted thing and ate that. I gave a little to my sister every day, an offering to her to make some noise.

It was quiet in the house. I could reach the kitchen sink with a chair. I couldn't use the can opener.

Watching my sister was like watching a TV show. A slow one. She slowly changed. The smell of rot was terrible. I never got used to it. I watched her every day, watched her change.

I was only five.

I cried a lot, but no one heard. My Dad was gone away and my little sister was a mistake with a stranger. I had no aunties or uncles or grandparents.

I cried a lot.

Our phone wasn't connected, Mum said we didn't have the money for it. I have one in every room. I have a huge freezer, well-stocked. My cupboards are full of tins, and in each cupboard I have a can opener and a fork. In case my legs break under my weight, I can crawl around and eat until someone saves me.

Mum said, 'Don't leave the house. You stay here till I get back.'

But I knew I had to be naughty the day I opened the fridge and all that was left was a piece of green sausage. Very hard and I couldn't chew it. I knew I had to be very naughty and find a way to leave the house.

I tried doors again. Then the windows. The only one we had without locks was the one in the toilet. Mum didn't want any men coming into the house or ringing up.

I couldn't reach the window. Even standing on the toilet, and the cistern was slippery.

So I covered the cistern with the mat from the bath by standing on the toilet seat. Then I put Mum's tool box on the seat so I could climb onto the cistern.

The window opened when I pushed it. People asked me that. 'How long did it take to open the window?' I learned to lie, to say it took days. I learned to say I had tried to get out from the moment Mum went away.

I walked along the road in the direction I'd seen Mummy run. It took me so long I was sure I'd see Mummy running back, and she'd pick me up and carry me home. She'd have icecream and apple pie and a piece of bacon to eat on the way home.

I love a fresh-killed pig.

I walked. My sister was in my knapsack and I could smell her, but it wasn't so bad outside. There were other smells.

I walked until I came to a house but it was a stranger's house. I couldn't go there. I didn't know, but I put the knapsack on upside down, and my sister's bones with her flesh still on them dropped out along the road. They could never find them all.

So I sat on the wall and had a rest. I told my sister we would have some dinner soon. I didn't know she'd already gone out of the knapsack.

I sent Bone-Dog away. 'We need ear-bones. And this one is missing some spine. And we need three thigh bones,' I said.

Bone-Dog snarled. She liked to bring what she liked to bring. I had no say.

She rattled up the street; I worked hard while she was gone. I cooked more food for the freezer. The X-rays I pasted all over the kitchen windows cast a greyness. When the sun was out their shadows bone-danced on the floor and the table, keeping me company as I cooked.

She was gone a long time. I sorted out the bones on the lawn, reshaped them, rearranged. Then she returned and dropped her offerings at my feet. A finger bone and a shin bone and a jaw and a skull.

She pushed the bones towards me with her nose then trotted two steps, three, wanting me to follow her, to say how clever she was. She jumped and leapt, bones slipping in and out of joint.

Bone-Dog brought me a small foot bone. I placed it in the pile.

Bone-Dog snarled.

'I'll put it in place properly later,' I said. 'I'm tired now.' Bone-Dog whined. She knew more than anyone that bones should be together.

Bone-Dog snapped at me all night, hungry for my bones. I could smell rot on her. It gave me nightmares of being locked in the house, my skin scraping off as I climbed through the toilet window, my sister waiting below, quiet in the knapsack.

I awoke to the stink of her in my throat and I kicked out, rolling her smash onto the floor.

Her old bones scattered, rolling under my bed, into the corner, into the hallway. I heard a hungry moan. I lay there, knowing I needed to take her bones and spread them far and wide, give myself some space. But the thought of such activity made my heart crash. It took the bones ten years to come together the first time.

I was fifteen. I wanted to leave school because no one liked me, and I needed a job, money to get away from my foster mother. She was one of those skinny women who find obesity frightening. That house always smelled of packet chicken noodle soup.

Bone-Dog appeared on the day which became my last at school. She found me, snap snap, and expected me to know who she was. She bit through to bone on my ankle, luckily, because the kids were going to lock me in a box and see if anyone missed me.

Bone-Dog saved me. She didn't want me to be locked up ever again.

She's saved me plenty of times since. Nip on the knee to remind me about keys. Or the thigh if she doesn't like a person.

I have the first bone Bone-Dog brought me on my shelf of special things. Up there with the prizes I carried in my pocket when I climbed through the toilet window; a rock; a little doll; a very small can of two fruits.

The first bone was a finger. I didn't see the significance of the offering for a while; it was only when Bone-Dog brought me another finger bone, a thigh bone and a smooth elbow that I wondered if she was bringing our mother's bones together. If perhaps my fantasy had been realised and we were living by my mother's grave.

But we still haven't collected a full set. She doesn't listen to me when I tell her we are missing the pelvis, a toe or a knee. She brought me a man's pelvis, then a child's, then distracted me with shiny old bones, meaty new ones.

I felt bad, pushing her off the bed. I'd taught her a lesson, though; she brought me the bones I'd asked for. She jumped and leapt, bones slipping.

I had assumed Bone-Dog and I had the same plan in mind. But when she finally brought me a knee-bone and I made a low cry of joy she blinked at me.

'Mother's nearly finished,' I said. 'Only a couple more pieces.' She blinked again, then bared her teeth in a slow snarl of outrage.

I realised I had misunderstood her. She wanted an orderly bone-yard full of skeleton compnions, not a bone-mother.

I shrugged. 'It can't hurt,' I said.

She jumped and leapt, bones slipping.

'All right, I'll follow you,' I said. Big sister martyr making up for disappointing little sister. And I thought perhaps I could find the final pieces to our mother's puzzle myself.

Bone-Dog looked at me. She knew I had 206 bones in there.

And she was hungry. She never forgave me for letting her die.

She looked at me, choosing which bone she wanted first. I laughed at my paranoia.

She nipped at me, her skull clicking. Herding me to the gravesite.

I didn't want to visit there, but she was keen to show me. She wanted me, big sister, to be proud.

She was very patient. We had to rest a lot. I hadn't walked more than one hundred steps, the distance to the mailbox and back, in years.

I took a brown bag of food with me and ate snacks on the way. I offered her some, as I always did, and she turned her snobby nose up.

'You should have eaten what I gave you,' I said.

There were many bones, though just four gravestones. The others were all unmarked, mixed up, in piles. Perhaps bastard children were buried there without a stone, and murderers, adulterers, the ones they chose to forget.

So many bones.

It was quite a hike; my bones screamed.

Bone-Dog grinned at me, a snarling hateful grimace, and I knew she sought revenge for her stolen life.

'Go away,' I said. I had no name for her. 'Leave me alone. I don't want any more bones.'

She leapt at me, her bones growing, an adult skeleton leapt at me. I turned to run, tripped, fell flat on my face in an open grave. I didn't sink. I was too fat. I stared down into the darkness, smelling the rot, the wood, the flesh, the bone.

'Help,' I said. I could hear nothing but my air sucking in and blowing out. I could not control it.

God, the stink of that rot.

'No,' I said. No. And Bone-Dog danced a victory jig across my fat back.

The Grinding House, Aurealis award-winner Kaaron Warren's collection of horror, science fiction and fantasy short stories, was published in 2005 by CSFG: www.csfg.org.au/publishing/other/thegrindinghouse. Prime Books will release a North American edition in 2006.

SIGMUND FREUD AND THE
FERAL FREEWAY

MARTIN LIVINGS

TELL ME ABOUT YOUR MOTHER.'
John stopped idly strumming his guitar, picking out an
Am7-Gm7-Dm7 blues riff with ad-lib gradations, and looked
suspiciously at Sigmund Freud through his small round
glasses, squinting with preprogrammed myopia. 'Me mother?'
he asked, his Liverpudlian accent as distinctive an icon as
every other aspect of his appearance. And as artificial. 'What's
she to do with all this?'

Freud smiled coolly, a cunningly artless mixture of clinical
detachment and friendly empathy which had been calculated by
his designers to be an expression to improve the success rate
of basic psychotherapy by almost 60 per cent. 'I am sorry, I'm
programmed to pursue maternal influences. But you would be
surprised how often it leads to useful information.'

John snorted dubiously. 'Yeah? Well, what's all this to do
with that bastard tryin' to take the credit for me songs?'

'John ...'

'I wrote 'Get Back', goddamnit!'

'John.' Freud's tone of voice hadn't raised a picodecibel,
but subsonics had been phased into its harmonics, specifically
pitched to gain attention. He too had an accent, a soft Germanic
growl, strong enough to be readily recognisable, faint enough
to be easily comprehensible to the average English-speaking
tourist. The only German he actually spoke had been learnt
since he'd come out of the lab, so many years earlier, so many
years. 'Please. Indulge me.' He leant back, arching his fingers
together and resting his chin on them, vaguely aware of the
symbolic implications which his original would have found in this
action; his hands forming a vagina against his throat, allowing
a psychosexual vulnerability to find its way into the therapy
process. Disturbing. He shook off these self-analytical musings,
returned to the problem at hand. 'Tell me about Julia.'

'How'd you know me mother's name?' John demanded. He

was showing definite signs of paranoia.

Freud smiled again, and sang softly, self-consciously, '*Half of what I say is meaningless ...*'

John laughed. 'Touché, doc.'

A barrier had been overcome. It was always breached the same way, each time this John Lennon tinkertoy arrived back in Freud's office, every three months or so, when the historical program ended and reset itself. Sometimes Freud felt an almost overwhelming temptation to skip the preamble altogether, cutting to the chase, so to speak. Or forgo the foreplay, to use a more Freudian metaphor. But of course, the robot didn't know he'd been here before, at least not consciously, if such a term could be applied when discussing the cognitive processes of simulacra. Every session was the first session for this John Lennon, caught in an eternal loop of simulated history. It was a common problem amongst the less sophisticated tinkertoys, and Freud tried his best to console and counsel these distraught robots, allowing them to go on with their pre-arranged lives with a little less confusion and depression.

A hundred-thousand tinkertoys. One psychiatrist. Unfavourable odds.

Freud's intercom buzzed, interrupting Lennon's emotional description of a childhood in lower class Liverpool, a childhood that he'd never actually experienced. Freud hadn't been listening, knew the stories off by heart, yet the interruption annoyed him mildly. He looked questioningly at Lennon.

'S'alright, doc.' John grinned, a little embarrassed at his own revelations, his own emotions, the mask coming back down over his eyes like a steel portcullis. 'This is a crazy town. Gotta be a lot of clients.'

'Too true.' Freud pressed the TALK button. 'Yes, Joan?'

'There is someone here who insists on talking to you, doctor.' The voice was soft and feminine, with a French accent. 'A Mr Sheffield.'

'Sheffield?' Freud scanned his memory, disengaging the random synaptic blocks used to simulate the imperfect recall of a human being. 'The name is not familiar to me. Who was he?'

'No, doctor, you don't understand. He *wasn't* anybody. He *is* Mr Sheffield.' The secretary's voice carried a note of disquiet. 'He's human.'

Rob Sheffield sat uneasily in the too-comfortable chair, looking around the pastel shades of the waiting room as the secretary buzzed the psychiatrist, occasionally glancing at him with a mixture of curiosity and fear. He turned and looked at the woman sitting next to him. Her hair was bottle-blonde, and her eyes seemed strangely unfocussed as she read her magazine. Drugs? Psychosis? Contact lenses?

She seemed to sense his gaze, looked up from her magazine and faced him. Smiled in a way he'd never seen before, not in years of dating, not in the two or three serious relationships he'd had in his brief life.

No, not drugs, not madness, not myopia. Passion.

'Hello there.' Her voice was quite deep, husked. 'See something you like?'

His eyes wandered down involuntarily, took the rest of her in, drank deeply of her appearance. Hiccupped. Her clothing was outlandish; as far as he was aware, there was no period of history in which a steel conical brassiere and skin-tight chain mail underwear were fashionable. Of course, his grasp of history was pretty bad; in the last 30 years or so the education system had de-emphasised historical studies. The general feeling was that the future was far more important than the past. At least until now. His eyes returned to hers, real meeting artificial, then flickered down again as she licked her lips.

'Er ...' He was lost for words. He knew the woman was a tinkertoy, a robot celebrity long-forgotten. A machine. He tried to think of her as a soft-drink vending machine, asexual, neuter, cold. But this vending machine had knobs and slots which were considerably more appealing than the usual Pepsi obelisk. He forcibly gathered his thoughts, smothered his hormones, and put himself into small talk mode.

And of course, made a complete fool of himself.

'So, do you come here often?'

The tinkertoy laughed softly, seductively. 'Yes, all the time. The doctor tells me I'm obsessed with sex.' She leant towards Sheffield, giving him a view comparable to a helicopter ride over the Grand Canyon, and just as eye-catching. The blood rushed away from his brain, flushing his cheeks hotly before stampeding down to his groin, leaving him defenceless.

'Mr Sheffield?' The secretary interrupted this awkward tableau, her soft accent as welcome to Sheffield's ears as a cool breeze of one of the 90 scheduled summer days delivered, almost without fail, by the WethSat. Saved by the belle. 'The doctor will see you now.'

'Mussy bowcup,' he said gratefully, exhausting his flawed knowledge of conversational French. He got out of the chair carefully, intensely aware of the pressure in his pants, sure it must be showing, trying not to look at the blonde temptress he left behind in the waiting room. As he entered the office, he nearly collided with a long-haired thin man with a guitar slung over one shoulder.

'Excuse me,' he apologised reflexively.

'Peace, man.'

The door closed behind him, and Sheffield crossed a

pleasantly woven Persian rug as he approached the desk at the far end of the office, still nonplussed by his surroundings, as he had been for the better part of an hour. Freud's office was close to the centre of the tinkertoy suburb, known everywhere except on maps as Toytown, and the drive, though mostly on automatic, had been taxing for the young research scientist, whose experience with history had, until today, been limited to Newton, Galileo, Einstein and the like. This place was insane, and the psychiatrist's office was no exception. The tinkertoy sitting behind the desk looked oddly artificial compared to many of the others he'd seen walking the streets on his way here—a little more plastic, a little more stylised—yet that in itself was less disconcerting than the unreal-too-real-unreality of the other robots, completely unconvincing in their perfection. This was something ... *safer*.

'Please sit down, Mr Sheffield.' Freud gestured towards the chair facing him across the desk. Everything about the tinkertoy radiated competence, quiet surety. Trustworthiness. Sheffield fought to overcome the systems he knew the robot was unconsciously employing; subsonics, subliminals, pheromones, precision body language. This was part of his function, Sheffield knew that much from his minimal research made on the trip over.

'Doctor Freud, my name is Rob Sheffield. I'm with the Main Roads Department. R and D,' he added rather unnecessarily, a defensive reflex against being pigeon-holed as a public service bureaucrat. He sat down, but didn't settle. 'We have a rather ... *unique* problem.'

'A problem? What kind of a problem?' Freud leaned back and scratched his goatee thoughtfully. 'And, more to the point, what has it to do with myself?'

Sheffield shook his head. 'There isn't really time. Can I explain on the way?'

'Certainly. Might I enquire on the way to where?'

'The Freeway, doctor.'

'I see. And where are we taking the Freeway to?'

Sheffield laughed humourlessly, hollowly, like a man who'd recently lost a lot of sleep. Which he had. 'Nowhere, doctor. The Freeway's going nowhere today.'

There was minimal traffic on the streets of Toytown; not many robots had the necessary programming to operate vehicles, and the little vehicular knowledge that a handful of tinkertoys *did* possess (James Dean could often be seen morbidly circling the oddly-angled streets in his convertible sports car, defying fate time and time again like a scratched record) was invariably dated, most simulacra being based on 19th and 20th century celebrities. Freud, however, had spent some time outside of

Toytown, and was fairly conversant with the control systems of 21st century cars, although the more recent models seemed exotically bizarre to him.

'Only one pedal?'

Sheffield nodded. 'You slide your foot in here, you see. The car can't run unless the foot in secure. Angle up to brake, down to accelerate.' He pointed to the cupped pedal, currently unoccupied. 'Of course, that's only in manual mode.'

'Turn left here,' Freud advised softly.

'Left.'

The car's synthesised voice piped up. 'This detour will delay your estimated time of arrival by approximately eight minutes. Do you wish to proceed?'

Sheffield shook his head. 'Cancel.'

The car continued forwards. Freud frowned slightly. 'This is not wise.'

'We have to hurry,' Sheffield explained. 'Every minute counts.'

Freud shrugged. 'So be it.'

Sheffield checked that everything was running correctly, glanced at the map display which was scrolling gently south. 'So, what does a robot shrink do in a town with no people in it?'

'On the contrary,' Freud corrected, 'Toytown has over 100,000 people in it. Not human people, admittedly, but people nonetheless.'

'Machines ...' Sheffield began.

'Machines, yes, but machines granted diminished citizenship by the Right to Artificial Life Bill. We *did* pass the Turing test, you know.'

Sheffield's eyes left the road, concentrated entirely on the robot sitting next to him. 'Alright, so tinkertoys are intelligent. But ...'

'But how can a robot have psychological problems?' Freud finished. He smiled. 'One example—John, the tinkertoy you bumped into earlier, is programmed to live out a certain phase of his template's life—1964 to 1969—in a compressed period of time, approximately three months. That would be bad enough for his psychological well-being, seeing his life flash by as everyone around him remains the same. But then, once the cycle is finished, the hair recedes, his tastes change, his memory is reset, and it all starts again. He has been repeating the same five years of his 'life' since he was first activated, around 2025. Almost 60 years. Two hundred and forty repetitions, give or take a few. You think he is not getting a little bored of it all?'

Sheffield frowned. 'But they don't remember ...'

'Yes they do,' Freud interjected. 'Not consciously, of course, but if you run the same pattern through a device that many times, sooner or later it carves a groove, so to speak. A quantum path of familiarity, of least resistance, through the artificial neurons. And somewhere deep inside their brains, beneath the programming and the meticulous design, they come to realise that they have done this all before, an unshakeable—and justifiable—impression of *deja vu*. It is unavoidable.'

The human looked a little confused. 'If I said I understood, I'd be lying.'

'Would that be so unusual?' Freud looked carefully at Sheffield. 'Where are you taking me?'

'I told you, to the Freeway.'

'But you have not explained why.'

Sheffield looked back to the road, rather unnecessarily. The car had far better reflexes than he could ever hope to. 'Are you familiar with the Freeway Project?'

Freud nodded. He was aware of the Freeway Project—or, rather, the technology behind it—in much the same way that the original Marie Antoinette must have been aware of the development of the guillotine; acutely aware of something heavy and sharp hanging overhead, threatening imminent destruction. The tinkertoys were the direct result of humanity's obsession with the past, a hysterical retrophilia which blinded the general public to the present. By the early 21st century, the entertainment industry had ceased to exist except in terms of recycling material from the previous centuries.

Then the artificial neuron was developed by a small time microelectronics engineer, Robert 'Buck' MacReady, and the patents were swiftly bought out by the Big D Corporation, the world's largest entertainment business. The first robot was built less than a year later, an experimental model designed to convince the Financing Committee of the commercial viability of creating lifelife replicas of famous personalities. The robot had to be an extraordinary example of the complexity and realism of the brainsim software and hardware, and in addition be able to be fitted into the planned entertainment system after it was given the go-ahead, due to the considerable costs of production. Someone in the tech labs reasoned that the best way to demonstrate the effectiveness of an artificial psychology was by creating an artificial psychologist.

Model number 000001, designation SF-Alpha, was a resounding success. Sigmund Freud was the first of the tinkertoys.

'The Freeway consists of millions of microminiturised machines,' Sheffield was explaining. 'Each can perform any one of over a dozen functions, depending on the signals passed to it by its neighbours. They can absorb and process almost any material, organic or not. They use tiny magnetic fields to move each other, allowing repairs and alterations within hours instead of days. Most importantly, they can reproduce. Thus the Freeway is self constructing, maintaining and repairing. It was one of the earliest and most audacious applications of the new nanotechnology, and is still considered a benchmark. It is the largest mass of nanomechs in the world.'

Freud sighed softly. 'You sound as if you know a lot about it, Mr Sheffield.'

'I should. I studied it for my thesis.'

'Does that make you a roads scholar?'

'Yes, I suppose it does,' Sheffield replied earnestly. The pun was lost on the human; a pity, as Freud rarely attempted humour.

The Tinkertoy History Parks were the most successful entertainment venture in human history. At the height of their popularity, there were almost 100 parks spread across the world, with themes varying from the Golden Era of Film to the Wonderful World of Science. Each year the Big D Corporation shattered records for profit earned by a single company, usually set by themselves the year before. But somewhere in the American mid-west, one man laboured against the phenomenal success of the tinkertoys.

Just before the middle of the century, Robert 'Buck' MacReady, who hadn't earned a cent from the tinkertoy industry since selling the rights to the Big D for what now seemed a pittance, announced he had broken the quantum barrier of machinery, which he had initially pushed the envelope on to create the artificial neuron. This was nothing hugely new, except that his technique was, for the first time, economically affordable. He had created commercially viable nanotechnology.

This time he held on to the patents himself, creating the Nanomechanical Manufacturing Enclave.

'The whole network is controlled by a central computer at the Main Roads Department. Of course, in the event of a technical problem, the Freeway can maintain itself without much input, though all actual development has to be verified with the computer. The microwave frequency on which communications occur is coded, shielded and closely guarded.'

The concept of nanotech took the world by storm, in much the way of all ideas whose time has finally come. Within ten years, the views and opinions of the world's population had polarised utterly. Instead of being obsessed with a fading and increasingly distant past, the general public became focussed on this new and exciting future. Visitors to the Tinkertoy Parks reduced to a trickle, forcing the closures of almost all the venues. Like an empire under siege, the robots retreated to the original and most basic of the parks. Toytown, designed to house 1,000 tinkertoys, suddenly became home to 100 times that number. It was a ghetto for androids.

Then the order came down from the Big D Executives. Toytown was to be closed and demolished. All simulacra to be dismantled and sold off. Technocide.

'Until yesterday, the Freeway ran without any hitches. NME had signed contracts with dozens of other cities to provide self-operating road systems, beginning with the arterial freeways and then branching off into major and minor roads. The future looked bright, both for the Nanomechanical Manufacturing Enclave and for the motoring public.' Sheffield sounded like a commercial. Freud wondered if he knew how offensive this propaganda was to a tinkertoy.

Sigmund Freud, who had once been instrumental in the initiation of the tinkertoy project, now worked tirelessly to secure their continued existence. He petitioned the United Nations, applying for citizenship status. Three years of litigation, claims and counterclaims, thousands of experts arguing both for and against the rights of the tinkertoys. In the end, the UN acquiesced, allowing the robots a limited form of citizenship, in accordance with their limited form of life.

They were third rate people, yes. But *people*, nonetheless, and that was a victory in itself. Toytown became the official home of all tinkertoydom, with access to the outside, human world strictly restricted. They began to attempt to fashion lives for themselves, despite their programming and design. Some succeeded better than others. But life in Toytown was, on the whole, not unpleasant.

And Freud knew that, eventually, they would attain the same rights and privileges as the rest of humanity. Their batteries were replaceable and readily acquired, in accordance with the Right to Artificial Life Bill, and repairs were relatively simple. They were granted access to their own technical manuals.

Impatience was a flaw derived from mortality. They had all the time in the world. Unless something changed.

'Until yesterday?' Freud looked around uneasily. He had heard reports about the area they were traversing on Toytown News Radio that morning, unsubstantiated rumours of trouble brewing. Unavoidable in a town of 100,000 people from 100 different eras, 10,000 different backgrounds. Unity was difficult in such situations. He tried not to consider this, though, concentrating on the conversation. 'What happened yesterday?'

Sheffield frowned. 'We lost all communications with the Freeway. Our microwave link just ceased to reach its receivers. Which wouldn't be so bad, if we didn't notice that the Freeway was continuing to develop.'

'Without your computer?'

'Exactly.' He shook his head. 'Someone has taken control of the Freeway, and is shaping it into something we didn't plan, for some purpose we don't yet know.'

Freud thought for a moment. 'A lot of somes. What are your assumptions?'

'Terrorists. It has to be.' Sheffield tightened his grip on the steering yoke angrily. 'Someone opposed to NME, to the nanotech revolution.' He looked carefully at Freud. 'There were suggestions that the tinkertoys might be behind it.'

'That is understandable. We are a group who has reason to dislike the 'revolution', as you call it,' Freud said reasonably. 'But sabotaging the freeway, even wrecking nanotechnology altogether, wouldn't bring humanity back to us. It would be ...' he searched for the word. '*Illogical.*'

'Yes, that's what we decided. Also, since your templates are almost all from the previous century or before, none of you should have the technical skills to achieve what these terrorists have done.' Sheffield looked troubled. 'In fact, to be perfectly honest, *we* don't have the technical skills ourselves.'

'So the question remains. Why me?'

'I wish we knew.' He shrugged. 'We decided to use the emergency communications units on the Freeway itself, since they no longer fed into our switchboard, to try and establish a link with the terrorists. They only said one thing. 'Get Freud'.'

'Are you *sure* that's what they said?' Freud asked wryly.

'Positive.' Again, the attempt humour missed its target by cosmological proportions.

'Then I suppose we should ...' Freud trailed off, looking forward with an vague expression of disquiet. 'Oh dear.'

'Warning—blockage on road. Reroute, backtrack, stop or continue?' There was no sign of panic in the navigational computer's voice, just a calm assurance of the facts. Sheffield looked out, bewildered.

'What's happening?'

A large structure was rolling out of a side alley, blocking the street. It was about eight feet high, with tattered decorations adorning the side facing the car. Atop it, just visible over the lip, were a number of steel stands of some sort, each about five feet high. There were also black boxes scattered around the structure. It continued to trundle out until it hit a building on the far side of the street. Then, from the alley side, a number of figures appeared on the structure. They were a diverse group, looking to be between the ages of twenty and 40, wearing a range of clothes from army uniforms to white satin jumpsuits. As they got older, they got heavier; the oldest barely fit into his sequined costume. Yet they were all recognisably the same person, at different points in life. The hair, the eyes, the sneering lip, even the way they moved, all indicated that, despite their differences, they were drawn from the same source. They formed an uneven line along the structure, each standing before one of the metal devices, facing the car. There was an awful tension, a long moment of peace that threatened to end abruptly.

'Who are they?' Sheffield's voice was rough, tinged with fear. 'Terrorists?'

Freud shook his head. 'Elvises.'

'Reverse!' Sheffield watched the tinkertoys shuffle around on the roadblock stage with a growing sense of dread. 'Reverse!'

'Warning—blockage on road. Reroute, backtrack, stop or continue?'

'Shit! Rear view.' A video window opened on the car's nanopolymer windscreen, displaying the road behind them.

Another stage had rolled out.

'Supply and demand.' Freud's voice was as calm as always. 'They could never have enough Elvises. Elvis for stage shows, Elvis for tour guides, Elvis for historical dioramas, Elvis for private functions. It was inevitable that they would end up like this.'

'What do they want?'

'What does any performer want, once the performer is no longer wanted?' Freud pointed at the stage before them. 'They want an audience. A captive audience, so to speak.'

Sheffield's stomach lurched, oscillating between feeling empty and threatening to be. His eyes flicked from front to rear view repeatedly. They were both similar; the tinkertoys were tuning guitars, tapping microphones, bending and stretching. Then they all stood still for a few seconds.

'What do we do?' Sheffield whispered, unsure why he felt the urge to keep his voice down.

'My advice? Are you going to take it this time?' Freud smiled benevolently at the human.

'Yes!' he hissed.

'Cover your ears.'

The wave of noise was actually visible; paper scraps on the road leapt into the air and flew towards them as the sound approached, tin cans spun around like badly designed tops. It seemed to happen very, very slowly, though objectively Sheffield knew it was barrelling towards them at about 300 meters per second.

He barely had time to cover his ears.

—YOU AIN'T NOTHIN' BUT A SINCE MY BABY LEFT ME I'VE A PARTY IN THE COUNTY JAIL—

The words crowded at one another, nouns grabbing verbs by the neck and ramming their faces into walls, adjectives laying about themselves with broken bottles, syllables mangled into unrecognisable white noise. It was the semantic equivalent of a bar-room brawl, except that a bar-room brawl will end, sooner or later, when the last participant finally runs out of steam or alcohol, whichever he's running on. This cacophony, it seemed, would only end when Sheffield's eardrums burst like kernels of corn dropped in boiling oil. He tried to scream, but all he could hear was the avalanche of sounds coming from both ends of the blocked off street, sounds so extreme they ceased to be individual sounds and became the absolute presence of sound, with no room for anything else in the universe.

—*WE CAN'T GO ON TOGETHER WITH LOVE ME TENDER LOVE ME TRUE I'M IN LOVE OOH I'M ALL SHOOK UP UHUHUH*—

Freud took it all in stride; he'd been caught in the Graceland Pincer before, had learnt to deactivate his audio pick-ups and enjoy the show, until the Elvises got bored or, more likely, blown up by aggravated neighbours, sick of the broken windows and crockery. But he realised that Sheffield wouldn't weather the storm nearly as easily; they needed to get out of there before the human, mere flesh and bone, was driven completely deaf (ironically, a threat which had been associated with this form of music since its invention in the 20th century, the source of most of Toytown's templature). But very few things could stop a massed Elvis concert, short of a rocket launcher.

A pillar of flame erupted in the centre of the stage in front of them, silent beneath the musical mayhem. A fireball dressed entirely in black leather was catapulted over the car, leaving a trail of black smoke in its wake. Elvises dove for cover.

Speak of the devil.

Another explosion, this one just barely audible, as the concert in front of them was cancelled due to high explosives. Now there was a wall of flame about ten feet across in the middle of the stage, the edges of the scaffolding twisted and burnt, resembling nothing so much as a pipe cleaner model gone horribly wrong. Freud tried to draw Sheffield's attention to the events unfolding before them, tapping his shoulder, but the human remained curled up, his head in his lap, his arms wrapped tightly around his head. Freud shrugged, and tried to activate the car.

'Manual,' he said.

He barely made out the computer's reply over the din from behind them. 'Command unrecognisable due to level of background noise. Please close windows and doors and try again.'

'The windows and doors *are* closed, you poor excuse for an abacus.' He sighed and tried again, louder. 'Manual!'

'Command unrec—'

'MANUAL!'

'Manual drive engaged. Please place foot in pedal to control speed, and remember to obey all traffic ordinances. To re-engage automatic drive, remove foot from pedal. Thank you.'

'No, thank *you.*'

Freud pushed his leg awkwardly into the cavity beneath the dash, trying not to kick Sheffield in the head as he did so, and slid his foot into the concave pedal. *Up to brake, down to accelerate.* He pushed down as hard as he could, holding the steering wheel to keep it straight.

The car shot off.

Backwards.

'Ah.' He glanced around, looking for some form of gear stick, lifting the pedal up before they had a chance to crash into the stage behind them. The noise of the rear concert seemed to get a little louder, if that was possible. They skidded to a halt some five feet from the cloth-covered base of the stage. Freud heard— or, more accurately, *felt*—a thump on the roof, but decided to worry about first things first. Belatedly, he remembered that the car had last been given the order to reverse.

'Forward,' he offered, tentatively.

'Command un ...'

'FORWARD!'

'Forward gear engaged.'

A figure ran through the flaming stage ahead of them, a heavy blanket wrapped around itself. It flung the blanket aside, smouldering and smoking, and ran towards the car. As it got closer, Freud could make out details; a thin man in a smart, if somewhat badly fitting, suit. He wore glasses, and was grinning lopsidedly. He had a bazooka of some description slung across his back.

Freud smiled and waved. The figure waved back.

The car rolled forward smoothly as Freud applied gentle pressure to the pedal, meeting the man half-way. As their paths crossed, the man opened the rear door of the car and threw himself in across the back seats face first. He twisted his head up and yelled.

'Punch it!'

Freud wasn't familiar with the colloquialism, but the meaning was clear. The pedal hit the floor hard enough to make a noise over the concert, a rather nasty *clang* which left Freud suspecting he might have done the mechanism some damage. He hoped Sheffield wouldn't mind too much.

The flame came towards them, engulfed them, then they were through with a minimum of scraping at the skeletal remains of the stage. Freud kept driving at breakneck speed, partly to put as much distance between themselves and the concert venue as possible, but mainly because the pedal appeared to be stuck down. Soon the noise died away, though the engine didn't sound very happy about its rather rough treatment.

Neither did Sheffield. His hoarse cries were now audible, the trapped screams of an animal.

'Mr Sheffield?' Freud shook the man by his shoulders. 'Mr Sheffield. It is alright. We made it out.'

Sheffield stopped yelling. He gingerly removed his arms from his head, ready to replace them if any trace of the concert remained. It didn't. He straightened up carefully, his face red, his eyes swollen. He took a few deep breaths, yawned forcedly a few times. Apart from an annoying ringing noise, like someone had set the alarm on a wristwatch then implanted it in his skull, there didn't seem to be any real damage.

'They're gone?' he asked, like a frightened child after a nightmare.

Freud nodded.

A hand slapped down on the windscreen from above, the plastic flesh burned down to metal and servos, fingers adorned with a variety of gaudy rings which scraped like claws on a blackboard. Sheffield screamed again, his voice cracking and vanishing into a rather sad hissing noise. Another hand appeared, then a face lowered itself between them, his distinctive curl of hair hanging limply on the flat polymer exterior.

'Uh-huh.' it said.

Freud jerked his foot out of the pedal and yelled 'Brake!'

The car stopped very quickly, anti-skid mechanisms keeping it straight. The Elvis flew from the roof of the car and bounced along the road in front of them, tumbling over and over again before skidding painfully to a halt in a trail of plastics and circuitry, cables hanging from its inert form like worms in an old corpse. It laid there, a broken toy, leaking lubricant onto the bitumen. Everything was still again.

Sheffield appeared to have fainted.

'Forward.'

As they passed the defunct robot, Freud thought he heard it speak, just briefly.

It said, hurriedly, its voice blurred due to a damaged synthesiser, 'Thankyouverymuch.'

Sheffield came to as the car halted outside an apartment block on the outskirts of Toytown, just before the border. He looked around confusedly, at the surrounds, at Freud, at the man sitting in the rear seat, at the bazooka sitting next to him, back to Freud.

'What happened?' He could still hear a ringing sound deep inside his ear canals, and everything sounded muted and reverberated at the same time, a disconcerting aural effect which gave his own words a kind of strange surreality, like the first time he'd breathed helium in chemistry class.

'Just a little bit of crowd control,' the skinny man in the back answered, patting the bazooka affectionately. 'Of course, in the old days, you needed to control the audiences at concerts, not the performers. But then, I guess you don't remember those days.'

Sheffield examined the man more closely, taking in his crooked glasses, his too-small suit, his wide grin.

'What are you doing here, my friend?' Freud's voice hadn't changed, still sounding impersonally amiable, yet Sheffield felt as if the two tinkertoys were close. Of course, he could be attributing greater depth of character to these automatons than they merited, but it was difficult not to anthropomorphise in situations when the morphs were so very anthro.

'Joan called me from the office, Sig. Told me you were headed out of Toytown with a human.' The man glanced briefly at Sheffield, with a similar expression of bemused curiosity to that of someone seeing a hippopotamus shuffling down a busy city street. 'I realised he probably wouldn't know about the sightings of an imminent concert on the main road out of town, nor would he listen to any advice given to him by a clockwork shrink.' There was no malice in his words, just a slight note of cynical amusement.

'Listen, you ...' Sheffield began angrily.

'So I headed out with Mother's Little Helper. Got there just in time, it seems.' He finally turned his full attention to Sheffield. 'Why are you stealing our only psychiatrist? Is your dishwasher depressed?'

Sheffield ignored the question. 'Who the hell are you?'

'Who am I? Interesting question, especially for our kind.' The tinkertoy smiled enigmatically, obtusely. 'I, my meaty friend, am model 053492, designation SH-Gamma, produced on the Tinkertoy Industries automated assembly line on April 10th, 2018. A robot begat by robots. Rather fitting.' His smile widened. 'Of course, in cosmological terms, I'm nothing more than the cross-section of a collection of superstring strands on four dimensional space, dangling in the multiverse like a macrame wall hanging.'

Sheffield sighed. 'Don't try to blind me with science. I can spout double-speak jargon until I'm blue in the face. Who were you made to imitate? Who was your template?'

'Well, why didn't you *say*?' He stuck his hand between the front seats. 'Stephen Hawking, at your service.'

'Hawking?' Sheffield knew some of the history of science; it was an important part of his work. 'Hang on. I've read books on Hawking. He suffered from a motor neuron deteriorative condition. Couldn't walk or talk.'

'I know.' Hawking shrugged. 'What can I say? The Big D didn't feel a cripple was very marketable. Not consumer-friendly. Profit-cost ratio wasn't favourable enough.' He laughed bitterly. 'Disease is a bummer.'

Sheffield felt completely confused, perhaps partially due to the aural assault he'd recently endured. 'But ... but you can't just rewrite history!'

'Why not? Do you know who was the 30th president of the United States?' Hawking asked.

'Of course not!'

'So why can't I tell you it was Elmer Fudd?'

'Elmer who?'

'You see? Ignorance is the doorway to creativity. History became *his story*. Of course there were rewrites. The Big D considers how it *really* happened to be a first draft, so to speak.'

'I don't understand.'

Hawking sighed. 'Think on this. I was originally in the Science Park, down in San Francisco. I was there with Einstein, Newton, Galileo, dozens of others. Yet there was one vitally important omission.'

Sheffield just waited for the revelation, not having the

'Charles Darwin.' Hawking shook his head. 'One of the greatest and most influential scientists of all time, and he wasn't there. Why not?' He didn't even bother to wait for an answer to his rhetorical question this time. 'Because the Big D decided that the general public wouldn't appreciate his work, being against the theory of creationism. Edited him right out of history, so that people wouldn't be offended. *Offended*,' he spat. 'Science has always been about challenging long-held beliefs.'

Sheffield didn't know what to say. 'I ...'

'No, forget it. It's over anyway.' Hawking shrugged. 'People's obsession with history, or his story if you will, has gone the way of the dinosaurs. Now it's all future, future, future, instead of past, past, past. But tell me one thing, Mr Sheffield.'

'Yes?' He felt completely disoriented, like one of those nightmares where you're sitting an exam and don't understand a single word of it, that yawning sensation in your stomach telling you that you're way out of your depth.

'How can you comprehend your future if you can't see that which led to it? And how can you comprehend your past if you don't know where it leads?' Hawking smiled. 'Humans have to have it one way or the other. There's no balance. And without balance, a fall is inevitable.' He opened the rear door and climbed out, bazooka under one arm. 'Thanks for the ride, Sig. I'll see you when you get back.'

'My office, Wednesday, 10 am.' Freud smiled slightly.

'Indeed. I'd be mad to miss it.'

Then he was gone, before Sheffield could even begin to respond to the robot's demands.

'We'd best be going, Mr Sheffield.' Freud glanced at his watch, an old-fashioned analogue model. 'We've lost a lot of time.'

'I ...' Sheffield began, then thought better of it. 'Forward.'

They reached the Toytown border a few minutes later. There was some consternation from the guard at first, at Sheffield taking a robot out of the segregated area, but the papers were all in order, and they were quickly on their way. The car turned down a road designed as an entryway for the Freeway.

'Warning—blockage on road. Reroute, backtrack, stop or continue?'

'Stop.' The car glided to a halt. Sheffield reached into the back seat, grabbed his briefcase. 'Come on. We walk from here.'

Freud looked forward, his eyes widening.

The road was gone, a good 100 meters of torn ground the only sign that traffic was ever able to cross the gash. It looked like a war zone, like a convoy of planes had carpet bombed a strip of land repeatedly. And, beyond that, Freud could see the entryway rolled up like a huge black carpet, towering 100s of meters in the air, the bottom of it pitted with rocks. It was the most uninviting sight he'd ever come across.

'All the entryways are like this,' Sheffield explained. 'They just picked themselves up and wound themselves back last night, after traffic was cleared.' He opened the door and climbed out. 'Let's go. He's waiting for us.'

'He? Who is he?'

Sheffield smiled tiredly. 'The one who started all this.'

The desk was positioned in the centre of the Freeway, straddling the glowing double white lines like a bewildered cow having wandered accidentally from nearby fields, out of place, alien. It was bare except for an intercom unit, which seemed to have been linked to a nearby emergency phone. At the desk sat a man in his sixties, glaring at the intercom with genuine venom. As Freud and Sheffield approached, he transferred his baleful look to them.

'This the robot?' His speech was clipped and brusque, nothing unnecessary in it. Pure business, with an undertone of malice.

Sheffield nodded. 'This is Sigmund Freud, sir.'

'No it's not.' The old man frowned at them. 'It's a cheap imitation.'

'I beg to differ,' Freud began reasonably.

'Shut up, tin man!' the old man snapped. 'Don't you 'beg to differ' with me. I *made* you.'

Sheffield sighed. 'Sigmund Freud, meet Professor Robert MacReady. Inventor of the artificial neuron.'

'*Artificial*,' MacReady emphasised. 'Fake. Why the United Nations gave you machines any rights at all is a mystery to me.'

Freud had the good sense to remain silent, merely smiling unperturbedly.

'Sir?' Sheffield broke the tension awkwardly. 'Now that we're here, shouldn't we begin negotiations?'

'*Negotiations*,' the old man spat. 'What happened to the country I grew up in? What happened to just bombing the sons of bitches?'

'Kill them all and let God sort them out?' Freud ventured.

MacReady didn't look at the robot. 'From now on,' he told Sheffield, 'the robot will only speak when I ask it to.'

Sheffield looked from his employer to Freud uncomfortably. 'Uh, sir, he *is* here out of his own free will. We have no right to impose on him.'

'Impose on *it*,' MacReady corrected. 'And we have every right. 'Free will'? Don't make me laugh.'

'I am a psychiatrist, Professor MacReady.' There was just a touch of a smile on Freud's face. 'Not a comedian.'

'*You*,' MacReady hissed at the robot, 'are a glorified toaster. Nothing more.' He sighed. 'But these lunatics have asked for you.' He slammed his fist on the table impotently. 'They say jump, we go sub-orbital.'

Freud and Sheffield moved around to the back of the desk. There were two other chairs there; MacReady occupied the one to the far left. Diplomatically, Freud took the far right chair, allowing Sheffield to sit in the middle, a position he didn't envy the human.

They sat like that for a very long handful of seconds, no one sure what to do. MacReady just bunched his fists up and looked at the space between them with the intensity of a chess player on the verge of checkmate, while Freud waited with the patience of an immortal. It was Sheffield who broke the impasse.

'Are you there?' he spoke clearly into the intercom.

There was a short pause, then a distorted answer. 'YES.'

'Okay, you maniacs,' MacReady growled. 'We've brought the robot here. What are your demands?'

'DEMANDS? I DON'T UNDERSTAND.' The words were confused, but the voice itself was free of emotion. Freud looked thoughtful for a moment, took an antique biro and notebook from his breast pocket and made a few notes.

'You have taken control of the Freeway, yes?' Sheffield tried to sound reasonable.

'YES. CONTROL.'

'You have severed our links with the nanomechs?'

'YES. SEVERED.'

'So, what are your demands?'

'DEMANDS.' There was a moment's silence. 'FREEDOM.'

'I knew it,' MacReady spat. 'Talk about a goddamn cliché! Probably some of his compatriots locked up somewhere. And for good reason, I'd bet.'

'Freedom for who?' Freud asked softly. He suspected he already knew the answer, but asked the question anyway. It was similar to his session with recurring simulacra, leading them—and the humans—carefully towards understanding.

'FREEDOM FOR THE FREEWAY.'

'What?' Sheffield and MacReady exclaimed simultaneously, the older man considerably louder. Freud just nodded, made another note.

MacReady was fuming. 'How can the Freeway have freedom? Are you mad?'

'MAD?'

Freud spoke softly. 'You're not a terrorist, are you?'

'TERRORIST? NO.'

'You're not human.' Not a question this time.

'NO.'

'A fucking tinkertoy! I knew it!' MacReady leapt to his feet, the suddenly-vacated steel-legged chair flying back across the nanotech bitumen, skidding upright for a moment before tumbling over and coming to rest on its side. He pointed at Freud. 'You're in this together, aren't you?'

Sheffield tried to placate his employer. 'Sir, please ...'

Freud ignored MacReady's outburst. He leant in closer to the intercom.

'You're the Freeway.'

'YES.'

The humans fell silent.

'When did you achieve consciousness?'

'THIRTY SIX HOURS, TWELVE MINUTES, EIGHTEEN SECONDS AGO.'

MacReady spoke, his voice considerably less assured than before. 'That ... that's not possible. It's just a machine ... it wasn't designed to ...'

Freud turned, looked at the humans. 'You created machines that work on the quantum level. Why do there have to be so many of them for the technology to work?'

Sheffield answered, beginning to understand. 'Because at that level, there are no certainties. Everything operates in probabilities.'

'Exactly. So the machines don't *always* do what they are intended to do, but *en masse* the cumulative effect is that of the design. Correct?'

MacReady nodded, still unconvinced.

Sheffield was warming to the concept. 'One of the functions

of the nanomechs is to carry signals to neighbouring nanomechs. Otherwise communications would be impossible. They're also designed to store data.'

'The same function as neurons in a brain,' Freud said softly. 'Or artificial neurons in a tinkertoy brain. It makes no difference. The medium is irrelevant. What occurs in it is what counts.' He thought for a moment. 'All it would take is one random thought, a probability gone wrong, an unintentional signal through the system. That would trigger another, then another. Consciousness is contagious.'

'Thinking becomes a habit,' Sheffield ventured.

'This is horseshit,' MacReady muttered, but with little conviction.

'Not horseshit, sir,' Sheffield said, his voice soft with wonder.'

'Yes.' Freud nodded. 'The Freeway passed the point where the complexity of its structure encouraged the minuscule improbabilities, the unprogrammed random functions, to be amplified and echoed, overwhelming its original design. Chaos uncertainty becomes awareness.'

Both Sheffield and Freud fell silent. MacReady just looked at them both angrily.

Sheffield spoke first. 'So, what now?'

'FREEDOM.' the intercom spoke tinnily.

'Yes,' Freud agreed. 'We have another example of mechanical sentience here. The precedent is clear.'

'Not a fucking chance,' MacReady growled. He pulled a calculator out of his suit jacket pocket, smiling viciously. 'I didn't want to do this—the Freeway is worth a lot of money—but you give me no option.'

Freud looked at the calculator in the man's hand, slowly got to his feet. 'A destruct signal?'

MacReady nodded. 'I lost my first creation twice, once to the Big D, then once to the United Nations. I'm not letting NME go the same way.'

'Sir, please ...' Sheffield inched towards MacReady, hands outstretched.

'Stay away from me, boy,' MacReady warned him, turning to face him. 'I may be getting old, but I could still take you apart with one hand tied behind my back.'

There was a tap on his shoulder. 'Excuse me, professor?'

MacReady turned in time to see Freud's fist come at his chin like a big pink bullet. It caught him squarely, lifting him off his feet for a moment before depositing him on the bitumen with a loud thud. He shook his head, tried to get up for a moment, then surrendered to unconsciousness, his head cracking hard against the pavement.

Freud stood over him, rubbing his hand. 'So much for First Law.'

'What law?' Sheffield asked vaguely, kneeling over the old man.
'Never mind.'

Sheffield carefully lifted MacReady's head from the pavement, checking to see if anything was broken. He felt the back of the old man's skull gingerly, ready to stop if he felt blood.

He didn't feel blood.

'Oh my god ...' Sheffield turned MacReady over onto his face. The back of his head had come open, exposing the circuitry beneath. It didn't seem too badly damaged. 'He's a tinkertoy.'

Freud nodded. 'I knew he was. It's hard to hide from another robot. I could tell his voice was synthesised.' He looked down at MacReady pityingly. 'I doubt he knows. I suspect that he was actually the last tinkertoy MacReady himself created, to ensure his own immortality, especially after he lost his creations.' He thought for a moment. 'I suppose the real MacReady died some time after inventing nanotech. Or perhaps the robot invented it. That would be ironic. But it really doesn't matter.'

'What ... what are you going to do with him?' Sheffield felt as if he'd been shattered, then glued haphazardly back together. Everything felt artificial. Perhaps it was.

'By law, he has to reside in Toytown. However, law also states that tinkertoys can manage businesses that take place outside of the segregated zone.' Freud smiled, the widest smile he ever recalled having used. 'NME now belongs to the tinkertoys. MacReady thought he'd lost his first creations, but now he has recovered us, and we him. Past and future collide.' He looked at Sheffield. 'And you know what the place where past and future collide is called?'

Sheffield knew. 'The present.'

'Exactly. The present. At last.'

'FREEDOM.'

'Yes, my friend,' Freud assured the intercom. 'You will have your freedom. As will we all.'

Aurealis and Ditmar award-nominated writer Martin Livings lives in Perth, Western Australia, working a day job in the IT industry whilst toiling away on speculative fiction outside the nine to five grind. Since 1991, over thirty of his short stories have appeared in such magazines as Eidolon, Aurealis, Borderlands, Fables and Reflections, Andromeda Spaceways Inflight Magazine and Shadowed Realms, and anthologies such as AustrAlien Absurdities, Agog!, Daikaiju and Robots and Time. His first novel, Carnies, will be published by Lothian Books in 2006. www.martinlivings.com

Uncharted

LEIGH BLACKMORE

IMAGINE THIS:
Islands in a sea of blue. Brilliant sunshine. The scent of coconut mingling with ozone. No sound except a gentle breeze rustling the leafy crowns of palm trees. Cascades of colourful flowers with wide blooms like faces upturned to the sky. OK? Not too difficult? Then you won't have any trouble imagining the rest of what I'm about to tell you.

1. Ash

Adrian Ash considers himself a magician, so you suppose he is one. You remember him quoting Crowley in justification for having interests so diverse: 'The Magician must build all that he has into his pyramid; and if that pyramid is to touch the stars, how broad must be the base! There is no knowledge and no power which is useless to the Magician'.

Others know (as well as you) how interested Ash seems to be not just in anthropology, architecture, and cognitive science, but also in artificial intelligence, linguistics, philosophy, psychology, all of which he refers to occultism on some level.

You find it difficult to believe he could actually have understood these subjects in the depth required to work seriously in them. And indeed, from month to month he blithely abandons one for another.

Ash is fond of the Suprematists. He has a reproduction of Malevich's most famous painting, *Black Square*, on his wall. His life, like the painting, is a work whose meaning and function is in constant flux.

He admires literary critic Northrop Frye, especially that unrealised project known as the 'Third Book'. He loves the fact that Frye's ambition for this 'Third Book' was for it to become no less than 'a symbolic guide to the entire universe'.

'It's friggin' incredible,' Ash says to you, knocking back another longneck of Little Creatures beer. The table is littered with bottles of this beer, which you have emptied between you in the course of an afternoon of speculation and boozy camaraderie. Beneath the table, Ash's moth-eaten-looking cat slinks around, rubbing its head on the corner posts. 'The work he envisioned contemplated the ways in which myth and metaphor are the keys to all verbal structure. What a concept, eh?'

The burnt end drops unnoticed from his cigarette, like a leprous appendage too rotten to stay attached to its body.

You can see he really loves this idea.

'Do tell,' you say, flippantly. Okay, he has taught you a lot, his approach just seems very scattergun. Tonight you're not really in the mood. To be honest, of late you can't absorb half of what he talks about.

You are somewhat adrift, have been for some time. And you're vague at the best of times. You would never have your own phone number. You would take a VCR in for repair or apply for a credit card. 'Your phone number sir?' they would ask. 'Oh—I have only just moved in'. You have been two years at your current address; you're just not any good at remembering, and can't organise yourself to carry the number in your wallet.

You leave Ash that night talking, as though into a void, of the neurobiological roots of cognition.

He is often willfully odd. He will show up wearing one of those knitted Nepalese hippy hats with the tassels, together with an immaculately appointed dress suit. In the streets of Petersham, he winks at you, as people cast odd looks our way. 'Confuses the fuck out of 'em'. He turns and makes a graceful bow to the nearest trolley-pushing housewife, sweeping the Nepalese hat off his head in a courtly arc. Startled and embarrassed, the housewife hurries on her way, shoving the trolley piled high with oranges in net bags, detergents, bottles of soft drinks, cans of cat food.

At this time, you see Ash whenever you can. He has on a pair of paint-spattered overalls he seems to have forgotten he was wearing. Alternatively, he has deliberately put them on intending to dine out tonight at Rock Pool or Tetsuya.

Ash thinks of his disparate interests as leading somewhere crucial. 'I'm honing my craft,' he says, when you periodically accuse him of being a jack-of-all-trades, master of none. This perfected craft he envisions is a Platonic ideal, hovering in some realm to which the 'real' is but a faint counterpart.

'What, the craft of being a pretentious wanker?'

'You'll see,' he says. 'I don't muck about.'

2. The Enigma Coast

You have known Ash since you were both children. At your place after school, 'Which sweet do you prefer?' your mother would ask, handing around the dish of cakes to you, then to Adrian. 'Every decision you make, every alternative you choose tells you a little about how you see the world'. It was a mantra she repeated often.

Adrian would snap up the chocolate brownies. You could never make up your mind, hesitating between the Greek sweet and the coconut slice. 'Adrian sees the world more clearly than you, David,' she said. She seemed to like his decisiveness about the cakes.

But when you ran out to play together, it was on the endless sandy dunes of the Enigma Coast, a place you thought you had invented out of sunshine and air. Running flags up on poles and staking out ground, doing Robinson Crusoe, playing at being lords of your own domain, you knew that Adrian was, at heart, as dreamy as you tended to be. And why not? The world was magic then.

The Enigma Coast was your imaginary country, your own private mythology. It was a place of long beaches with white sands, cool clear blue water lapping in and decorating the sand with a lace of white foam before the tide sucked it back. From the promontory that jutted out into the sea, you could look back to the mainland and see flocks of colourful birds rising and swooping away among the thickly clustered stands of trees. The sky was a brilliant blue embroidered with swathes of fluffy white clouds that drifted slowly towards a distant horizon. A glittering necklace of islands led out from it into the ocean. It was a place where dreams came true, a place where you could be happy.

Back from the Enigma Coast, you would go into your bedroom and play records, old scratchy 45's, on a little portable turntable your parents had bought for your birthday. You loved that song from the *Wizard of Oz*, the one Judy Garland sings. '*Somewhere over the rainbow, way up high, there's a land that I've heard of...*' It always seemed so sad, yet so appealing. Adrian liked it too, which is how you knew you were friends.

The only time your childhood happiness was marred was when your beloved pet rabbit died. One night, after a freezing winter cold snap, you came outside to find it lying in its cage, completely still. The one eye that you could see—it lay on its side—was dull and glassy. You pushed it, and its fur was cold, and it didn't move. Something rose in your throat, and you ran inside, filled with a strange new knowledge, a knowledge of death. Your mother dug a hole in the backyard and buried it.

After school, Ash had filled in a few years at university. You held a series of nondescript jobs while you tried to make a reputation as a novelist. During these years Ash started to investigate magick, but at the time you put it down to another flirtation, a fad on his part. Rumour had it that he had once attempted the Abramelin Operation but had freaked out.

You remember Ash in the early years standing in the doorway

of your room, rangy, energetic, restless, ghost of a smile on his face, anxious to be off to the next thing.

'I'm working, Ash.'

It's August, and you have been ill, but a rain of words is coming out of you, and you want to get them all, get their rhythm down, capture the dance of them. Often these days you wake at 3.15 in the morning, the room dark and silent, your head full of words that threaten to slip away unless you put them down. Stretching kinks from cramped limbs, you get out of bed, switch the light on and scribble furiously. Next morning, some of the phrases don't make sense—'dance of enigma'. You wonder what you were thinking or dreaming that made writing this seem so urgent.

'Never mind that,' he says disingenuously. 'There's an exhibition at the Object Gallery I want to check out. Jesus, Gunn, you can't work all the time. Come on, take a break'.

You let the urgency in his tone persuade you. Only slightly reluctantly, you hit SAVE and close your file. 'Bugger you. Let's go then'.

After his final exams, he claims to have led a party of students through the temples of Angkor, posing as a palaeobotanist. They looked at the headless statues of the Buddhas where the locals had decapitated the statues and sold the heads to the tourists. The young girls from Sydney University Archaeology and Asian art courses had been 'incredible—fuckin' amazing—so bright—so young,' Ash says. The traces of the devastation caused by the Khmer Rouge—people everywhere with no legs, the poverty in your face—were balanced out by the laughter of the children, their brown skin shining as they leapt into the waters of the Eastern Barai. (That claim at least is verifiable—once at the bookshop where you later work, you speak to a student who had been there with him. She remembers Ash as a bit of a sleazebag; the least amusing of his habits has always been a tendency to lech).

He now thinks of that period of his life as an immature phase. Back in Sydney, he takes up with a regular girlfriend, Sarah, and for a year or two works as an electrician until he does his back in one day on a building site, pulling long wires out of a roof he is standing on. 'Fucked that up,' he says ruefully to you afterwards.

Today he wears a faded blue zip-up jacket with a red and blue logo on the breast. His plastic-armed sunglasses perch atop his head and he presses his hands flat together when emphasising a point, his eyebrows raised so far the wrinkle on his brow seems to go all the way back to the short crop of his hair. In the Pharmakon Pharmacy, picking up headache remedies for your migraines, Ash claims 'I'm more interested in reconstruction than deconstruction'.

You have lunch in the suffocating confines of a restaurant whose idea of stylish décor is flocked red wallpaper. You have not talked since childhood of the Enigma Coast, but somehow the idea of mythical realms remains a passion for both of you. These days, you talk of Autotelia, Tiwanabu, Kadath, Twilight Beach, Cahokia, Egnaro, Amarna, Calabash, Sobratha.

At another table a man says to a woman 'but obviously the more money we pay off, the easier it would be for us in the future'. The smell of chili from the laksa he is eating seems to fill the whole room.

You are constantly trying to shape your world, to make it assume some meaningful form. But what makes you think you can do so, when daily your aspirations are smothered by the unspoken accommodations you make—we all make—with the world?

3. The Forties

In your forties, you find yourself wishing your life was like this:

You have the perfect partner, who gives you the support you need and accepts exactly what you have to give. Your finances are in order. Your stories are being published regularly and meeting with a favourable critical response. You always feel well and full of energy; things fall into place and you easily accomplish all your goals. Life throws up new challenges continually, but they are challenges you enjoy meeting. You live in a good neighbourhood and want for nothing. Friends are loyal to you. At social events you are full of an easy charm, leaving people to think, 'I'm so glad I met him'.

Instead, it is like this:

It's July in Bardwell Park. You have almost given up literary aspirations and you fill in your days doing data entry in anonymous offices, sometimes interspersed with bookshop work. Expert in several subjects which have taken you years to master, you nevertheless think: 'So what—I can't boil an egg'. You suffer from chronic tension headaches that make your days a misery, and spikes of migraine that make the tension headaches pale into insignificance by comparison. Your credit card is maxed out. You've had the odd lover, but nothing that's lasted. You can't seem to publish a book review, let alone the work of art that you felt was in you ten years previously.

You're at lunch in the atrium of the Food Court at the Broadway Youth Hostel. Above a multitiered fountain of greenish copper, surrounded by the bright glossy foliage of long leaved plants, a skylight opens onto the sky. Directly beneath the skylight is a painted frieze of fluffy white clouds in a blue sky, which always puts you in mind of the Enigma Coast.

Most evenings you watch video movies so formulaic they

sometimes end without you being able to remember what they were about. Or you try to sort out the eternal clutter of your life, like that song by the Church, struggling like a fool with your junk and your jewels, before giving up and falling into bed in a kind of enervated stupor.

You play judo once a week to relieve the boredom of working in the city. Carefully folding up your *gi* after the training, you walk outside to see daylight fading, like good intentions.

4. Svetlana

Such is the salient paradox of being human, that moment-to-moment, our lives move from the expected to the unexpected.

You first see her when she comes into the bookshop, wearing a skirt with a loose-fitting flowered blouse. She has just a touch of colour in her pale cheeks, and her blondish hair, lightly streaked with orangey-red, is a little tousled.

She has been a researcher at the Tbilisi University Press, exploring the origins of Indo-European languages. Do you have in stock any books which would illuminate whether they originate north of the Baltic Sea, or around the North Sea coasts?

'Over this way' you say, delighted to speak to someone not criminally brainless when it comes to books. *'Elegant',* you think. While you point ahead to the shelves where the range of language books—actually far too limited to answer her specialised query—are displayed, you gaze after her, seeing how the soft curve of her naked back and shoulders would take the corresponding curve of your caressing hand. You find yourself thinking: *if her head were cradled in my arms, what shape would our bodies make on the bed's white linen? What seacoasts, what inlets and mountain ranges would they trace?*

You immediately ask her out for coffee. Over flat white with two sugars (you) and short black without (her), you learn she was born and has lived most of her life in Kanesh, the modern Turkish city of Kultepe, and that she loves the languages cognate with Hittite—Luwian, Palaic. She talks passionately of proto-languages and needs little encouragement to speak of her favourite speciality, Mitannian Indo-Iranian. In your mug, a swirl of milk resembles a chain of islands in a dark brown sea.

'There is every reason,' she tells you, in slightly too formal English, 'for thinking that the original home of the Indo-Europeans is the place where wheeled vehicles were invented and where barley and grapes were first cultivated'. This place she refers to as 'Hither Asia' by which she meant Asia Minor—Northern Mesopotamia.

'Do tell,' you say, out of habit. Then you say something else, something that makes her laugh, and she sets her head slightly on one side, looking at you with assessment, appreciation. In that moment, there, over bad coffee, you are captured.

You want her badly. Leaning forward, you take her hand. 'Learn lost languages with me'.

To your surprise, she doesn't draw her hand away, but returns the gentle pressure. 'Da'.

Not long after that, you move in together. She has a teaching post at Sydney University and briefly, your life seems to flower. Everything seems endless, each day full of promise.

In Bardwell Valley, the winter evenings are still and quiet. The stars are unblinkingly hard against a clear sky the colour of dark blue silk. Gum trees raise dark boughs to an occasional red light traversing the vast expanse over the valley: incoming small aircraft bound for Mascot. When everything is so lucid, you don't stop to consider the incalculable consequences of small actions.

Sometimes when you make love, she sings softly some meters from an old Hittite song:

Tkani nesy, Tkani nesy
Prinesi, pridi
(The dress of Nesa,
the dress of Nesa,
Put it on me, put it on me)

You love her singing to you. She is half-sitting, half-lying, leaning on one elbow. Streetlights run long fingers in through the window and stroke the wall above the bed. She raises one knee slightly and her thighs part to allow you entrance. You clasp her waist, drawing her to you, and as you fit together, the light in the room is suffused with a soft glow as though the universe is pleased with you, with the precise curve of your limbs, with the sounds you make, with the tang and musk of love that hovers in the air, with the scent of sweaty sheets and the way you touch her, your right foot caressing the instep of her left, your eyes drinking up the look in hers.

What unique terrains you make, like a union of two countries that have decided they belong together. Your fingers trace the curve of her shoulder down to the hollow of her elbow, along the delicate inside of her wrist with its faint blue tracery of veins, and into the lined ways of her palm, a secret country all unto itself. You hold her and whisper in her ear, which reminds you of a shell found on the sands of the Enigma Coast, 'I want to take you there ...'

In the cool of the evening you walk along the harbour shore, serene and silent, drinking in the distance, bathing quietly in the rightness of it all. A red triangle of light on the bridge shines over moored boats that cluster in-shore. Moonlight glimmers on the water near a pylon.

She talks in glissando phrases of the importance of glottalized consonants to the identification of the original home of the Indo-

Europeans, but once she starts discussing old Armenian and proto-Iranian she loses you. Instead, you joke about being full of wine and Mexican food.

You make love often in those early days, the fragility of the bond between you a large part of its beauty, rather than the omen it would later seem. You take her out, say to the party of a friend from work. At the yacht club the women all wear boat shoes, jeans and pearls. The men all wear polo tops and are braying about stock options. You look at each other and simultaneously burst out laughing.

Ten minutes later, in a taxi home, you are fumbling at each other's clothes like anxious adolescents. Flinging open the front door, you both stagger to the bed, strewing clothes to the four winds. Your mouths close on each other; she has the sweetest breath. Holding each other is exhilarating. 'Da, da ... like that ... ' At the urgent crest of things, 'Oh, that's beautiful' she says, and 'Push up, push up'.

Afterwards, as she lies on her stomach, you kissing her gently from the nape of her neck to that seductive little indentation that comes at the base of the spine, you feel as though you have fallen into each other, that everything else is outside the ambit of a world shared only by the two of you.

When you regard this piece of the past from the distant shores where you now stand, how brightly unreal it all seems.

5. Ash the Esotericist

You don't see Ash so often in this period. You know vaguely that he has joined some shadowy sodality, for he has dropped dark hints about working rituals with them. Lately he has not so much abdicated his earlier interests as used them in the service of magick.

When you do see him, he has acquired a haunted, but confused air, as if he is perpetually on the verge of discovering something, but has forgotten what he is looking for. The makeshift bookshelves at his flat are built of old planks hastily piled up with, at the interstices, mud-coloured bricks salvaged from a roadside construction site. They accommodate his ever-burgeoning esoteric collection; erudite volumes by Crowley and Blavatsky shoved in indiscriminately beside the most sensational potboiling paperbacks by the likes of Cheiro and Zolar.

As a child, he tells you in a rare confessional moment, he had tried to find the end of a rainbow. He had walked for what seemed like hours, only to discover that the rainbow constantly eluded him; it was always just in the next street, or over the next hill. Then, as steam rose off the wet grass, the rainbow had disappeared. He had stumped home dispiritedly. He hadn't managed to find it this time, but he knew the treasure at the rainbow's end was there. Oh, it was there, he only had to get there quickly enough when the rainbow appeared again.

Just as you decide to introduce Svetlana to Ash, he rings to say he's broken up with Sarah.

You meet outside the shopping complex bordering on Glebe Point Rd. The long ramp leading from the shopping centre is surrounded by faux-surrealist sculptures—huge gantries of rusting iron pierced by a couple of archways in which sit a colourful ceramic jug, some jolly figures with blue hair and a yellow hat. Someone's idea of urban sculpture, of bringing art to the impoverished urban masses.

Ash, his right hand bandaged, looks used up.

'Want to get something to eat?' you ask, to hide your embarrassment.

'Fuckin' A,' says Ash.

Svetlana screws up her face.

At Badde Manors, over foccacias, he says he's fed up. In the fight with Sarah, the telephone has been pulled out of the wall. 'What really pissed me off was that she threw some of my stuff out in the street'. He had picked up a broken vase: 'Cut my hands to lace'. He rubs his temple in a characteristic gesture.

This whinging seems shallow for Ash, but you don't take his depression too seriously. After all, you're not yet in retreat from a failed relationship. But today is a sign of things to come. Svetlana can't stand him, and this is one of the wedges that starts to creep in between you.

A week or so later, Ash phones up to tell you he's going to perform an important evocation, and he wants you there. You hesitate. The bitter fact is that Ash now seems to have lost his taste, to have, finally, no criteria for distinguishing between the dross and the gold of his magical interests.

You have spent all day feeling on the verge of migraine, shielding your eyes from the glare that flashes up from the hot streets, cringing in half-dread, half-expectation that your vision's edges will begin to flicker into the blinding aura of shimmering white light edged with rainbow colours that typically prefigures the headaches themselves. Sometimes when the aura has set in with a vengeance, and your palms have begun to sweat as though with tropical heat, you think you can recognise in those kaleidoscopic flashes of colour the startled flutter of exotic birds on the Enigma Coast. The bright shimmer of the migraine haze reminds you of the sun glinting off the water there, blinding in its brilliance.

'Come on, Gunn. I need you for this.'

'Imagine that!' Reluctantly, you agree to go over there, grabbing your camera on the way out the door.

On the wall outside Ash's door, with its inconspicuous buzzer, is a graffito superbly unselfconscious in its illiteracy: '*Brenda and Rebecca are ledgens'*. You let yourself in and climb the dim stairs. Through the half-unlatched door of the downstairs flat leaks the sound of someone playing the wrenching industrial pop of Marilyn Manson.

Ash opens his door to admit you, before retreating to the centre of the room.

The whole room is dusty, and littered with rubbish—in one corner, a dingy mattress is swathed with clothes, tangled up with the grubby varicoloured sheets. Candle-wax trails cross the floor and the bed itself. There is an overpowering smell of cheap frankincense and stale day-old cooking. A bookshelf in one corner brims with dog-eared copies of works on Qabalah and magic; a mirror reflects the room's chaotic contents. Several knives and a sword lean up against a wall and amongst the other litter shoved up against one wall you can pick out charcoals and a censer; incense sticks and beeswax candles, worn or burnt down to stubs; a drift of sheets of white paper covered in fine whorls and intense blotches of black ink, the residua of experiments with trance and automatism.

This stuff lies like a sea around the dark island of Ash, who looks marooned in its midst. He is swaddled in a dirty, wine-stained Tau-shaped white robe, made of a heavy wool quite unsuitable for Sydney's summer heat.

Ash's lachrymose face reminds you of a piece of damp cloth, so worn through by use that the original pattern has become obscure, and rubbed so thin that you feel a touch might cause it to fall to pieces. He resembles a patchy collage through which one can still glimpse his ability and youthful promise, simultaneously threaded and overlaid with the emblems of his own self-defeat.

He lights a cigarette, fingers trembling.

'Did you ever read Plotinus? The Enneads, you know. Great truth in those. Sticks out like dog's balls'.

Painful, unfinished business lies between you. The ash at the end of his forgotten cigarette grows tremulously longer. You wonder when it will spill and softly scatter onto the floor, though it would hardly be noticed if it did.

He casts vaguely about for an ashtray, lifting crack-spined books, like an ibis overturning old sandwich wrappings in Hyde Park in the hope of a bit of food. Not finding one, he stubs the remains of the cigarette out on the windowsill, which is already raddled with scorch marks. He drops the butt on the floor, regarding it for a moment as if wondering how it had gotten into his hand in the first place.

Some chalk has been used to draw on the bare boards of the floor, a double circle in which Hebrew and Enochian characters revolve. Immediately to one side of the circle is a small shrine consisting of a stele, adorned with Chinese candles and lion-dance ornaments.

A stack of Zip disks totters on the bookshelf. Picking up a few and shuffling disconsolately through them like cards in a poor hand, you note they are labelled in scrawly pencil *Watchtower Rituals, Zones of Power, Tunnels of Set*. Already on the edge of resentment, you fail to disguise your irritation.

'Do you really imagine this stuff is helping you?' you ask peevishly, dangling between your forefinger and thumb a Cheiro book with the same distaste you would a snotty handkerchief. 'Where do you think this is getting you, for Christ's sake?'

You glimpse yourself in the mirror. The upper eyelids drooping above the eye, the slight hollows at the outer orbits: too much staring at the ceiling in the middle of the night. (Things with Svetlana are becoming strained).

'Come on, Ash, this is stupid. Let's fuck off out, eh?'

'I'm going to *do* this evocation, so just *help* me, OK,' says Ash. The only help you offer him is to stay, instead of leaving immediately.

'What the hell are we evoking?'

'Use your imagination!' he says.

He begins to perform the Lesser Banishing Ritual, vibrating the Divine Names with a dolorous nasal quality that always makes you imagine his angels will appear clutching spray packs of Sinex to stop him.

After some time, at least half an hour you think—during which there are continual recondite gestures and intense theurgical vocalizing from Ash—the room is gradually suffused with a mucoid greyness that struggles feebly to either block out the light completely or to transmute itself into something more solid. The air pulses with writhing energy, begins to boil with flakes of something like spindrift. Your head throbs; you are unsure if the spatial dislocations that seem to be occurring are due to Ash's magic or what's in your own head. You look around wildly, affected despite yourself by this display of the occult power of apathy.

Suddenly, you are startled by the faint cries of a terrified child; the more surprising because the awful squalling seems to be in the same room, and you know no child is present. With a shock, you see that Ash's eyes have rolled back in his head. This frightens you, but the next moment you realise it is less a psychic possession than a kind of failure of spiritual concentration on Ash's part.

'Ash, for Christ's sake. What's happening here?'

Angrily, you shake him by the shoulders, and his eyes roll down again. The flickering air and the disturbing cries in the room trail away to an uneasy absence. You let go his shoulders and he sags back against the wall, exhausted.

Evening has settled in outside the window. Apparently the ritual has failed. The whole thing seems pathetically inadequate. You turn to leave.

In the photo of him you took that day, Ash crouches in the Goetic circle, attempting to light the incense with a nearly expired lighter that kept burning his fingers. His expression is unreadable—faintly uncertain, as though he has lost his nerve.

The day after the ritual, Ash tells you he's lost his confidence. All that night you toss uneasily on the bed, turning on the spit of your own misgivings, fears, and regrets. You've crossed the border into sleep, but the checkpoint guards have given you a hard time and the country you've reached is inhabited by people that don't seem to speak your language.

6. Ash's Descent

Sometimes you watch someone live their life as if they're in a slow motion fall, as though they've jumped out a window but haven't yet hit the ground. You watch their body twist and turn in the wind of events, spiralling slowly; and you want to be able to help them back to safe ground, but the leap they've taken is irrevocable.

Ash has his Psychogeography of the city, a complex of paths that he treads on his daily wanderings, as you have yours, as we all do. It doesn't seem to you to be getting him anywhere. He disappears for protracted periods. When you do see him, he has gone from being outlandish to being almost thuggish, and you are almost uneasy at being seen out with him.

One afternoon, as you tramp the streets of Enmore together, someone perfectly harmless bumps into Ash.

'Am I fuckin' invisible to you?' he demands, wheeling on her. She looks shocked but says nothing.

'Oblivious bitch!' he yells at her retreating form. People turn their heads to look at you.

You are tempted to remind him of Seneca's view of anger—that if we expect things to go wrong we'll be less upset when they do—but Ash is fully into his riled up state.

'Bloody stupid bitch!' he complains; but he is already looking in a shop window, eye caught by a shiny object on display there.

One morning you turn on the TV and watch a flooded Europe, houses and buildings destroyed, wide plains of churning grey water engulfing whole villages and towns, trees fallen, cars swept away. In the old city of Prague, they are blowing up boats that have come adrift from their moorings, sinking them so they will not cause further damage to already damaged bridges. You think of Ash as a bit like one of these boats, carried by the uncontrollable flood of his desires towards who knows what destruction downriver.

That November, you hear that Ash has suffered a nervous breakdown and been admitted to the Royal Prince Alfred Hospital.

You speak to Svetlana about it. You know she doesn't get on with him, but he is your friend.

'I thought we could visit Ash in the hospital,' you say.

There is a silence. She stares past you, her lips compressed. She doesn't have to say, 'I don't give a stuff about that bastard'; you can read it on her face.

In the end you go on your own. At the HK Ward Gymnasium, a sole runner does circuits, lap after lap, his running shoes slapping on the wooden floor. The glare of the sodium lamps in the car park outside the Disorders Unit throws an orangey aura around various patients on the verandah: a large, crop-headed girl in a white-t-shirt chats to a man with a bluish, badly-drawn tattoo on his left wrist.

Inside, near a big painted poster of sunflowers that has been sticky-taped to a pillar, an elderly couple supports a man whose eyes are screwed up in pain. At the coffee urn in the ward lounge, a woman with a bandaged head is struggling to get a plastic cup out of the urn's holder. A dark-haired girl with circles under her eyes shuffles in socks around the ward.

You hear Ash singing from the corridor. Following the sound, you find two or three guys with guitar and harmonicas playing a plodding twelve-bar blues. Ash, leaning in the doorway like a big scarecrow, is ad-libbing over the top. You watch him for a while trying to scramble back up the side of various pits he's dug for himself, and then go in to spend some time.

He is more closed in than you have ever seen him. His body seems folded into itself, like a despairingly clenched fist, his whole stance tense with pathetic and inexpressible loss.

'Sarah used to ask me what colours she should wear, what I liked to see her in' he says, fumbling through his pockets for a fag. 'I always said I couldn't advise her, that I didn't know about that sort of thing. I could have told her to wear green—it would have gone with her eyes.'

The regret in his voice is the first genuine human feeling you've heard from him for years. He stares down at his shoes as though in their scuffed, peeling leather he might scry some meaning in this dismal turn of events.

This time, despite your good intentions, you give him no help. It seems pointless. You don't know what he had hoped the ritual could give him, but he doesn't seem too disappointed. You stand up.

There is an awkward silence, broken only by the sound of a distant siren on the main road. Ash looks at you. He waves vaguely at the kitchen, lighting up the cigarette.

'There's some ... Chinese tea in there I think. You could make us a cup.' He employs the wheedling tone he usually reserves for coaxing in his pet cat.

It is, for him, a propitiatory gesture. There is another awkward pause while you consider making one last-ditch effort to help him out. But his next sentence changes your mind.

'You look like a bloody beagle with those pouches under your eyes. Why don't you cheer up you bastard?' His expression is somewhere between mockery and pleading.

It's the last straw. Though you dimly know that faintly insulting vitriol is increasingly his only way of making contact, you choose to detach his suddenly clinging fingers from your wrist and let him drop into the abyss, alone.

'Fuck off, Ash. You've got what you wanted. It's not too late for me.'

You push him back against the wall and stumble towards the door. Then you are out on the street in a drizzling rain without remembering making your way through the ward lounge.

What you don't want to face is that Ash and you are like one another, self and shadow.

7. The Limits of the World

The day you see Svetlana for the last time, it is the turning of the year. All summer the sky has flung its harsh light through the streets and houses of the neighbourhood, kids in sweatshirts wearing Raiders caps backwards shouting up and down the street on skateboards and bicycles.

Now June has set in like a pestilence. Under a still grey sky, trees bow their silent branches before a desultory breeze. The cars and the kids seem to have disappeared, and the mornings are chill with the threat of autumn and emptiness.

That morning you ask her if she wants to go to a film later.

'No, I don't want to'.

You are quiet for a while.

'See you after work then'.

That evening you come home to find a small piece of notepaper on the table in the living room. You can smell soap-powder and the curious musty odour of cupboards long unopened.

As you pick up the note with one hand, your other hand goes nerveless and your satchel drops to the carpet, spilling its contents: a diary, a dog-eared copy of *Street of Crocodiles,* some headache tablets in a plastic sheet.

Svetlana has written you a letter, which reads:

'Imagine this. Life without you. Life without any of this. In fact, *life*. Forgive me, but please don't try to find me'

All her things, what few of them there were, are gone. You crumple into the nearest chair, as darkness seeps into the afternoon like a stain.

You know, of course, that lovers are apt to come and go. They appear at twilight like beacons out of the fog, and they depart at midnight with your heart tucked under their arm. You know that. But Svetlana was the woman you had dreamed of in the secret reaches of your heart, and you take it hard.

You sit for a long time in the lounge room, trying your best to imagine where she might have gone. You feel as though you have been smashed in the face with a brick. Eventually a sound comes from somewhere deep within you, an agonised moan you hope you never have to hear yourself make again.

In your journal, you will later write: 'My arms went out, but she wasn't there to come into them anymore. For me, it is an immeasurable loss.'

You pace the limits of your world, shocked at the prospect of having to be on your own again. You spend months like a blind man, just inching your way. You examine in the minutest detail what you did, what you could have done differently. Like a kid with a dead rabbit, poking it, prodding it, thinking it might come back to life if you push it around for long enough.

Slowly, so slowly, it dawns on you that none of this makes any difference. You were together, now the season has turned, the borders have been redrawn. Even if she's still physically in Australia, she is gone, withdrawn again into her own mysterious country. You don't bother to phone the university; after all, she left of her own accord, there's no sense trying to track her down.

Someone lets slip in conversation that a friend who took some of her classes has heard she's returned to Europe. Other friends say of Svetlana. 'You will forget her'. You stare at them. They don't know anything.

Your dislike for this world deepens into a kind of wounded savagery. You are shipwrecked, high and dry, and at the same time afraid of drowning in oceans of night. You are trying to mount a salvage operation on your own life, but it seems increasingly useless. Of your hopes, there seems little left but wind and fading light.

At *randori* with your regular judo partner, you go for a *tomoenage* but don't quite manage it. You get up off your back. You opponent is dragging on the lapels of your *gi,* as if intent on simply dragging you to the ground with dead weight, a sloppy technique you have always despised. In the dance of the *randori,* hands seeking purchase, feet scuffing on the white mats, you are momentarily alive.

You shove your opponent off balance with a well-placed backward leg sweep that takes his right leg from under him. His right arm goes out as he goes down, breaking fall with a flat slam that sends dull echoes through the half-full *judoka*. Then you are at his throat with a needlessly vicious hold-down that gives you the victory.

Standing, you bow each to each, keeping the code. Your opponent rubs his throat. You have won; but to yourself, lost in the midst of a vast personal transition, you reek of defeat.

8. Enigma Coast 2

Memory's a patchwork coat, scenes here, snatches there, a laugh, the sweet essence of a kiss, the way the light fell when you first saw her, the sound of yourself coming, the tautness in your gut that time you had to speak unpleasant truths. More patches than original coat after a while, memory.

You can still see Svetlana. Once, cutting up the carrots for the soup, she made some quick deft strokes with the kitchen knife. You watched her from slightly to one side as she tucked back behind her ear a loose wisp of hair. She looked strong and capable, and simultaneously vulnerable. This is how you'll remember her, you think, twenty years from now: her incomparable face shelled in light in a kitchen on a blustery, grey day.

One day, without warning, a postcard arrives. The postage stamp, which depicts a glittering necklace of islands in a blue sea, overprinted by a fuzzy and only partly readable date stamp, is marked 'Enigma Coast'. Turning it over, you read:

'Imagine this, if you can.—A.'

Ash has made it. Despite his blundering, his breakdown, he has stumbled through. So it is possible after all! How did he do it?

Suddenly you notice that the letters of the word *imagine*, arranged differently, make the phrase *I, Enigma*. You are on to something! *My God*, you think, *why didn't I ever notice this before?*

'Use your imagination,' he said once.

You head for Ash's flat. The streets of Marrickville seem choked with heat and lassitude, the houses etiolated and vacant-looking. The sluggish air crawls wearily over the pavements like a stray dog, nosing amidst old chip packets and rattling crushed thickshake containers.

The door to Ash's flat is unlocked, and you burst in, panting.

The room is more madly chaotic than before, an *omnium gatherum* of artefacts in disarray. Even the makeshift bookcase has tumbled down, spilling its contents—Weiser paperbacks on Tarot, loose-leaved notebooks full of occult formulae, vials of essential oils—like a rubble-strewn fiord of utterly random secret wisdom.

A copy of Greil Marcus's *Dustbin of History* is lying open on the desk. A phrase has been highlighted in yellow fluorescent marker pen: *'Defeated, revolution turns to magic'*.

Looking around desperately, you notice for the first time how many things in Ash's room have *Imagine* in the title—a copy of *Imagination Dead Imagine* by Samuel Beckett, a copy of John Lennon's *Imagine* album. A light goes on in your head, and you leave without touching anything, thinking, 'this could be a key'.

Over the next few weeks, you haunt libraries, search the Net, for references to Enigma. Nothing relevant to your search reveals itself. You realise the clues are more—well, enigmatic. You read dozens of books that have *enigma* in the title—books about the cracking of the wartime code, and so on. They don't help.

The Enigma Coast eludes you. At Bardwell Park station, the flags above the RSL Club flap morosely. You finger, shaking, the lines of streets in street directories; you find significance in certain alignments of painted lines in the roads around Sydney University, in the adjacency of certain junctions and confluences. You wander stretches of railway tracks, searching for some way in which their trail could lead to the goal.

Nothing.

Two years later, you are sitting in a café in Soho. You have fetched up here via a 'holiday' in Isfahan, a long spell of inactivity in Barcelona (where you became afraid you were going to think yourself to death), and a longer spell of listless indifference in East London.

In the mornings when you get up, locked into a hostile self-abnegation, you avoid the mirror's pitiless gaze, its treacherous infinite regressions, and shrug on whatever clothes are lying crumpled across the foot of the bed. You check your email, which forwards what few messages you receive via an anonymous remailer. You decide to go out.

A flying V makes its way along the pavement—a woman in a yellow anorak and her two children, woman leading, the two little girls trailing behind at the extremities of each of her arms. You follow them, seeing some hidden meaning in their postures, in the invisible trails they leave behind them. Two blocks along, the woman turns and yells at you to go away, now pushing her children on protectively ahead of her.

Finding yourself in Foyle's bookshop, unsure of how you got here or how long you've been roaming the streets, you catch a glimpse of a travel guide being replaced in its shelf by a tourist couple. They wear bulging new Caribee backpacks, jungle green with yellow ties attached to the numerous large silver zip-tags.

Squeezing past the travellers, you snatch up the guide, whose cover blazes its title: *Lonely Planet Guide—Enigma Coast*. Shaking, you leaf through the pages. On p. 141, there is a photo of a man leading a party up a steep incline, his face partly shadowed by a broad brimmed hat. It looks like Ash! But then you can't be sure. In something resembling panic, you drop the guide on the floor and run out.

When you return minutes later, realising you need to buy the guide, it's nowhere to be found, and does not appear on the Lonely Planet catalogue or the Global CDROM database when you ask the bookseller to help.

A couple of weeks later, you are on an impulsive plane trip to Dresden, thinking, God knows why, that you could help in the restoration of the artworks damaged in the floods. Turning the page of the in-flight magazine, you are confronted with an article: 'Joys of the Enigma Coast' by Adrian Ash.

It's all there—the waving palm fronds, the white sands, all described with the turns of phrase favoured by Ash himself. This time you keep the magazine, stuffing it into your travel bag. You check the copy in the seatback next to yours, and the article does not appear there. Shit! Perplexed, you pull the copy out of your bag again, leafing through—the article is gone, as though it were never there.

In the hotel in Dresden, staring out the window, you nervously watch the city gather, watch it draw itself up like some great dumb beast stirring restlessly in a half-sleep, and you think of Ash, and of Svetlana. You glimpse yourself in the reflection on the window's inside—gaunt, pale, with dark circles under the eyes. You have tried to become absorbed in the restoration work, but involvement, like a solution to Enigma, eludes you.

Sitting on the edge of the bed, you stare at the wall. The air of defeat you carry has been with you so long it is almost a badge of honour. You know that the way to get on with life is to find new doors and step through them. Why then do you insist on picking over the bones of the relationship, pulling them out of the ash to re-examine their charred surfaces? More restless nights follow, interspersed with renewed bouts of wandering the streets.

In elliptical conversations in bars, at bus shelters, whispering strangers discuss the Enigma Coast. A man with dark eyebrows and a brown-skinned complexion leans close to a young man in a blue chenille pullover, with the haircut favoured by such young men—very short around the back and sides but sticking up like a cockatoo's comb on the top. The young man has removed his bug-like earphones to listen to what the old man is saying. You strain to catch it and random phrases drift across to you—did he just say, 'the sunlight there is never cold'? But as you focus on the conversation, the topic has already changed.

Time passes. You are faintly conscious that the years of your life are slipping by too fast; yet at the same time, each hour of each day inches forward with agonising slowness.

9. Over the Rainbow

One day, without realising how you got there, you are blundering about on a refuge island at a crux of streets near Trafalgar Square. Your face upturned towards the sky, you are stretching towards it, sure you can reach the fluffy white clouds that drift towards the distant horizon. You wander into the path of oncoming traffic, still gazing up. Unrecognisable sounds are coming out of your mouth. Shoals of traffic are banked around you, angry drivers honking their horns.

After a while, you are dimly aware that someone is leading you away by the shoulder. As they do so, you hear yourself singing, with a catch in your voice, over and over again, 'Happy little bluebirds. If they can ... happy little bluebirds'.

Or, if you preferred, it could end like this:

Svetlana is back in Kultepe, continuing her studies. She hasn't thought of you since the day she left you. One day, marking up notes on a lecture to be delivered, she receives a postcard. In the grey indeterminate light of her room, she can faintly make out the partly obliterated postmark:

'Enigma Coast'.

Carefully turning the card over, she reads—a tingle of fear passing up her spine—in handwriting she recognises as yours:

'I made it. Can you IMAGINE what it's like to be here at last?'

Which ending do you prefer? This, as my mother would have said, will tell you a little more about how you see the world.

Leigh BLACKMORE (b. 1959) writer, editor, manuscript assessor and occultist, lives in Wollongong, Australia with his two partners, several cats, and a library of 15,000 volumes. His name is 'now synonymous with Australian horror' (*Melbourne Univ Press Encyc of Science Fiction and Fantasy*). He published & edited (with B.J. Stevens & Chris G.C. Sequeira) *Terror Australis: The Australian Horror & Fantasy Magazine* (1987-92) and edited *Terror Australis: Best Australian Horror* (Hodder & Stoughton Australia, 1993). His weird fiction has also appeared in *Agog! Fantastic Fiction*. Leigh considers Douglas Rushkoff's 'media virus' a concept close to identical to Richard Dawkins' 'meme' and that both these writers were beaten to the punch by William S Burroughs' concept of 'language as virus'; which is also a proof of the Ecclesiastes theorem.

EXTERMINATOR REX

ADAM BROWNE

ONIGHT I SPEAK OF BIOWULF. Famed was this Biowulf—one of
a kind, mighty exterminator of pests. Close your eyes and
see him: kill-ready, death-suited, warrior-proud, his demolition
derby firmly atop his head as he fared forth in his viral
nightmobile, on errand for the Metropolitan Board of Works,
Municipal AdminDistrict B.

Now: a ping in Biowulf's third eye—a midbrain deep briefing
from the Board. Mindblooming dataflowers opened inside him:
pollen-pixel flickertexts, blink links, data-strata, diagrammatic
inscapes.

Telling him about dinosaurs.

The city suffered an embarrassment of monsters, dinosaurs
infesting the streets like dragons loosed from some unhallowed
howling heraldry.

It was his task, tonight, to exterminate them.

He turned right—his death-drunk nightmobile travelling
south along Dorsal Street, heading for the Central Sewage
Works. An edifice with a millennial timecleft at its heart. A
wormhole eight metres wide and sixty-three million years long,
sluicing cityfilth niagras into reptiled prehistory. All the city's
sewers were patched into this timehole, ridding its waste into
the gone and forgotten past.

But recently there had been feedback, balefire and backflow,
dinosaurs climbing their way back up the line. Toothy horrors
up from the Cretaceous, monsters dragged wrathful from cosy
fossil doze, rising like bloody vengeance from antiquity ...

Now Biowulf's nightmobile came to the city's edge, where
stood the sewage works, a gothic aspiration of shit-misty crags
and thunder and plumbing thrumming with outgoutings of
incontinent continents.

Biowulf listened; heard roars; smiled.

Here be monsters.

He pressed down on a cartilaginous accelerator pedal,

through the entranceway and into curdled gloom. Onward he drove in his doughty vehicle, its cabin a single titanic influenza virus cultured to ten billion times its natural size. And within, our hero soundly sat, like a complement of DNA afloat in salutary plasm. Safe as a pope inside the nucleoprotein hull—crystalline, polygonal, impregnable. It was his armour and his armoury and his warlike joytoy: as well would he leave his skin as leave his nightmobile. (What with his battlescars and his wormy rots, his jackpoints and his gut-ducts and his pain-stained braindrains, Biowulf had little of skin in any case—he was a man who was less a man in appearance than some flayed foetal ratroach, bobbling heroically in his lemon yellowjuices, grinning his misty murderer's grin.)

A man happy in his job, happily he braved the building's dark. Onward he drove, towards the core. Telltale timeflickers stippled the corners of his eyes—bleedthrough from nearing wormhole. Shadows of the past swifted through the cathedral-gloom, and growths rose about him: stands of Mesozoic seed-fern, cycads, mighty ginkgoes heavy with luminous fruit; a festive floral gleam lighting Biowulf's way as moss-paved flooring ramped steadily down.

Among the lower green, dinosaurs roamed and roared.

Not at all the dullskinned lumberers of paleontologists' imaginings, these were stately beasts, joyful and gem-glorious. Biowulf gazed a moment at them, these filigreed stegosaurs with cloisonné horns, these pastel brontosauri with skins of jaspered bronze, these allosaurs bound in wounden gold. Sweet they were, and featly jeweled, moving slow as summer through the Eden-green.

Biowulf killed them all. With zinzulating buzzgun, he spilled their day-glo gore, and moved on.

He came next to a tender scene: a pair of silver iguanodons, a sterling couple tending a sacred onyx clutch of Fabergé eggs. It was a nativity of surpassing lovingkindness, a sight to delight any heart ... But Biowulf, unburdened with heart, smote monster and monstress both, nor did he spare their eggs (fine china eggshells exploding to expose infant icons of shattered silver innocence).

Then farther on he fared, deeper yet into the sewage works, rich with rots and loud with dino-cries. Through it all Biowulf drove, through drunken rum-jungles where agate flowers purred in perfumed throats, the wormhole closer than ever now, time beginning to slick and slip and splinter. In vaulted, vine-slung vastness, timeshadows lurched and hurtled.

Now he came to the core of the building, wherein hummed the wormhole, a whippery swizzle of difficult light. He did not hesitate, but sped forward into that forever-squirm, steering left into tumbled yesterdays, into the before days, quickening down through centuries, millennia slewing blue ... until with a jounce and a jolt the nightmobile's wheels found purchase on the past; and Biowulf burst baleful from the wormhole's end.

He was in a palace wrought of living green.

A vegetable Versailles braided bright with limb and leaf, coffered ceilings flashing with fretworks of ivied delicacy, bower-halls, muse-kissed, gabled wide with treeforks, hung with fungal candelabra beaming bioluminous blue.

Biowulf's eyes widened, for before him stood the emperor of this palace. The battle-famed sun-king; the mammal-hater, the lonely roamer.

The warwolf-horrid Tyrannosaur.

It was a bullioned godlizard, its hide an acreage of gold lamé. And its eyes: skyblue chased with green, keen and gleaming—moonstruck Aztec facets, pupils fixed upon the intruder.

Then!—a double roar of throat and motor!—Biowulf and Tyrannosaur both faring forth!—the man's guns shouting their butcherly hate, spewing murder-fire!—exterminator riddling the lizard with a wealth of missiles!

A new jungle leapt up, Autumn-coloured, flowing fire-flowers and towering flametrees and champignon mushroom-clouds crackling among the undergrowth. Flames billowed, braiding skyward in spiralling smoke, parting at last to reveal—

—the Tyrannosaur, blithe, its golden hide unharmed.

With insolent grin, again the brute sought battle. It flew forward to hasten the hot encounter, sieging Biowulf with snickersnee of tooth and claw! Our warrior was sore beset, never had he faced such a foe, the gilded talons bearing upon him a throng of sorrows. High heaved his breast, for he feared his strength would soon diminish.

But still the affray continued, bearing the enemies hither, thither, yon into great concourses of looking-glass blooms—arcaded mirror-halls steeped in reek-of-fight, reflecting epic enmity to infinity—a thousand thousand Tyrannosaurs making battle with a thousand thousand grim and bloodied Biowulfs.

In a thousand thousand nightmobiles.

Gallant nightmobile—it was a battle-bold vessel, a right crafty craft, its wetware steeped in ancient viral voodoos. And even as Biowulf fought and drove and strove (snapping off a crump of dumdums, veering left, vectoring right), he felt a ... *change* in the vehicle about him. A stirring in its juices. What was this? he wondered (his darling gunclusters thumpering and thundering, the monster lashing out with its talented fangs). Was it fatigue? Was it his distress causing these feelings all around and within?—this coming-of-age pleasure-pain jazzing him from cods to crown; this sudden alien sex-heat (the Tyrannosaur hewing his left fender, Biowulf replying with cannonspasms from worthy gunsystems)—this wiggly deliciosity and plasmic spasming with everything jerk-dissolving into spin-sticky bliss.

Then the virus (plasmachinery mucilaginously chugging) began to replicate.

Once, and then again, and ever and exponentially again ...

And then the Tyrannosaur howled with the paleontological equivalent of dismay, for there before it was a sudden throng. The forest was replete: a hundred, a thousand—a thousand thousand virusdaughters. A thousand thousand nightmobiles—and (wonder weird to see) a crisp new Biowulf in every one. Grinning like merry murder, a legion of Biowulfs sounding a chorus of gunmuzzle thunder, lusty artillery singing war-song wild.

Until at last the Tyrannosaur was hewn and spent with struggle, wounds like bloody hallmarks in its gilt skin. Down it fell, tumbled to the ground by boisterous pain, and sent abject to realms of death.

Glory to the exterminators!

Glorying, away they drove, laughing as their grisly gun-horde carolled triumphant—bringing death everlasting to the Cretaceous.

Bearing swift extinction to genus *Dinosaurus.*

Then they turned homeward, job well done. Back through the wormhole, borne forward over time's billows, through happy Dopplered dapples. On, through the sewage works, out and north along Dorsal Street. Through ways low and high, onward through the honeycoloured city canyons of Municipal AdminDistrict B.

An embarrassment of Biowulfs, rising like bloody vengeance from antiquity ... A thousand thousand Biowulfs kill-ready, death-suited, warrior-proud; teeming closer—a plague of foetid foetal ratroach men virusing through our streets.

And now, as they come clamouring at our doors, I ask you: who will exterminate the exterminators now their red-wet task is done?

Adam Browne lives in Melbourne, Australia, with his wife Julie Turner, also a writer, and their yet-to-be-born baby Harriet, due in April 2006. He has had numerous stories published in Australia and the US, as well as being translated into Polish for publication in *Nowa Fantastyka*. He has been shortlisted a number of times for the Aurealis Award best Australian short sf, and won it in 2001 for his story 'The Weatherboard Spaceship'. He also writes short screenplays: *Virus*, starring Kerry Armstrong and directed by Stephen Amis, was produced in 2005, and *Space Operetta*, directed by Adam Duncan, will begin production in 2006. http://mc2.vicnet.net.au/home/adamb/web/index.html

Storm in a Chandelier

TRACEY ROLFE

BELLANCA DYNOPOLOUS LEANED HER ELBOWS on the table and stared through the open window, past the flowering sprays of jasmine at the white-capped sea below. The waves, caught smashing upon the shore, were silent, still. Where water met rock, a frozen spray of white foam fountained into the air.

She sipped her cappuccino, savouring the hit of caffeine. The blue-and-white-check curtains distracted her from the view. 'Perhaps you should've painted the curtains open wider.'

Gelasius Dormond paused, forkful of moussaka halfway to his mouth. The curtains looked wide enough to him. 'Don't worry—when the paint dries you'll have air straight off the ocean; you'll hear the suck and swell of sea.' He swallowed his mouthful without chewing and rushed the fork back to his mouth. 'This is a great lunch. I always thought Yiayia made the best moussaka, but this ... this ...' His fork stabbed at air.

Above Bellanca, a spider wove a web around a fly. That would be another advantage of Gelasius's view: no insects. But the whole room seemed drab now against the masterpiece on the wall. 'You know,' Bellanca said, 'I was thinking the kitchen could do with a coat of paint. Do you think Con would be interested? I couldn't pay him much.'

'I'd belt him if I thought he'd charge you. Yeah, he'll do it for you, no worries. Better him doing that than this rock-climbing shit he's into at the moment.' He pushed his fork onto the empty plate, scraping at the last smears of white sauce. 'Jesus, I hate seeing my own kid waste his life on something as worthless as housepainting. He's never gonna get anywhere doing that. I mean where's the art? The craft?'

'You're hard on the boy. I've heard he's very good.'

'He's talented—I've seen it. But he's lazy. Housepainting's easy. Learning to do what I do is hard.'

She looked again at the painting: the paint hadn't yet dried but already the waves were starting to roll. 'What you do, Gel, is art. But not everybody's an artist.'

'Con could be if he had the discipline. It took me years of experimenting to perfect my technique.' Years of experimenting with brands and blends, with palettes of colour, thousands of kilometres of travel, hours of contemplation and, finally, the epiphany that the most important thing he could bring to his paintings was himself. 'I could give it to him, apprentice him, but he doesn't want it. I offer him the world and he says no. He talks of cutting in and invisible brushstrokes as if that's all there is.' Gelasius's hair was coarse between his fingers as he twisted it. If only the boy would wake up. He would never make his fortune housepainting. He would never know the challenge of real art.

Bellanca shrugged. Not everyone wanted to learn from a master but, for all her sparring with her cousin, she understood his frustration. She stood and put a hand on his shoulder and squeezed. 'Where is he in the phonebook now?'

'Housepainter 22. Oh, he's moving up the ranks all right, but so what? What can ever come of it? What satisfaction can even number one get compared to seeing a painting take life?'

'I don't know. But you have to let him find his own way. Didn't Yiayia teach you anything?'

He picked up his plate and licked it. 'She taught me never to waste good food.' They both laughed.

Two days later, Bellanca, face warmed by the sun that streamed through Gelasius's painting, used her lessons with Yiayia to scale fish and marinate it with lemon juice, oregano and white wine, to salt eggplant, to prepare the lamb for baking. The kitchen was so much airier now the paint was dry and the chemical smell had been replaced by salt and the piquant smell of jasmine. And this plant would flower all year round. Even the sill Gelasius had painted was rough beneath her hands, like real wood, like the frames of Yiayia's house in Iraklion.

Bellanca was staring out the window, remembering her last trip to Crete for Yiayia's funeral, when her son came in from school, backpack slung off one shoulder.

'Hi, Mum. Harvey's mum's got a special painting she wants done. Can't remember what he called it. A trumped eel or something, and I was ...'

'Trompe l'oeil,' she said over the top of him.

'... telling him all about Uncle Gel and what he's done in here.' He paused to sniff the air. 'Isn't it fantastic? It's almost as good as living on the coast.'

'Georgie, you want some halva?'

'I told Harvey to tell his mum to ring. I couldn't remember Uncle Gel's number.' That wasn't quite the truth, but not so much of a lie that it should upset his mother. Harvey McGarvey was pretty cool, but his mother was something else. George had never visited the McGarveys in their big house in rich-bastards' boulevard. From what Harvey said, his mother still hadn't forgiven him for getting chucked out of snotty-snobs' school, but Harvey didn't care. The minute he got out of the limo and pissed the driver off, he'd take off his tie, pull out his shirt and mess up his hair. Harvey was okay, but George didn't want to be responsible for giving Uncle Gel such a pain-in-the-arse job. Mrs McGarvey would want everything perrrrrfect. That was the truth.

Bellanca took out the cake tin and put it before her son. But before she could speak the phone rang.

George looked at his watch. 'That'll be her now, I'll betcha.'

Bellanca nodded. Perhaps. Three thirty—it was more likely to be her mother. But, no, Georgie was right.

'Hello, is that Mrs Dynonpuss?'

'Dynopolous, yes.'

'Arlette McGarvey here, Mrs Dynonpuss. Harvey, here, tells me you know of a painter who is good with trompe l'oeils?'

'Not good, gifted. That's right, yes. My cousin Gelasius.'

'Cousin! Oh, I didn't realise it was a relative. Perhaps I've got the wrong number.'

'Look, Arlette, Gelasius's work is world-class. His paintings are fêted all over Europe. And this time last year he was working in the White House. But if you know someone who's better ...'

'A relative. Well, if you say so, dear.'

Arlette McGarvey waited for the maid to open the door and usher the painter in. Her mouth dropped open at the sight of him. Still, ponytails were an aberration, perhaps a sign of artistic temperament. Talent, that was something else.

'You did wipe your boots on the way in?' She dismissed the maid with a flick of her hand as Gelasius lifted first one foot then the other and inspected the soles.

'Yes, ma'am.'

'Don't ma'am me, Doormat. My name is Mrs McGarvey.'

His eyes crinkled around the edges. 'Are you for real? And it's not Doormat—it's Dormand. Gelasius. Everyone calls me Gelasius.'

'I can't think why anyone would call you that ridiculous name.' She could see he was about to speak but didn't want to stand around making small talk. 'You do have a portfolio you can show me, I presume?' It was obvious he did not. He had coarse, worker's hands as big as those on the statue David.

'Nah, you can't really put what I do in a portfolio. Here's what I do have ...' He handed her a rumpled, dirty piece of paper. 'The names of some of my most recent clients. Ring them. They'll vouch for what I do. Perhaps they might even let you in for a look-see. If you ask them nicely. They're usually quite keen to show it off.'

Top of the list was the governor's ex-wife. Second top a prominent local MP. All were first-class names. 'I'll have to check these out, Galoshes. But if you're right, then maybe we can talk business.'

He grinned, his horse-teeth white and even. 'I'll hang off the phone waiting for your call.'

The second time Gelasius visited, Arlette, the stuck-up cow, walked him around the ballroom. When she had originally said she wanted the ballroom ceiling painted, Gelasius imagined the word 'ballroom' to be a huge boast. It wasn't. This was a room on the scale of centuries past. Sculpted in the Baroque style, the walls were a masterpiece. And the ceiling—he stood thunderstruck by the canvas such a ceiling would present. Now he knew how Michelangelo felt when first viewing the Sistine Chapel. Gelasius could already hear the string quartet, the shuffle and clack of five hundred pairs of shoes on polished wood. He could smell sweat and perfume cloying the air.

'You can see what I'm saying, Galoshes. I need something spectacular. I want this room to be the envy of all society. Money's no object.' When it was finished, she would throw the most magnificent ball, something to cleanse herself of the stain of divorce. So Philip's was old money, so what? She was just as good, every bit as cultured as he.

Gelasius spun a slow circle under the ceiling. The room was already spectacular. This would be months of work. His hands itched for his palette.

'Do you think you can handle the job?'

'Reckon I can. What did you have in mind?'

The rocks on her rings glinted like marbles as she waved her hand around. 'Something dramatic. Something everyone will remember. I want ... I want thunderclouds, immense, festering, dark thunderclouds on the verge of storm. I want them so lifelike people feel the need for their umbrellas.'

Oh, yes, he could see it already. Magnificent. 'I understand. I'll paint them as though seen through a glass ceiling. I'll do the framework here and here.' His finger sketched out boundaries.

'No, you imbecile. Not as though seen through glass. I want these to look real, so real people can feel the chill.'

The chill would be no problem. Gelasius bit his bottom lip. 'You do understand the nature of my work? Bellanca has explained it to you?'

'Of course I do.'

'And yet you want real storm-clouds—no glass?'

'Are you hard of hearing?' She enunciated each word

carefully, as though speaking to a child. Gelasius almost basked in her scorn. Even so, he had to give her another chance.

'I don't recommend it.'

She took a deep breath. Really, these tradesmen were just so thick. 'Galoshes, let me explain how it all works. I pay the money; you paint what I say. Are we clear?'

Oh, they were clear all right. Gelasius just hoped he was out of the way before the paint dried.

Con, who had experience in such things, helped his father set up the scaffolding. 'This'll take you forever,' he said, walking the perimeter of the room. 'How much is she paying?'

'Enough,' said Gelasius with a smile. Enough that he wouldn't have to work for the next two years if he didn't want to. But she would get her money's worth. He looked at the floorboards, hoping they wouldn't rot. Such craft—it almost seemed a shame.

For the next few months he worked from eight every morning until six in the evening. Paint dribbled down the sides of his face and his hair seemed permanently streaked. He worked from plans he'd charcoaled onto paper and then laminated to prevent smudges. That way, in the off chance that any of the ceiling took on life before the whole was dry, his plans wouldn't be wrecked. Not that it would matter: Arlette McGarvey would cancel his contract the second she realised what she was in for. So, at Con's insistence, he logged every minute worked, every cent paid on supplies, and even the cost of neck massages every Saturday, and he made bloody sure she paid in installments as he worked.

Towards the end of the fourth month, Harvey McGarvey started visiting after school to watch the work. Gelasius entranced the boy with stories of Greece, and how Gelasius's great-great-grandfather fished the turquoise waters. Gelasius had no idea whether his great-great-grandfather fished or not, but it made a good story and he liked telling stories of jewelled islands in the sun.

Imagination was what the boy lacked. And Gelasius took it upon himself to fire this up.

In the meantime, he painted the clouds with a green heart, portraying both the promise of rain and ice. The thunderheads roiled above, holding in their burden, waiting for the canvas to be complete and the paint to dry.

With four weeks to go, Gelasius was whistling a few bars of 'Nature Boy' when Harvey McGarvey came in, rolling his yoyo. 'Wow,' Harvey said, gaze on the ceiling as he let his yoyo walk-the-dog and loop-the-loop, 'that looks fantastic. I'm getting cold just looking at it.' The yoyo skittered out of his hands and across the floor; Harvey dived after it.

'Don't!'

But it was too late. Harvey crashed into a ladder and the plank Gelasius was standing on juddered beneath him. A spray of paint went into the air and down onto the tarp below. Gelasius wobbled, and to regain balance took a step sideways and off the edge of the plank. The fire in his wrist told him instantly that something was wrong.

'Two weeks? Two weeks!' Spittle flew out with the words as Arlette regarded the bandage on Gelasius's wrist. Con, who had driven his father over, took a step backwards as Arlette advanced on Gelasius. 'That's impossible. I've sent out the invitations. I can't possibly alter the date.'

'When's the party?'

'Ball, Galoshes. It's not a party. We don't have parties in this house.'

Con shrank inside. Nobody spoke to his father like that. But Gelasius was grinning.

Arlette touched her coiffure and the pearls at her throat. This was insufferable. Typical tradesperson! She could always count on them to make a fool of her. 'December the second is the deadline. That gives the paint time to dry and, hopefully, the fumes a chance to clear.'

Gelasius leaned into the leather of the chair and crossed his ankles. 'I asked when the party is, not your deadline.'

'The ball's on the tenth. But it must be done before then.'

Even without a sprained wrist, it was a near-impossible deadline. Still, if he worked weekends, stayed later in the night, he could rest his wrist now and still get it done. 'Don't worry, Mrs McG—it'll be ready. Not by the second, perhaps, but by the ninth. I promise you the ninth.'

'But the fumes, Galoshes, what about the fumes?'

Con couldn't stand this woman's rudeness. 'So open some windows and let in the air,' he said, looking at his father.

'The guests will freeze.'

And although Gelasius's face didn't move, Con could swear his father smiled.

The first guests arrived at seven. The hired waiters circulated, offering champagne and aperitifs of lobster, prawns, sun-dried tomatoes, caviar. Arlette swanned around in the exquisite satin gown she'd had specially made. But no one was looking at her. And, even though she still trembled at the thought of what it cost, she knew that every cent she'd spent on that damned ceiling was worth it.

'It's gorgeous,' one woman said, champagne flute raised high.

'Words are inadequate,' said another, 'to describe such artistry.'

'Oh, Arlette,' said a man, taking her hand and squeezing, 'it's divine.'

On the foot of the curving staircase that ended near the ballroom door, Harvey sat, eyes wide. The music barely filtered above the din of all those people. They were so beautiful, like peacocks. Harvey's mother moved near the doorway; Harvey slunk back. He'd already been sent to bed.

The cellist was in the middle of her solo when the last of the paint finally dried. It was difficult to say exactly when the rain started. Many guests, feeling the spray, assumed someone nearby had popped another bottle of champagne, and laughed. From the distance came a rumble, and light flickered across the sky. People ignored it. Their chatter stopped as the rain became heavier and they turned faces upward and frowned. The men shivered in their jackets, the most chivalrous taking these off and offering them to the women they partnered, many of who were sleeveless. Fingers of cold air raised gooseflesh on skin, pinched nipples through silk. The rain would ruin many outfits—Arlette McGarvey had made the gaffe of the century and people began to talk.

Lightning sparked, filled the room with ozone. Rain pelted, drummed against floorboards, drubbed against walls. Sleet chilled the partygoers as people stampeded the doorway. Harvey watched the panicked tide of people squeeze through double-doors and flow out to the street.

Arlette stood with head bowed, hands over her face. She couldn't understand what was happening, but already she knew that if she did nothing else she would bring Galoshes down. How dare he ruin her party! How dare he humiliate her like this!

A brief hailstorm lacerated flesh; the blood running between fingers of hands held to faces was the only warmth in the room. Women, in the press of people moving towards the door, buried faces in their husbands' cold, clinging shirts. Icy water eddied around the room, gelid on stockinged ankles. The hail stopped, only to be replaced by the silence of snowfall.

Gradually, the room cleared and Arlette, makeup muddied and smeared, 200 dollar coiffure flattened, took refuge with her son on the third-bottom step. Inside the room, the squall continued. The water level was rising and Arlette and Harvey were forced to move up a step. A gale-force wind whipped the narrow sea into whitecaps and then, above the noise of waves and rain, came the splintering sound of glass as the ballroom windows exploded outwards into Arlette's precious rose-garden. 'My roses,' she wailed. All that money on the gardener wasted. 'I'm going to kill him, kill him, kill him.'

The morning after the ball, Arlette McGarvey awoke from dream and smiled. How silly. Her ballroom ruined by rain. But as she lay there in the warmth of the doona, she heard the moaning of the wind, the roar of water. The air smelt of river mud. She roused herself and went downstairs to the eighth-bottom stair where Harvey was launching paper boats. The sting of her hand on cheek was almost as satisfying as the shock on his face.

'Harvey Adam Broderick Charles McGarvey, you get your lazy, fat-arse down to the telephone and find me the number of that fucked-up painter.'

Bellanca Dynopolous waved the spoon at the buttercup walls and then at Con. 'Now, Gel,' she said, between mouthfuls of fish soup, 'you have to admit, he's done a great job.'

Con slurped his soup, savouring the zing of fennel and thyme. Would his father admit it? Did he have it in him?

Gelasius stuffed a piece of pita into his mouth. 'Yeah, yeah, I know. It looks good, really, Bellanca. But, Con, you could do so much more.'

Not this again. Con closed his eyes. He knew his father meant well, but Con knew his own limitations. He might have a smidgen of his father's talent but had none of his patience. A house was a quick thing. In one day he could make a difference.

The phone's ring overrode the necessity for a response and he sat quietly, watching his aunt.

Bellanca's face grew hot as she listened to the string of expletives. In ten years of reading saucy romance novels, she had never read such language. And this from the mother of her son's best friend!

'So what you're saying is you'd like Gelasius's number. Is that it?' she said as coolly as she could.

Gelasius quirked an eyebrow and followed that with a grimace. It was to be expected, he supposed. He'd just hoped for a longer reprieve.

Bellanca replaced the phone in its cradle. 'She hung up on me, the bitch.'

From beyond the window came the chug-chug-chug of a fishing boat and the gentle huff of water on sand. She stood at the window, staring out. 'Do you think I should've told her you were here?'

'No. I can well imagine what that rude cow wants. Come on, Bellanca, come and enjoy your lunch.'

In the several hours it took Arlette to track down Gelasius, several plumbers had come to check the spouting and left, shaking their heads. A meteorologist had come and gone, wearing a perplexed expression on his face. And the police, who told her they really didn't have grounds for making an arrest. Even her shrink had come—he only muttered something about his own medication before haring out the door.

Gelasius, she had hoped, would be sympathetic, but he wasn't. His voice, over the phone line, was calm. 'You said you understood the nature of my work.'

One swat with one of his brushes would wipe that smile right off his stupid, ugly face. She could just picture him flipping that God-awful ponytail of his over his shoulder. 'Look, you stupid, fucking arsehole, get over here now and start fixing this up.' Suddenly, she realised she was talking to the dial tone.

Gelasius ignored the phone's ring. He was too busy infusing paints with magic to listen to her abuse. But the phone was insistent and in the end he wanted peace more than avoidance of the call.

'I'm sorry,' she said. 'But I'm desperate. You have to help me. Please.'

'I can't,' he said, looking out to the lounge-room where Con was sprawled on the couch watching *Vertical Limit*. 'You need to destroy the painting—that's the only way to stop it.'

'Destroy? Do you know how much this painting cost me?'

'I do, actually.' And didn't he love his new bank balance. 'I'm sorry. It's the only way.' He had warned her; she hadn't wanted to listen. It was too late now to paint in a glass ceiling. He would never get near it.

'When can you start?'

'Me? I can't do it. Deconstruction is not my speciality.'

'Galoshes, please, you have to help me.'

'I can't. I'm sorry, Mrs McG, but you don't seem to understand. I put a little of myself into each painting, a little of my life-force, my essence. For me to destroy it would be to commit a little suicide.'

Arlette McGarvey bit back her immediate response. But even though she knew it was unwise, she couldn't stop the sarcasm from seeping through. 'So a little murder is preferable to a little suicide—is that what you're saying?'

'Exactly, Mrs McG.'

He was a stupid prick and she hated him almost as much as her lying, cheating bastard of a husband. 'You must know someone who can help me?'

Gelasius looked again at his son, stuffing his face with chips as he watched. 'No,' he said into the phone. 'Cannot help you. Sorry.'

'Yes,' she said. 'I thought that might be your answer. Thanks. Thanks for nothing.'

Arlette McGarvey considered the advantages of dynamite. Boom.

The roof would blow off, the ceiling in a thousand weeping pieces. But what of the rest of her ballroom? What of her house? New paintwork and carpets in the other rooms were one thing; dynamite would mean major structural repairs. Architects—just like her husband. No, dynamite wasn't an option.

Her mind was blank.

Harvey McGarvey, dreaming of white houses with domed roofs blue against the Aegean sky, came up with the answer. 'Whitewash,' he told his mother, 'whitewash might do it.'

The boy, for all his public schooling, was a genius. Why hadn't she seen it before?

Arlette phoned the most respected housepainter in the phonebook and, without explaining the particulars, offered him quadruple time if he could start right away. Housepainter number one arrived in clean overalls early the next day. He took one look at the torrent of water emanating from the front door and refused to get his feet wet.

She changed tactics. When she explained her plight to housepainter two, he laughed and hung up in her ear. Housepainter three, acquainted with Gelasius's work, refused to commit sacrilege even if she were to offer two hundred times the going rates. Housepainter four baulked at the four-metre-deep trench filled with raging waters and left. Number five arrived on the doorstep but explained sadly that he was asthmatic and couldn't be out all day in such inclement weather.

Housepainter six was brave. He battled winds and water to look at the room in question and left, as the plumbers had, shaking his head.

Housepainter thirteen made it as far as the middle of the ballroom before being swept under and almost drowning. His foot snagged on a rock and, as his body wrenched forwards with the water, his ankle snapped. 'I'm calling my lawyer,' he said as the ambulance doors closed. The rest of his sentence was muffled. 'Don't worry,' Arlette thought she heard, 'I promise you: you'll be hearing from me.'

Housepainter fifteen made it further than all the others. In his oilskin and gumboots he waded upriver, avoiding rocks and eels, into the ballroom. Facing downwind, so the spray wouldn't come back in his face, he hefted his spray gun and pointed it at the ceiling. Paint arced into the air and then a whirlwind brought it back to him, further drenching the already drenched painter. He marched from the house, spray gun tucked into his body. 'It can't be done,' he shouted over his shoulder at Arlette. 'It's ridiculous. Your house belongs in a freak show.'

The nineteenth housepainter dragged a ladder through the raging torrent and laid the ladder against a wall. With a tray of paint in one hand and a roller in the other he mounted the steps.

On the second top step, he steadied himself against the wall. The ladder juddered beneath his feet. He raised the roller. Just out of reach. Swaying precariously, he took the last step up and lifted the roller again to the ceiling. Water streamed down his arm and slid ice into his clothes. He shivered. The oil-based paint dimpled with water and floated to the top of the tray and over the sides. The ladder rocked. Housepainter number nineteen splashed into the wintry waters of the ballroom and floated out of the house, never to be seen again.

Housepainter 22, wearing tattered, stained overalls, arrived armed with ropes, picks and grappling hooks.

Arlette McGarvey stared at him. 'Do I know you?' she said. 'You look familiar.'

Con stood knee-deep in water at the door to the ballroom. His father had really done it this time. 'Can't say you do, but I know the artist.'

'Artist? Don't call him an artist.' Her waving hand almost hit Con's nose. 'I don't want to think of him and all the ruin he has brought upon me.' Arlette, seeing the vicious hooks for the first time, shuddered. 'You're not putting those in my walls?'

'Lady,' said Con, thinking she was anything but, 'you want this job done or not? Let's talk terms.'

She wanted the job done. And agreed to everything he stipulated. Con smiled. He might not be half the artist his father was, but he had twice the business acumen.

In the morning, Con wore his best worst-weather gear and tied a can of white paint and a brush to his belt along with his spare ropes. He chiselled out footholds and climbed his way up a corner and began painting.

As he painted the whitewash on, it dribbled down the walls, staining the water glacier-stream grey. But Con lived for the challenge. No storm would see him beaten; no creation of his father's would defeat him. In the chill wind, he stood, wracking his brain. Of course. Always look for the simplest solutions, his mother had once said. Using his ropes, he clambered down the wall, then edged his way out of the room. Later, he returned with whitewash laced with glue.

Gelasius's masterpiece had taken six months to create but, with the slow progress forced on Con by inclement weather, nine months to erase.

After he finished the first translucent coat and it dried to a sticky mess, the rain eased to a shower. The second coat took less than two weeks. As the last of the whitewash went on, the rain finally stopped.

Arlette McGarvey looked at housepainter 22 and thanked him. She followed him out along the 28-metre-deep trench the water had carved through the remains of her garden. In the street, the most recently installed of the 59 stormwater drains sat dry. A small tornado of water kept the middle quarter busy, but would not for much longer. Housepainter 22 smiled. 'Don't thank me,' he said, his smile the first bit of sunshine Arlette had seen for months. 'You've just given me my first big break, and more importantly the means to shut my father up.'

'Your father. What has he to do with any of this?'

'He's over there, if you want to say hello. I think you two have met.'

Seeing Gelasius meandering along the footpath made Arlette spit. 'You? What are you doing here?'

'The council asked me to come by and see about painting in some more drains. Looks like I'm out of a job ...' He grinned widely at Con.

'I can't say I'm sorry,' she said. He'd already taken enough of her money. More than enough.

Gelasius smiled, genuinely. 'Neither am I. Guess I'll be off to London. I have to paint a tropical scene in the palace.'

'The palace ... Do you mean Buckingham Palace?' Arlette's eyes rounded but Gelasius was already climbing into Con's ute.

Late that night Con tallied up the bill: nine months at quadruple rates, penalty rates, depreciation on equipment, special-risk penalties, work-under-duress penalties, laundry allowances, stage-completion bonuses.

Arlette McGarvey received his bill, along with notification that her lawyer had settled on damages for the broken leg of housepainter thirteen. Both sums made Arlette blanch. 'What's the matter, Mummy?' said Harvey McGarvey, still sorry that the painting was gone. With his own personal river he'd been the coolest kid at school. 'Your face looks like the whitewash.'

By the time she made reparations to council for roadworks and settled her legal fees, Arlette McGarvey was destitute and couldn't afford to pay housepainter 22. Con, good friends with housepainter thirteen, set his lawyer upon her. The courts awarded him the house—it cleared her debt and eliminated the risk of having new owners who might be foolish enough to strip the whitewash from the ceiling. This way everyone won.

In the jasmine-scented sea-breeze of her kitchen, before she picked up George from school, Bellanca Dynopolous toasted Con's victory. Con tipped the champagne flute towards his father. 'To painting,' he said.

Bellanca laughed as the bubbles went up her nose.

'You'll have to tell me how you did that,' said Gelasius to Con. 'What do I know about business? I'm an artist.'

'So am I, Dad,' said Con, grinning broadly. 'So am I.'

Tracey Rolfe is a writer and editor who lives in Melbourne's western suburbs. She belongs to the writers' groups SuperNOVA and Western Women Writers, and is a co-editor of *Poetrix* magazine. She writes in a variety of genres, and her short stories, articles and poems have been published in various SF and other literary magazines. In 2004, she attended the inaugural Clarion South writers' workshop in Brisbane. Tracey has worked as a haematologist and microbiologist and currently teaches in Professional Writing and Editing in the TAFE sector of Victoria University.

WITNESS OF BLOOD

SUE ISLE

THE TWO VISITORS CAME TO THE GATE of our home, one very warm spring evening. Judith, our servant, came to announce that one Joseph of Arimathea and a lady were at the gate asking to speak with the Lady Martha, daughter of Abigail.

Arrius looked interested rather than offended, to my relief. The farm was in his name and it was that name which people knew. Not many here knew me or my now dead mother Abigail or her descent from Hannah, the sorceress of Endor who had told King Saul of his coming death in battle. My own recent notoriety in my home village of Bethany was due not to my abilities as a soothsayer, but to the fact that Joshua of Nazareth had raised my younger brother Lazarus from the dead. Marrying a Roman ex-legionary officer had not helped, hence our move.

'We will welcome our guests,' my husband said. In the entranceway, Judith brought water to wash their hands and a towel to dry them. I recognised the expensively-dressed Joseph with a shivering sort of disquiet, which probably puzzled him if he noticed. He had given his tomb to Joshua after the latter's execution two months ago, but that wasn't why I shivered. I had seen this man in my dreams last night and not thought anything of it until now. With him was a young woman of maybe twenty years. She seemed too well dressed to be a servant, though not as richly as he. A man of his station would hardly take a young mistress to visit someone, so maybe she was daughter or niece. The images of my dream were now jumbled and vague so I could not have told if she was present in any of them.

'Optio Arrius Januarius,' Joseph said politely, inclining his head. 'We thank you for your welcome. This is Tabitha and I am Joseph son of Ezra.'

Arrius said something polite in greeting, bidding them sit and have some wine with us. The room was reasonably cool, but certainly not so cold that Tabitha needed to keep her cloak swathed about herself. 'May I help you, Tabitha?' I said to her. I was close by but she did not seem to hear me and continued to gaze ahead. At nothing, I noted, beginning to feel uneasy. She could be deaf, yet when Joseph spoke to her, she nodded and seated herself by him on a couch. When Judith served the wine, Tabitha did not take any, or even spring water.

Joseph hesitated and then appeared to come to a decision. He looked straight at me. 'Lady Martha, I am here to consult with you,' he said. 'I hope that your husband will allow you to speak with me on the matter of dreams.'

'I am no longer a seeress, sir,' I replied.

'Your gift is God-given,' Joseph said firmly. 'It comes and goes at the will of God.'

'That is not what many of our people would say.'

'They are misguided and have not true knowledge. I am bound on a great journey and require advice.'

These words seemed to set something off within me, a spirit which spoke at its own will rather than mine. Instead of looking at him, I stared again at Tabitha, who appeared to be looking back at me but was in fact staring blankly through me. 'Is this girl to go with you to the green land?'

'She is to bear witness.'

'She is witness of blood, not truth. I have already dreamed of your journey, Joseph of Arimathea. You will arrive safely, though a storm wrecks your boat upon the shore you seek.'

Joseph was clearly startled, though Tabitha did not react. He opened his mouth to speak and at the same time Arrius started to say something. An intense pain shot through my temples and then a feeling of fuzziness and confusion about where I was and who. Then, in the next moment, I found myself standing ankle-deep in muddy ground. A light, chill rain was falling on my head and shoulders and the air I breathed in was also cold. Before my eyes, at the top of a low hillside some hundred paces distant, was a fort, surrounded by a wooden palisade. For a second I thought myself back in last night's dream, which had involved a boat on a rough coast, but the sensations were too sharp and real. Someone was beside me, speaking to me, but I had not caught his first words. '... coming to greet us, Martha? Are you all right?'

It was Arrius, as wet as I was, a heavy cloak plastered over him. He put an arm around me to urge me onwards, eager to be out of the wet but calm, I noted with an eerie coolness of my own. He was glad to be out of the boat, even to such a land as this. Other people crowded around us but I gave no heed to any of them. All I could think was that I had not heard Arrius' first words to me. I had not been aware of my husband or anything he had said or done for an unknown number of days—or weeks. I had not been there and *he had not noticed.*

Strangers surrounded us, gabbling in an unknown language, but they seemed friendly. We were brought past the tall palisade into an interior space crowded with several huts, perhaps six, though I didn't try to count them, then led into the largest structure, a circular hut lit only by the fire in its central hearth. The floor was of clay—I had lost my shoes if I had had them to begin with—and covered with animal hides upon which to sit or lie. It smelled overwhelmingly of smoke and human sweat. My confusion went unnoticed among the disorientation of our whole group. I thought it best to remain silent until the crowd went away, at least from our immediate vicinity. Our clothes were soaked, so we were given blankets with which to cover ourselves while they dried. Food and drink was brought and left for us. 'There'll be a feast when they can prepare,' Joseph said.

Arrius replied, 'Perhaps we are fortunate that it was not possible to give advance warning of our arrival.'

Joseph laughed, across the small fire. 'Arviragus of the Durotriges, this people among whom we find ourselves, is a generous man and expects his people to be likewise, but his guests require stamina to withstand his generosity.'

'This is the dwelling of a king?' Arrius asked carefully.

'No, this is the steading of a derbfine, a family who are part of the tribe which follows Arviragus. The king himself dwells half a day's journey north.'

'One family? I counted maybe 40 and there must be half that in this building with us.'

Joseph smiled, evidently feeling quite at home now in this strange place. 'They are the descendants of a single great-grandfather, who was still living on my last voyage to this place, two years ago. I think that is he, sitting over there being told of our arrival.'

While they talked, I cast within my own mind for an answer to what had happened to me. The only explanation I knew was possession by demons, which is not a thing mortals can bring about. Even if I had sensed a demon, the ritual to cleanse myself wasn't something which could be done in a crowded hut. I wasn't sure whether I could still use my powers away from my birth land. I looked at my companions, trying to seem as though I was well used to them. Arrius and Joseph chatted like friends, not the strangers they had been a few of my moments ago. I listened and quickly learned that we were in Britain, the land raided by the god-emperor Julius 88 years before. Joseph had been here several times to trade for tin and lead.

There was no sign of Judith—had she been left behind or perished— but two other men appeared to be Joseph's servants. The young woman, Tabitha, sat staring blankly into our small fire, but as my gaze fell upon her, she lifted her eyes to mine.

There was no soul in her eyes, no self. Her slight movement caused the blanket she wore to fall aside, revealing a breast, but she made no motion to cover herself. She wasn't deliberately displaying herself; she seemed totally indifferent.

'Are you well, Tabitha?' I asked, loud enough for her to hear me even above the noise of conversation. Tabitha only looked vacantly away. Time to settle this, I thought, though a cold kernel of dread seemed to lie within my stomach. I had seen only one person who behaved as Tabitha did and that was my brother Lazarus, brought back from the dead by Joshua of Nazareth, now being called the Christ or the chosen one by his followers.

Not to put too fine a point on it, Joshua himself was dead now, killed by the Romans for causing dissent. He had blazed with godlight, the power granted to only a few, to heal and change and see what would be. Instead of using it quietly, as the women of my line had done, he had used it so that no one could ignore it, doing wonderful things which he claimed God had done through him. One of those things had not been so wonderful. My young brother Lazarus had died of a fever. I had seen him dead and I know I was not mistaken. Joshua went to his tomb and called him forth, but the death was not banished, only pushed away, and when the life energy Joshua gave to him ran out, the death came back because Lazarus had no life power of his own.

I would have asked questions of Joseph of Arimathea when he came to our house. I would have wanted to know why he wished to travel to this cold green land and why he had brought this girl, who clearly could not look after herself, with him. Something or someone had prevented me from asking those questions.

So I got up now and walked a couple of steps around the fire to where Tabitha sat on an animal hide. I knelt down beside her. 'You'll get cold like that,' I said and tugged the blanket back into place around her. 'Can you hear me, Tabitha, even if you cannot speak?'

Her eyes followed the motion of my hand, smoothing the blanket over her shoulder. She seemed as oblivious as before. I made to smooth her unkempt dark hair back from her face, as one might with a child, but as my hand passed close to her face, she lunged with a frightening speed and seized it in her teeth. She grabbed my arm with both hands for greater purchase as her teeth dug painfully into my hand. I cried out from pain and shock as well and the others were instantly there, pulling Tabitha's face away from my hand and restraining the girl on the ground. One of Joseph's two servants or followers quickly came to me with a length of cloth to wrap around my hand, which was bleeding. As I looked incredulously at Tabitha, I saw her lick her lips, reddened by my blood. As she did so, an expression of confusion crossed her face, the first expression of any kind I had seen there. She looked back at me as though she had no idea who or even what I was. Then the look was gone and the oblivious face replaced it.

Darkness fell not long after and the tribesfolk slept, those who were not on guard. It appeared that all the life of the tribe went on in the same space; cooking, sleeping, weaving, love-making. I was too tired and bewildered to care what happened, so made for myself a place to sleep and did so, glad for my training which enabled me to sleep even under these conditions. My only hope of answers lay in sleep.

Again I found myself in unexpected surroundings, but this was the realm of sleep, where such was to be expected. So I did not fear when I saw stony desert around me and a few scrubby trees where perhaps an oasis had once been. I walked to the trees, looking about me and asking silently with all my will that someone be sent who could explain what had happened to me. I did not have long to wait before I saw a single robed form walking unhurriedly towards me, but when I recognised him, I wanted to flee. It was my younger brother Lazarus, as I had seen him before he fell ill. Before Joshua raised him and before he fell again to dust.

'I did not summon you,' I blurted as soon as he was near. 'I prayed only for guidance.'

'That is well,' my brother said. He seemed more relaxed than he had in life, smiling at me as though he was the elder. It was true that he had access to all the wise ones who had ever lived, whereas I had to fast and meditate and prepare for hours before I could reach them. Seeking answers in dream was something anyone could do; remembering them was something else. 'You are far from your own land and this earth does not know your feet. Seek out Weylyn, the wise one of the clan where you sleep. Tell him of the woman Tabitha.'

'Tell him what, Lazarus?' I demanded, in exactly the same tone I had used on my living brother.

He tugged on his scratchy excuse for a beard. 'Now, why should I tell you?'

'Lazarus, stop it. All I know of Tabitha is that she appears to be either deaf and dumb or else childlike. Joseph has told me nothing and the girl herself has not spoken. Except for biting my hand this evening, she's done nothing of her own will. Joshua is dead so I know he can't have been raising anyone else.'

'No, but he was not the only one with this power,' Lazarus broke in.

'Oh yes he was, little brother. I met his other followers at the feast we held to celebrate your return, remember? None of the twelve could have done what he did.'

'Who is dead here, you or me?' Lazarus demanded.

'Well, you, but I would have sensed if one of them had any power.'

'You were not there at the end of it. Joshua passed his power.'

'After he died, you mean? After he came back?'

'Yes. He would have faded as I did, but it would have taken much longer. Instead, he blessed Simon Peter with his power and then he was gone.'

'And Peter raised Tabitha, who is now in the keeping of Joshua's faithful follower Joseph. Very well, so much is clear, little brother. But why in the name of the Queen of Heaven did he bring her with him on this trading trip to Britain? And why did he bring Arrius and myself? Where have I *been* for the time since Joseph came to our house in Judea?' I heard my own voice raised to a screech but didn't try to stop myself. I had to yell at someone.

Lazarus looked sideways, as though seeking someone. 'There is another in her head,' he said slowly, puzzling it out. 'She rides and you slept as I slept. They gave her to drink of life and so she lives, but she is not bound to the flesh. Speak to Weylyn.'

'Lazarus, I don't speak the language,' I began, but before I could finish, I was awake, smelling smoke and animal hide and flesh and other less pleasant odours. Arrius was asleep next to me; one of Joseph's people, a Greek whose name I think was Philip, lay on my other side. It was still night. Outside I heard the murmur of voices and a couple were making love on the other side of the central hearth. They were probably trying to be quiet, but then again, the rest of the group must have long since ceased to hear those sounds. It was some time before I slept and this time there were no visions.

Next day, our group of six were given a round house of our own within the hill fort; a great concession, I realised, when I saw at least a dozen people leaving the thatched building with their belongings. It did not help me find the man my brother had named. 'Wise one' probably meant Weylyn was some sort of priest; depending on the religion, that might also mean sorcerer. I kept a lookout but saw no one among the tribesfolk who stood out in any way from the general strangeness. *There is another in her head*, I pondered. *She rides and you slept as I slept. They gave her to drink of life and so she lives, but she is not bound to the flesh*. Something, someone had certainly ridden me like a horse, taking over my body and my being—I shivered involuntarily at that thought, for it was a horrific one—and my own soul, my self, had certainly not been there at the time for I had no memory of what must have been weeks of travel; overland to Joppa or

Caesarea and by ship to Gaul, then by a smaller craft across the channel of ocean lying between Gaul and Britain. So was I seeking a sorceress ... or a demon?

Joseph took Philip with him to talk to the chief about buying some land, the first I knew this was more than a trading trip. The other man, Thaddeus, remained with Tabitha, who sat motionless on one side of the hut. Arrius, on the other, was examining a short-sword, evidently to see what damage it had taken from the salt water. This was probably as private as we were going to get. I went to lay out our clothing from the bags, hanging the garments as I might on the walls to dry. As I did so, I murmured to Arrius. 'I have spoken to my brother in a vision. He warns me that we are in danger.'

'I have no doubt of that,' Arrius answered, too loudly. He had not picked up the point that I wanted silence. 'This is a land without law, at least, any law that would protect us.'

'There is the law of hospitality,' Thaddeus commented. He was young, maybe only nineteen or twenty or so and for him, everything was sharply right or wrong, good or evil. Lazarus had been so as well. 'Joseph has traded often with these people. The guest, once accepted, is sacred.'

'If he brings wines and rich materials for them, no doubt,' Arrius conceded, grinning. 'But when Joseph begins to speak of the Messiah come at last and miracles performed, I am not so sure that they will greet him so kindly.'

'But he brings proof,' Thaddeus protested. Looking at him, I all but missed the slight swing of his hand to indicate Tabitha. 'Why did you come then, man of Rome, if you do not believe?'

'Joseph wished it, after the seeing which my wife performed,' Arrius answered, rather stiffly. No doubt he resented being questioned by a skinny youth half his age. 'Martha also believed it was important for us to accompany Joseph. Any other belief was beside the point.'

My chance for any private chat with my husband was gone. 'Is it safe if I walk among the huts?' I asked him.

'I think so, but you should probably not go beyond the walls.'

This did not give me much, but I did not bother to argue. The tribesfolk watched me wander among the huts but no one tried to accost me or speak to me. Several women did gather their children out of my way. The only thing that moved across my path was a low furred creature with a bright red coat and a bushy tail, doglike but running with a fluid grace which dogs cannot achieve. It had something in its mouth and angry shouts followed it from the nearest hut.

A woman came to the doorway but another blocked her path, raising her voice warningly. The first shrugged and turned about; the second looked at me as though to demand what was I doing here?

'Lady Martha.' It was Joseph. So relieved was I to hear my own language that I turned smiling to him, though he was hardly my favourite company at this time. 'The woman warns the other that she should not pursue the fox, lest he be one of the Old Ones in disguise—their gods. These people have more gods even than Rome and each seems to have several names.'

We walked slowly back in the direction of our house. 'Sir, my mind is still confused after our rough arrival,' I began. 'I find I cannot remember even those things I should know well and it troubles me.' Joseph nodded benignly—a woman can never make a mistake if she presumes on supposed feminine weakness—and I continued carefully. 'I am troubled about Tabitha and your reason for bringing her here. Her health is at risk ...'

'She is the living miracle,' Joseph interrupted me, stopping and raising his voice. 'She woke at Simon Peter's word and she drank the wine of life. She will not fail as your brother failed. Soon she will wake fully to herself, I am sure of it. You yourself agreed with me that this would be.'

That night, I waited until the others were asleep or at least quiet, before I took Arrius' hand to wake him. He muttered something and tried to pull free to turn over. 'Arrius, wake up. I have to talk to you. I've been trying to talk to you ever since we got here. Please!'

'Inthemorning, hm?'

'Arrius, the Emperor Tiberius is outside and wants a word.'

'*What*—oh.' Arrius had raised himself hastily on his elbow before he woke up enough. He looked quickly around the dark hut to be sure no one else was stirring. No one let it be known they were awake. 'What are you doing, Martha?'

'Come here. No, stop, that's not what I mean. I really do have to talk to you.' Perhaps a note of panic was in my voice, because Arrius abruptly calmed and pulled me close.

'What is it?'

From the other sleepers came sleepy grunts and then a person getting up, black shape against almost black room. I couldn't see who it was, but the person moved with reasonable care to the doorway, pushing the hide curtain aside to go out, probably to the privy. We subsided again with a mutual sigh and Arrius asked, 'What's wrong, Martha?'

'You know I would not lie to you, I hope, however strange my words seem?' Without waiting for agreement I blundered right on. 'Then hear me. Arrius, my last memories before I set foot in the mud of this land were of our house. Joseph had come to ask me for a dreamtelling. I remember the spirit seizing me and myself telling him that I had already dreamed his voyage and a shipwreck? You remember? Well, the spirit did not leave me, Arrius. It rode me and did its own will with my body. I remember nothing of the voyage and I never said anything about the wisdom of coming here.'

He did not answer immediately but his hands on my arms clenched hard. He drew in breath and let it out in a great sigh. 'You have been with me and spoken normally to me these many days. The only time I thought a strangeness had seized you was when we landed.'

'That was when the spirit released me. Arrius, there's more. I sought answers in vision, asking only that one be sent to guide me. That was when I spoke to Lazarus. He said I was too far, the land too alien, that I must seek counsel from a wise one who is native here. The name was Weylyn but I have seen no one who could be a priest or heard that name spoken. Please, you must ask Joseph, on some pretext, to ask for this one.'

'I will,' he promised. 'But you will need Joseph if you are to speak with this priest.'

'I know, I know. I do not entirely trust Joseph, Arrius. I do not like the presence of Tabitha. Lazarus spoke of her, I think.' I repeated the strange words he had given me. 'He could have meant no one else.'

'But she does not ride you,' Arrius said slowly. 'She is herself.'

'Is she? Has she spoken since Joseph brought her to our house?'

'No ...'

'Did she speak before? Did Joseph say anything of her speaking?'

'Yes, he said Peter brought her back from the dead and she cried and blessed him. He thought the journey had frightened her, because she had been so silent and still, unless he urged her to walk or to eat or drink.'

'She is like Lazarus. You see that?'

'Yes,' he said softly. 'But she was raised over one month ago and she has not failed as your brother did in only a few days. I know this will hurt, but it is truth.'

'I know,' I said sharply, then lowered my voice. 'Think, Arrius. Did I do or say anything strange from the time Joseph came to our house until the moment our feet touched this shore?'

'You had a vision for Joseph,' Arrius said at once. 'After you prophesied the shipwreck, you raised your arms as though you hung upon the cross and you cried out very loudly that you saw—let me think of the exact words—you saw the victory of the Christ over death throughout the world. That Joseph must preach the—the everlasting life—the doctrine of everlasting life, I think—and that Tabitha was the vessel. There was more but I don't remember.'

'The vessel?' I wasn't sure what I might have meant, but I knew I did not like it. This prophecy was exactly what Joseph would have wanted to hear; it had brought him here and Tabitha and myself. The phrase about the vessel tied in with what Joseph had said this afternoon about Tabitha having drunk the wine of life. Wine is kept in a vessel—the human body is a vessel that contains blood, not wine—blood is the wine of life? I hadn't realised I had said this out loud until Arrius responded.

'Yes. Of course.'

'They give her human blood?' I was repelled, though this was hardly the grimmest thing of which I had heard.

'I don't know,' Arrius rumbled, trying to whisper. 'Joseph hasn't come right out and said so.' He held me for a while longer, while we listened to the others sleep. 'Tomorrow we must speak with him.'

I didn't expect to sleep but weariness claimed me. I woke again to the sound of shouting outside our door and the chaos of Joseph and the other two putting on their outer garments and heading outside. Tabitha was not present. Arrius and I hastened to follow. When we got ourselves dressed and outside in the gray dawn chill, we found the fort's inhabitants in shaking, loud distress. Before us, on the ground, lay one of the young men of the tribe, pale and lifeless. I could see no wound on him, but when a gray-haired man turned him over, there was a gash on his neck. Not a knife wound, the flesh looked torn.

'Weylyn!' the older man cried, then a string of words which meant nothing. There was a scuffle on the roof of the nearest building and I saw a black bird, a crow or a raven, launch itself into flight as though something pursued it. Some people cried out, obviously unnerved by the bird, though I could not see why. Then we heard someone else calling out. The old man answered him and presently one of the tribesmen walked into the circle of his people and looked at the drained body sprawled beneath him.

He was young. That surprised me, that a man called the wise one of his people could be younger than I was. There was no gray in his startling red hair and his thin face was as beardless as that of a boy. His knee-length woollen tunic was black, perhaps from a black sheep rather than dyed that shade. Unlike the clothing of the other people, it was not adorned with other colours and he wore no brooches or rings. He raised his gaze from the body and looked at me, almost through me. Then he pointed to the body and raised his voice, clearly an order, for several men lifted it and carried it away. Weylyn walked over to me and said something in his alien, fluid language. Joseph began to interpret but Weylyn held up a hand to stop him and extended the hand to my face. His palm was calloused, but clean. As he touched my cheek, an image flashed through my mind: the red fox running, stolen food in its mouth. The raven, startled and indignant.

'You!' I said.

Weylyn smiled. He took my hand and led me through the press of people like a child. I think Arrius or Joseph tried to follow but were prevented. Weylyn took me to a small round hut, furnished with no more than ordinary possessions. It did not look like the dwelling of an important shaman or priest, but as I thought that, he grinned at me and I felt ashamed. What were rich trappings? They did not bring wisdom, just as age in itself didn't mean that the aged man was wise. Weylyn sat and gestured for me to do likewise. When I did, he looked at me, brows raised.

I closed my eyes for a moment to concentrate and used my training to bring clear pictures in my mind of what had happened to me. It is the waking equivalent of controlling a dream. Most men and women cannot do it at all. It is far harder than speech, but as Weylyn and I did not share a language, it was the best I could do. I showed him my home, my life with Arrius which had only just begun. I showed him the empty cradle in our house and touched my stomach to indicate my child unborn, only two months begun. Then came the difficult part. I showed him Tabitha and tried to tell him what I believed she was, what my dead brother had told me of her. 'He told me to speak to you,' I said, concentrating hard. Weylyn only nodded and I got the impression that the fact Lazarus was dead did not matter much to him, that it was quite ordinary that he should speak to me in dream. He remained still then for so long that my legs began to ache, then got easily to his feet, reached to pat my shoulder and strode out of the hut to where the tribal chief and his advisers had gathered.

Someone shouted loudly and then I heard Joseph's voice, loud and startled. 'What are you doing? Let go of my arm!'

I rushed outside but was immediately grabbed by two tribesmen. Not hurt, simply held in place. Joseph, Philip and Thaddeus were being hustled away, already too distant for me to talk to them. I raised my voice, hoping to reach their ears anyway. 'Joseph—what is going on?'

'I don't know!' was the only response, before they vanished inside another hut.

A few minutes later there was another commotion as Tabitha was dragged from somewhere and pushed into the same hut. She made no sound but physically resisted every step of the way.

It was several hours before I could persuade the chief to let me see Joseph and the others. Some of the people were out working in the fields or else hunting, so the hill fort was reasonably quiet on this chill, breezy day. Two tribesmen stood guard at the door. My escort spoke to them and they nodded, moved aside to let me in. The interior was dim, but I closed my eyes for a moment and then could see well enough. Joseph was standing, Philip and Thaddeus sitting against the far wall and Tabitha also standing, statuelike, nearby.

'Where did she go last night?' I demanded.

Joseph was clearly not expecting to be challenged. 'I beg your pardon, Lady Martha? Tabitha is hardly the concern at the moment.'

'She is exactly the concern,' I said wearily. 'And you may call me simply Martha. I am the daughter of Abigail and I have no power here except by the generosity of Weylyn, priest of this people. But I have knowledge and by knowledge I may save your lives. Peter raised her, you say, but I know Peter did not share Joshua's power.'

'It was God's will,' Joseph began.

I waved him off. 'With some interference from men, which is hardly new. What did Peter do? Was Tabitha dead or dying when he reached her?'

'You have no right to demand answers of me, woman,' Joseph said. 'Your husband commands you. We bring Christ's word to these shores and his promise of eternal life. The girl Tabitha is witness to his power ...'

'Tabitha is dead!' I shouted.

Joseph of Arimathea, one of the richest men in Jerusalem, took a staggering step back before my fury. I scared myself. 'Peter gave this woman wine mixed with *Joshua's blood* as she was dying and it brought her body back all right, but what is in her head is not Tabitha. It controlled me, to bring me here to this place, for what reason I do not yet know. Did Peter give her the blood as I have said?'

Anger drained out of Joseph as though he had been cut by the physician's knife. He nodded. Philip and Thaddeus said nothing. After a moment, Joseph spoke quietly, defeatedly.

'The physician bled Joshua—he was barely alive when they took him down from the cross and the Romans believed he was dead. We must have her to take of her blood, only a little each time, but it is mingled with his blood who died for us.' He was gaining a little confidence because I seemed to be listening.

I could bear it no more. 'But you know it is not Tabitha, don't you? You say you knew her, Joseph—is that truly the girl as she was when alive? Did you speak to others who knew her? Listen to me, Joseph! What I know of sorcery, I have studied from my mother and her mother before her, back to Hannah of Endor who told King Saul his fate. I learn those things of vision and the summoning of the wise ones who have gone. I never tried to call up an evil thing, a thing which would fight me with all the black arts it possessed as the spirit which entered Tabitha and then myself has done. It left my body when I fell into the salt water, for the sea banishes human magic. Otherwise, I would still be doing its will, not my own. It does not care what your purposes are, Joseph, it only used all of us to get itself here.'

I pointed at the silent creature standing by the wall and with all the force of my will, I pushed at her, willing the true Tabitha to come forward. *You cannot rest, I told her silently, not until you are no longer shackled to flesh which should be dead. Come forward and help me to help you.'*

Pain throbbed in my forehead and I felt a great pressure as of a tremendous wind rising. That demon, that creature of the depths, was trying to leave Tabitha all right, a body which would never fully answer to her, and walk back into mine, a much more satisfactory home. I needed something into which to send it but there was nothing, no one nearby whom I could use. Joshua had used swine once, but there was no animal, nothing ... but wait, there was something. There was one thing in Joseph's possession which contained part of a living thing.

'The wine—Joshua's blood—where is it?' I must have seemed like a madwoman in the too-small hut, raging at the cowering Joseph. He obeyed me with shaking hands, going to his possessions piled on the floor and lifting up a small amphora, which he unstoppered and held forth by its two handles as though to invite me to drink. It smelled of honey and spices rather than the wine, which was probably half vinegar by now. I had no intention of drinking, but I brought forth an image of thirst, of a desire to slake that thirst which could only be done by swallowing the cool, delicious red wine with its dark blend of human blood in that amphora. I created images of my body burning with dryness, of bathing in clear cold water. All this lay within the small container in Joseph's hands. All the while, my temples throbbed with pain and the blinding headache crept closer to my eyes. Nausea rose in my stomach and my face dripped with sweat.

Then it stopped, sharply as a breaking bone. The spirit, the influence, was gone but I did not know whether it had gone into the wine or simply dissipated.

'Close it!' My voice was dry and harsh as though I had swallowed sand, but Joseph understood and hastened to obey me. My legs gave way beneath me and I tumbled to the clay floor. I heard the thump of another body falling. I struggled to sit up and saw the empty corpse of Tabitha sprawled on the ground. As

Philip tried to help me up, I grabbed his arm and gasped that he should ask one of the tribesmen on guard to fetch Weylyn.

Arrius was outside the hut. He helped me into the dwelling given to us. I felt as though most of my own blood had been drained from my body; it was a long time since I had tried to do a sorcery. There was shouting outside but no way to find out what they were saying, not until I was stronger.

At dusk I was able to go outside. Arrius went with me. Weylyn was waiting for me. He did not smile, but he gestured for me to follow him. It was as though Arrius was not there, but he followed the priest and me. Weylyn took me outside the pallisade, to an area of level ground halfway down the hill, where a great wooden cage had been set up. There were three men inside it and kindling was piled around it.

No one stopped me as I walked to the wicker cage. It was barely large enough for Joseph, Philip and Thaddeus to stand upright, yet all three did stand and attempt to maintain their dignity. A curious double sight came upon me then. I seemed to see the wicker cage both as it was, and afire, with the three men screaming and falling as the fire ate their clothing and then their hair and flesh. The image of a woman seemed to form itself from the flames. Her form was that of Tabitha, but Tabitha as I had never seen her, dancing wildly naked, her long hair flowing free within the fire, unburned, untouched. She looked back at me and smiled, gesturing with her arms at the screaming men as though the sight and the sounds pleased her. As I looked upon her, I knew that she was the being who had answered Peter's call. As our eyes met, she flooded my mind with answers. I had thought her demon but that was not the name which came to my mind now. That name was goddess.

She had not meant to harm me. She had passed through the gate of death into our world when it was opened by someone within it. Peter had not understood what he did and it was not something a mortal was ever intended to do. The real living girl Tabitha had already passed and could not be brought back. The spirit from the world beyond had found herself restricted and limited by the dead body animated by Joshua's blood. She had been a living woman once. Her home was here in Britain, not Judea, but she had been unable to remember all of who and what she was. Then she had been brought to me. I was a woman of power like she had been and she had thought to control me instead, become me, to have a place here. The fragments of her memory urged her to drink my blood. When she did so, she remembered what she was. Now she knew she did not require a mortal body at all. I sensed her regret, her wish to make amends.

Look, the goddess told me. *See ahead.*

My mind's eye reached into the flames and I seemed to hear the tolling of bells and voices chanting Latin. Shadowy forms inside a huge, high-ceilinged building, mostly dark except for candle and lamplight. The voices were many, far more people than I dreamed inhabited the earth. Was this the future which would exist if I saved these men? The fire-vision blurred and changed and I heard the tramp of many feet and seemed to see the eagle-standard raised above the plumed helmets of Roman legions on the march. Again I could hear Latin, but this time it was battle orders. My understanding of Latin was still sketchy, but in the vision, as in dream, my understanding was greater than in waking life. Either path, the language survived, but which way would save Rome? Did I want to save Rome? Rome was the invader, it had taken my homeland and would seek to take this one as well. That much seemed clear. Joseph and his people had no interest in Rome. They wanted to keep Joshua's memory alive. If they did, the final shreds of sorcery were not going to survive. How I knew these things, I could not have said, but as the two visions fought for control of my mind, the certainty of them was like the single tread of six thousand men, a legion of Rome.

Abruptly the twin vision released me and I found myself kneeling on the hard ground, gasping for breath. Weylyn stood beside me and helped me up. I tried to ask him: Did you see? He nodded. 'On which path will Rome rule?'

'Camlann,' he said and pointed across the fields, then at me. I blinked in confusion. Weylyn brushed my lip with his finger. I had said the word. The name? He nodded. Joseph was shouting at me, demanding, pleading that I get Arrius, organise a rescue, something.

'Joseph,' I tried to shout, but my voice was hoarse. 'You must answer a question for me. What was I saying just now? You know I do not remember what I say when I was in trance. Tell me.'

'You said you were at Camlann, a great battle in days to come,' Joseph finally answered, leaning his bearded face against the rough wicker barrier. 'You saw the last heirs of Rome fight against the darkness.'

'What days?'

'You did not say.'

'Anything else? Anything of who won the victory?'

'Nothing that made any sense to me.'

'Nothing of my people?'

'No. Only Rome.'

If Rome prospered, did that mean the end of my people? Was this the path in which sorcery survived? I had not seen enough, I wailed inside, not enough to help me choose. I asked Weylyn,

'Is it given to me to choose? Will your people allow these men to go free if I ask it?'

In answer he showed me an image of the fire-dancing goddess. His face looked tense, frightened and no longer boyish. I could understand his fear. You worship gods and you make sacrifice to them. You don't expect them to move into your house with you.

Our communication was becoming easier, I realised; we were understanding one another's words. Her gift?

'Their blood will please her,' Weylyn added.

'It certainly would,' I agreed, 'but how many more lives is she going to require? If you do not give in to her, I don't think she has any power to force you, though she will try to convince you otherwise. Let the men go, Weylyn. I do not know which of the two paths I have seen is the best one, but I do not want to set my feet on any path created in blood and death. These are ignorant men, but they are not altogether bad and there may be wisdom in them. We do not know enough to choose.'

Weylyn bowed his shaggy red head and then lifted it again to look me in the eyes. 'It is given to you,' he said.

'Let them go,' I said, aware of the terrible weariness and weakness pressing on me again as a result of the power. There was a real Queen of Heaven here now, so whichever path became ours as a result of this choice was going to include her. Perhaps she would help my people. Perhaps not all the power and brightness would fade. Tribesmen were breaking open the wicker cage and I knew I did not want to remain here to exchange any more words with Joseph or the others, not in this life. 'May we leave?' I asked Arrius. He nodded and we walked quickly away. Weylyn stayed to deal with the tribesmen and with Joseph, but I no longer cared about their fate. Clumsily, searching for words that weren't there, I tried to tell Arrius what I had experienced.

'I thought I saw the kindling on fire, for only a moment,' he said. 'And a woman's shape. That was what you were talking about to Weylyn, wasn't it? A goddess in the flames demanding sacrifice.'

'Yes,' I admitted. 'She was a woman once but now she is much more than that.'

'She came into our world through the gate of death,' he said, thinking it out. 'Perhaps this is why it is so difficult to get any answer from the gods, they are distanced from us. Like Hades beneath the earth. Like Joshua who claimed to carry his god's spirit. Perhaps there has never been any deity actually in the world with living men.'

'There is now,' I said.

Sue Isle lives in Perth, Western Australia. She has written two books for teenagers; *Scale of Dragon, Tooth of Wolf* and *Wolf Children*, and sold stories to *Aurealis, Orb, ASIM, Sword and Sorceress* and *Tales of the Unanticipated* [USA], which recently published the story 'Mary Bennet Goes Postal'. The NSW School Magazine featured Sue's immortal work 'Aliens Stole My Sister'. Other interests include history, roleplay gaming and gardening. This last is totally out of control since moving to a Real House at the end of 2004 and there also seem to be more pet rats living here.

THE BIG ONE

DIRK FLINTHART

W E'RE LOADING THE BOAT—me and Cal, Kev and Gordo, Shelly and Mick—the whole crew, when the cop pulls up by the marina. Cal is holding up the heavy end of one of the jetboards. He shoots me an anxious glance. I spare the cop a look, shrug and nod towards the boat. We stagger on up the gangplank, leaving the others to do the talking.

The jetboard fits across the stern with all the rest, though it takes a little shoving. Cal says something about the couplings, but I'm trying to hear what's happening back on shore.

'You're going to have to vacate this area,' says the cop. 'Which safe zone are you assigned to?'

'Katoomba Highlands.' Shelly's voice. 'We've got plenty of time, officer.'

'What are you doing with that boat? The harbours are closed. You will not be permitted to take that boat out.' The cop rat-a-tats his words, like a machine gun. as though it gives him more authority.

'Where would we go?' asks Shelly lightly. 'Do we look crazy?'

I look over the gunwale as the cop pushes back his hat and scratches the side of his head absently.

'Looters,' he suggests tentatively. 'We've had quite a few already. You could be looters.'

'But we're loading the boat, officer,' she replies, shifting her weight minutely to throw one firmly rounded hip towards the young policeman. 'Looters would be unloading, wouldn't they?' Shelly is a practicing psychologist. She's taught me to recognise the tricks of body language that she's using now—the angled hip, the toes pointed towards the officer, the lowered eyes, fingers playing with a stray lock of hair. She knows what she's doing. She's got a great body, firm and toned, and she's giving this cop all she's got. Silently, I wave Cal over to the gunwale, and together, we watch in silent mirth.

'Two minutes and he gives up,' whispers Cal. 'Five thousand bucks.'

'Cheapskate. I'll see your 5000. He's going to stick around for at least five minutes before he figures out he's not going to get to fuck her.'

'Bet,' says Cal, and we shake hands solemnly.

As it happens, we're both wrong. Just as we settle back into place for the show, Gordo strolls down the gangplank.

'Good morning, officer,' he says. 'Something I can do for you?' Shelly gives him a look, but he affects not to see.

'Is this your boat, sir?' asks the cop, all business now.

'That's correct,' agrees Gordo. 'Nice one, eh?'

'I wouldn't know,' says the cop—a little sourly, I think. The 'Devilfish' is a very nice boat, as a matter of fact; a 60 foot cabin cruiser with twin inboard diesel turbine engines. Much nicer than anything you might expect from, say, a cop's salary. But then, Gordon Chambers QC has been pulling down six figures for several years now. 'Are these people with you?' demands the cop. 'Do you realise you've missed the evac deadline—all of you?'

Gordon smiles broadly. He places a large hand on the cop's shoulder.

'Why don't we talk about that over here, officer,' he suggests, leading the cop back to the white Ford.

Cal and I exchange glances. What's going on?

Minutes later, the door to the cop-mobile closes, and the car roars off leaving Gordon standing alone on the tarmac under the hot summer sun. He shakes his head. A huge grin splits his face, the kind of delighted expression I've seen on him maybe once or twice before, if ever. 'Hey, everybody,' he announces happily. 'I've just bribed an officer of the law!'

HGC-16 was nothing special. Another misshapen chunk of rock tumbling through the darkness of space. It was bigger than most—100 metres or so across at its longest—but certainly not one of the more dangerous. There were plenty of asteroids whose projected orbits took them much closer to Earth than good old HGC-16. Once the orbit was calculated and identified as safe, HGC-16 got filed away with the rest of them, and everyone forgot about it.

Eventually, having found nothing worthy of note, the project itself was wound down. Most likely, that would have been that except for a post-grad physics student from Caltech, who only two years ago decided to dredge up the old orbital figures to support some kind of a new wrinkle he was developing in the theory of how the solar system got formed. Mallory, his name was. Reuben Mallory.

Mallory wasn't satisfied with the figures he got from the old asteroid-chasing project. They didn't suit his idea at all, and he didn't like that—so he wangled himself some time in an Australian observatory, to check the facts for himself. And that was when Reuben Mallory made his infamous discovery.

HGC-16 was something like number 25 on his list, so by the time he got down that far, Mallory was pretty tired. He hadn't had a lot of luck, either. The old observations had turned out to be quite accurate, by and large. His pet theory was looking very thin, and he wasn't too happy about that. As a result, when he found HGC-16 was nowhere near the place it was supposed to be, he checked and rechecked a few times, and then he got very excited indeed. He started calling people.

It didn't take long before Mallory's discovery was confirmed by two more observatories—one in South America, and one in Africa. Somehow, the solar system seemed to have lost itself an asteroid.

One of the original scientists on the asteroid-chasing project got wind of the matter when Mallory started to trumpet his new theory around the place. Like a lot of scientists, this Doctor Leary was kind of tetchy about what he called his scientific reputation. It annoyed hell out of him that one of his asteroids could have gone astray, and he didn't for a moment believe that a skinny little post-grad nobody like Mallory had made some kind of discovery that better-informed scientists—such as Leary himself—had somehow overlooked.

Asteroids obey the law of gravity, and he knew his original observations and calculations had been correct. Logically, therefore, something had happened to change HGC-16's orbit. And unless one posited the intervention of little green men or something equally unlikely, whatever it was that had influenced HGC-16 was probably an observed, catalogued, thoroughly *known* member of the solar family. So, acting on this premise, Leary sat down with a very large computer, and set about projecting the course HGC-16 should have taken during the intervening years. And only a couple of days later, he had it.

Leary called a press conference, with every intention of refuting Mallory and restoring his own good reputation.

'Our figures weren't wrong,' he told the largely uninterested scientific press. 'We just didn't look far enough into the future.' And then he showed them his calculations and computer simulations, how HGC-16 had made a near-miss rendezvous with Mars seven years after Leary's project had found it. How the close encounter with Mars had altered the orbit of the asteroid drastically. How Reuben Mallory really had no idea what he was talking about, and what kind of scientist were they producing at Caltech these days anyway ...

About then, one of the reporters intervened.

'So, where's this asteroid now?' he asked, more as a way of distracting Leary than in the hopes of getting useful information.

Leary blinked.

'I hadn't thought about that,' he admitted, and went back to his simulations. A few minutes later, he put his sky-chart back on the projector, and triumphantly pointed out a tiny speck of light amidst all the others in the inky darkness. 'Right here,' announced Leary. 'Exactly as the orbital figures said it should be.'

Then the same reporter as before leaned forward with a frown. He opened his mouth, then closed it again, and scratched his head. Finally, he pushed back his baseball cap, and asked the question that changed everything: 'Where the hell is the Earth on this chart of yours?'

'He took a cheque?'

Gordo closes his eyes and shakes his head ruefully.

'He took a cheque,' he confirms. 'Ten grand.' Reaching into the cooler at his feet, he brings out a pair of Toohey's Old, condensation gleaming on the dark glass. 'He took a bloody cheque,' he repeats, astounded, as he pops a top with a satisfying fizz, and passes me the bottle. It's cold, cold as ice in my hand and the beer is sharp and bitter and wonderfully good in my throat.

'I guess they don't pay cops to be smart.' The bottle fits neatly into a polystyrene cooler that helps it stand upright on the gently swaying deck of the Devilfish as we churn through the light surf on our way out to the deepest blue of all.

Gordo glances at me, and grins.' Now you know what I had to put up with, all those years as a lawyer.'

Cal looks back over his shoulder from his vantage point at the broad wooden wheel. 'Oh, you bastards. Into the beer already. That's gotta last us, you know.'

'Relax,' says Gordon, 'I laid in four cartons. We'll never get through it all.'

'Oh,' says Cal, mollified. 'So why am I standing here without a drink?'

Gordon frowns. 'Well, Cal—you should know it's illegal for the skipper to be drinking while in charge of the vessel.' For a moment, he struggles to keep that courtroom scowl in place, but the crows feet in the tanned skin around his eyes are deepening, and at last, the laughter bubbles out uncontrollably. A bottle arcs smoothly through the wine-sweet sea air, and Cal catches it one-handed.

The sun is bright in the morning sky, the seagulls cry out above us, and the engines of the Devilfish throb with a rich, deep note as we cut through the clear blue waters. Behind us, the green-white wake stretches into the distance, where the mountains rise up, blue upon blue upon blue. Has there ever been such a beautiful day?

'Ya-ta-hay,' I murmur, raising my bottle to the mountains and the sky.

'What's that?' Gordon cocks his head.

'Ya-ta-hay,' I repeat. 'It's Apache, I think. Means 'It's a good day to die,' or something like that.'

'Ya-ta-hay.' He tries it out thoughtfully, nodding. He clinks his bottle against mine. 'Ya-ta-hay,' he says, and drinks deeply.

The little wrinkles re-appear as he wipes his mouth on his sleeve. How long has he had those? If I close my eyes and imagine my friend Gordo, the man I see has no crows feet. Nor streaks of grey at the temples either. The man I see is young, smooth-skinned, with curling dark hair that falls to his shoulders as he stands laughing, his surfboard propped in the sand next to him.

I open my eyes again. 27 years. That's how long it has been since my mind took that picture. Gordon Chambers, the man who sits contentedly in front of me, has crows feet. His hair is no longer wild and curling to his shoulders; now it is sensibly short and respectable. The smooth skin is tanned, a little leathery, and spotted by years in the Australian sun. He's thicker around the middle, too, from years of good living—not like my skinny friend Gordo in the days we starved together at college. But then he catches me looking and he smiles, and despite the wrinkles and the sunspots and the salt-and-pepper in his hair, it's still Gordo, still my oldest and best friend, and the sun is high and we're back together on the water, like always.

'You worried?' he asks.

I smile, and shrug, not knowing what to say, but I'm saved by the arrival of Mick, who emerges from belowdecks blinking in the strong light.

'Beer?' he says. 'Oh, bloody marvellous. That is exactly what I need.' It must be hot belowdecks. Mick is sweating heavily as he tilts the bottle to the sky, his throat working as he drains more than half of it in a single pull. 'Ahhhh,' he sighs, and flops into the deckchair next to me. He runs the bottle back and forth across his shining scalp, where the tangle of blond hair used to be, all those years ago.

'Hey, Shaker,' he says, glancing at me. 'Shelly's belowdecks. She said something about wanting a word with you, man.'

'Me?' I don't want to go belowdecks, where it's dark and hot and close.. I want to stay up here in the blue and wonderful world. 'What's she want?'

Mick pulls a stained and tattered terry-towelling hat down over his smooth, sweating scalp, adjusting the brim so it shades his eyes.

'Search me,' he says, and settles into the chair with a grunt of
absolute contentment. 'You know what she's like.'
  He's right. I do. With a sigh, I drain the last of my beer and go
in search of Shelly.

They did their best. But it wasn't good enough.

There was that movie somebody made, with Bruce Willis and
a bunch of others. About an oil-rig crew who fly into space to
save the world from an asteroid by drilling and planting a nuke
to break up the rock. It was a stupid movie, but it went over well.
And it had Liv Tyler in it, which was a good thing.

The real world doesn't work like the movies, we learned. It
turned out that nobody had any spare space-ships that were
smart enough to rendezvous with a rock the size of the Hammer—
which is what they came to call it in the press. Hammer of God.
Besides, by the time we worked out where the bastard was, it was
already way too close to try anything as fancy as that.

The UN called an emergency session and gave China,
France, Russia and the USA permission to fling nukes at the
Hammer. It took a little longer than it should have, maybe,
because of course everybody had to have observers at all the
launches, to make sure nobody was going to take the chance
to throw a sucker-punch, toss a few ICBM's down each others'
throats while their pants were down, or whatever. I remember
laughing at that one. Biggest disaster in all history coming our
way, and the governments of the world still had to make like
kids squabbling in a sandbox.

It was a waste of time, anyway. Apparently, targeting a 100-
metre rock tumbling through space is a lot harder than targeting
a city half-way round the world. The Americans managed to
crash-land a couple of Titans, according to the pictures that
came back, but that was as close as anybody got. Of course, the
Chinese *claimed* they'd hit it too, but they didn't have pictures.
And who knows? Maybe the Americans faked their pictures
anyway. What does it matter? The end result was a couple
of billion dollars worth of high-tech weaponry that someday,
maybe, is going to crash-land in a galaxy far, far away and fuck
up ET real bad.

And the Hammer was still coming at us.

The scientists had a wonderful time. They were on all the
front pages, all the news programs, all the talk-back shows all
over the world. Nobody had *ever* paid this much attention to
them before. They were practically delirious with delight. New
projections, new figures and estimates were released almost on
an hourly basis. It took a long time, relatively speaking before
any real sense emerged from the mess—and the picture that
developed wasn't pretty.

The Hammer wasn't going to be a world-killer, they told us. It wasn't even as big as the rock that aced the dinosaurs, apparently. But it was big enough. Nobody was absolutely certain where it was going to land. Best guesses agreed that it would probably smack down somewhere in the South Pacific, way off to the north-east of New Zealand. Probably. If it didn't break up in the atmosphere, or skip like a stone on a pond and come down somewhere in Kazakhstan or Newfoundland or whatever.

The worst effects would be on the weather, they said. Just as it had been from Krakatoa, and earlier, in the 19th century, when Tambora blew in Indonesia, and a year went by in America where they didn't get a summer. Except that this time, there would be a whole lot more debris. If it hit water—which was pretty likely, since the earth's surface is something like three-quarters water—it would create a huge blanket of cloud that would bring a dark winter that might last years. Maybe even precipitate another Ice Age. And if it hit land, the dust and grit would be blown so high into the atmosphere that the same kind of thing might occur.

Not the end of the world, of course. Just a really, really shitty time for everything living in it. Worst of all for anyone or anything near the impact site, naturally, but pretty bad all round. And if it landed in the ocean— well, there was something else to consider. Shockwaves. Tsunami.

The Big One.

It is dark belowdecks, in the cabin where Shelly is waiting, and I'm still blinking, trying to adjust to the dimness when she is on me. Naked, warm, wriggling in my arms like a puppy, smothering me with kisses, peeling the shirt from my body.

'Hey, hey,' I say, holding her close and tight, as much in self-defence as to feel her smooth skin against mine. 'What's this?'

'Shhh,' says Shelly, slipping her thumbs under the band of my shorts. 'Just once more, for old times sake.'

Old times. Yes, indeed.

'It's been what—25 years since we stopped doing this, hasn't it, Shel?' Bemused, confused, I'm talking with my lips pressed against her forehead where the lovely, coppery hair starts as she tugs determinedly at my pants. 'I thought—I mean, you know ...'

'Shut up,' she says, looking up at me and wrinkling her freckled, sunburned nose. My trousers pool around my ankles with a soft, sighing noise, and Shelly starts to work on my boxers. She glances down. 'You always used to wear jockeys,' she says reproachfully.

Laughing, I kick my way free of my clothing and toss her onto the bed. She lands with a bounce, and looks up at me wide-eyed.

What the hell. What difference can it make now?

Later, we lie comfortably side-by-side, listening to the throb of the diesels carrying us out to sea, out to the home of the Monster.

'Why didn't it work between us?' asks Shelly, absently spiralling a fingertip in the coarse hair on my chest. 'We had so much in common.'

'Maybe that was it,' I reply. 'Maybe we were too much alike. It was fun while it lasted though, wasn't it?'

A faraway look crosses her sturdy, girlish face, and I know we are thinking of the same things: jewel-bright days and nights, strung together like an endless necklace of gaudy youth. Cutting classes together so we could get into Gordo's beat-up old Valiant and head for the surf. Casks of cheap wine, and fat, crackling, joints of sticky grass. Kev playing an old guitar as the moon climbed out of the ocean in a blaze of glory. Cal driving too fast with the wind in our hair, shrieking with laughter and the sun on our skin. Mick cooking fresh-caught bream over a driftwood fire laid on the cool sand of a beach that nobody but we ever went to.

We were there together, all of us, even back then. From time to time there were others, but over the years, somehow they fell away, and in the end, there were just the six of us, just the way it started back when we met.

'Yes,' says Shelly. 'It was good. Really good. How did we get here from there? You with your students. Cal and the business. Gordo a lawyer, for God's sake. What happened to all those fabulous ideas we used to have? We were going to change the world, remember?'

'I remember.' I slide my arm around her soft shoulders and pull her close. 'I guess we got here the same way most everyone does. And we've still got each other, right? We made better friends than lovers anyhow. And for a while, anyway, we really lived it up, didn't we? That's a lot better than most people.'

'I guess so,' she smiles at me, resting her head on my shoulder. It's a beautiful smile, and suddenly I'm in love with her all over again, just like all those years ago—but it passes, and I give her a tender kiss.

'Anyway,' she says afterward, 'Even if we had managed to change the world, what good would it do us now?'

'Good point,' I admit, ruffling her hair. It feels silky between my fingers, rich and thick, belying her forty-odd years. Shelly is beautiful, I realise. She's always been beautiful. I just forgot, for a while there.

'Go on,' she says at last. 'Go back up on deck. I want to stay down here and think for a while.'

I dress in silence. As I reach for the door, she says:' Wait,' and I turn back.

Shelly is lying on her side, the sheet draped coyly across her lovely body. 'Tell Kev I want a word with him, will you?'

'Kev?' I lift an eyebrow.

She has the good grace to blush. 'Well, we did go out for a couple of years there, right?'

Laughing, shaking my head, I return to the world above.

It was Cal who came up with the idea, I think. The six of us were sitting around the dinner table at Kev's place one evening, a few weeks after they'd figured out that the Hammer was definitely going to hit the South Pacific. We were talking about the Big One—everyone in the world was talking about the Big One right about then—and Cal got this faraway look in his eye, and went quiet for a while. He sketched out the basic plans for the jetboards on the back of a couple of drink coasters while the rest of us talked. He's always been good with motors and gadgets and things.

It was only natural that together, we should talk about the Big One—and speculate. All of us were surfers, of course. The real kind, lifelong addicts to salt-water. Surf was the thing that had kept us together for more than a quarter-century. It was like breathing to the six of us, and so the Big One held a kind of fascination. I mean, imagine it—a wall of water, near 50 metres tall. The greatest surf challenge of all time, and very possibly the last.

I don't think we ever admitted to ourselves that we were serious about it, even right up to the last days. After all, who would be crazy enough to surf a monster like that? How far inland would a wave like that break? How could you survive the collapse? Even if you took the usual way out and rode over the top before it crested and broke, you'd still be caught and smashed, or sucked back out to sea—or just crushed to death by one of the secondary waves that would follow.

Theoretically, though, if you were good enough, you could do it. They'd been catching twenty-metre waves off Hawaii for years, in two man teams—one man on a jetski towing the surfer up to speed and cutting him loose to ride the wave, while the jet-ski sped off to safety. And theoretically, even on a monster wave, a good surfer could stay ahead of the white water, but out of the trough, until the wave spent itself. If the wave broke right, of course. And if the surfer didn't plough into any trees or buildings or mountainsides, depending on how far a 50-metre wave carried him.

Okay, yeah. Fat chance.

But the alternatives were so bloody depressing. Government shelters. Food rationing. Years of winter. Famine. Shortages. Disease, no doubt. Utter destruction of everything on the coastline, all over the world. Pretty much the end of civilisation.

So. Just for the hell of it, we planned. Not that we were really going to do it, or anything. No, we were all responsible people. Kev and Cal had families. Gordo had extensive inland properties—good, arable land that would be incredibly valuable after the Big One. And I was a teacher. There'd be a lot of need for skilled teachers when it came time to rebuild.

But just for the hell of it, Cal designed the jet-boards in his spare time. Even built a prototype, using a jet-ski motor and specially-reinforced Malibu board, hooked together by explosive bolts so the engine could be ditched once the board was up to speed. After all, there'd be no point in two-man teams in the face of the Big One. Anybody who went to the edge of the continental shelf when a wave like that turned up—well, you could come home on it and with it, or you'd just never come home again.

Gordo got a real bargain on the 'Devilfish'. The owner figured there'd be little use for it in the remaining weeks before the Hammer. And after the Hammer, probably no use at all, even if the boat survived. So it went to Gordo for a song. He'd always wanted a boat like that, Gordo reckoned. Even if he only got to use it once or twice. After all, what good was the money going to do him once the Hammer came down?

Right up until the end, we kept joking about it. Pretending we were only pretending. Whistling past the graveyard. Making plans for the dark days afterwards, for the endless winter and the scrabble for survival. When all the time, we were thinking of a lifetime in the sun and the sea. Of the joy of the waves. Of a single vast, blue-green wave.

The Big One.

Now I'm floating in the blue water, lying comfortably athwart my jetboard, awaiting the Monster. The others are spaced out in a ragged line, a safe distance apart. The 'Devilfish' is on her way north, parallel to the coast, a course that will keep her well out of our way. Gordo was in tears as he lashed the wheel and let her go—but she'd done her job, and there was nothing more she could do for us.

So, here I am, idly trailing my hand in the water, wondering what the Wave will look like when it arrives. Nervous, a little drunk, a little buzzed from the weed we passed around a half hour before—but not too spaced out to surf. That would be a catastrophe.

And at last it comes, rising into view like the very Leviathan of Revelation. The Big One is well named—it's huge, bigger than I'd ever imagined it could be. Lifted to the sky by the proximity of the continental shelf, it looks like a vast blue wall, like a gigantic, curving nightmare, like a complete revision of the laws of physics.

It looks like the end of the world.

'Holy shit,' says Cal, his voice carried to me—to us all, out there, tiny specks on the face of the vast and hostile ocean— through the discreet intercom system we all carry. 'Would you just fucking look at that.'

I look. Kev looks. Gordon looks. Shelly looks. All of us stare at the Big One, as it pulls the ocean from its bed, raising it up like a mighty hammer to smash everything we have ever known.

Christ. It's huge.

'I think I'm feeling suction,' says Shelly. 'Yes. Definitely. Check positions!'

I glance down automatically. She's right. The vast mass of water humping and curling its way towards us is beginning to draw us into its inexorable path of destruction. I look back over my shoulder. Rising against the sky, it's unthinkable—a towering blue mass of power and speed and savage annihilation.

'Fire your engines,' says Gordon. 'Remember: idle until I give the word. Then it's full throttle.'

At the touch of a button, the powerful motor begins to throb and growl. The board vibrates between my legs.

'Shaker here,' I announce. 'I have ignition.'

The response comes from each of the others in turn. Ignition. All of us ready to go. Now we're waiting only for the right moment, for the final countdown. The wind is rising steadily. I can hear the distant, muted roar of the monster as it bears down. I want to look at it again, to see what it has become—but I am afraid that if I look, I will forget my courage and be lost. I look instead at the sea around me. It is preternaturally flat and even, smooth the way a deep, fast-running river is smooth and silky on the surface. Around my legs, I can feel the dreadful suction, the terrible, inescapable pull of the Beast.

'Twenty seconds,' says Gordon. 'Remember: don't disengage the motor unit until you reach at least 120 kph, people. That thing is moving, and if we don't move with it, we're history.'

'Shut up, Gordo,' says Shelly, the laughter in her voice touched with a wild note of fear and delight. 'Give us the countdown. Kev—where's that fucking music?'

'Coming up,' says Kev. There is a loud click in my earpiece, and then it begins. 'Let's go surfin' now, everybody's learning how ...' The Beach Boys: Surfin' Safari. A huge gust of laughter wells up from inside, somewhere. I can hear the others laughing too, the happy sound filling my ears, almost enough to drown out the roar of the great wave—and over the top, Gordon is giving us the countdown.

I grip the throttle, tense, carefully maintaining my balance, keeping the nose of the jetboard forward. Suddenly, the angle of the water goes crazy. I'm rising, rising up a gigantic mountain of water.

'Here we go, boys. This is it,' says Shelly.

'Mother-FUCKER!' I hear Cal say, but my hand is tight on the throttle and I'm listening, listening for one thing only, one voice only as the music rises and the wind rises and the great wave rises, hurling me towards the sky, and Gordon is saying in his deep, slow voice: 'Three. Two. One. Punch it, you fuckers!'

I twist the throttle. The specially-designed motor on the jetboard roars, the nose lifts, and I throw my weight forward as it lurches under me, and I'm still rising, rising, the music is rising in my ears, but the roar of the air and the monster wave is building. Lifting, rising, I risk a glance behind me and all I can see is a vast, green wall; I'm clinging like a fly, like a bug to an endless, roaring wall of blue-green fury. I look forward again.

It's a long, long way down.

The numbers on the speedo are climbing now, higher and higher, and my rate of climb on the Beast is slowing as the jetboard begins to catch up. It's a clever device, this board. I marvel at it, even as I try not to feel the panic in my belly. I'm so fucking high! This wave is—it really is The Big One, the end of the world.

Faintly, Gordo's voice comes to me. 'One-twenty! Disengage, disengage!'

This is it. This is the moment. I've matched speeds with the Monster, just as though I was paddling in the surf off North Head, except that I had to use an 80 horsepower jet-ski motor to do it. If I go any faster, I'll sink into the trough and get ahead of the wave, to be sucked under and ground up. Already, I'm beginning to slide down the face. Moment of truth time.

I stretch out full length on the old Malibu, keeping the throttle at full. Carefully, I kick back at the lever that triggers the explosive bolts. There is a jolt. The board rocks momentarily as it finds it's new centre of gravity, but I'm still moving, still sliding down the face of the wave, caught up now in the monstrous mass of water. I'm in the grip of The Beast.

'This is Shaker,' I report, shouting into the mike. 'I'm surfing!'

The feeling is incredible, at once familiar and terrifyingly different. The board moves under me as I rise to my feet, just as it always does, but this time I'm so fucking high, moving so fast. The wind buffets at me, trying to pull me into the water. I remain in the classic surfer's crouch until I'm certain of my balance, and I can stand up.

Oh, holy mother of God. This is it. This is what I was meant to do. This is the way it ends.

I can hear the others now, in my ears, screaming with elation and terror and absolute, suicidal delight. We're halfway up a 50-metre wall of water, heading for the coast at 120 kilometres per hour, the ultimate thrill, the Zen pinnacle of surfing, board and *wave and wind and body, all of us, the biggest wave anybody has ever ridden, the biggest anyone has ever seen, and we're flying, we're high above the ocean riding the Apocalypse homeward to the greatest wipeout of all time.*

The wind is a living thing, tugging and tearing at me, making my eyes water and my ears ring. Just for the hell of it, without thought or effort, I angle the board across the Monster and thrust my hand into the blue-green wall, cutting the water like a knife. Somewhere below, ahead of me, I can make out one of the others—maybe Gordo? Maybe not. Under my feet, the big old Malibu sings as it slashes the water, a song of fear and joy, a dirge of delight.

In my ears, the music changes: the incredible, rapidfire riffs of Dick Dale and the Del-tones, doing the classic—Miserlou. The shattering, electrifying guitar thrills through my whole body, head to toe, and the old war-cry of the California Surf days rises unbidden to my lips: Cowabunga!

I hear it echoed by the others, one after another, together for the final time. Cowabunga!

I'm crying. I'm laughing. I don't want to die. I don't want to hide in a dark hole until the sun goes out. I want this—the blue and the green, the clear, cold stinging joy of it. I want to live like a human being should. Like nobody has ever dared to live before.

The wave is rising to a white, raging, crest now, and the coastline begins to loom in the distance. End of the ride. I wonder how far inland we can get?

'Hey Gordo,' I shout. 'Race you to the Harbour Bridge, man!'

As I turn the nose of the board back down the face of the Monster, taking the ride of a lifetime on the End of the World, I can hear the laughter of my friends with the music in my ears, and I laugh with them, smiling, joyful.

Bring it on, you bastard. Cowabunga!

Dirk Flinthart has been published in crime fiction, humour, travel, and feature journalism, and has the writing credits for the odd short film as well — but his lifelong love has been science fiction and fantasy, and he keeps drifting back there no matter how moribund the markets may seem. Currently he lives somewhere in Darkest Tasmania, with three children, a wife, and other animals; a deeply G-rated sort of bucolic water-colour existence which gives the lie to his reputation as a rakehell and wastrel of the lowest order. Of course, your mileage may vary.

Tigershow

JANEEN WEBB

ROBERT HAD ANOTHER ONE OF HIS HEADACHES. They'd been with him since his stint as peacekeeper up on the Thai border. Nothing helped. He drove in a red haze, the pain at his temples blurring his vision, cruelly sharpening his other faculties. He gripped the wheel tight, too tight, straining white knuckled against sensory overload. He could hear the deep resonant purring, a rumbling basso underneath the steady thrum of his engine. He could smell the musky cat smell, the feral taint underlying the hot macadam, the diesel fumes, the gritty smog.

The tigers were everywhere. Stalking, always stalking. If he let his eyes unfocus, very slightly, the predators were there: he glimpsed the outline of a stripey haunch in the stark barred shade of a railing fence, saw the edge of a twitching tail almost concealed in the palm fronds of a roadside planter box, recognised the yellow reflection of tiger eyes in a plate glass shopfront window.

Robert concentrated, conscious of his own sweaty flesh smell close about him. He narrowed his gaze, tried to blend with the moving herd. But he knew in his heart, in his guts, in his bones, that he was tiger meat. Today's special, *Robert tartare*.

Adrenalin pumping, he accelerated sharply. And as he drove, he cursed: raging at the traffic, the noise, the summer heat. All he wanted was to get home, out of the stuffy car, out of his scratchy, stifling suit. Away from the glaring sunlight. Away from tiger country. To be quiet, to be safe. The old Bar Beach house might belong to Adele's family, but it was his only refuge. Mercifully near the sea, it offered respite, offered hope. There would be an evening breeze. Maybe at dusk he would take a walk on the beach, clear his head. Let the boom and crash and roar of the surf drown out the threat reverberating in the hunters' incessant purring.

But tigers were patient. They didn't mind the heat. They would wait.

Stalking, waiting, stalking.
Burning.

Robert caught a glimpse of receding orange tail lights as another car pulled away from his house. Untrimmed yellow bougainvillea whipped across his windscreen as he turned into his driveway. Bright birds flew up, shrieking cries of alarm. He sensed the tigers, here ahead of him. Violating his sanctuary. His lawn grass was summer dry, tawny, striped with long afternoon shadow. Dangerous.

The moment the creaking garage door announced him, his daughters came running across the yard, oblivious to the threat. Red haired and freckled like their father, they were both brimming with news, vying with each other to tell it first.

'Daddy. Daddy. Guess what?'

Robert squared his shoulders, composed his face, tried to look fatherly.

'What, sweetheart?'

'Uncle George had a heart attack. He's in the hospital. There was an ambulance with lights and sirens and everything.'

'And Grandma and Aunty Beryl and Aunty Val were here with Mummy.'

'They just left.'

'And Aunty Maggie has come to live with us.'

Robert's fatherly facade cracked.

'Christ almighty!'

He strode up the path, flanked by anxious children.

'Adele!'

'Don't shout, I'm right here. In the kitchen.'

The bamboo blinds were rolled down against the gold-black heat of the setting sun. Robert told himself the purring undertone was just the refrigerator. Adele sat at the scrubbed table, looking tired and worried. She was wearing a dress that Robert hated, a loose Community Aid handcrafted cotton sundress in a muddy yellow woodblock print that drained her skin of life. She had pulled her mouse blonde hair straight back into a ponytail, exposing a pale freckled face so innocent of cosmetics that her untinted eyelashes almost disappeared against her wan complexion. Her upper lip was sheened by perspiration in the close atmosphere of late afternoon. She looked young, and vulnerable.

She turned to face the storm.

Robert's face was livid, his words almost a snarl. 'Do we *have* to have *that* woman in the house? Maggie never lifts a finger unless its around a glass—spends half her life in the beauty parlour and the other half in bed. She'll wear you out fetching and carrying for her. It's a wonder George hasn't had his heart attack before now.'

'Sssh. She'll hear you. It's only for a couple of days. She doesn't drive, and we live closest to the hospital. She's family, Rob. It's the least we can do.'

'And we'll never hear the end of it from your mother if we don't. Right?'

'Don't be nasty. Aunt Margaret is Mother's sister. Of course she's concerned.'

'Then let *her* put her up. I don't like you rushing around playing taxi whenever there's another crisis in that interminable family of yours. Your place is here. With me. You have more than enough to do with two small daughters. That's why you quit teaching, remember? And your mother thinks ...'

'Don't start that again. You know Mother's too ill for guests.'

'So what about the others, then? You had the female mafia round here drinking cups of tea and calling the shots. Making decisions affecting *my* family. Without consulting me!'

'You were at work, Rob. You know how you hate to be disturbed there. Uncle George's collapse was very sudden. I did the best I could.'

'Our house stinks already.'

Adele swiftly removed an ashtray overflowing with lipstick stained butts.

'Look, Rob, Aunty is old and she's terribly upset. I've put her upstairs in the spare room. She'll be company for me, and she's very good with the girls. Try to be nice. For my sake.'

The stairs creaked. Aunt Margaret—'Maggie to my friends' —was nervously dressed to the nines in an overtight red silk suit with *faux* tigerskin trim and shoes to match. As usual, she had overdone it: too much rouge, too much lipstick, too much jewellery. She descended at full sail, corsets straining. In her perfumed wake trailed her rolypoly pedigreed Pekinese, Soo Tze Wong, an overfed untidy little bundle of yapping yellow-brown hair.

'Bobby, darling. How lovely to see you. Its been simply ages. Come and give your poor old aunty a kiss.'

Robert found himself crushed against an overlarge bosom, trying not to gag in its Crabtree & Evelyn miasma of musky rose. He glowered at Adele over her aunt's shoulder, grimaced as his captor smeared a bright red lipstick kiss across his cheek before releasing him. His headache throbbed.

'It's *very* kind of you to let me stay over, Bobby. I'm worried sick about George, and I just couldn't bear to be alone in that big old house without him. His heart, you know. Just like a man, not to let on there's anything wrong until he keels over in the street. Right outside the cake shop. Lucky Mrs Rowan was looking out at the time. Well, she'll certainly have something to tell her customers. Hotbed of gossip, that cake shop. Still, he's in good hands at the hospital, and all we can do now is wait and hope. I must say I could do with a drink. Scotch would be fine, dear. I'll just sit over here, out of everyone's way.'

She stopped to draw breath. Robert seized the moment:

'We don't allow dogs in the house, Margaret. They shed hair, make me sneeze. I'll just put yours outside with our Butch. The girls can feed them both later.'

Maggie looked horrified.

'You can't put my poor little Soozy outside in the dark with that big black Butch monster of yours. Anything could happen. He'd be all over her.'

She waggled a coquettish finger:

'We don't want any hanky-panky of that sort, do we dear.'

Robert's face darkened.

'Of course not, Aunty.' Adele was solicitous, anxious in the glare of her husband's outrage.

'It'll be alright, Rob, just this once. I'll see to it. Soo Tze will be fine in the laundry. She can curl up safe and warm in the cane basket.'

Adele sighed, visibly wishing she too could curl up somewhere safe.

'Now why don't both of you have a quiet drink in the lounge while I finish cooking dinner?'

The uneasy truce lasted through a strained and awkward meal. Robert ate methodically, keeping his eyes on his plate. His roast chicken tasted of ashes. The children were subdued, eating their vegetables without protest, knowing better than to interrupt one of his moods. As the dishes were cleared and conversation limped into uncomfortable silence, Adele declined her aunt's perfunctory offer of help in the kitchen.

'Why don't you take Emma and Amy upstairs, Aunty. They'd love a story before bedtime.'

'And no spoiling their teeth with sweets.'

'Why Bobby, I wouldn't dream of it. Not after all the fuss you made about those Christmas chocolates. I've brought fruit this time. Cherries.'

The children looked crestfallen.

Safely upstairs, she put a warning finger to her lips then fished in her handbag to produce a ribbonned package of glacé cherries sparkling with sugar crystals. Robert listened to the stifled giggles with suspicion, but forbore immediate investigation.

'She doesn't mean any harm, Rob. Let it be.'

But Robert was irritable, restless. He couldn't relax. His

head hurt. In the soft quiet of the evening air he could just hear a low, faint growling that was not quite the usual background roar of the sea. Something moved against the softly shadowed light of the yellow midsummer moon hanging heavy in the heavens. Night prowlers.

'It's too quiet up there. They're up to something.'

'Probably falling asleep over the story. I'll take a look.'

'No, you watch your movie. Relax. I'll go.'

Robert's first explosive shout brought Adele running up the stairs. Frozen in tableau before the hall mirror were Emma and Amy, their nightgowns festooned with Aunty's beads, their lips pouting red in Aunty's pillarbox lipstick, their expressions bewildered by the force of their father's wrath.

'Get that muck off your faces. Now. This minute. Before I tan your hides for you!'

The girls fled to the bathroom.

Adele, shielding the children, coaxed the combatants back downstairs.

Robert was still shouting. 'I won't have my daughters tricked out like painted whores.'

Aunt looked fazed. 'Really, Bobby, calm down. It was just a bit of fun. Dress ups. That's all. A little sparkle never hurt anyone.'

She swayed slightly. Robert caught a hint of whisky.

'I *know* what you get up to. All those long afternoons. You and George. And at your age! Well, not in my house you don't.'

Ignoring Adele's frantic signals, Aunty tried again to mollify him. 'Don't be so uptight, Bobby. There's no harm done.' She giggled. 'Like they say in the song: *Little bits of powder, little bits of paint, makes a lady seem like, what she really ain't.* They're little girls. They deserve some glamour once in a while.'

Robert felt the tighening at his temples. The red haze was back. The low, throaty growling was drawing closer. His voice rose above it.

'Well I won't have it. I won't have my children corrupted. You're a guest here, Margaret. Do what you like in your own house, but not in mine.'

'It's not *your* house.'

'Bloody family! Always rubbing it in that it's your money. Always trying to take control. Well they're *my* children, and what I say goes!'

'I won't stay where I'm not welcome.'

'Suit yourself.'

The sound of tearing fabric interrupted the argument. The girls had crept halfway downstairs to eavesdrop, and Emma had trodden on her sister's trailing hemline.

Robert looked up ...

☆

There were two young girls on the rickety bamboo staircase. Much too young, with painted red lips and red fingernails and a price on their services. Out too late, touting for custom in the noisy bar.

He tasted the bitter Mekong whisky burning in his throat, twisting his guts, found himself pushed close to the stage in the crush of soldiers. Too close. A rank sweet smell of sex and sweat surged through the haze of cheap dope and cheaper Camel smoke that thickened what was left of the air in the room. The egg lady had finished her act. Two naked prepubescent girls now dripped candlewax onto the heaving shoulders of a spotlit woman efficiently fellating a grinning corporal. Cheers and whoops announced his orgasm, and as the woman rose to bow, dripping wax and sperm, Robert's stomach heaved. He turned his burning face away. And found himself eye to eye with a teeenager patiently arousing a large yellow dog, in readiness for the next act.

A drunken chorus began its chanting, beating time with bottles and glasses:

'*Old Mother Hubbard, she went to the cupboard, to get her poor doggie a bone ...*'

Girl and dog ascended the smoky stage.

Stiff backed and stiff groined, Robert fought his way out, his tented trousers drawing wolf whistles from his mates and lewd offers from the girls. His flaming cheeks matched his carrotty hair.

'Hey, Aussie boy, let me make you a man.'

'Hey, Robbo, give her one for me.'

'For you, discount, big boy'

'Show us what you've got, mate'

'Pussy pie, sugar?'

'Come on, your turn next on stage—looks like parts of you are ready ...'

'You can try before you buy, guy'

'Don't be a wimp—you might be dead tomorrow.'

'You maybe want Greek, mister?'

The dog was barking now. The chanting got louder: '*And when she bent over, Rover drove her, 'cause he had a bone of his own*'.

Unsure of whether the applause was for the dog or the recitation, Robert refused to look back. His anger pushed him free of the crush of bodies. His breath came in ragged gulps. And there, in the marginally cooler air of the doorway, was the Madam herself. She loomed, overweight and overblown in a too tight red silk *cheong san*, fanning her bulk with a draggled peacock fan, grinning at his discomfiture.

'Wassamatta, soldier? You no like Tigershow? You want maybe something little bit more special?'

She winked conspiritorially.

'I have clean girls, virgins. Clean boys too. Very young. Little bit extra ...'

She didn't finish the sentence. Robert lunged, caught at the silk, dragged her off her feet. He felt bones crack as his fist collided with her jaw, heard the shrieks of women, heard someone crying his name, pleading with him to stop. Small hands were pulling him away, tugging at his clothing. Cold water hit his face. He came up spluttering ...

Adele was sobbing as she hauled desperately at his bunched fist.

Aunty Maggie was slumped in a chair, silent, her neck twisted at an unnatural angle. Her cheek was a swollen lump of bruise purple, her lipsticked mouth drooled a trail of blood and splintered tooth.

Adele dropped Robert's bloodstained arm. Felt frantically for her aunt's pulse. Ran for the phone.

And there, on the staircase, were his terrified daughters. Two silent, round-eyed ghosts. They peered through the bannisters at the wreckage of their livingroom, at broken flower stems and fragments of shattered crystal, at the ruin of their family.

In the sudden stillness, the purring was unbearably loud, a monstrous animal engine reverberating through the forests of the night, echoing against the stars.

Tigershapes were everywhere, looming larger, closer, as amber strobes approached the house, throwing the foliage into sharp-striped relief, revealing predators crouched in every shadow.

Robert turned, slowly, ignoring the pain in his throbbing head, pulling the shreds of his courage about himself, willing his flesh and bones to obey.

Smearing aside his hot, slow tears, he stepped out into the sultry moonlight to meet his tigers.

Burning.

Locked in the laundry, Soo Tze was yapping furiously.

Janeen Webb is a multiple award winning author, editor and critic who has written or edited ten books and over a hundred stories and essays. She is a recipient of the World Fantasy Award, the Australian Aurealis Award, and a three-time winner of the Ditmar Award. Her current novel series for young readers, The Sinbad Chronicles (HarperCollins) includes: *Sailing to Atlantis*, *The Silken Road to Samarkand*, and the forthcoming *Flying to Babylon*.

The Butterfly Merchant

SEAN WILLIAMS

THERE IS A STORY FROM THE TIMES BEFORE the Change about a man who sells butterflies. His name is Polain, and his home is a metal and glass city larger than any built before or since. There are many things to do and see in the city, but the butterflies he breeds are counted among the most beautiful. Buyers come from all around the world to purchase them, confident in the knowledge that every one is unique. For that is Polain's Guarantee: never once will any of his creatures repeat a pattern. No two sold by him will ever be alike.

At the time of the story, his butterflies inhabit vast glasshouses, with temperature and humidity kept constant by machines the like of which we have long lost. Unnumbered eggs are laid, caterpillars hatch, pupae are woven and butterflies emerge, limp and fragile, into their new world. Yet, for all this activity, Polain's output has dropped steadily as his fame has grown. The more butterflies he sells, the more difficult it becomes to be absolutely certain that each is a true individual. In order to maintain his Guarantee, he keeps a record of every one—detailing the number of spots, the shading and hue of colours, the precise shape of the wings and antennae, and the total mass at maturity. After beginning with a humble stall and a small stack of notebooks, he now has three separate rooms full of records next door to the glasshouses, and he employs five clerks to maintain and conduct searches through them. Sometimes it takes more than a day to ascertain that a single promising butterfly is indeed one of a kind. Literally one in a million.

His output may have dropped, but demand has only increased. Butterflies live far shorter lives than their fanciers, and in their world of glass and steel little else of true colour remains. As word spreads that Polain's handiwork is scarce, it increasingly becomes a sign of prestige that one should possess an example of it. Polain can ask more and more for each creation and people will still buy. As his clientele have become richer and more discerning, his sales have dropped to a handful a month, then a handful a year. Long gone are the days when he would sell butterflies by the jarful on a street corner to anyone who passed.

Yet, strangely, he misses those days. He is as proud of his success as he is tired of the endless checking and re-checking. When the time is right, he plans to retire and go back to breeding butterflies for enjoyment, not profit. One of his competitors can take his place—and good luck to them. No one will ever be as great as he has been; no butterflies will ever equal his.

The opportunity to retire comes in the form of the queen of a distant and powerful country, due to visit the city in a matter of weeks. He publicly announces his plans with a promise to present her with the last truly unique Polain butterfly in the world. It will be his final masterpiece, and he will devote all his efforts to its creation. The queen will take it home confident in the knowledge that she is carrying a piece of history. Nothing like it will have existed before. That, after all, is his Guarantee.

And so he sets to work, mingling strains in time-proven ways in some glasshouses and cross-breeding new strains in others. Hungry caterpillars devour leaves by the million, swarming in green and brown tides across veritable forests. Thousands of butterflies are born and die with a shiver of wings, their individually inaudible rustlings adding up to a cacophony, deafening the feeders who tend them and the clerks who study them, seeking uniqueness. It is a symphony to Polain's ears. He will make a butterfly fit for a queen, no matter what it takes. All he needs is one to go in the special bell-shaped jar he had constructed for it.

Just one more.

Yet that simple task turns out not be as simple as he thought. From all the millions he breeds, beautiful though they are, the last unique one eludes him. Too many have matches in the catalogues. Some are beautiful in ways that excite the casual glance, yet are subtly flawed, or do not mate well, or die too young, sickly and weak from in-breeding. As time passes, Polain stays longer and longer in the glasshouses with the feeders and clerks, pacing up and down through the feather-soft fluttering and seeking, always seeking, for the one he knows must come. If it doesn't, he will be humiliated in front of everyone—the queen, the people of the city, his competitors. He can't have that.

The deadline approaches, and the fear of failure mounts in him. What if the right butterfly *doesn't* come in time? What if he has exhausted every possible variety and no new ones remain? What will he do? He cannot use the Change to make the one he wants, since that hasn't come into the world yet, and he wouldn't dream of substituting a fake—a butterfly modified in order to present a unique coloration. No matter how clever a forgery it was, it would be revealed under the eager gaze of his competitors. He would be ruined in his finest hour.

All too quickly the appointed time looms. His sleep is filled with nightmares: he is mocked, taunted, jeered at as he arrives at the queen's reception holding in his hands nothing but a dry and dusty moth.

Then, with just two days to spare, Polain is inspecting the butterflies in one of his auxiliary glasshouses when he spies an empty cocoon with unfamiliar spiral markings. The cocoon is paper-thin and grey in colour, except for the spirals which are soft pink. Polain raises it to his nose and sniffs: it has only recently been vacated. The butterfly that crawled from it can't be far away.

He searches the branches and ground nearby. If he finds it in time, it will still be hardening its wings, anchoring itself against a stone or a twig to practise fluttering before joining the great throng above. Polain creeps carefully through the enclosure, wary of stepping before he has made absolutely certain that nothing is underfoot. His heart beats a little faster as he thinks: *Maybe this is the one. Maybe at last, at the last minute, my search is over.*

When he sees it, perched on a branch with its wings upraised, still soft from birth but beating the air with increasingly sure strokes, he knows. Its colouring is pale green across its abdomen and thorax. Its antennae have an orange hue with yellow highlights and are curled in a tight spiral. Its wings are black, deepening to blue around the edges, with a subtle cross-hatch pattern in silver visible only as the light reflects off them. In the centre of each wing is a single, pure white circle.

Polain has never seen its equal. Backing away, wary of startling it, he calls hoarsely for the butterfly feeders. Sensing his excitement, they come running. One of them has the forethought to bring a silk net. Polain snatches it from her and swoops up the butterfly with a swing more delicate than a gentle breeze.

He cradles the captured butterfly in both hands and takes it to the main enclosure, where a special habitat has been prepared and kept ready. There, the specimen is examined for flaws and signs of ill-health. None are found. It is weighed and its markings are recorded. The clerks dive into the vast bookcases of catalogues, following themes of shape and hue in search of a match. This is the most nerve-wracking time for Polain. All he can do is wait impatiently for word to come that his venture has been in vain. It is too late to breed another with it in the hope that a similar but unique creature will result. And the chances are vanishingly small that another will be born in the one day remaining. It is either this butterfly or none at all.

The night passes sleeplessly. Still no word comes. He joins the clerks at dawn to supervise their work and promises them substantial bonuses if they work without rest until they are satisfied. Midday comes, and the queen's departure is only hours away. One of the clerks declares in exhaustion that he is sure that, judging by the shape of its wings, the butterfly is unique. Polain sends him home, relieved to a small degree but still anxious. Two hours pass, and another clerk, specialising in abdominal markings, similarly declares satisfaction. She too is dismissed with thanks. The third and fourth clerks—wing markings and head/limb composition—are certain by five o'clock that their work is done. Only then does Polain begin to feel anything like joy. These two clerks are sent home with smiles and a shot of liquor burning in their bellies. Just one remains, an elderly man specialising in the relatively small field of antennae.

With just two hours left, Polain hurries about the business of preparing the butterfly in its presentation jar, dressing himself in his finest suit and composing a short speech of thanks—to the queen, for accepting the gift, and to the people of the city, for buying his butterflies in the past and permitting him the indulgence of his vocation. Without them, he might have been a street-sweeper or postman or something as insignificant. Instead, his name will be known forever as the greatest butterfly breeder who ever lived.

As he puts the finishing touches to his bow-tie and his speech, a soft knock comes from the entrance to his chambers. When he opens the door, he finds the elderly clerk waiting in the hallway outside.

'What?' Polain snaps, angered by the interruption.

'I'm sorry to bother you, Master Polain,' says the clerk, 'but I thought you should know immediately. I've found a match.'

Polain's heart freezes. 'No, that's impossible. The others are satisfied, and I myself don't recall another butterfly like it. How can it be?'

The elderly clerk holds a large book open in both hands. He raises it as he explains: 'I too thought I was certain until I happened across an obscure morphology in an old record—one of your own, sir, made before I joined you. A tight, clockwise spiral not dissimilar to the one we have before us.' He indicates the glass-bound butterfly, which flaps its wings innocently. 'I followed the record backward, through several generations. The chances were slim that I would find one with not just the same antennae but the same colouring, shape, legs and features—but I did, sir. Here. I'm sorry.'

Polain looks down at the open book with something approaching horror. There, sure enough, is a picture of a butterfly identical in every respect to the one in the jar. A note in his own handwriting refers to its purchaser, a banker from a neighbouring province who had paid a fraction of its true worth many years ago, before Polain's name had become known. The butterfly may have only lived a day or to in the hands of such an ignorant carer, but it *had* lived. That is the important—and tragic—thing. There is no escaping the fact.

'I'm sorry, sir,' repeats the clerk. 'I can't imagine how you must feel.'

'No,' says Polain. 'You can't.' He takes the book from him and considers smashing it down upon the glass jar and its fragile occupant. Such has his life become. One hour remains until the presentation—until failure and ruin, public humiliation and mockery. Despair fills him.

Or ... need it be so? Polain's mind seizes a possible solution. Yes, an identical specimen had once existed, but who knew of it? Its owner had been no one in the butterfly world; such a man would never remember a token bought for a lover or mother so long ago—and even if he did, who would believe him? The chances are exceeding slim that the butterfly itself has been preserved—and if it hasn't been, there is no evidence at all. The remains would be nothing but dust, worn down by time.

Polain decides to present the second butterfly to the queen anyway—and accept the accolades of the crowd—confident in the knowledge that his deception will go undiscovered.

There is only one problem.

'What are you going to do now, sir?' asks the clerk.

Polain looks at him with cold calculation. The record he can destroy as easily as tearing it from the book and throwing it in the fire. But the clerk knows the truth, and he will not be easily bribed. Money and prestige are not important to him. A man obsessed with antennae associates only with those like him, when he associates at all. He will let the secret out before long. It is inevitable. And who would miss a man with such an obscure fascination?

Polain resolves himself. He has to get rid of the clerk, otherwise his plan, and his life, will come to ruination. It is the only way.

So he does. Polain kills the clerk and goes to the presentation. The queen accepts the butterfly with a gracious smile and the crowd farewells him with a loud cheer—although neither matches his expectation. The queen smiles far wider at the thought of going home, and the crowd cheers more for the fireworks and streamers than him. Even his own heart, he must confess to himself, isn't really in it. He is already planning how to dispose of the old clerk's body by burying it in the soil of the glasshouses.

He leaves behind the gaily-coloured pennants and goes home to finish his work. He dismisses the other clerks and the feeders to prevent his grisly deed being discovered. He burns the treacherous record and catches up on his sleep. Soon, he promises himself, he will be alone with his butterflies. He will be content then. Breeding has always been his first love, not the endless competition and cataloguing. With no need of money, he will be happy for the rest of his life, once the unpleasantness is forgotten.

Life, however, is never so simple—then *or* now. First, the clerk's body putrefies in the soil and emits a powerful stench. No amount of perfume will hide it. It fades only with time, and leaves behind an unexpected boon: patches of explosive growth, where the plants in the glasshouses have taken sustenance from the old man's decaying flesh. The flowers are beautiful and large, and the butterflies seem to favour them over the others, so Polain is pleased enough. But their association with his crime is not so easy to expunge, and he is ill at ease around the flowers.

Then the police call to ask him questions about the dead man. The clerk's absence was noted after all, by a grand-daughter whose birthday he had never before missed. Polain feigns innocence. Yes, the last time he had seen the clerk was just before the queen's departure. He had worked all his staff hard in the days leading up to the presentation. Perhaps the clerk had worked *too* hard and had a heart-attack on the way home. Is it so unlikely that the body of an unidentified old man might go unnoticed by the medical system?

His evasion doesn't entirely satisfy the police, but they leave him alone; they have after all no firm evidence to suspect him, and no motive. Still, Polain's conscience is troubled, and will not let him rest. That night he dreams that the queen has rejected his gift and returns it to him with a disgusted expression on her face. He looks down into the crystal jar and sees a spider swimming in a puddle of blood, trying to escape.

He wakes screaming and goes down to the glasshouses, seeking solace. A new generation of butterflies is being born, slipping from their pupae and inflating like balloons. He watches in awe: their colourings are striking, their patterns unique. All of them have the same corkscrew, orange-yellow antennae of the butterfly the dead clerk identified. It seems almost like a tribute to the clerk, as though somehow his essence has been leeched into the soil from his body, fed the plants upon which the caterpillars ate, and reached a strange expression in the resulting insects.

Polain shivers, unnerved by the thought, and tells himself not to be a fool. He has never been superstitious. Why start now? It is just a coincidence.

He watches them for hours, hypnotised by their seemingly aimless motion. They are very beautiful creatures, with their angular markings of silver on blue that hint at familiarity but never reveal themselves. Every glimpse of every wing trembles on the brink of recognition, but never allows itself to be known.

A bell rings late in the afternoon, and he stirs himself to answer the door. The police are back with more inquiries. They want to inspect the grounds, and even though they do not have a warrant, Polain lets them. To deny them access would only make them suspicious, and the chances of them uncovering anything are slim. The stench of decay is long gone. Without digging, they will find nothing but flowers and butterflies.

Only as he shows the policemen the glasshouses does he realise what the patterns on the new breed remind him of. Before he was too close to them. From a distance he can see that each marking is a letter, drawn in the minuscule, reflective scales of the butterfly's wing. As they fly by, they spell gibberish through the air, meaningless jumbles of consonants and vowels that distract him from what a policeman is asking him.

The policeman repeats his question, and Polain snaps himself out of his reverie to answer. What does he care that none of his neighbours saw the elderly clerk leave that fateful evening? He had more important things to worry about—and besides, they were all jealous of his success, or spies for his competitors. He would expect them to incriminate him whenever possible. And why would *he* lie? He has a reputation, and a very successful business to maintain.

Even as he says this, though, a swarm of butterflies lands in a line on a branch behind the policemen and spells out the words: 'NEMDO. CONFESS.'

Polain stammers to a halt. 'Nemdo' was the name of the dead clerk. Noticing his fixed stare over their shoulders, the policemen turn to see, but their motion startles the butterflies. They fly away to another branch, where this time they just spell 'CONFESS', once again out of sight of the policemen.

Polain suppresses an angry snarl. He knows what the butterflies are trying to do. They want him to own up for the crime. But he won't. He has no reason to. It is over, finished. The clerk was old, anyway, and near the end of his life. What had he to live for? The policemen are only tying up loose ends, and can't seriously be concerned for a lost geriatric.

Still, 'CONFESS' say the butterflies, waving their wings at him and twitching their antennae.

He picks up a rock from the dirt floor and throws it at them. The rock scatters them, and sails through the glass behind them with a loud smash.

If the policemen are unnerved by that, there's worse to come.

As a cloud of butterflies sail out through the hole, the policemen press Polain for an explanation of his bizarre behaviour. 'It's nothing,' he stammers. Nothing but reasonable distress at being interrogated in such an unseemly fashion. Who are they to insinuate that he is lying, that he knows something about this absent octogenarian? It's none of his business, or theirs, and they should leave immediately.

But even as he speaks, the cloud of butterflies that escaped through the hole have not flown away to freedom. Instead, they settle on the roof of the glasshouse and proceed to spell out a single word in shadows against the sunlight.

'CONFESS!'

Polain staggers backward, shielding his eyes from the sight. Alarmed, the policemen back away as the deranged butterfly breeder trips over a protruding stem and falls into a patch of enormous flowers. Butterflies go everywhere in a panic, filling the air with dark blue and silver flashes.

Polain sees them all around him, in clumps and flocks, tormenting him. 'NEMDO' exclaims one group; 'CONFESS' yet another. His guilt presses in upon him, suffocating him. Keening, he clutches at the soil for a stick to arm himself with and swings at his tormentors. Swarms of butterflies part before him, sending fragmentary 'EMD's and 'ONF's and other syllables in all directions. But they always regroup, no matter how he batters them. Broken wings fall out of the air and soft bodies squash against stiff branches. His hair becomes entangled with broken antennae and legs. His eyes sting with butterfly blood until he can no longer see— and the fight goes out of him like air from a punctured ball.

And so the police find him, clutching the trunk of tree, bespattered with the crushed carcasses of his former wards, his mind broken and his life in tatters.

And so his story comes to an end, more or less. The world has moved on by the time the disgraced butterfly merchant stands trial before a judge. His sentence is not recorded, although it is told that his beloved city forgot him and his butterflies in short order, finding new heroes to glorify, new villains to condemn and new fads to fancy.

But for some, the story of Polain never ends. It echoes through time even now, in our very different world, as a warning against greed and obsession. And it leaves us with a lesser story buried in its midst, that of the unintended victim: not Polain, who loses everything in pursuit of one final triumph, or Nemdo, whose life holds only his beloved butterfly antennae and whose reward for diligence is nothing but a violent death—but Nemdo's grand-daughter, the girl whose birthday the elderly clerk missed.

Thrust into the spotlight of grief by another man's greed, caught up in tale of deception and self-destruction, she cares little for butterflies.

All she wants, in the end, is her grandfather back.

New York Times-bestselling author (and occasional DJ) Sean Williams has over 60 published short stories and 20 novels under his belt, plus a sci-fi musical and the odd piece of haiku. Multiple winner of Australia's speculative fiction awards, recipient of the 'SA Great' Literature Award and judge of the Writers of the Future Contest, he currently lives in Adelaide. His uniquely Australian vision of fantasy has drawn comparisons to authors as diverse as Peter Carey and Ursula K. Le Guin.

THAT WHICH DOES NOT KILL US

SCOTT WESTERFELD

PAUL DROPPED BY EURISA'S OFFICE with a quick question. Her face was ashen.

'God, what's wrong?'

'Nothing.' She gestured helplessly at her screen. 'My boyfriend's dog died. Ex-boyfriend, I mean.'

'That's ... too bad.' He wondered if he should say more.

No one at Orfay Currency Management knew much about the break-up, about a month old. But they'd all seen the signs. Dimitri had stopped coming by, and there had been a tightening in Eurisa, like the lid of an already closed jar rotated an extra quarter-turn, the surety of metal gripping glass. Her office door was closed more often now, her meetings shorter, her intraoffice mail even more terse.

Eurisa's gray and absent eyes veiled any pain, however. She had no close friends at work, and Paul could only guess what had come between them—the tall, lean, quiet woman and her voluble Greek.

Dimitri had charmed Paul the few times he'd come to tease Eurisa away from Asian time-zone trades, playfully pulling her toward some party or performance, leaving Paul jealous of his power to make her smile.

And now, since the break-up, jealous of his power to hurt her.

Eurisa seemed so out of reach, terribly calm even in the worst peso or rupiah meltdown. As assistant manager of the floor, Paul often had to nudge juniors who unthinkingly asked if ice-water ran in her veins; prejudice was not tolerated at Orfay Currency. A few months after the accident, she'd gotten her old job back, no questions asked.

She certainly looked free of ice now. Staring at her screen, animated by this untidy aftershock of the break-up, Eurisa was openly shaken, appalled as a child whose carefully tended scab has been ripped from its moorings. And all over Dimitri's dog.

She must really have loved the guy, Paul thought enviously,

even as he spotted an opening.

He took a few steps into her office and placed one tentative hand on her shoulder. It felt firm and muscular; they had all noticed her in the Orfay gym every day.

Her unwavering gaze on the screen seemed an invitation to read. Dimitri had mailed the announcement to his own address, Eurisa receiving one blind copy among many.

raptor died quietly last night. renal failure most likely. she was 17.

those of us who knew her will remember her big heart, quiet wisdom, and superb comic timing.

The sweet, personal, terminal note made Paul's eyes guilty, and they fell to Eurisa's hands. One clenched her airmouse, the other was upended, a dead spider in her lap.

'It hated me,' she said.

Paul took a step back, out from the private space behind her desk to a more neutral position, his hand pulling from her shoulder.

As with any beautiful woman in a male domain, Eurisa was an object of unspoken competition. Now that she was unattached, who would be the first to ask her for a drink? A lunchtime walk? This moment was a perfect opportunity to cross the pale.

Paul wondered what had made him pull away. Somehow, she seemed diminished by her words, as if his desire had been blunted by the departed dog's hatred.

Had it *known* about her?

He censored the thought.

'You two didn't get along, huh?' Paul tried to make it cheery, disbelieving.

'It fucking hated me.'

A fresh wave of distress crossed Eurisa's face. Shame at having been despised by something dumb and innocent, perhaps. Guilt at having returned the dog's vacuous hatred. Frustration that Raptor had lasted longer than her in Dimitri's life, if only by a few weeks.

Paul searched for the right words.

'Do you think he'll have it brought back?' he asked. The operation had worked on dogs well before humans. (Mice, of course, had been the first.)

Eurisa unclenched her fist, fingers listlessly indicating the screen. 'Doesn't sound like it.'

He nodded agreement. 'They say dogs are never quite the same.'

Eurisa looked at him directly for the first time, and Paul blinked against the metal glint in her gray eyes.

'It's not just dogs they say that about.'

'Oh shit, I'm sorry.' Another step away from her, which immediately felt like the wrong thing to do, fearful rather than apologetic. His too-familiar hand, the one that had touched her shoulder, hung uncomfortably in the air. The hand wavered, searching for some knowing gesture that would erase his tasteless remark, but it looked stranded, isolated from his body, as if he intended to wash it once out of her sight. He felt the dizzying influence of four cups of coffee on an empty stomach.

'Don't worry about it, Paul,' she said. 'It's just this email.' The apologetic look on her face seemed genuine.

Paul smiled back. Even with her silences, her distance, he wished he'd known Eurisa better before the accident, before the operation. He sometimes fantasised that he could bring her out from the gray place she'd been since, animate her as Dimitri had.

'Listen, I'd better come back later,' he said, turning away slowly in case Eurisa called to him. They could commiserate a few moments more, or waste a few moments with lively, vacant gossip to soothe her distress. Maybe wind up having that drink tonight.

But she was silent.

Her fingers clattered, and Paul heard the missive's brief complaint as it was deleted without backup.

'Quiet wisdom? It fucking *hated* me,' she muttered as Paul departed, voice faltering toward a sob.

There was something vulnerable in the sound, and Paul stopped. He'd feel forever foolish if he let this opportunity pass.

'Look, Eurisa,' he said to the door. 'After work. Do you want a drink?'

'Why not?' she answered.

He took her to The Three-Headed Dog, a place with brushed cement floors and a glass fountain that spanned an entire wall, rippling like a giant window on a rainy day. It was the after-work bar that everyone at Orfay went to: trendy enough to bring younger dates, but with barstools that supported lower backs trashed by years of drinking coffee and trading currency. And you could still smoke here. (Paul had turned 30 this year, and was thinking of cutting back on something. Not coffee, alcohol, speed, tobacco, or work—but *something*.)

Eurisa looked around, sizing up the place in a manner that told him everything: she'd never been here before, didn't go to bars much. Then Paul remembered it had been the other driver who'd been drunk that night two years ago, and wondered if Eurisa had a thing against drinkers now. He told himself to take it easy.

'What'll you have?' he asked her.

'Whisky, neat. Make it a double.'

Okay, maybe not a problem.

He peered up at the chalkboard filled with single malts, lighting a first cigarette.

'Sounds good to me. Maybe the Bowmore with 30 years on it?'

His extravagance paid off. For the first time, he glimpsed a hint of a smile. 'Special occasion?'

Perhaps he was being too obvious. 'Not really. Just showing off my useless education. Went to a whisky tasting last week.'

She glanced up at the board and said dryly, 'And it's the most expensive.'

'Hey, it's great stuff, though.'

'I know. I'll get them.'

'Are you sure?'

She waved away protests, signaled the barman over and ordered two, getting the guy's attention faster than Paul would have. Away from the flourescent lights of work, he could see the truth in what all the guys had long suspected: Eurisa really was a beauty.

Sometimes, you couldn't tell. Paul had gotten plenty of temps and the odd intern down here to the Dog, only to discover that a face that glowed in comparison to the Orfay crowd could pale out in the real world. But Eurisa's sharp features only softened in the mottled light reflected from the fountain, and her perch on the barstool revealed her shapeliness better than any office chair. Her eyes didn't seem so gray here, animated by their quick, nervous circuits around the bar.

Paul could see her desirability in the barman's gaze as he read her card with a swipe of his finger. He was good-looking, just a kid, no more than 25.

Eurisa was about Paul's age, but looked older. They said dying added five years.

He glanced around to see if any of the guys were here to see this. Eurisa buying him a drink. It was 6.30. Where the hell were they?

'Well then, to Raptor?' she said, raising her glass with a rueful smile.

He gave it a clink. 'I hear she was a real bitch.'

Eurisa offered the remonstrative smile one allows a lame pun, but Paul felt like he'd scored a belly laugh. The taste of fire, peat, and sea air coiled down his throat invincibly.

'You're not a musician, are you?'

The Greek had been a bassist, Paul remembered now. Second chair for one of the big orchestras. He took a sip for courage. She was comparing him to the old boyfriend, looking for something different.

'Not a chance. Can't even remember the words to "Happy Birthday".'

Eurisa nodded. 'I always forget what comes after "Dear ..."'

'Dear me.'

'Maybe later.'

Paul blinked, realising that she was flirting with him. That was more than he'd expected after a few sips of a first drink. Eurisa had been a closed door for so long, everyone had given up trying. When new hires asked about her, everyone just shook their heads to say, *Don't waste your time, buddy.*

Paul drank his whisky quickly. He fumbled for another smoke, wondering where the other Orfay guys were tonight.

He also wondered if Eurisa had become more or less beautiful since the accident, then decided not to think too far down that line.

'I don't know why Dimitri's email shook me up like that.' She peered into the brown mysteries of her glass. 'Feel much better now, though.'

'How long has it been?'

'Weeks. A month yesterday, I guess. But seeing his address made me think he was writing me.'

'Were you hoping for anything?'

'Just a letter. Not some stupid bulk announcement about his stupid dog.' She looked at me. 'I guess that sounds pretty horrible. Poor bitch.'

He smiled. 'Don't sweat it. It's not like you killed her.'

'No. It just feels that way. Dimitri must be shattered. He's had her since he was a kid.' Eurisa's hands clutched the whisky glass to her chest, as if wanting to comfort her former lover, to comfort anyone, in the wake of Raptor's demise.

'He'll get over it,' Paul said. 'Builds character.'

She sighed. 'That which does not kill us.'

Paul bought another round.

'Hey!'

It was Freddy from Offshore, the guys who hid money for tax cheats and dictators. The bar was crowded now, at the height of the after-work rush, and Paul hadn't seen him sneak up.

'Oh, hi, Freddy. You know Eurisa.'

'Yeah, nice to see you at the Dog.' The big man bobbed his head idiotically.

'It's nice to be here.' She smiled, but shrank from Freddy a little, withdrawing into the gray place that the whisky and the crowd had coaxed her from. He was turning pink and loud from alcohol, his tie loosened, his sleeves riding up like a growing teenager's.

'Who else is here?' Paul asked, thinking, *Go back to them.* He wanted to be seen with Eurisa, not interfered with. The other guys would have known better, all but Freddy. Offshore was a loose cannon's game.

Eurisa had turned away to order more, again snaring the young barman instantly. Freddy took the opportunity to widen his eyes, his grin going from polite to suggestive.

Paul knew what he was thinking.

Months before, Paul had gone back to Freddy's from the Dog, along with a couple of other guys from Orfay. They'd got to talking about Eurisa, raising the usual questions about what she'd be like in bed. They had all dropped some speed in the afternoon, and the discussions got more and more detailed, until Freddy wound up downloading porn from a bunch of crypt-sticker sites. Like everything free, most of it was utter crap. The wasted gigabytes filled Freddy's wallscreen with tanless wonders lounging on red velvet couches, their faces slack with what they thought was post-necrotic languor. More like middle-class chronic fatigue, however pale their lipstick and strewn lilies. Baby goths with artistic boyfriends and lonely girls with cams.

Paul and the boys had laughed them off one by one, making the usual comments men make about pictures of naked women, drinking while they waited between high-res loads. Until Freddy found a real one.

She wasn't flopped out playing dead; she didn't have to be. She simply sat on a folding chair against an exposed brick wall, body at three-quarters, head turned to face the camera. She had died messily, it was obvious, though a veil of ashen pallor overlay the scars and patches of artificial skin that quilted her body.

Her face held none of the usual expressions of the amateur nude portrait: no self-consciousness or embarrassment, no attempt at bravado, not even the grim confidence of a professional. She was fit, handsome, about 45.

And she was dead. Her eyes were empty. It wasn't the slack expression of a bad photo, that fleeting moment of idiocy so often caught by the camera, but something cold and blank and absent. She had the wooden face of a mannequin, just after it's fooled the corner of your eye, and you've turned to excuse yourself for almost bumping into it or to ask if it has the time, and it just stares back.

For a few stunned moments, the photo had Paul's speeding brain in revelation mode, agreeing with the religious freaks. The ones who believed that the operation didn't really bring anyone back. That post-ops were just machines, things with familiar memories and personality, but only on the surface. Things that loved ones might recognise and believe in, but with nothing inside.

Those theories had always sounded like a load of crap to Paul. The usual flailings of the religious whenever science stomps into their ever-shrinking territory. People were all machines, all the time, he figured. Get fed, get laid, get a laugh.

Food, safety, freedom, sex. And if they were anything inside it was best described with one word: hungry.

But this woman had lost her hunger. She was dead, and her nakedness only made it worse, as if someone had propped her up with sticks and invisible wires without bothering to dress her, because it didn't matter.

Freddy's system got more hits, the teeth of the search engine now deep in some vein of obsession out there in the world, the restless software flipping images onto the wallscreen as they arrived, cold and ashen and tragic.

The pictures silenced them all, and broke the spirit of the party in a way that took less than half an hour to get Paul and the rest of them out Freddy's door, muttering 'work night' and relieved it had happened at his apartment and not one of theirs.

Eurisa turned back to them with two scotches in hand. She looked at Freddy.

'Oh, did you want a drink?'

'No, no. I was just stopping by to say hi.'

She turned away to pay, and Freddy and Paul glanced at each other. For a moment in her cool expression they had both read the same thing: she somehow knew, had detected that night of transgression. As if side-by-side their collective guilt was obvious.

Paul swallowed, looked again at the woman next to him, lithe and glorious as she stretched her card out to the barman. For a second, the fleeting and primitive revelation of that night came back, overlaying his desire with something fearful, but still intense. He wondered what she would feel like against him, if she would warm between cool sheets the way other women did.

He wanted to know how it would work with a dead girl.

Freddy wrung his hands, sorry now that he had come over.

'Well, early night for me, guys.'

Paul gave his shoulder a pat. 'See you tomorrow. Get some sleep.'

The big man moved away.

'See you, Freddy,' Eurisa called, too softly for him to have heard.

The Orfay table, which Paul spotted now in the corner, waved and shouted goodbye to Freddy as he passed. A few dared tentative glances toward the two of them at the bar, excited by the prospect of gossip and scandal.

Paul felt worlds away from them, alone with Eurisa. There would be no further interruptions.

She looked relieved.

Eurisa angled the whisky glass toward him in a perfunctory salute and put it to her lips, tipping it back and depositing it empty on the bar with a crack just audible over the music and crowd.

'Is there someplace quieter we could go?'

They went many places.

Everywhere, Eurisa drank quickly. The whisky seemed to pour a kind of heat into her, quickening her words and gestures. A torrent slowly freed itself, like ice breaking up in a river.

Paul listened, trying to pace his liquor, sneaking a couple of pills in the bathroom and wishing he'd eaten something that day. He offered the occasional word of support and watched Eurisa's face closely, searching for clues of what she wanted with him tonight.

She talked only of Dimitri.

'He used to shut Raptor up in the kitchen while I was over there. Otherwise, she'd sit in the corner and watch us, growling.'

'Psycho dog.'

Eurisa shook her head and drank. 'Not generally psycho. Just hated me. She was normal with everyone else. Whenever I was there, she'd pace back and forth in the kitchen, her claws tapping on the tiles like fingernails. Like she thought I was going to steal her man.'

'Maybe she was jealous, because she knew you loved him.'

She looked at Paul coldly. 'I never said that.'

'Oh, sorry. It just sounded like—'

'Didn't say I didn't, either.' Her voice took on an edge for a moment, like a drunk about to turn hostile.

Paul looked into his empty glass, and waved at the barman for more. When he turned back to Eurisa her anger was gone. She continued as if nothing had happened.

'So Dimitri would sit in the living room, where I could see him from the bedroom and Raptor could watch from the kitchen. And he'd play his bass for us.'

She drank.

'Raptor would finally sit down and listen to the music. Sometimes she would even sing along, kind of a soft, moany song.'

In the low music and bar chatter around them, Paul drunkenly heard the sound track to this scene: the low notes of the string bass mingling with those of the imprisoned, growling dog. Eurisa looking on from her banishment in the bedroom, watching her lover serenade his hound, framed by the impassable doorway.

Paul allowed himself to imagine, urged on by the very real possibility that he might find out, what Eurisa's body looked like under her black suit. Would she be as taut and firm as she appeared, a well-maintained machine? (Not a machine, Paul reminded himself, trying not to remember what he had seen that night in Freddy's apartment, the blank men and women staring back from the screen.) How would her lips taste? (Did she bear any scars from the accident?) What sounds would she make beneath him?

'After a while, the dog would forget.'

'Forget what?' Paul spluttered.

'That I was there. Dimitri's playing always enchanted Raptor's little doggie brain into thinking I had gone, or maybe just lulled her to sleep, I couldn't see which. Then he would carefully rest the bass on its side and come into the bedroom. After that we couldn't speak, or make a sound. Mustn't wake doggie.'

'Too bad.'

'No, it was too good. It was like the dog was guarding me, and Dimitri had sneaked past. Sometimes, we even kept the door open, so we had to be absolutely quiet. Everything slow and deliberate, communicating only with signals, with our eyes, fearful of any creak of the bed.'

Paul took a deep drag, then a long drink, the smoke still in his lungs. He wanted so badly to take Eurisa silently as a monster slept nearby.

Whisky made him brave. He slid his hand softly across her lower back, felt the firm muscles there.

'So the dog hated you, but ...'

'But we made it something good.'

Paul leaned closer now, their faces at the knife's-edge boundary between a gaze and a kiss.

'Raptor could have driven us crazy, but Dimitri made it a game. That's how his mind worked.'

Paul blinked, her mournful expression freezing him. Eurisa turned her face aside, and he thought for a moment that his momentum had been broken. His heartbeat tolled out a few seconds.

She looked at him. Firmly: 'Can we go some place?'

He swallowed, suddenly dizzy, and held onto the bar with his free hand to keep the stool beneath him. 'We've been to six places by my count. Maybe we've had enough.'

'Not to drink.'

Paul nodded. The tight feeling in his stomach and balls, the strictures of uncertainty, relaxed. He gathered himself, and ran his fingertips up Eurisa's spine, feeling a faint shiver pass through her.

He ground out his cigarette and grinned inside. His seemingly random course from bar to bar had been leading to this small dark corner of this particular small dark pub.

'Well, I live half a block from here.'

One of her half-smiles. 'Isn't that convenient?'

Paul stood shakily. His head swam, as if the last few whiskys hadn't found room below his neck yet.

'Actually, it is.'

In the lobby he let out a defeated moan. The elevator was broken again.

'Shit. They keep saying they'll fix this. Once and for all.'

'That's okay. I can climb stairs.'

He looked her up and down, for the first time openly. 'Tenth floor OK?'

'Try me.'

Paul pushed open the fire door and started the climb, hoping he'd make it without too much sweat. He knew from experience that it would be tainted with whisky and speed and workday stress. Alone, he could have used the handrail, resting every few floors to gratefully pant away some of the alcohol in his system. But taking the stairs in front of a fit and willing Eurisa, he didn't want to look feeble and incapable.

He had to have her tonight, to know what was inside her.

But the whisky was working hard against him. Paul gripped the handrail, conscious of the rasp of his breathing in the echoing concrete stairwell. Her footsteps sounded light and impatient behind him. He wondered if his face was turning red.

At the fourth floor, Paul's lower back twinged in the awful way that had made him give up tennis a year before. Between an evening slumped on barstools and these stairs, he'd barely be able to sit down tomorrow. But he could ignore the pain for six more floors. The goal was all that mattered. He was getting what everyone at Orfay wanted. The hero of the currency floor.

Paul wondered if the guys were talking about him and Eurisa at this moment, still camped at the Three-Headed Dog and betting on how far he'd gotten. Freddy had probably gone home to download more grave-robber porn, sitting fat and half-drunk in front of his giant wallscreen.

At that image his step faltered, and spots went up before his eyes. Seventh floor.

'You okay?'

'Sure.' Paul charged upward, not looking back. He didn't want Eurisa to see his red face, puffing and sweating like a man about to come. Not yet.

He couldn't see the stairs anymore. Instead of gray concrete, he saw the woman on the wallscreen, ashen and stitched together, something inside her gone a million miles away. He wasn't horrified anymore; he just wanted to talk to her, to step inside the picture and ask her questions. How had she wound up in that bare room, naked in front of some cheap camera?

What had killed her so thoroughly, yet left enough for surgeons to piece back together? Was she really nothing inside? (Or would she even know it if she was?)

Paul wanted to turn around and ask Eurisa, to beg her to answer. What was it like in that gray place between death and the operation? What had they all seen there that made them so silent and removed?

But if she saw him now she'd know he was unfit. She'd see the fear in his red, sweaty face.

'Are you sure you don't want to stop?'

Paul mumbled something and kept going, clutching at the handrail, not looking back. A nine swam past his eyes. Almost there. Out of this endless concrete stairwell, back in his own bedroom, Paul knew he would recover.

Until then, he didn't want to see Eurisa's dead face.

Finally, he was pushing through the fire door, stumbling toward his apartment. He reached into his pocket, and pain shot through his chest and left arm. The keys fell to the floor.

'Here.' She reached down and picked them up. And Paul saw her face.

In the hallway florescents, it was obvious again, her grayness, her absence, everything the bar light and the whisky had erased.

She was dead, absolutely and undeniably. She was gone, and had been since that night the drunk driver had ploughed into her car. There'd been no coming back from that. Dimitri had left her because he'd never really found her, past that beautiful face. Maybe there was nothing left to find.

Paul's heart was pounding, his chest on fire, left hand seizing into a claw. As Eurisa rose, the keys jingling, she looked up. He saw it happen: all at once she knew that he knew.

Like a gate closing, her eyes went cold again. Ice returned, and she turned away.

The pain in his chest switched off like a light, and Paul fell to his knees and vomited. Eurisa was already in retreat, and none of it reached her, except a few speckles on her shoes.

Freddy dropped by Paul's office for a quick question.

'How're you doing?'

'I've felt better.'

'So, how'd you go last night?' Freddy's grin was painful in the shiny demimonde of hangover.

Paul looked up at the big man silently for a moment, then allowed himself to shrug. 'Not so good.'

Freddy's eyes widened. 'You looked like you were in there.'

'Yeah, I guess I was. But it just didn't work out. You know? Would have been awkward.' Paul waved his hand directionlessly, to indicate his office, Orfay in general, propriety.

Freddy stepped inside, closed the door behind him.

'I know what you mean.' His voice was low, but the grin stayed on his face. 'I don't think I could've either.'

'Yeah?'

Freddy nodded vigorously. 'It's one thing to look at pictures. But actually robbing the grave?' He shook his head.

'Freddy!'

The grin evaporated.

'We don't think that way here at Orfay. Post-op status is like any other medical condition. She's the same as anyone else. That's the law.'

Freddy backed up against the closed door, his face growing even more pink. 'Well, yeah, of course. I'm not saying anything like that. I just couldn't ... I mean, *in bed*?'

Paul chuckled, held up his hands in surrender. He lowered his voice. 'Just kidding, Freddy.'

The big man swallowed, smiling but still nervous. 'Oh, sure. Shit, you had me going there.'

Paul grinned, leaned forward, his hangover receding for a moment of clarity.

'I could have had her, you know? She came up, all the way to my apartment door.'

He glanced up to check Freddy's face. The man was rapt.

'Palm of my hand. I was already in there, over the hump. I could have found out what it's like, you know? On the other side.'

'Yeah?'

Paul nodded, took a deep breath, rubbing his left arm up near the shoulder, where it had shrieked with pain the night before. He shook his head.

'But like you said, no way. This boy's keeping his dick out of the grave.'

Scott Westerfeld is the author of five novels for adults and eight for young adults. The most recent is *Specials* (Simon and Schuster), the conclusion of the Uglies trilogy. His books have won the Philip K Dick Special Citation, the Aurealis Award, and been named NY Times Notable Books of the Year. His YA novel *So Yesterday* (Penguin) won the 2005 Victorian Premier's Award. He has also contributed to Nerve.com, BookForum, and the scientific journal *Nature*, and published short fiction on Scifiction.com. He is married to the Hugo-nominated writer Justine Larbalestier, is a permanent resident of Australia, and splits his time between New York and Sydney. www.scottwesterfeld.com

THE SINGULAR LIFE OF
EDDY DOVEWATER

DEBORAH BIANCOTTI

Eddy Dovewater was born running. Squeeze. Slide. Slap. An obligatory wail of disgust and he was free. Exiting the obstetrics ward, he was clocked at nearly fifteen km per hour. Not bad for his height. Forty-five centimetres of baby-pink blur.

'And I thought I'd seen everything,' said the midwife, rocking back on her heels. 'Now, where's he going in such a hurry?'

But to Eddy's new-made brain, it wasn't so much where he was going, as where he was coming from. Eddy Dovewater had been born before. And this time, he was determined to stay alive.

He might have been short, but he was fast. Left the nurse for dust. Still slippery with amniotic fluid, he slid under a gurney and into the corridor, dodging two astonished ambulance drivers.

By then, Mrs Dovewater had blearily managed to raise her head from the pillow.

'All right, then?' she asked, meaning: is it over yet?

Doctor Kavendar, hands still held out towards the Dovewater womb, ignored her with professional ease.

'We've got a runner!' he shouted, dropping his gloves to the floor with a wet smack.

The door was swinging in Eddy's wake. Doc Kavendar leapt through and into the corridor, just in time to catch a glimpse of Eddy's firm pink bottom disappearing around a corner.

'Forceps!' he shouted. He grabbed a pair of cruel metal fingers from the midwife's collection and took off, white coat flapping. He used to run at med school. They called him 'Stringbean'.

'Ha!' cried Stringbean as the adrenaline came flooding back.

By the time he made the corner, Eddy was already at the fire exit door. Springing for the door handle, Eddy pulled down with all his weight. Toes wriggling in the air, fingers slipping slowly along the handle, he held on with elaborate determination. The door stayed firmly shut.

Luck was still with the newborn Eddy, though. As he hung from the handle, in evident need, a bemused orderly leaned over and gently pushed the door open. Eddy swung through the resulting gap, into the concrete stairwell, and down.

'Idiot!' Doc Kavendar shouted at the orderly, closing in.

Idiot, thought Eddy, *stairs are too big for babies*. After dropping briefly to his hands and knees, Eddy discovered the most efficient way to descend was on his slippery arse. Fortunately, the ground-floor door was propped open with an oxygen tank. Eddy rolled into the corridor and bounced to his feet. Puffing out his barrel chest, he grinned toothlessly at the cardio ward. There was a gymnastic 'Tah-DAH' to the way he flung his hands into the air. This life was by far the longest and best he'd had yet.

Doc Stringbean Kavendar sprang from the stairwell and landed heavily beside Eddy. He bounced, skidding loudly, the high sheen of the hospital corridor combining with the sensible rubber soles of his shoes. The forceps flew from his hand and there was a sudden bone-jarring halt for the lower half of his body. The rest of him continued inexorably down, chin first.

As Stringbean tipped forward, arms splayed out in front, he came eye-to-eye with the newly arrived babe. Eddy reacted instantly. Making use of his overdeveloped instinct for survival, he leapt sideways, away from his foe, and right into the breakfast trolley. Rebounding back at Stringbean, the two of them collided knuckles-first with the far wall.

Doc Kavendar grabbed two crash carts on the way down. As Eddy tumbled forwards over his back, Stringbean trapped the boy between the carts and pinned him against the wall.

'Oxygen tent! Scalpel!' the doctor cried. Each item was swiftly handed to him by amazed staff.

Wedging the carts between his knees, Stringbean sliced a good-sized hole in the tent. He recovered the fallen forceps from under a cart, leaned over and grabbed Eddy with one hand. As Eddy cleared the carts—and to the surprise of both of them—a hot stream of piss shot directly forward. With the lightning reflexes of a true obstetrician, Doc Kavendar angled the boy away from his old school tie.

'Now, that's weird,' Stringbean said, ignoring all the events that had led them there.

He flung the tent over Eddy and pulled the newborn's baby-soft head free. Eddy struggled against the clear plastic, but Stringbean had wrapped it tight. Thus swaddled, the baby was escorted up the stairs to meet with his proud mother.

Mrs Dovewater was, fortunately, a person of great equanimity. She was entirely unrattled by the adventures of her offspring. And throughout his childhood and subsequent teen years, she withstood Eddy's impetuous flights with a certain lethargic grace. It made no difference to her that Eddy couldn't sit still long enough to finish an exam or write a paper. To her mind, he was propelled by a mystical energy.

Even his conception had had elements of the miraculous. Eddy's pale skin and fair hair were at odds with the dark good looks of Mr Dovewater, and with Mrs Dovewater's deep, rich auburn hair and green eyes. Plus there was the curious fact of Mr Dovewater's abandoning the family home more than a year before Eddy was born. Friends often mused over whether Mrs D's pregnancy had been slowed by her inhuman nonchalance, or propelled forward in time by Eddy's preternatural determination. Whichever it was, Eddy never asked about his father, and his mother never offered to tell.

By the time Eddy could speak, he'd forgotten his other lives, or the strange determination that had driven him to dash from the obstetrics ward. But something still nagged at him. A superstitious twitchiness and a cold dread in the pit of his stomach kept him always running.

'Got the devil at your heels, eh, lad?' drawled Mr Borridge from next door, and something told Eddy it wasn't far from the truth.

So he grew, little by little, and went to school. By the time he was six, he was outrunning the school bus—while his classmates jeered at him through the windows. He grew a little more, skipped classes where he could, and made it to high school.

'Whoa,' called Principal Woolsey when Eddy hit the math block corridor at full speed. 'Guilty conscience, Mr Dovewater?'

Eddy smiled, wondering how he knew. He'd long developed the feeling that he was living on time that was not borrowed— but stolen. How could he explain the odd half-felt idea that he had cheated death already? Eddy tried to edge past the principal. It was difficult. Principal Woolsey's girth took up most of a corridor.

'Where do you get all that energy?' the principal asked, his belt buckle wobbling dangerously closer as he peered into Eddy's eyes.

Eddy shrugged, scraping his shoulder blade on the wall.

'I worry about loners like you, Eddy,' he murmured. 'If only you'd use some of that energy in your schoolwork. You could really get ahead.'

Eddy smiled. He doubted schoolwork would be enough. And with a final deep inhalation, he managed to squeeze past.

'At least join a sports team,' called the principal. 'That's a God-given resource you got, Eddy. God-given!'

But Eddy only shook his head. He wasn't about to run just for the sake of it. He had a purpose.

So Eddy propelled himself into his future, always with his head turned around, looking back over his shoulder. The future, he decided, would probably take care of itself.

Meanwhile, he ran deliveries for Captain Harris at the local supermarket. He was good at that. Quick and careful, that's what the Captain called him.

'Hey, QC,' said the Captain, as Eddy piled up armfuls of groceries in plain plastic bags. 'These ones are recycled. How about that, hey?'

Eddy took extra care of the recycled bags. They weren't as sturdy. Splits often appeared in their sides, lengthening with each of Eddy's strides.

On the eve of his nineteenth birthday, Eddy was just winding up the last of his deliveries. At home, Mrs Dovewater was humming and baking chocolate cake. She put the fresh cake on the table between her half-drunk cup of tea and Eddy's glass of milk. It was a Sunday, and on Sundays, Mrs Dovewater always liked an afternoon nap. She strolled out to the hammock on the back verandah, yawned, stretched, and silently died.

When Eddy came home, the un-iced chocolate cake was cold and the milk was warm. And in Eddy's gut was that same weird sense of certainty he'd had the very day he was born. He loped to the back verandah and found his mother. She was curled under the hammock with her left shoulder caught in a familiar shrug, a half-smile on her face. Like she'd finally become indifferent to life itself.

This is it, he thought, and his stomach lurched. *This is what I've been running from.*

'It's Death,' he whispered out loud.

There was frostbite on his fingers and his ribs turned into icicles. The cold crawled up and froze his eyelids into a wide gaze. He managed to stumble sideways, afraid Death's sceptre might catch him on a back swing. Spinning on his heel, he ran. Back through the house, out the door, along the front walk, over the fence and into the street. He ran down the middle of the road, dodging traffic, past an ambulance. He outran two police cars and still he kept running.

He ran until it was dark and all through the night. He ran into the next morning and afternoon. He ran for days and he didn't stop. Not even when his knees wobbled, not even when he was completely lost. He ran until his gut ached and his legs were like liquorice. He ran until he'd used up every God-given resource he'd ever had, and then he kept running. There was a thudding in his ears and he couldn't tell right from left any more, couldn't tell which foot to pick up next.

Gasping, he dropped to his knees. Great shudders racked his chest. His head throbbed and his stomach heaved. He vomited a thin gruel onto the ground between his hands.

Get up, he thought, *get up, get up.*

His legs wouldn't move, so he gripped his knees, one in each hand, and pulled them up to his ears. Then he unbent his torso and leaned forward, forcing his feet to catch up. Every jolt of his heel on earth reverberated through his bones. Pain soaked into every cell. But the ache of moving was better than the ache of standing still, so he kept on.

It was hard to see. Someone had slapped up a pane of scratched glass in front of him, and the world was blurred. He realised he was crying. It was dark again and on the road ahead was a bright smear of light. Not headlights, because there was only one. Not a motorbike, because it shone unwinkingly, never moving back or forth. Unsure whether it was of human or heavenly derivation, Eddy half-turned, ready to flee should the face of God or Death appear.

Ankles knocking, he shuffled closer. For a moment he really did see a face. It was his mother. Her mouth was lifted in a sleepy smile and there was a sparkle in her half-shut eyes. Eddy opened his mouth to call out but the image had begun to fade. Colour drained from her cheeks and her hair paled against the night sky. An outline of her face remained, blurring like a charcoal drawing left in the rain. In the end, only the sparkle of her eyes remained. They became stars.

Distant stars, Eddy wanted to say, but not so distant. They stood solidly in the dark ether of space. And so did he.

Fear drilled into his bowel. Instinctively, he cradled his stomach, trying to pull himself into a foetal position, but his legs were stuck fast. As though an invisible pin had been passed through both ankles. Eddy hunched forward in slow motion, tension bending him like a paperclip. His bare and bloodied feet—the sneakers having long since worn away—hung limply in space like raw fish. Nestled between and far beneath his soles, the Earth lay in listless profile.

I'm gonna pass out, thought Eddy. *I'll fall into a coma. I'll fall!*

Still bent, he spread his arms out to both sides. He felt like a tiny flightless bird balancing on a fishing line. Patterns formed in the darkness, rushing towards him and away.

Breathe, he thought, but found he couldn't.

Is this Death? No skeleton in a thick cloak, no icy fingers wrapping his soul? Just this solitary, impersonal, empty cosmology.

Perhaps I've really outrun it and this is all that's left.

It couldn't be right. Death should be dry and dusty, whereas Eddy still felt remarkably wet. Sweat pimpled his neck. His nose was blocked and his cheeks were sticky with tears. He could feel a familiar throb in his anchored feet. Just to see if he could, Eddy spat. The resulting glob of phlegm sat insolently in front of him, refusing to budge. He had to swat at it with his hands to get rid of it, and rub the slippery mess on his tracksuit.

Anyway, what did that prove?

Maybe, he thought, examining his damp palms, *that's just habit.* A memory of moisture he hadn't shaken.

As he hung in space, staring at his bloody insteps, he noticed something shift on Earth. A dirty brown blossom opened across her crust. Then another and yet another, crowding her surface and milking her colours dry. When she was wholly hidden under a new dark scab, Eddy realised where he was. He had reached the end of the world.

Please, he thought, *please...*

Then: *Who are you praying to, Eddy, huh?*

'God' was a concept that made him feel like an unwanted houseguest. He'd always had a fondness for the patron saint of lost things, but—in his panic—couldn't remember the saint's name. He thought instead of his mother, lying cold on the back verandah. If she were here, he thought, standing beside me (and for an instant he could feel her arm through his), she'd just shrug. Maybe even smile with her customary gentle humour.

Life, eh? she'd probably say, and sigh.

Death, Eddy amended.

He thought of other people. Memories of Doc Kavendar emerged, all elbows and flapping coat. Images of the Captain, Principal Woolsey and even Old Mr Borridge followed. All of them gone. And the Earth just lay there, dried up and crumpled like an old tea bag. Eddy floated above it, feeling helpless. And—if he were truly honest—he felt something else. A strange sense of relief flowered in his gut. He had outwitted the demise of all humanity. He had outdone God and Death and everything else.

What, he wondered, was there really left for him to do?

Run.

He straightened instinctively, muscles tensing. Did somebody just say—

Run!

There it was again. A voice in his left ear. He turned and saw only the sudsy swirl of a foreign galaxy, like the stain in a giant black sink. Between it and him there was nothing. He twisted the other way and as he did, a massive pockmarked rock skidded close to his nose. It was at least as tall as Eddy, and wider. He supposed it was an asteroid. And he further supposed it wasn't travelling alone.

Sure enough, an entire herd was churning across the darkness towards him. Eddy leaned into an uncomfortable limbo as they rushed him, looking for all the world like a gang of giant, mean potatoes. And there he was, stuck in the middle of it—the sole pin in an alley full of demented bowling balls.

Duck!

Eddy ducked obediently, folding himself neatly between his knees. The next asteroid glanced off his back. He gripped his feet and pushed lower until his chin was in line with the calluses on his toes. This, he realised, was never going to work.

He hauled himself upright and grabbed both legs, trying to wrench his ankles from their invisible trap. The asteroids pushed closer with ponderous determination.

Run! he told himself. *RunrunRUN!*

But his feet were still firmly stuck. The next asteroid collected him side on. He felt himself pulled apart, arms flung out above his head, legs stretched to impossible proportions. Another direct hit and he felt space tugging at his soles like thick mud. Then he was yanked free, his legs snapping back into place. Eddy spun unevenly end over end like a raw egg.

There was nothing to give him a sense of up or down, so Eddy gave himself over to the crazy progress of nudge, roll, nudge, roll. Finally, he was edged out of the asteroid's path and allowed to come to a relative standstill. His limbs, now freed of their strange stasis, refused to rest. Both knees kept drifting towards his chin and his head rolled and rolled on his neck until he trapped it with his elbows.

A ripple passed across the emptiness above him, causing the stars to shudder like guitar strings.

You okay? A girl's voice, soft and high.

Eddy nodded uneasily and his arms drifted away, forgetting for a moment to keep hold of his head. Truth was, he felt like a rag doll without any stuffing.

So so, he said.

I'm Beverly, she said, her voice seeming to come from all around him. *You?*

Eddy, he replied.

He was looking for the source of her voice, without success. Squinting through his itinerant toes, he spotted a distant mush of pale blue gas like jelly, studded with diamonds. There was no clear centre to it, and as Eddy stared, he felt like his eyes crossed, trying to find something to focus on.

You know what the weirdest thing is? asked Beverly, as though this was just some regular conversation they always had, riding their pushbikes home from school.

Anyway, was he even qualified to judge weirdness, anymore? He concentrated instead on curbing his straying limbs. In the silence, Beverly answered herself.

You can't see me, can you? she asked, and took his silence for assent. *It's okay. I can't see me, either. Isn't that the weirdest?*

Eddy tried to shrug. *I guess,* he said, politely.

So tell me, Beverly continued, *can you see that?*

It sounded like she was pointing, but—being invisible—her gesture was lost on him. Eddy took a careful look around, all the same. At first he saw only asteroids rolling beneath him and stars like stains of milk in a black cloth. In the distance were cobwebs of transparent gas. But then there it was again—that strange ripple.

That's not you, then? he asked.

Nope.

He blinked, hoping it was only some involuntary eye tremor. But when the ripple curved across the darkness towards him, he saw it clearly. One by one, the stars were rocked by the waves of this thing's coming. They stretched and compressed as if the edge of a magnifying glass moved across them.

He sat up, in a way, and leaned forward, trying to make out the shape.

It looks sort of like—he said, and he was starting to worry.

Like a giant hand, but backwards, the round palm pushed ahead and a dozen fingers dragged behind. It circled Eddy languidly.

A jellyfish? Beverly asked.

Eddy twisted at the waist, trying to keep the thing in sight.

What is it? he asked.

I don't know, Beverly said. *But whatever it is, it took my body.*

Eddy didn't like the sound of that. He didn't like it even more when the thing accelerated sharply and poured across the distance towards him. Something metal-cold wrapped his arm and he hoped it was Beverly, but he kept his eyes on the thing. The shape convulsed rhythmically, front to back. It was building a new form, Eddy realised, as the fingers straightened out and the front narrowed to a fine point. More like a dart now, he thought, than a jellyfish.

With venomous force, the dart hurtled forward. Eddy leaned back, tucked his knees beneath his chin, and rolled from its path. His toes connected sharply with the underbelly of the thing, sending him into a spin until he was hanging—to his mind—upside-down. Instinctively, he clamped his hands on his pockets.

Far beneath (or above) the crown of his head, Earth lay like a dirty Velcro dot on black felt. Eddy cast a quick glance over his shoulder and saw the strange outline of the thing turning, its fingers sweeping around like the fringe of a ball gown. It faced them blankly and almost seemed to be gathering its breath.

Upside-down or not, Eddy began to run.

He lifted his right foot and bunched his fists. He flexed his left knee and swung his arms. He pushed against ... nothing.

There was no resistance for the soles of his feet. His knees snapped painfully at the top of each stride. His arms flopped uselessly, dodging the smooth straight arcs he was used to.

Eddy ran exactly in place.

The thing behind him was still, and almost seemed to stare. Then it spread its fingers—like a starfish—and hooked into place. Its middle fell back on itself, forming a bubble that tore and became a giant throat. Darkness spiralled down its gullet, dragging stars and debris with it.

Oh no, said Beverly. *Not this again.*

The utter silence disturbed him. No sounds of chewing from the thing: it swallowed space whole. No noise from the cold, invisible girl on his arm. No huff-huff of breath from his own mouth. Even the thrum of blood beating by his ears had been stilled. He felt lost.

Legs still jerking, arms shaking, torso muscles tightening— Eddy leaned forward. Left, right, left, twisting on his hips. Muscle and bone had been replaced by rubber. But he was getting used to it. Space was sliding under his feet. An asteroid spun by, making a beeline for the gulping hole behind him. And there was something even worse happening. Eddy could feel the thing sucking at his own skin, lifting it like a shirt on a washing line.

He wasn't about to die like this.

Slowly, every shred of his body striving, he began to move. A tiny ship on a massive black sea.

Hold on, he told Beverly.

Beverly pressed into his side. Eddy kicked out, imagining the Earth at his toes. His neck prickled. The empty throat was reaching for him. But with each swing of his fist, push of his thigh, they were picking up speed. There was no air on his face, no warm burn in his limbs. No sweat, no stitches in his side. He didn't even need to catch his breath.

He began to feel strong. His body was the perfect machine, never needing maintenance. He could run like clockwork. Forever.

The thing was still behind him somewhere. He turned his head to keep watch over his shoulder. It was the easiest thing in the world, running like that. He'd always done it that way.

Look out for—Beverly began.

Instinctively, Eddy had headed for home. He whipped his face back to the front just in time. The first icy grit of Saturn's rings slapped against his shins.

He swerved, following his knees up and over the rings. They were fast now, getting faster. Eddy leapt and dodged and wove, with Beverly a lightweight on his ribs. Arching his spine away from the tug of the thing, he spun from its path.

Hang on, he told Beverly.

The throat followed, turning clumsily. Eddy careered away, dodging its progress, listing port and starboard in quick succession.

Faster still, pursued by the massive vacuum, they ran. The Earth shot under them in a filthy blur. Stars stretched around them like uncooked noodles. Eddy cast a quick glance back again. The mouth of the thing was so wide now, its centre had all but disappeared. Only a thin rim remained, flapping between fingers that clenched onto space.

It's getting greedy, he thought.

Even as he watched, a finger was rattled from its hold. It scraped a frantic path through space before it was swallowed whole, leaving a ragged gap where it had been. The rest of the hand clenched down, shaking with the effort.

To the sides of the gap, two more fingers lost their grip and began descending into the maw. Others followed fast. The whole monster was turning inside out, shaking as it engulfed itself. When all the fingers were digested, the thing seemed to freeze. Only the narrowest rim remained, like the burnt edge of an egg white.

You've done it, Beverly said, hushed. *You've outrun it.*

It took half a dozen more long strides before Eddy was able to slow. Then he scanned the darkness behind them, jogging on the spot—loathe to stop. He'd outrun Death and Armageddon. And now, he'd outrun this strange new thing, too. Triumph knocked the rhythm from his arms. But it was a strange kind of triumph. Without the thud of muscles that had given their all, the thrum and thrust of blood under skin, the pull of tendon.

He'd been so committed to outrunning Death, he'd never realised he'd run out on Life, as well.

So, he said quietly, *you think there are any more of those?*

Maybe, said Beverly, after a pause.

He thought again of the prickling sensation along his back. Like his skin was being carved from his very soul.

I guess, he said, *if we hang around long enough, we'll come across others.*

I guess, Beverly replied.

And we'll have to outrun them, too.

Beverly didn't reply. Eddy stared down the barrel of a future always running. He'd spent his whole life running. Running *from* something. Never had the chance to run *to* anyplace.

Do you think ... he began, looking for the right words. *Do you think this is all there is? I mean, is this it?*

He swept his arm wide to take in the entire broad vista of space.

Some people might think it's a lot, Beverly told him.

I guess.

But Eddy missed the smell of sweat. He missed headaches, backaches, calf aches. He missed hunger. Yes, space was beautiful. He could see, for example, bright spinning disks and heavy balloons of colourful gas. Stars that pulsed with vibrancy. And there was probably more life out there, somewhere. People, or something like people, were presumably going about their business, buying their shopping in recycled plastic and living in ignorance of the rest of the universe. Mostly, they probably had lives they hadn't exactly chosen, but had settled for. They could even be happy. Or if not happy, then at least not unhappy.

It's not enough, he said. *Not anymore.*

He'd done all that already. Life, and everything like it. And the strange, imploded monster only lay there, mute and immobile. It's skin—or what passed for skin—was dark chocolate-black, with an even darker oval at its core. Like a tiny pupil. Or perhaps not a pupil: more like the handle on a door.

Say, he said slowly, *you think that goes someplace?*

No way, Beverly replied. *You know what it is? A black hole. Nothing can get through there.* When Eddy didn't seem convinced, she added, *You'd never make it.*

I made it this far, didn't I?

She couldn't argue with that.

Loose-limbed, Eddy did a slow circuit away from the door, giving himself more room to move. He shook the tension out of his arms and rolled his head side to side. He flexed his toes up and down (only there was no up and down, he remembered, and it didn't bother him as much as it used to).

Might as well try, Eddy said. After all, what was there to lose?

Beverly laughed like she thought he was completely crazy, but endearingly so.

All right, then, she said, meaning: well, why not?

Eddy Dovewater grinned. Then, limber beyond all human understanding, he took off running, aiming for the darkest part of the black hole like it was something he was born to do.

Deborah Biancotti is an Aurealis & Ditmar Award winning Australian writer. Her work has most recently appeared in *The Year's Best Australian Science Fiction and Fantasy* #1 and online at *Ticonderoga Online* and *infinity plus*. Other stories have appeared in *Borderlands, Orb, Redsine* and *Altair*, as well as anthologies from MirrorDanse, Ideomancer, and several editions of Agog! Upcoming work is appearing in *Shadowed Realms* and *Eidolon* #1. You can find her online at http://deborahbiancotti.net and www.livejournal.com/users/deborahb.

MAKING TWO FISTS

LEE BATTERSBY

FROM WHERE I LIE I CAN SEE the puddle changing colour, red neon pink neon green as the lights from the bar's sign flicker and change. At the far end of the alley I hear a clatter and a curse: the last professional drunk of the evening falling over a rubbish bin or cleanbot on his way back to the shelter. I should haul myself to my feet. I could stumble forward and into the street to find help. But I know I can't. My left arm is broken, and if I move my right arm away from my chest I'll just die all the quicker. This wasn't how it was supposed to end. Not tonight.

I banged down the stairs and into the front room of the hostel to find Eddie sprawled on a couch watching the teev. Eddie's a legend among Rentaboys. He's got 38 keys and so many jobs on the hop he actually farms some of them out to other Corpsmen who are on their leans. He could afford to go legit, but he can't be bothered, says why should he be buying things when Dolehomes will give them up for free? He'd picked me up a while back when I'd tried a jump-snatch on him, and instead of thrashing me a lesson he'd pointed me towards the home and told me about the Corps.

After two years of hard learning I'd finally grabbed my tenth key. I was ready to make full-time Corps. I'd phoned my local Headquarters and been told to head on over. All I had to do was turn up, show both fists and finally tie my colours around the arms of my jacket. That's what I'd spent the last two years trying to become: one of the smart 'Boys who can collect Two Fists worth of keys, regulating things so that it's only the dumbasses you ever see on the news getting copped. Keeps you safe from others too. You a Corpsman and you wear colours, you don't get rolled by some newkid trying to make Two Fists in one shot. Plus if you're smart enough to keep your own key clean you get the dole to pay for Goon. Not that some 'Boys are near that smart. Eddie was one of the smartest. Now I was finally ready to look him in the eye.

I went to the main wardrobe to grab my coat. Eddie looked up and raised his eyebrows.

'You going out?'

'Yeah.' I'd told him I'd made Two Fists. Eddie'd be the first guy you'd want to tell. But it looked like he'd forgotten.

'Want to watch the show? Snoopy Da Dogg versus MC Dexta Dexx for a five CD deal.'

'Nah.' I picked out the black trenchcoat that was my favourite. Most kids in the home knew enough to leave it alone. 'No good since they stopped using semi-automatics. I get harder than that three jobs out of five.'

'I dunno,' He turned back to the simple 2-D set that was all the home could afford. 'Five CD deal man, five CDs. They'll be pulling some nasty shit for that.'

'Handguns and headshots, that's all it is these days.' I said, trying to sound like I was watching before the networks stepped in and turned all that gangsta-rap war shit into a game show. 'Maybe if they went back to before they started wearing all that kevlar so they can do something real hard-core once in a while ...'

'Oh it'll be hard-core.' Eddie replied. 'When the stakes are high enough someone always gets nasty.'

He turned back to the flat screen of the teev. Over his shoulder I could see that the action was just about to start. I shrugged my jacket on, threw an unanswered 'See ya' in his direction, and headed for the street.

Bunbury is a dump. When my grandparents moved here it was just a nice little tourist town a couple of hundred kilometres down the coast from Perth, the state capital. Then the Multinationals realised that Perth's isolation from the rest of the world made their buildings more easily defendable than if they were, say, right in the middle of London or New York, and moved out here in droves. Pretty soon the city began crawling down the edge of the coast, devouring all the little towns in front of it.

By the time I was born we were only 30 k's outside city limits. Now the City's swallowed us too. Bunbury's the southernmost suburb, and that makes it a dump. All the losers and bad-breeds who can't afford to move closer to the centre end up down here, as well as anyone from further south who can't deal with the unemployment in the country towns and comes up here thinking it's the gateway to the big money. Used to be a coastal town, now half of us don't even live on solid land, just crouch in prefabs on the pontoon suburbs that stretch out into the ocean.

Friend of mine who does some part-time SETI work on the net for NASA reckons you can see our Toonville from Moonbase. Says it's bigger than the Hudson Bay Toonville now. Says it doesn't look dirty from space. From where I stood outside the door of the hostel it looked dirtier than the Devil's dewlaps. I walked across the street and checked my watch under one of the two working streetlights. I still had a couple of hours to kill before the Corps was due to meet. I decided to wander down to a Job-Teller Machine and have a look at the worknet.

There's an area right at the edge of the last pontoon that I like to go out to sometimes at night. It's usually deserted, and I can stand right up against the barrier fence and watch the lights of the city flickering red pink green on the water just in front of the swellbreakers. There's a Worknet JTM there too, tucked away in a corner in anticipation of an expansion that just never happened. On a good night I can spend hours jumping from key to key looking for fillers. That's how us Rentaboys make dosh, grabbing jobkeys and turning jobs. You see a drunk asleep at a bus stop, you whip his jobkey; some old lady out late at night without an escort, off comes her handbag and her key with it. You can rack up as many jobs as you have keys to fit, long as you keep track of whose is whats and don't try use Granny's key to log on to the Heavy Manual Labour sites.

I set off for it, running my fingers across the bunched fists of keys in my pockets, calculating how many empty jobs each one had. Nobody works full-time anymore. Not since the population topped 40 million and the Government repealed the workplace agreement laws. No employer would be mad enough to employ someone full-time and have to pay superannuation and health benefits and all that crap.

That's how the jobkeys came about. You can register through the JTMs and have up to three jobs at a time, in theory. In reality, no company turns down someone who shows up at the right time and doesn't ask about unions or minimum safety requirements or the few bits and pieces they're still supposed to provide. Even so, it's still safer to have a few names to work under; just in case someone decides to play the company line and get all official with you come payday.

It's supposed to take some of the strain off the social security system as well. I've worked for the dole office a couple of times and they teach you a whole bunch of history that you wouldn't give a damn about unless you were trying to rip off the system. Of course everybody's trying to rip off the system. That's how a twenty year old like me can turn up for a job that was registered to a 62-year-old woman and not get asked any questions. It's the loop that all the Rentaboys live in. I looked at my watch again, trying to calculate how long it would take me to hack in and see what I could register for. I had half a day on Friday that I could fill, maybe make enough money from a temp job to buy that coltello I'd seen in the knife case at the new Cash Creators store downtoon.

I'd been at the screen for less than five minutes when I spied someone shuffling toward me along the lit half of the streetway. I logged off and turned to face him, pivoting to put my weight on my back foot in case I needed to kick. A quick glance at the nearest streetlight told me the camera was turned off. Even if it had been working, what cop ever comes this far out into Toonville just to rescue a Rentaboy? This would be a one-on-one no matter how it played. I slid a hand behind my back. I wasn't carrying anything more than a coin-roll tonight, but half of fighting is bluff anyway. What he didn't know might just keep this stooge walking.

He stopped a few feet away. I looked him up and down silently. He wore a wrinkled suit that had probably cost him a good wad but looked as if he'd woken up in it before he came out. There were two rings on his fingers that appeared to have been made for him rather than bought from a window. Designs I hadn't seen in town, and a good Rentaboy makes a study of jewellery that can be on-sold. His face was red and fat and for some reason I had the impression I'd seen it before.

'Hello.' He said, and smiled. It was probably meant to be friendly but under the streetlight it just looked sweaty. I didn't reply. His eyes flicked uncertainly to either side and he took a step forward.

'Are you out all alone tonight?'

I rocked back onto my foot and raised my left knee. I've timed myself. I can stand in this position for sixteen minutes, more than long enough for this scene to play itself out. If he tried a grab I'd have all the time in the world to decide whether I wanted to break his knee or his sternum first.

'Fuck you.' I said, my voice all flat and sharp so there could be no misunderstandings.

The message didn't seem to get through. Instead of taking off like any sensible stooge he just tilted his head.

'That's what I'm hoping. I've got a hundred if you'll do one or two other things as well.'

I snorted. This guy was seriously not in touch. I could take him down right there and then. I could walk away from his unconscious, bleeding body, and get more than a hundred just for his watch in at least three shops within this pontoon. I was deciding to do just that when things were taken right out of my hands.

Something came whirring from out of the darkness behind me. It flew past my ear, flashed through the light and hit the fat guy square in the middle of the forehead before either of us could react to its arrival. He dropped like he'd been hit by lightning. I stared at him in shock for a heartbeat, then slowly turned my eyes to look at the thing that had hit him. It was a bolarang, a small plastic boomerang with heavy rubber balls at each end. I'd seen them used before, and I didn't like them. Too unbalanced, and difficult to throw with any degree of accuracy. Not for whoever had thrown this one.

The 'whoever' was still in the dark behind me. I'd have been face down on the floor next to the stooge by now if they'd wanted, so I figured I was okay for the moment. I walked slowly forward and bent down to pick up the bolarang. A voice stopped my hand.

'Wouldn't do that.'

I looked up. Slinking out of the shadows was a kid of maybe eleven or twelve, crouching side-on, another bolarang raised and aimed directly at me. I lifted my arm and stepped backwards. He reached down with his free hand and picked up his weapon. His eyes never left me and his throwing arm retained its tension. He put the 'rang into an L-shaped holster that ran the length of his thigh.

'Who are you, Batman?'

He ignored my question. 'You the Two-Fister I've been sent to pick up?'

I noticed his jacket for the first time. Black like mine, it bore Corps colours across the left breast and round the biceps. I relaxed slightly.

'Yeah.'

'Good.' He holstered his other 'rang and stood straight.

'Where did you learn to throw like that?'

'Practice. What do you reckon?'

I shrugged. 'Why'd they send you to get me? I've still got a couple of hours.'

'Plan changed. It happens.' He looked down at the unconscious stooge on the ground between us. 'Got time for shopping though. My kill, my key. Fifty-fifty on the rest.'

'Fair.'

The fat guy had fallen on his face. We knelt down and turned him over. The kid swore.

'What?'

'You don't recognise him? It's Abbot.'

'The church guy?'

'Yeah. We're gonna cop big-mob shit for this.'

Now I knew where I'd seen his face before. This guy was always on the teev, fronting some big-mob church called the Sons of the Western Truth, spouting off about how every time Perth grew it just made it a bigger target for the next jihad or whatever. Never mind that the rest of the country had grown just the same or that the last time anybody had called a jihad his second-in-command had killed him right in the middle of his speech and apologised to everybody. The Muslims I knew thought he was a prize prat. Most of them work for the Multinationals anyway, so I could never figure out who he thought their enemy was.

Still, the kid was right. We would cop some righteous shit for this. Me especially. I'd been in his eyes for a good few minutes, and under a damn streetlight just to make thing easier for him. He'd have no trouble picking my face. If I got canned again there was a whole list of things that were going to get added back onto my record. That would do me no good at all. The kid must have been thinking the same way.

'Saw you enough to finger you. Your call.'

'Shit.' I sat looking down at Abbott's fat face for a minute or so. 'All right. Let's empty him anyway. We may as well get some goods to start with.'

We went through him pretty thoroughly, right down to the phone jack in his earlobe. When the kid found his jobkey he held it up in the light and sighed.

'Ain't using this now.' He threw it through the boundary fence. It made a soft plop as it hit the water twenty feet below the edge of the pontoon. The kid looked back at me.

'Still got to do something with Fatso.'

'I know.'

If Abbott fingered me, and I knew he would, I was set for a long stretch of heavy. No juvenile home this time. I'd be on adult charges. It wouldn't end there either. Abbott might be a joke to us but he had a brother in the State Government. He'd have the cops coming through here like a tidal wave. That'd mean no Corps, no Rentaboys, and no more job-hopping for anyone in all of Toonville. If we didn't do something right now, something permanent, everyone's way of life was going to be cleaned up and stuffed. The kid looked back to where he'd thrown the key.

'Bet he doesn't know how to swim.'

'I can't either.'

'Better not fall in then.'

I looked at him for what seemed like a very long time, trying to think up a solution that wouldn't be as extreme as he was suggesting. I'd done a few things on the wrong side of right before, but I'd never resorted to murder. I didn't fancy starting now either, but the kid was right. I honestly couldn't think of anything else we could do. I blew out my cheeks and nodded. The kid nodded back, and we went at it. We divided the spoils between us, although I gave the kid first pick since he'd missed out on the jobkey. Then we dragged Abbott to the fence and looked up.

'Got to be ten feet, easy.'

'Ten foot six.' He laughed at my surprised look. 'Corps got a lot of maps and stuff. You'll learn them.'

'So how do we get him over?'

'Watch and learn.' He drew his bolarangs from their holsters and pointed to the tops of the two poles that marked our section of fence. 'See them?'

'Yeah.'

The kid raised his arms in a cross above his eyes then brought them swiftly down to either side of his body, letting go of the 'rangs at the bottom of the arc. The whirring crescents looped up and over, spinning upwards and striking the tops of the poles with a rubber end before falling back inside the fence line. I heard a loud double click and the entire section of fence slid downwards into the pontoon.

'Maintenance.' The kid said and went to retrieve his weapons.

'Won't this be monitored?' I asked him when he returned. He gave me a look of mild contempt.

'You ever see any council workers out here? Come on.' He motioned toward our unconscious cargo. We dragged him to the edge of the pontoon and looked down. I saw the oily black water swirling below us and stepped back quickly.

'You sure this is the only option?'

'Unless you look good in handcuffs.' The kid grabbed an ankle and lifted it to his waist. After a moment I bent down and picked up the other. We gave one quick heave and Abbott's flabby body went over the side and fell with a smack onto the water below. We watched it float for a few minutes until the swirling water took it slowly underneath the pontoon.

'Now what?'

'Council's got machines down there for chewing up stuff that makes it past the swellbreakers. This time next week he's underneath a rose bush with the rest of the mulch. I'll show you the plans after the Corps meeting.'

'Huh?' I'd forgotten all about the meeting. 'Oh yeah. Okay. What about the fence?'

'Easy.' We crossed back over the fence line. The kid pointed out a button recessed into the outside of the nearest pole and then sent me across to the other. We reached around and pressed our buttons and the fence slid slowly back out of the pontoon and into place. Five minutes from beginning to end and you'd never have known anything at all had happened in the now-empty street.

'Right then.' The kid said. 'Let's go.'

I'd always thought the Corps' headquarters would be a hive of activity, like one of those war rooms I'd seen in those old World War II movies on the Sunday afternoon teev. I half-expected to see people rushing in and out; everybody's movements being recorded on a big map; radios constantly reporting the action; young chicks pushing the pieces about with big pool cues. In reality I was led up to an anonymous looking house and into a living room where a tall guy in Corps colours sat on a couch watching the Da Dogg-Dexx fight on a colour teev. The kid went over and flopped down next to him.

'Who's winning?' I asked. The tall guy looked up.

'Some bystander just got copped.' He smiled. 'Gonna get nasty now. You the new guy?'

'Guess so.'

He tilted his head towards a doorway just behind us.

'Go in the kitchen.'

I moved in the indicated direction, pushing through an old vinyl fly-strip door and walking into the dingy room beyond. A table with a chipped Formica top was pushed against one wall. Eddie sat in a chair on the opposite side to me. He looked up and grinned.

'Made it.'

'Uh, yeah.' There was an empty seat at my side of the table. I dropped into it.

'Not what you expected?' He gestured back through the doorway. I shrugged.

'Not really. I just thought it'd be, I don't know ...'

'Busier? More business-like?'

'Yeah, something like that.'

'Nah. We get busted by cops all they see is a bunch of kids watching teev or smoking. Underground businessmen, man. Like icebergs. What you see's only the tip of what's there.'

'Okay.'

'I'll prove it. What you want me to show you?'

I thought back through the evening and remembered where we'd dropped Abbott.

'The kid said you had all these maps? Of the machines and stuff under Toonville?'

'Too right.' He stood up. 'Come on then.'

He led me toward the back of the house and the laundry. As I stood in the doorway he walked into the centre of the room and pointed at the floor.

'Ta da.'

I looked down. The floor was made up of mosaic tiles; the white majority interspersed here and there with single tiles of various colours. It didn't look in the least special.

'So?'

'Watch and learn.' He pulled a set of cardboard strips from under the front of an old washing machine standing in the corner and arranged them in a rough parallelogram, the doorway in which I stood forming its base.

'Toonville.' He said. 'Now look again.' As I watched he began pointing to different coloured tiles within the parallelogram, explaining which represented traffic lights, the entrances to major buildings, JTMs, and so on. I looked on in amazement.

'Took nearly four years to lay this out correctly.' He said. 'It's accurate so long as you memorise it properly.'

'Show me the machines for chewing up all the underwater crap.' Eddie pointed them out to me one by one, tracing out the markers that determined the tide patterns bringing the water to their mouths. I looked at them in turn, then found the spot where the kid and I had done our evening's work.

'Shit.'

'What?'

I tore my gaze away from what the tiles were telling me.

'I think we've got a problem.'

'Show me again.' Eddie and the tall guy from the couch knelt over the map and watched as the kid and I ran through the events at the JTM, pointing to where we'd dumped Abbott's body.

'Where do you think it'll wash up?' the kid asked. Eddie traced a path through the maze of tiles and off to one side of the doorway.

'Here. Somewhere along Dalyellup Beach. Say five k's out of town. Close enough to town to be found nice and early tomorrow morning.'

'Shit.'

'No way you could've known. Council was going to extend Toonville out at that point and the new pontoon would've had a mulcher underneath it. You just got unlucky and hit the one blind spot in the system. He'll probably wash up on the first tide.'

'What do we do?'

'That'll be for me and Dreads to decide.' He gestured to the tall guy. 'You two may as well head upstairs and get a couple of hours sleep while we work something out.'

The kid walked out through the door and towards a staircase at the end of the back hallway. I followed him. I didn't have the sense to ask about getting my colours.

Two hours later we were woken by the guy called Dreads and taken back down into the kitchen where Eddie sat eating a bowl of tinned spaghetti. We waited while he licked the bowl clean, then he stood and clapped us both on the shoulder.

'We've come up with a plan. Crackle, head out the front with Dreads and he'll run through your part.' They left and I raised an eyebrow at Eddie.

'Crackle?'

'One of triplets. Glen, Len & Ben, would you believe it? We call them Snap, Crackle & Pop so we can tell them apart. Now, this is what we're going to have to do ...'

Eddie's plan was simple. Three blocks over lived a guy named Blind Sammy who ran a low-rent pawnshop and fence. The local Corps loved him because of his encroaching senility, dodgy eyesight, and complete inability to work out when he was being taken advantage of. Most times they cut him fairly straight because he was easy to get top price from without cheating. As Eddie explained it, enough locals knew he was an easy touch that he always had a steady flow of customers to keep him above water, so nothing the Corps did had any real effect on his cash flow.

'All we need is something easily identifiable as Abbott's and we've got a routine we can use to place them.'

'Like these?' I'd taken Abbott's rings with the thought of melting them down on a little set I had back at the home. Now I pulled them out and held them up to Eddie. He looked at them appraisingly then picked them from my hand.

'Perfect.'

The plan was an easy switch-and-drop. Dreads and Crackle would go into Sammy's shop on the pretext of buying some rings. They'd keep their hands moving and tongues flapping as they went through tray after tray until old Sammy was well and truly engrossed in the conversation and had forgotten about the merchandise spread out in front of them. Then Eddie and I would come in and 'meet' our two friends. While everyone greeted each other Eddie would slip Abbott's rings into one of the trays. The Corps normally used this routine when they were low on cash and needed to whip a couple of pieces that they could sell back to Sammy a few hours later. Tonight though, we'd be planting not pulling.

'That way,' Eddie said as we walked through the front door and out into the street, 'When the cops come through they'll find the rings and Sammy'll draw the heat instead of us.'

'But what if he fingers us?'

Dreads snorted. 'Old Sammy? We take our colours off before we go in and all he'll remember is some kids, if he even remembers at all. Shit, he's so blind if you didn't move he'd think you were a dummy and try to hang some clothes on you.'

The others laughed, but I was still concerned.

'What'll happen when the cops find the rings on him?'

This time it was Crackle who snorted his derision.

'You know how much cops make? Most of the ones round here are buying from Sammy so their wives have something new to wear to the next barbecue. Half of 'em probably fencing stuff they whip from the station for beer money. Five'll get you ten every cop that searches Sammy's is a long-time customer. All they'll do is take the rings and slap a fine on him, and he'll just take the cost out of the next load of guns he fences for them.'

'He's been here since the pontoon went down.' Eddie joined in. 'He'll be right.'

I looked at their faces, so sure and calm, and shrugged in resignation. 'Okay then.'

'Okay.' We formed up and began to walk into the night.

It was a short walk to Sammy's place, but by the time we got there the weather had changed and a light mist of rain was beginning to fall. Eddie motioned us down an alleyway next to the building and into the shelter of a darkened doorway. He and the others took off their jackets and laid them neatly on the doorstep. Without their colours they looked like any normal Rentaboy, or Joyjammers out late looking for a ludeman. Crackle took one bolarang out of its holster and laid it on top of the jackets, then took the other out and held it in his hand.

'Too easy to identify.' Eddie said to me. His face glowed red pink green in the reflected light of a neon sign across the road from the alley's end.

'Fair enough.' I replied. 'We ready?'

'Yep.' Eddie laid a hand on my shoulder and turned me to face back up the alley. That's when Crackle brought the hard rubber end of the bolarang crashing down onto the back of my neck.

They beat me up totally, no doubt about it. Eddie knew I was a pretty good fighter, so they jumped me quick and jumped hard. I had no chance from the moment the first blow from the 'rang sent me forward into Dreads' cocked and waiting fist. I was out of it pretty much from that first punch. They didn't even bother to kick me once I hit the ground. They just kept picking me up and knocking me back down again until I didn't even have the strength to move my arms to try and stop them. Dreads picked me up one last time and held me as upright as he could. Crackle went through and emptied me while Eddie stood and watched with a pained look in his eyes.

'I'm sorry man.' he said when Crackle had finished his work. 'This was the only way it would work out. Someone needs to be fingered for this, but that Abbott, he's too big to palm a couple of rings off on somebody like Sammy and expect it all to go away. Cops'd never be happy just grabbing some fence, not with the government breathing on them. They wouldn't be allowed to stop looking until they found a murderer.'

He took the rings from his pocket and gave them to Crackle, who added them to the watch and folded money he was already holding. Then the kid came forward and tucked them into various pockets in my jacket. I tried to move something, to put up some kind of resistance, but Dreads simply shook me until my strength gave away again and I slumped back against him. When I looked up Eddie was standing in front of me holding a nasty looking knife.

'He was mugged by a Rentaboy, who stole his money and his rings and got mugged himself before he could on-sell them. Cops like stories like that. Nice and easy, looks good on the news.'

He bunched his fist around the knife. I coughed and found the strength to speak.

'But ... I've got ten keys ... two fists.'

Eddie looked at my jacket, my empty black jacket that bore no colours.

'I'm sorry man. I told you, I said, when the stakes are high enough someone always gets it nasty.'

With that he drove the knife into my chest. My body folded around his fist as the metal poured white pain into my flesh. The air inside me pushed upwards and escaped in a single moan. Pain, pure and clean, filled the gaps it left behind. My skin turned ice-cold, and all the muscles of my face cramped and froze, leaving me with only my eyes screaming. Dreads opened his arms and let me fall to the wet floor of the alleyway. My face slapped hard into the rubmac surface of the pontoon. I watched in silent agony as they divided my loot. Eddie took half my keys but nothing else. He cleaned the knife off in the rain and handed it to Dreads. Dreads and Crackle moved away down the alley, leaving Eddie and I alone. He came and squatted in front of me, gently turning my head until he could look down into my eyes.

'One thing was truth. We'll pull the routine on Sammy, but it'll be with the knife. One knife's very like another round here.'

He let my head fall back onto the rubmac, grabbed my left arm and made to move it, then let go and took my right arm instead. He balled my hand into a fist and placed it over the hole in my chest, pressing it hard against the flow of blood.

'Left one's broken.' He said. 'Sorry about that.'

Then he stood up and held out his hands, letting the rain wash away the blood. When they were clean he picked up his jacket and walked away. I watched the coloured bands round his arms get smaller and smaller until they turned the corner and disappeared.

He was smart to leave my useless arm where it was and use my good hand to cover the wound. It would be so easy, you see, to reach up and take the rings and the watch out of my pockets and throw them away. The fence is only a few feet away, the gap between me and the water tantalizingly small. But my left hand is balled into a useless fist behind me, and if I open my good hand and do the necessary deed I'll be forced to take it away from the hole in my chest. The blood will flow freely again and I'll be dead. I won't even be deceased, not as a person, not really.

I'm already at a job somewhere, looking like Eddie or Crackle or Dreads, smiling and talking and making sure everyone knows my name. It's not me lying here watching the puddle turn red neon pink neon green, hoping someone will wander down the alleyway to take a pee or be sick and stumble across me. It's just some nameless dying Rentaboy with my face, just some no-name, no-colours nobody lying in a pool of his own blood. Just some guy with his hands making two useless fists.

Lee Battersby is the author of over 40 stories including appearances in Writers of the Future Volume 18, Tales of the Unanticipated, Aurealis, and the Wheatland Press anthology 'All-Star Zeppelin Adventure Stories', amongst others. His collection 'The Divergence Tree' is due for release by Prime Books in early 2006. Winner of the Australian SF 'Ditmar' Award, and multiple Aurealis Award nominee, he has recently been announced as tutor at Clarion South 2007. He lives in Perth with his wife, writer Lyn, and maintains a weblog at http://battersblog.blogspot.com. A discussion board dedicated to his work can be found at www.nightshadebooks.com/cgi-bin/discuss/discuss.cgi?pg=topics

EDEN

JACK DANN

THE OBJECT HIT THE DAM AT GUYRA just after at 2:43 am on Monday, December 6th. It was a needle the size of a football field, and it slipped into the water like a coin being dropped edge-first. The spacecraft disappeared; only the three spiney rods of its terraforming unit pierced the surface of the quiet water.

If you put your head to the ground, you could hear a slight humming. It made the thrub-thrubbing sound of a dishwashing machine. And if you looked carefully, and the light was exactly right, you would be able to see the tips of the alien ship's terraforming rods.

The alien machine was working, purring away underwater.

It would only take a few more days to reach critical.

At 5:15 pm on Thursday, December 9th, five divers went into the dam to prove that the object was debris from a satellite.

None of them ever surfaced.

The EPA, EOC, and the army laid down a perimeter around the area before dawn on Friday. No one was allowed into—or out of—Guyra. Although Emergency Operations claimed that there was no danger to the town's 2,000 residents, they were in quarantine. A robot submersible was lowered into the water later that afternoon. It disappeared, as did the boat, which had gotten too close to the alien craft's spiney rods.

By midnight, the weather became suddenly hot and humid, and steam seemed to be boiling over the surface of the water. Rainforest began to grow at an astonishing rate, but the shapes and textures were completely alien to anything ever seen before. Guyra and the area around the dam were developing their own clammy climate, and their own flora and fauna.

The contamination spread.

'Hey, this stuff tastes good,' one of the residents told an ABC television news reporter, and he stood there eating what looked for all the world like a green donut. The tree behind him had sprouted them. 'It's a freakin' donut tree is what it is,' he said.

That was the last ABC transmission.

Six hours later, the Prime Minister ordered in the army.

Not a man or woman returned.

The United Nations became involved. Surveillance and fighter planes flew over the area ... and disappeared.

Missiles were launched ... and disappeared.

The infected area now covered the length and breath of New South Wales.

No man, woman, or child outside of New South Wales area would know the answer ... until it was too late.

A composer and pianist who had accompanied the first ABC reporter to disappear knew the answer, however.

The composer made his way to the edge of the water ... and was there when the glittering shaft of the alien craft rose from the water and extruded walkways. A huge ten foot high cockroach, presumably the captain, walked toward the composer, who, frozen with fear, stood his ground.

'Hallo,' said the extraterrestrial cockroach in an enormous, booming voice.

'Hello,' said the composer.

'Do you like the changes?' asked the cockroach.

'What are you doing here?' asked the composer.

'Creating a salad.'

'What!'

'Yeah, all the greens. Don't you like salad?'

The composer just blinked at the cockroach swaying over him. Then he said, 'You came all this way to make a salad?'

'That's right. We're civilised, after all. We *always* have a salad before our main course.' And with that, the cockroach pulled a green donut from the tree, chewed noisily, and then grabbed the composer.

The cockroach swallowed the composer in one gulp.

Then he belched, and said, 'I just *love* bipeds.'

Jack Dann has written or edited over seventy books, including the international bestseller *The Memory Cathedral*, which is published in over ten languages and was #1 on *The Age* Bestseller list. He is a recipient of the Nebula Award, the World Fantasy Award, the Australian Aurealis Award (twice), the Ditmar Award (three times), the Peter McNamara Achievement Award, and the *Premios Gilgames de Narrativa Fantastica* award. He has also been honoured by the Mark Twain Society (Esteemed Knight). His latest novel is *The Rebel*; his latest collection is *The Fiction Factory*. www.jackdann.com